Nick stood leaning against the windowsill with his arms crossed over his chest watching her sleep. The rain outside had stopped, but the downpour of guilt and remorse inside him still persisted.

He'd slept for a few hours. Long enough for Vicki to have finished her shower and fallen asleep in the bed opposite him. She slept in her underclothes. Nick could see the strap of her pink bra peeking at him over the edge of the blanket. She looked peaceful in her deep slumber. But he was wide-awake, and his whole body ached for her.

Despite his self-condemnation, despite her obvious—and now he understood—justified feeling of contempt toward him, he still needed her, maybe now more than ever. Only she could heal the hurt inside him, only she could stop the emotional bloodletting he felt in his very soul.

He moved before he had time to reconsider. Before his mind could catch up with his heart and remind him that she despised him. Before he remembered how horribly he'd failed her.

Dropping his towel, he bent his knee and crawled across the bed. Lifting the cover, he aligned his body to hers, he lowered his heavy form with the greatest of ease.

Vicki's eyes opened immediately, causing Nick to wonder if she was really asleep to begin with. She stared up at the man lying on top of her. Nothing in her eyes reflected surprise in waking to find him there.

BOOK YOUR PLACE ON OUR WEBSITE AND MAKE THE ARABESQUE ROMANCE CONNECTION!

We've created a customized website just for our very special Arabesque readers, where you can get the inside scoop on everything that's going on with Arabesque romance novels.

When you come online, you'll have the exciting opportunity to:

- View covers of upcoming books

- Learn about our future publishing schedule (listed by publication month and author)

- Find out when your favorite authors will be visiting a city near you

- Search for and order backlist books

- Check out author bios and background information

- Send e-mail to your favorite authors

- Join us in weekly chats with authors, readers and other guests

- Get writing guidelines

- AND MUCH MORE!

Visit our website at
http://www.arabesquebooks.com

DÉJÀ VU

ELAINE OVERTON

BET Publications, LLC
http://www.bet.com
http://www.arabesquebooks.com

ARABESQUE BOOKS are published by

BET Publications, LLC
c/o BET BOOKS
One BET Plaza
1900 W Place NE
Washington, DC 20018-1211

All Kensington Titles, Imprints, and Distributed Lines are available at special quantity discounts for bulk purchases for sales promotions, premiums, fund-raising, and educational or institutional use. Special book excerpts or customized printings can also be created to fit specific needs. For details, write or phone the office of the Kensington special sales manager: Kensington Publishing Corp., 850 Third Avenue, New York, NY 10022, attn: Special Sales Department, Phone: 1-800-221-2647.

First Printing: August 2005

10 9 8 7 6 5 4 3 2 1

Printed in the United States of America

Dedicated with love to "Big Mama."
You are called by many names, but historically
your role has been the same.
To serve as the symbol of feminine strength and beauty
in the life of every young woman.

ACKNOWLEDGMENTS

To the source of all things, My Lord and Savior Jesus Christ, thank you for inspiration and perseverance and the miracles of your everyday blessings.

To my family whose love and support in this endeavor have been more than I could ever have asked for. Especially to my sweet son, Stacey, for your patience and understanding while I pecked away at the computer.

To the Michigan chapter of Romance Writers of America, for your supportive words and encouragement. Also, to the organization at large for providing excellent information about the trends in the industry, and tools for writers both published and not.

Thank you Julie Beard for writing *The Complete Idiot's Guide to Getting Your Romance Published,* the best book I have seen so far regarding getting your writing dreams off the ground.

And finally, thank you to Demetria Lucas and BET/Arabesque Books for giving those dreams wings.

PROLOGUE

Little Rock, Arkansas
Eight years ago . . .

"Who are you going to believe, Nicky? The woman you love or an accused murderer?"

"Don't go there, Vicki. You know as well as I, the man is innocent until proven guil—"

"How can you look me in the eyes and say that? Me, Nicky! This is *me* you're talking to."

His dark eyes, usually filled with passion, now seemed devoid of all life. Vicki Proctor felt a cold chill run down her spine as a realization dawned on her. The man she loved, the compassionate advocate for the underdog, was no longer residing in the body before her. All that remained was the cold-blooded, calculating glory-hound.

"I know who I'm talking to." His mouth twisted into a smile, but it was not the warm and loving smile Vicki knew so well. This smile was cunning, and ruthless. Vicki had the feeling of being a sparrow caught in the jaws of a hungry cat. "I know you better than anyone, Vicki. And you know me."

"What's that supposed to mean?"

He crossed the room at lighting speed, stopping within a few inches of her. He rose to his full height of six feet, two inches and glared down at the woman standing almost a foot shorter than him. "It means, if you put that crackhead on the stand, I will tear her to pieces."

Vicki let out a long sigh, but it did nothing to relieve the heavy weight bearing down on her heart. "Regardless of whether she's telling the truth or not?"

"You have your job to do and I have mine."

She shook her head. "What happened to you, Nicky? I don't recognize you."

"Maybe you don't know me as well as you think."

Vicki turned to pick up her small tote bag. "Good-bye, Nicky. Have a good life."

She walked out of the bedroom and toward the front door.

As if awakened from hypnosis, Nick stared at the solitaire diamond ring cradled in his palm as if he'd never seen it before. Twirling it between his fingers, he felt a fury like he'd never known building in his chest.

There was much he wanted to say, so much he could've said, but his pride would not allow it. Instead, he took the role of aggressor, which felt as comfortable as a second skin. "Vicki, cut the dramatics! Put the bag down, you're not going anywhere and we both know it," he snapped while trailing behind her.

Vicki did not answer. She needed every ounce of her strength and concentration to keep her unwilling feet moving in the direction of the door, and as far away from Nick Wilcox as she could get. The front entrance seemed miles away, and the few seconds it took to reach it felt more like hours. As soon as her hand reached the knob and turned it to open the door, his larger hand reached above and slammed it shut again.

"Vicki, don't do something you'll regret."

Vicki could not remember ever feeling so completely exhausted. She leaned her forehead against the door. "I could say the same about you."

He grabbed her by the shoulders and turned her to face him. "Don't you see? I'm not just doing this for me, I'm doing this for us. This case will make my career, baby. I'll be famous. This case can *make* me."

"And break me," she whispered. "But that's not nearly as important. Is it, Nicky?" The question was met with dead silence. She released a single, harsh chuckle. "See you in court."

Vicki opened the door again, and this time Nick made no move to stop her. She walked out, and away from the future she had once been certain would be hers.

Never once did she slow her steady stride or look back. It was the hardest thing she'd ever had to do, but she was certain she was right, and equally certain that after this trial ended, regardless of the verdict, she would never see Nick Wilcox again.

And she did not, until eight years later in the case of *The State of Illinois v. Tommy Morrison.*

CHAPTER ONE

Chicago, Illinois
Present day

That lousy bastard, Vicki thought, watching as he removed his light wool jacket. The coarse fabric fell smoothly off his broad shoulders, down his muscular biceps, his sinewy forearms, and into his large hands. With one fluid motion he flipped it onto the back of his chair.

His ash-gray silk shirt clung to his well-developed torso. His perfectly creased charcoal-colored slacks fell neatly over his lower portion. He was a vision to behold: everything from the top of his shiny bald head to his wing-tip shoes. His full lips and high cheekbones, accentuating his African ancestry, were in direct contrast to his more European characteristics—his patrician nose and dark brown oval-shaped eyes. Such contradictions in appearance were common in African-Americans, but in this man the divergence was stunning.

The trial hadn't even begun, and already he had every female eye in the courtroom trained completely on his every move. Vicki cast a glance at the jury. She was regretting her decision to accept the six young women, who all now sat slack-jawed watching the handsome defense attorney with a body like an ancient Zulu warrior. Even the sixty-nine-year-old retired schoolteacher had a look of lust in her eyes. Vicki sighed wearily, already feeling defeated. It was going to be a long trial.

Nick knew she was watching him; he could feel her eyes on him. Good, all those late hours at the gym had served their purpose. Of course, physical attention wasn't the only thing he wanted from her, but he knew he had to start somewhere.

He turned abruptly. Caught with her eyes on his derrière, Vicki jumped like a guilty child. "Good morning, Victoria," he said evenly, fighting to hide the overwhelming emotions he felt every time he looked at her.

"Morning, Nicholas," she answered. "I see you've been working on your . . ." she let her eyes roam over his long form, ". . . defense."

He chuckled. *Still a smartass,* he thought, *albeit a beautiful one.* Her coffee-brown complexion tinted with a touch of cream, and classically delicate features were as refined as the lady herself. Voluptuous in form, she moved in a way that animated her feminine curves. Nick was certain that on more than one occasion when she'd walked away from him, her supple hips had waved bye-bye.

"My defense is ready, although I won't be needing it, considering my client is innocent and you have nothing more than a few minor pieces of circumstantial evidence."

"Innocent, huh?" Vicki looked past him at the thug slumped in the next chair. Everything about the young man said it had been a long time since he was innocent. "Would that be the Andrew Pallister kinda innocent?"

Arkansas State Representative and pillar of the community, Andy Pallister, was the asteroid that crashed into their perfect world eight years earlier. Vicki was the prosecutor assigned to convict the man of murder, and Nick had defended him and won.

But in the end they both lost, when their strong feelings regarding the case came between them, and ended their lifelong friendship and year-long engagement. Andy Pallister was dead now. A drunk driver forced his car off the road and straight into a tree. He was the drunk driver. Most of the country felt they had lost a great man with a bright future. Only Vicki and a handful of others felt that it was karma.

Nick felt his jaw tightening. "That was a cheap shot."

"So was strutting in here like a *GQ* stud!" Vicki exploded.

"Don't get self-righteous with me," he shouted back. "If that skirt was hugging your hips any tighter, it would be skin."

"I'm not the one trying to seduce the jury."

"I don't need cheap tricks, lady. I'm a damn good attorney, and like I told you, my client is innocent."

"Who are you kidding, Nicky? You'd represent the devil as long as his checks didn't bounce."

The quibbling pair fell silent, realizing theirs were the only voices being heard. The fifty-odd people that filled the courtroom were all listening intently. Both parties stood paralyzed, clueless as to how to regain some semblance of civilized behavior.

The problem corrected itself. The silence was shattered when the deep baritone voice of the bailiff reverberated across the room.

"All rise." The two simple words turned everyone's attention toward the small man entering the courtroom. "In the case of the State of Illinois versus Tommy Morrison. The Honorable Judge Thomas Scott residing."

Everyone stood patiently while the man climbed the

stairs leading to the bench. The sign of his advanced age showed clearly in the hunch of his shoulders and his measured pace. At his age, Judge Scott felt he deserved certain liberties, one of which being the right to not be rushed. After several minutes, he finally straightened his long black robe and settled behind the high ledge.

"Please be seated," the bailiff said.

For a few moments, the only sound heard was the noisy shuffle of people sitting. Judge Scott's shrewd brown eye took inventory of his courtroom. He methodically surveyed everyone from the deputy sheriff guarding the doors to the transcriptionist at his elbow.

"Aww jeeze," he whispered to himself as his eyes flicked over the legal representation for both parties. *Not these two again*, he thought. Last time they squared off in his courtroom, for the arraignment, they almost came to blows. He silently berated himself for not recognizing the names on the docket. If he had, he would've seriously considered calling himself off.

He thought for a moment, considering whether to go forward with the fire and ice combination. But what cause did he have not to? They hadn't actually done anything—yet. He sat thinking for several moments, but his mind could come up with nothing. He had no choice but to move forward. He nodded to the bailiff to recite the case and file.

"Victoria Proctor for the prosecution, your honor."

"Nicholas Wilcox for the defense, your honor."

So far, so good. After all the preliminaries, including instructions for the jury, Judge Scott was ready to begin. "Ms. Proctor, your opening statements, please." Judge Scott nodded and slipped his bifocals over the edge of his nose.

"Yes, your honor." Vicki adjusted her skirt, now

self-conscious of the tight fit. *Okay, so it's snug,* she thought, but that wasn't *why* she wore it.

She crossed in front of the defense table, moving toward the jury. *Ignore him,* she silently scolded herself. "Ladies and gentlemen of the jury, we will present evidence today to clearly prove, Mr. Morrison, on the day in question—"

"I object!" Nick was out of his chair.

Judge Scott frowned in disapproval, the battle had begun. "Mr. Wilcox, this is the opening statement. What is there to object to?"

"I would like Ms. Proctor to be specific about the dates and times. She tends to forget details."

"No problem, your honor," Vicki smiled. "If Mr. Wilcox is having trouble following along, I'll try to *simplify* it for him."

"Considering I scored fifty percent higher on the bar exam than Ms. Proctor, I don't believe I'm the one with the trouble keeping up. But she has been known to ignore details."

"Your honor, would you please advise Mr. Wilcox that this is a trial and not his personal infomercial. I mean, really, who cares what he scored on an exam taken over ten years ago?"

"I was just stating that—"

"Approach the bench!" Judge Scott roared.

They came toward the high counter with heads bowed. Both realized how badly they were behaving, but neither seemed capable of *not* behaving in such a way with each other.

Judge Scott let them stand there for a moment, studying them with the eyes of a parent trying to determine punishment for his disobedient children.

They both stood silently, knowing better than to speak

out of turn. Vicki was thinking how much Judge Scott looked like a black George Burns.

Nick was taking advantage of the opportunity to look down Vicki's cream-colored blouse, which was slightly open. Standing almost a foot taller than her, he had a clear view of her tawny cleavage. It had been a long time since he'd seen her beloved breasts. *The twins*, as he affectionately referred to them.

Seeing what he was doing, Judge Scott cleared his throat, loudly. Nick jerked upright. Never had he be been so grateful for the rich mahogany-brown skin that concealed his embarrassment.

Judge Scott covered the microphone with his hand and leaned forward. "What seems to be the problem?"

Vicki shrugged. "Nothing, your honor."

Nick decided to follow her lead and play dumb. "I don't have a problem, your honor."

"If this turns into another *War of the Roses*, you will." Judge Scott fought to control the level of his voice, but his anger was making it difficult. "This is a court of law, not a battlefield for your personal, petty conflicts. Do we understand each other?"

They both nodded, refusing to make eye contact.

"Now, can we proceed with this case like the professionals we are, or should I rule a mistrial and have other counsel appointed?"

"No, your honor," they said in unison, both voices together registering just above a whisper.

"Good, let's get on with this." He sat back and released the microphone. Judge Scott watched Mr. Wilcox return to his seat, and Ms. Proctor continued her opening remarks without interruption. He watched as they exchanged a quick glance, and places, as Mr. Wilcox gave his opening. He noted how intently Ms. Proctor studied her opponent, the way her eyes lit up when he smiled. He wondered if she was even conscious of it. He watched Mr. Wilcox spill a stack of files all over the floor when his opponent, bending to pick up a pencil, greatly distracted him. The Honorable Judge Thomas Scott silently wondered why the pair didn't just get a hotel room and get it over with.

Nick took another bite of his hot dog and sighed heavily. Sitting one hip on the second level banister, he watched Vicki across the large half-moon shaped mezzanine. She sat with her head buried in an open file, and a cell phone pressed to her ear. Nick knew she was aware of him, although she was pretending not to feel the intensely heated stare coming from the other end of the corridor.

When they were standing in front of the judge that morning, Nick could smell her familiar perfume. She'd worn the same thing for almost fifteen years. Smelling the sweet scent had been like coming home. It was such a warm, well-known feeling.

"Nick?"

The sound of a woman's familiar voice startled him. He turned around and smiled. "Veronica! Wow, strange meeting you here."

"I know." Hungry eyes skimmed his long form. "You look great."

"So do you," he said, taking in her cultured appearance.

Tall and thin, Veronica Cole had always been a fashion plate. She made no secret of her love of money, and her even greater love of men with money. Nick had never believed the pleasure of her company would be worth the damage to his wallet. So, although they worked together from time to time, Nick had made a point of steering clear of her romantic advances.

"What are you doing in Chicago?" he asked.

"My law firm is representing a corporate client," she said, with a flip of her long dark hair. "What about you?"

"A family matter." He glanced back over his shoulder to confirm Vicki was still there. Much to his surprise, she was not only there, but watching his conversation with Veronica. Vicki tried to look away when she realized he'd seen her, but it was too late. He stood and embraced Veronica. He kissed her cheek, and toyed with a few strands of the hair falling over her shoulder.

Veronica was enjoying every moment of the attention. She'd tried for months to turn Nick's eye, without success. She smiled widely, now that he appeared to have had a change of heart. Veronica, knowing she would have to remain in Chicago for several weeks because of the complex nature of the negotiations, had envisioned many boring nights. But running into Nick now, things were definitely beginning to look up.

Nick knew Vicki was probably wondering what his relation was to the pretty woman conversing with him. *Let her wonder,* he thought, laughing loudly at something Veronica said.

The pair talked casually for a few more minutes. When they exchanged phone numbers and addresses, Nick shifted his body so that anyone across the mezzanine could clearly see he was writing something down. He kissed Veronica again, hugged her tightly, and sent her on her way.

He tossed the last bit of hot dog into his mouth and cast a sidelong glance across the balcony. Yes, Vicki was still watching him. Was that anger or frustration on her face? Whatever it was, he decided he liked it. It showed caring and concern. Things she was trying desperately to pretend she didn't feel.

Lunch was almost over, and Nick wanted to prepare for the next three witnesses. He headed back into the courtroom. After six frustrating weeks, it seemed he was finally making progress.

Judge Scott called a recess at 5:15 P.M. After the brief reprimand, both counselors had been careful of their remarks to one another. He was feeling hopeful that they might get through this thing without any bloodshed. This was a high-profile case, and Judge Scott knew the press would have a feeding frenzy if they sensed the intense animosity in the courtroom.

He glanced back over his shoulder at the pair, who obviously had a history. He shrugged and exited through his private entrance, his mind already focused on the thought of reaching home.

The room emptied. The sequestered jury was returned to their hotel and the defendant was removed. The spectators filed out, reporters returning to their home offices to make the late run, and concerned relatives making their way back to their respective homes. Soon, Nick and Vicki were the only two in the courtroom.

Vicki packed her briefcase hastily, trying to avoid just this situation, but unfortunately her assistant had managed to mix up her files, and it took time to sort them out.

"My Aunt Tilde says hi," Nick said, watching her pack up out the corner of his eye.

Vicki couldn't hide the smile that the familiar name brought to her lips, Miss Tilde having been one of the fondest memories of her childhood.

"Tell her hello for me." She snapped her briefcase shut.

"You called me Nicky."

"What?"

"This morning, you called me Nicky."

"So what?" She wondered where this was leading.

"No one calls me that anymore. I've missed hearing it."

"I've always called you that."

He tilted his head to the side to look directly into her eyes. "I know," he mumbled, hating his sentimental heart.

She paused for a long moment. She knew what he was saying, but was unsure whether she should acknowledge it or let it pass. She decided to pass. "Whatever." She picked up her briefcase and turned to leave.

Nick stood staring into his open case, listening to the clicking of her heels fade away. He wondered again, for the hundredth time, why he insisted on making a fool of himself for a woman who'd made it perfectly clear she didn't want him. Everything he'd done in the past six weeks had been to win her back, and she'd rebuffed him at every turn. Why did he keep putting himself through this?

He slumped down in the chair, realizing he was the only person left in the courtroom. He stretched his long legs out in front of him, reclined, and closed his eyes. It had been a long day and the trial had just begun. Given all the witnesses that were scheduled to testify, he knew it would be a grueling trial. Day after day of being within inches of her, and not being able to touch her. He shook his head in silent defeat.

Suddenly, images of a slightly younger Vicki filled his mind. She was smiling; he could hear the happy echo of her laughter. She was dodging him; a teasing sparkle lit her soft brown eyes. She darted left and right, barely avoiding his long reach. She was happy and in love. Finally he managed to grab hold of her; her hearty laughter was like music to his ears. She pretended to fight him off before finally succumbing to his hold and his hungry mouth. He pinned her against the wall; she was the sweetest tasting thing he'd ever known. He lifted her legs, and she eagerly wrapped them around his waist.

He loved her.

He saw her storming across the room toward him, fury burning in her eyes as she debated some controversial topic; he dared to disagree with her. She was so beautiful when she was impassioned.

Speaking of passion . . . the picture in his mind shifted. It was late at night, the room lit by the moonlight streaming in, she was twisting and writhing beneath him, her face contorted in pleasure and pain as she fought to prolong the inevitable climax.

He saw her, sitting across from him at the kitchen table; her small hands flailing through the air as she tried to make him see her point of view. He wouldn't agree, but he'd say he did, just to make her happy, just to see her smile again.

She was sleeping beside him, curled against his large frame like a baby with a blanket. She'd been happy there once; he was certain she could be again.

He saw her high on a ladder, reaching higher to paint a wall. It was their bedroom; she'd chosen the colors. Ivy-green and cream. She had such good taste. She looked back over her shoulder to say something to him about his lack of participation in the project. He simply laughed in response. He was too busy enjoying his view of her from the foot of the ladder to concentrate on the actual painting project.

The images were coming in quicker succession. Picture after picture of her lovely face, her melodious voice, her clear brown eyes. *So many memories, and all of them good,* he thought.

He stood, feeling rejuvenated. He snapped his briefcase closed and turned to leave the room. Why did he keep trying? He flicked the light switch off, and slid the door closed. *Because,* he thought determinedly, *she's worth it.*

Nick sat typing away, his long fingers flicking at lightening speed over the keys. The sun had set hours ago, but he usually worked well into the night. He barely heard the phone ring over the sound of the keys clicking.

He paused, his fingers inches above the keys. He heard it again. He spun around in his chair and grabbed the cordless. "Hello?"

"Why are you here?"

Nick sunk down in the chair, stunned to hear the soft voice on the other end. He didn't even know she had his number. "What do you mean?"

"Here in Chicago. Why are you here? And why Tommy Morrison—and why now?!"

He tapped the tip of his pen to his lips and tried to think of a reasonable excuse. He had nothing. "Chicago's as good a town as any, and Tommy's a distant cousin of mine. He needed help, and I was available."

"Chicago's a long way from Hope, Arkansas."

He chuckled. "Ain't it though?"

"Ain't?" Vicki said, unable to resist the tease. "Did you say *ain't,* Mr. Phi Beta Kappa?"

He laughed. She had him. After four years at Fisk and three years at Yale, he realized some habits couldn't be broken.

"I'm serious, Nick. Why did you move *here?*"

"For the reasons I gave you . . . and more. I could tell you the more, but you wouldn't like it."

"Try me."

"You won't like it."

"Tell me."

"Okay, but you won't like it."

"Tell me, damn it!"

"I wanted to be near you again."

The phone fell silent. Nick could hear the faint buzzing of the line connection in the background. He waited a few beats to give her time to breathe.

"Vicki, you still there?"

"Yes."

"Told you you wouldn't like it."

"It's never gonna happen, Nick. Please don't try."

"Why?"

"I try not to make the same mistake twice."

"Now I'm a mistake?"

"You know what I mean."

"I love you."

"It's over, Nick. It was over a long time ago."

"I understand that, but my heart just keeps on loving you."

"That doesn't matter."

"Didn't you hear me, Vicki? I said, I love you."

"Stop saying that."

"Why? Can't you handle hearing it?"

Click. The line went dead.

Nick turned the telephone off and returned it to the base. He sat staring out the window at the flashing lights of the busy city below. *Okay,* he thought; he'd told her. It wasn't the way it was supposed to go down, but it was done.

It was supposed to happen over a nice candlelit dinner, after a long drawn-out speech consisting of a bunch of back-in-the-day memories, and a handful of where-did-we-go-wrongs?

But instead it was done over a phone line, and he

didn't even have the benefit of watching her face to see what she was really thinking. Her heartfelt "no chance" statement didn't mean much to him, not until he could read it in her eyes. How many times had she declared she hated him, and then followed it up with some of the hottest lovemaking he'd ever experienced?

No, he decided, *she doesen't mean it.* Sometimes she just didn't know what was good for her. He swung back around to the computer and continued working on his brief, not the least bit put off by her cold rebuff. He'd moved to Chicago to right the greatest wrong of his life, and he wasn't about to let Vicki get in the way of her own happiness.

CHAPTER TWO

Vicki was fuming. This was exactly what she'd feared. She knew once the national press got wind that famed defense attorney Nick Wilcox was defending Tommy Morrison the case would become a circus. Hidden inside the door leading to the courthouse stairs, watching the barrage of people crowded on the sidewalk, Vicki realized the clowns had come to town.

There, in the center, with his hands lifted as he tried to control the mass of microphones and cameras, stood the ringmaster.

"Mr. Wilcox, what about the blood?" A young, male reporter in the back bounced up and down trying to be heard over the masses.

Nick gave his full attention to the young man. "The blood evidence is circumstantial," he answered. "They have yet to prove conclusively that it is indeed the blood of my client."

The man seemed satisfied, and Nick turned his attention to another reporter. Vicki shook her head, probably the one person there who understood why Nick would choose an obvious rookie over the more experienced and influential reporters in front.

Was that rule number five? Vicki thought. She could almost hear him saying, *"Pick your friends for the future not the present, Vicki."* The young man was probably flattered at having been acknowledged, and he would no doubt write a story that was favorable to Nick. And who knows, in ten years the young man might be a force to be reckoned with, and who would he remember gave him his first break?

"Mr. Wilcox." A pretty, female reporter in the front was giving him a winning smile and flaying her hands madly. Nick turned to her and smiled. *Always smile, Vicki, even if you don't mean it.* That was rule number three.

"Is it true that your client confessed and recanted?" the reporter asked. The sparkle in her brown eyes seemed to contain more than a professional interest in Nick.

"No, they do not have a confession from my client."

Vicki huffed; he'd effectively avoided answering the question.

"Hey, Hawkeye," someone else called out.

Vicki twisted her mouth in disgust, thinking what a ridiculous nickname. The media had crowned him with it after a 1998 case, when the press claimed his sharp perception and ability to see the importance of the tiniest bits of information had won the case. How Vicki wanted to tell them that their hawk was nearsighted and wore corrective lenses.

"What about the rumors that you may be running for attorney general for the state of Arkansas?"

Vicki's whole body stiffened. This was the first she'd heard of any such rumors.

Nick's brief glance in her direction revealed that

he'd known she was there all along. "No comment," he answered briskly.

Vicki listened as he fielded a few more questions before deciding she'd heard enough. It had been a long day, and so far none of the reporters had spotted her. She wanted to keep it that way.

She shifted along the side of the building, well concealed behind the huge alabaster columns, and attempted to slip away unseen.

Nick saw her moving out the corner of his eye, and wrapped up the interview quickly. "That's all I have to say today. No more questions." He took off after her. "No more questions," he said firmly, to a few of the more insistent reporters who attempted to pursue him.

Vicki rounded the corner and breathed a sigh of relief that she'd managed to escape that madhouse. So Nick was up for the attorney general slot.

"Vicki, wait up," he called behind her.

She kept walking, hoping she could make it to her car and get inside before Nick caught up with her. But, considering his legs were almost twice the length of hers, it didn't take him long to gain on her. She slid into the driver's seat, and was about to close the door when she felt him pull on it.

"Hold up." He came around the door, smiling at her.

Vicki wondered if there would come a day when that smile did not melt her insides.

"Who'd think you could move that fast in those heels?" he teased, enjoying the view of her rounded calves stretched out under the steering wheel.

"What do you want?" She kept her voice icy cold. Indifference was her only weapon.

"Just to say hello. We haven't spoken all day," he said,

mentally weighing his next words carefully. "Look, about that attorney general thing—"

"Forget it." She snapped when she meant to sound nonchalant, but it was hard to be nonchalant about something that once meant so much to her. "If the state of Arkansas feels you're the best person for the job, I wish you the very best." She was losing the struggle to keep emotion out of her voice. "But in order to take that job, you'll have to live in the state of Arkansas, won't you?"

He watched her face, the hurt written clearly across her lovely countenance, but what could he do about it? She'd chosen to leave the state of Arkansas—and him— behind. She'd chosen to turn her back on everything they'd shared, including their dreams. And yet, he didn't doubt for a second that the other emotion he saw in her eyes was blame. As if he'd intentionally set out to steal the position she'd coveted since her sophomore year at Fisk.

He knew there was nothing he could say at that moment to change what she was feeling, so he moved on to what he felt was a safer topic. "The other night, when you called, I didn't get a chance to explain what I meant."

She looked directly into his dark eyes, something she normally tried not to do. The butterflies she now felt in her stomach were the reason why. "There's nothing to explain," she said, and pulled on the door.

His strong hold on the door did not loosen one bit.

"Nick, I don't know what you expected to happen between us, but nothing will."

He stood, leaning into the car, silently watching her eyes.

"Besides," she tried to reason with him, "I'm already involved with someone."

His full lips twisted into a devious smirk; he'd already researched the competition. "Preston, isn't that his name?"

Her eyes widened; she should've known. *"Know thine enemy, Vicki."* "Rule number twelve, right?" she said, trying to remember where the bit of information fell on the Nick Wilcox chart of Rules to Live By.

His eyes widened in surprise. "Very good. I can't believe you remember."

"If you know I'm seeing someone else, why bother with this?" Vicki snarled in tired irritation. Nick's revived presence in her life was making a mess of her neat little world.

"Because, you belong to me," he stated as a matter of fact.

The statement was met with dead silence. Finally, she asked, "I beg your pardon?"

"You belong to me. You always have. I was just too ignorant to realize it."

Vicki stood suddenly, her body rigid with disdain. Her head was pounding so hard she thought it might pop off. "Are you insane?" she roared. "What is this? You Tarzan, me Jane?! I don't *belong* to you or any man. So just take your pompous, caveman attitude back to the ice age where it came from!"

She got back into the car, and this time managed to pull the door free of his hold. She peeled away, leaving a still-smiling Nick behind.

"I can't wait to get you back to my tree house, Jane." Nick laughed. He turned on his heels, and headed toward his jeep parked on the other side of the lot.

After leaving the courthouse, Vicki drove aimlessly around the city. She did her best thinking behind the wheel of the car, but at the pace her mind was racing she would need several hours to sort everything out.

It had been almost two months since she arrived in

the very same courtroom and almost fainted at the sight of Nick standing behind the defense table looking like something out of one of her dreams. Which was the only place she'd seen him in the past eight years. He'd made it perfectly clear—from the seductive glances to the sensual way he spoke to her—that he was expecting to walk away from this trial with more than a "not guilty" verdict.

And she'd made it equally clear that she had no desire or intention of repeating the past. They'd parted company eight years ago with a few very ugly final words, and neither had ever looked back. Why now, after all this time, did he feel the need to have a fling with her? And she was sure that was what he wanted. In her opinion, Nick was simply too self-absorbed to be capable of anything more.

The large metal skeleton of what would eventually become another Chicago skyscraper appeared, and Vicki realized where she'd unconsciously arrived. She decided to take it as an omen and turned into the dirt road leading to the construction site.

She came upon a group of workers who looked to be preparing to end the workday; she asked for directions. Vicki exchanged her striped brown pumps for the athletic shoes she kept in the back seat. Glancing at her watch, she began to move faster across the large open area, never noticing the group of men who watched her with male appreciation.

"Angela!" Vicki called loudly to a woman standing in front of a large Dodge Ram truck.

The tall, slender woman fit perfectly into the setting, dressed in a pair of denim jeans and flannel work shirt. Vicki often wondered how any woman fared in such a male-dominated workplace. But Angela could give as good as she got, a skill Vicki herself had never mastered.

Angela stood talking to a man, probably a member of her ten-man crew. She was pointing up at the tall skeleton frame and gesturing. She turned away from the man at the sound of her name and waved to the approaching woman. The man signaled his departure just as Vicki reached them.

"Hey, girl," Angela said with genuine surprise. She squeezed her friend tight. Angela hadn't heard from Vicki in almost two months, and feared what Nick's arrival may have done to their long-standing friendship. "What are you doing here?"

"This trial is really getting to me." Vicki shrugged. "I don't want to go home just yet. Wanna get something to eat?"

"Sure. Giovanni's?"

"Sounds great. I'll follow you." Vicki turned and raced back to her own car.

Shortly after, the two women sat devouring their second basket of bread, and wondering what was taking their order so long to arrive. Vicki loved dining with Angela, who had no shame in eating like the hungry woman she was. Most of Vicki's female friends stopped eating long before their stomachs were full just for the sake of decorum.

Not Angela; she ate until her stomach cried for mercy. Vicki wasn't the least bit envious that Angela ate like a starving lion and yet still fit perfectly into a size four dress. She'd known the woman most of her life, and swore there was a great hole in her belly that swallowed everything she'd eaten for the past twenty years. Vicki had gotten past the jealousy thing in high school. Now when she looked at Angela, all she saw was a dear old friend.

"What are they doing back there?" Angela asked, looking around the corner of the booth toward the double doors leading to the kitchen. "Killing the cow, so they can cook it?"

"Apparently they have to raise it first," Vicki said, tearing into another bread roll.

Angela chuckled, happy to see that the arrival of Nick had not had too bad an effect on her friend's sense of humor. She'd been afraid to call or visit, not knowing what she would find when she did. It had been a very pleasant surprise for Vicki to show up at her worksite the way she did, her presence clearly stating that there were no hard feelings. But still, Angela wondered. "How are things?"

"Just say what you're thinking, Angie." Vicki tossed another bit of bread into her mouth.

"Okay, how are you holding up?"

"You mean since that damn brother of yours came riding back into my life?"

"Watch it with the 'damns.' He is my favorite brother," Angela retaliated.

"He's your *only* brother."

"Still, watch it."

"What is he doing here, Angie?" Vicki pleaded.

"Don't know," Angela looked around the corner of their booth again. This was not a conversation she wanted to have, but had known from the moment that Nick showed up on her doorstep six weeks ago, was inevitable.

Vicki waited patiently for her friend to turn toward her again. When she did, Angela's dark face was riddled with guilt. "Liar," Vicki whispered, and took a sip from her water glass.

She hadn't expected Angela to betray her brother; she knew how close they were. But she had at least hoped for some kind of reassurance that Nick's plan to win her back was pointless. For some reason, she needed to hear it from someone other than the voice in her head.

"I'm losing the Morrison case," Vicki said, looking away from her friend. She didn't want to see pity in her eyes.

Angela sat contemplating that statement, knowing how important her response would be, and what a thin line she was walking. They had been friends since they were old enough to share a seesaw. Angela knew better than anyone what a fragile ego Vicki had where Nick was concerned.

Vicki, who usually exuded confidence with ease, became a bumbling imbecile when put in the same courtroom with the infamous Nicholas Wilcox. Despite the fact that the two had been friends as well as lovers, all that seemed to fall by the wayside when they stood on opposing sides of a courtroom. Other than the Morrison case, in which they were currently squaring off, this anomaly had happened only once before, and that had been one too many times as far as Angela was concerned. Vicki felt like a second-rate attorney when compared to Nick; she always had.

Angela personally believed it all began with Yale. After four years at Fisk University, both Nick and Vicki had applied to Yale's school of law. Two months later, Nick received an acceptance letter; Vicki did not. Angela knew Vicki's insecurities had less to do with Nick, and more to do with Vicki herself. Her feelings were completely unjustified, especially considering that their win-versus-loss ratio was almost the same. Nonetheless, when Nick squared off with her in court, Vicki's self-confidence faltered. Her prosecution wasn't good enough, her witnesses weren't believable, and her evidence wasn't strong enough.

Angela remembered years ago, Vicki had confessed to her that during the first case she and Nick had tried together, the Andy Pallister trial, she'd gotten almost no sleep and had broken out in some sort of strange hives. According to Vicki, Nick, who was living with her and sleeping beside her every night, never noticed a thing. And for some reason she never confided her feelings to him. Even at the end, when everything had turned bad, she'd kept silent.

Leaving Little Rock eight years ago had been the hardest thing either of the two women had ever done. But the friends were both feeling stifled in their current situations, and needing a change in scenery. They chose a city at random, based on some positive comments from a coworker of Angela's who'd grown up in Chicago.

The pair had shared the expenses of a small apartment and dined on lots of lunchmeat until they could afford to do better. Soon time had worked its healing, giving Vicki space to rebound from Nick, and Angela a new career that gave her great satisfaction.

Angela had watched as Vicki, out from under Nick's shadow, blossomed into the attorney she'd always wanted to be. And although she could've left the prosecutor's office long ago to work in one of the posh law firms on Michigan Avenue, Vicki stayed, putting life's purpose ahead of personal gain. But now Nick was back, and that newfound assurance was floundering.

"You'll find your footing, just stick to the evidence," Angela said, trying to bolster her friend.

"I wish it were that easy. Nick's tearing my evidence to shreds. He found a DNA specialist who confirms that after being exposed to the air for forty-eight hours, you can no longer get a positive read on a sample. My blood evidence had been out for nearly three days."

"Well, find an expert to counter that."

"I tried."

Angela reached across the table and took her friend's hand. "Don't do this to yourself. You're as good an attorney as Nick, if not better. Don't let him undermine your confidence in your evidence. You've built a solid case, and despite his flaky experts it's still solid." Angela loved her brother, but Nick Wilcox needed no pep talks. Vicki, on the other hand, needed all she could get.

Vicki could see the genuine concern in her friend's eyes. "Thanks," she said.

The food arrived, and no more words were spoken as the two tore through the platters of steak and potatoes. Only the sounds of forks clanking, wine being poured, and the pungent aroma of A1 steak sauce filled the air.

Vicki listened carefully to the music of the song. She turned off the CD player and tried to find the key on her piano. She played half a chord and paused on the C-minor, tapping it repeatedly. *No,* she decided, *that wasn't it.*

She pressed the rewind button on the CD player once more and replayed the same refrain. She listened again, until the sound of the phone ringing interrupted her concentration.

"Hello?" Vicki sighed heavily, unable to hide the agitation in her voice.

"Ouch." The cheerful sound of a woman's voice came through the phone.

"Hey, Peaches."

"Who ticked you off?" Peaches chuckled.

"Nobody. Just working on a new song for the choir. What's up?"

"My spirit for one," the woman practically cooed into the phone, "I'm finally getting my own show!"

"No way," Vicki jumped up off the piano bench in

excitement, her own personal frustration quickly forgotten. "Congratulations!"

"I feel like celebrating."

"I'm all for that. What do you have in mind?"

"You know what," Peaches said slyly.

"No way!" Vicki barked. She was determined not to be baited by her friend this time.

"You know you wanna," Peaches's voice dripped with temptation.

"No, Peaches," Vicki insisted. "After the last time, we vowed, remember? Under no circumstance were we ever to return to the Cheesecake Factory again. It took ten minutes to put on ten pounds, and a month to get it off. That place is evil."

"Sin has its purpose," Peaches replied. "Besides, how often do I get my own show?"

Vicki reluctantly gave in. "Okay," she said, knowing full well how hard her friend had worked for this moment. "I'll get my shoes on, you drive."

Vicki was bent over the end of her bed tying up her laces of her running shoes when the phone rang again. She expected it to be Peaches letting her know she was waiting out front.

"Hey, baby." The Southern voice of Maude Proctor came through the phone.

"Hi, Mama," Vicki said, her voice sounding strained as she bent to tie her shoes. Maude made a point of speaking to each of her children at least once a day. For Vicki, it was usually twice a day. This was call number one.

Over the years, Vicki and her two siblings had abandoned their hometown of Hope, Arkansas, and scattered to various parts of the country. But that did nothing to deter Maude from speaking with her children regularly. It always amazed Vicki how easily her mother picked up a phone and called across the country like she was calling her next door neighbor. Vicki cringed to think what her monthly long distance phone bills looked like.

"What are you doing?" Maude said.

"Peaches got her own show, we were going out to celebrate."

"Oh, that's wonderful. Tell her congratulations for me."

Maude also prided herself on knowing all the important people in her children's lives: close friends and significant others. Vicki, her sister Rhonda, and her brother Carl Junior, often joked that Maude's spy network could easily rival the CIA. Given her resources, it was not surprising that Maude knew Nick was in Chicago almost a week before Vicki did.

"I will."

"How's Nick—and Angela?" Maude asked, realizing her slip too late.

"Like you give a flying hoot how Angela's doing," Vicki said smugly. "As for your precious Nick, I wouldn't know. We're not that close." She wondered when her mother would stop nursing the hope that they would reconcile.

Little Nicky Wilcox had wooed Maude Proctor twenty years ago when he showed up one Mother's Day on her doorstep with a handful of half-dead dandelions. His hands were stained yellow, and his white dress shirt was ruined, but both had been well worth the effort. For on that day, Nick Wilcox won an ally for life.

"Well, I understand you're on your way out. Call me back when you return."

"Is this about Big Mama's birthday party?" Vicki asked. Her grandmother's one-hundredth birthday was coming up, and what had started out as a small family gathering was becoming the social event of the year. Vicki had been delegated the responsibility of organizing it.

"No. I need to talk to you about some business," Maude said, trying to sound casual, but her daughter knew her too well.

"What kind of business?" Vicki asked, standing upright, her full attention on the conversation.

"Well, this land developer has been coming around, and he made an offer to buy the farm. I understand he's made offers on a few others in the area, too."

Vicki knew her family's chicken farm wasn't doing well. When Vicki's father, Carl Proctor, died ten years ago, Maude took over the family business herself. It had been an uphill battle to keep the small farm both profitable and competitive. The signs of that struggle showed in Maude's tired eyes and strained back. Those closest to her knew her reasons for keeping the farm up and running had less to do with money and more to do with her husband's legacy.

Over the years, Vicki had seen some of the financial statements and forecasts. The lawyer in her understood why her mother might want to sell, but the child in Vicki thought of the sixty acres as home. "Are you considering taking the offer?"

"Don't know, that's what I want to talk to you about," Maude said. "But go have fun with your friend. This isn't anything that can't wait."

Vicki hesitated, wanting to hear more about the offer; her mother heard the hesitation.

"Go," Maude insisted, and hung up the phone before Vicki had a chance to protest. She knew her daughter was too cheap to call her right back.

Vicki considered it for a moment. She heard the

familiar sound of Peaches's car horn, so instead, she grabbed her purse and coat and headed out the door.

Vicki and Peaches ate like gluttons. What was supposed to be a small celebration treat turned into a three-course meal with dessert.

The two women had met purely by chance almost five years ago at a dinner party of a mutual friend. They hit it off right away, and had been the best of friends ever since.

For Vicki, Peaches broke every stereotype of white women she'd ever heard. To the art community, the mysterious young artist was known as Peaches, but the handful of people she called friends knew that her birth name was Vivian Silverstein. It was one of the few things she knew for certain about her origins. She had been abandoned as a child, and raised in foster homes until an attempted rape caused her to flee her last home at the tender age of thirteen. After that, she'd survived by wit, determination, and, as she herself often stated, the grace of God.

Through it all, the one constant in her life had been her love of art. She worked, hustled, and stole art supplies over the years, and never once questioned her obsession. She sold her first piece ten years ago, and never took on a regular day job again.

Given her hearty appetite, Vicki often wondered if Peaches's petite size was in any way attributable to malnourishment as a child. Her sky-blue eyes were open and friendly, despite the harshness of her childhood, and her blond hair hung in locks to her waist. Her hairstyle tended to cause stares wherever she went, but Peaches never seemed to notice.

Vicki was only partially listening as Peaches went on

about the pieces she wanted to display in her show. Vicki's mind was still on the conversation she'd had with her mother. She wondered if the farm which sat adjacent to theirs had been one of the ones an offer was made on. And, if so, what would Nick recommend to his aunt Tilde.

". . . that's my only hesitation." Peaches hunched her shoulders. "But it's probably all in my head anyway."

What was Peaches talking about? Vicki's attention was drawn back to the table. She sat blinking dumbly at her friend, a partially chewed bit of cheesecake in her cheek.

Peaches twisted her mouth in annoyance. "You didn't hear a word I said, did you?"

Unable to speak with a mouthful of food, Vicki shrugged apologetically.

"I said, the down side to this whole show is that it is being sponsored by Mr. Yoshimoto."

"Who's that?"

"My newest patron," Peaches said in a less than enthusiastic tone. "He showed up at my studio about six months ago and has been stalking me ever since."

Vicki scrunched her arched brows, "I thought having a patron was a good thing."

"It is." Peaches shook her head in frustration. "But the man gives me the creeps. Nothing I can put my finger on, I mean he hasn't actually said or done anything that could qualify as creepy. It's just him. Something just doesn't feel right about him."

"Why do business with him?"

Peaches erupted in laughter. "You're joking, right? The man is one of the richest businessmen in the country, maybe the world. And he's chosen to promote my work. I'd be crazy to chase him away. For the first time in my life, my *own* show, Vicki."

Vicki knew Peaches lived by her instincts. Having practically raised herself on the streets for most of her youth, she had to. That "creepy feeling" had often been the only thing standing between her and a bad situation. She trusted it without question. So, for Peaches to ignore her instincts was evidence of how much this show meant to her.

Feeling completely stuffed, Vicki sat back in her chair, staring regretfully at an uneaten piece of chocolate chip cheesecake. "Well, be careful in your dealings with him," Vicki warned her friend.

"Always," Peaches answered off-handedly. Her attention was riveted on Vicki's plate. "Um . . . are you gonna eat that?" She pointed with her fork.

Vicki frowned. The selfish little girl in her cried, *"Yes, I want it, it's mine."* But the weight-conscious woman simply slid the plate across the table. There would be other cheesecakes. She tried and failed to stifle a yawn, the evidence of her gluttony. It really was a sin for something to taste so good.

"Bring the salt," Angela called out while setting up the Monopoly board. One of the benefits of Nick's arrival had been the renewal of their ongoing Monopoly battles. They'd played relentlessly and ruthlessly since they were children. They took pride in stealing each other's property when at all possible, and never passing up an opportunity to send the opponent to jail—straight to jail—without passing go.

Nick strolled back into the room, his arms filled with all the extras his baby sister needed to complete her gourmet popcorn. "Here you go." He offered her the cup of melted butter and box of iodized salt. He reached past her and set the two cans of Pepsi on the coffee table.

"Coaster," she howled, watching him out the corner of her eye while standing her horseman upright.

Nick tilted his head to the side. "You were such a messy kid, when did you become a neat freak?" He reached over and placed a coaster under each can.

"When I became the one who had to clean up the mess." She laughed, and reached into the game box for the dice. "Ready?"

"Roll the dice, and prepare to meet financial ruin," he teased, while settling back on his forearms.

The pair spent the next two hours playing. Angela was winning, but she knew it was due in part to Nick's lack of concentration. He was so busy watching the door and the clock, he hardly watched the game board.

"You know . . . ," she started, while shaking the dice in her fist, ". . . if I didn't know better, I'd think my company was less than stimulating."

"Shouldn't she have been here by now?"

"Contrary to what you believe, Vicki doesn't spend nearly as much time here as you think," Angela said.

Up until a few weeks ago, Vicki had customarily stopped by almost every day, since she passed that way going home. A habit she gave up, once she realized Nick had caught on to it and began making a point of being there when she arrived.

Angela tossed the dice and moved her man four spaces. She decided to spend five hundred dollars on the real estate.

He cocked an eyebrow and twisted his mouth in disdain, "She's probably with *him.*"

"*Him* has a name. It's Preston," Angela said, reaching into the popcorn bowl. "Anyway, he's out of town until the end of the week." Angela regretted her words as soon as she saw the twinkle in her brother's dark eyes.

"Oh, really?" He smiled.

"Nick, no. Please, don't go over there."

"Why not?" he asked, already rising and picking up his keys from the coffee table.

"Because, she doesn't want to see you."

"She's just mad, she'll get over it." Nick figured Vicki would probably still be angry at the way his expert had torn her evidence to shreds earlier in the week. But when would he get another opportunity like this?

Angela jumped to her feet to confront her brother. "It's been eight years, Nick. And guess what? She's not over it."

Nick reared back, surprised by his sister's anger. "What's gotten into you?"

"This whole situation has gotten into me. I'm tired of always being the referee between you two!" Angela finally released the frustration she'd felt for almost a decade. "I'm tired of defending you to her. I'm tired of hiding her from you. I'm tired of this whole damn thing."

"What are you talking about? I love Vicki."

"Do you, Nick? I mean, do you *really*? Or is she just another conquest? Your Moby Dick. You know, the one that got away."

"Is that what you think?" Nick slammed his keys back down on the wood table, "That this is some kind of game?"

Angela took a deep breath; her next words were crucial. This conversation had been a long time coming, and she needed desperately for him to take her seriously.

"You have a hard time with losing, Nick. I was here. I saw what Vicki went through getting over you. I'm afraid you want her back for the wrong reasons. I won't watch her suffer like that again."

"Do you think it was easy for me? Letting her walk out of my life?"

"No, but you did it, because you understood it was the best for both—"

"No, Angela, that's where you're wrong. I did it, because I had no choice," he snatched up his keys again.

Seconds later Angela heard her front door slam shut.

Nick drove aimlessly around the city for over an hour. He hated to admit it, but Angela was right. As much as he wanted to see Vicki, it had to be at her invitation. Otherwise it would be a hollow victory. *Not that it was a victory,* he silently scolded himself. This wasn't about winning, this was about love.

He'd spent the last eight years in empty, meaningless relationships, trying to find that something special. He finally realized that what he wanted could be found in one place only, in one woman's arms, and he had every intention of getting back into those arms.

Vicki still loved him; he saw it in the fire of her eyes. Now all he had to do was fan that flame into an inferno. He'd done his research, and knew her schedule better than she did. Every day after work she stopped by Angela's, almost religiously. The fact that she didn't show tonight meant she'd caught on that it was more than coincidence causing them to meet there at the same time every day for the past few weeks. She was intentionally avoiding him.

That's okay, he thought. He knew this wouldn't be easy. He'd hurt her worse than he realized at the time. But he was certain he could make it up to her, if she gave him the chance. But in order for that to happen, they had to have more contact than as rivals across a courtroom, or chance meetings at Angela's house. Nick understood that attempting to win back the woman he loved was the greatest gamble of his life, and as he pulled into the parking garage of his apartment building he had resolved to up the ante.

Nick was feeling much better by the time he entered his apartment. He picked up the phone and dialed his sister's number.

"Hello?"

"Hey, it's me."

"I'm sorry I blew up like that."

"Don't sweat it. You said what you felt."

"You're my brother, Nick, and Vicki's my friend. Sometimes I feel—"

"I know. Are *we* okay?"

"Always. See you tomorrow?"

"Yeah. Leave the board up, we'll finish our game."

"See you soon."

Nick replaced the receiver and slumped down in his leather desk chair. He stared out into the darkness. Angela's words played over in his head like a recording. *"Do you Nick, I mean, do you really?" Yes,* he thought, *I absolutely, and completely love her.* It had taken him almost a decade to come to that conclusion, and he wasn't about to let anything turn him away from it now.

CHAPTER THREE

Vicki stood under the cascade of the showerhead, loving the feeling of liquid warmth running over her body. With the Morrison trial and Nick's arrival in Chicago, her whole body ached with the tension of the past several weeks. She closed her eyes and leaned into the pulsating water, wishing she could stay there forever.

She wanted to go shopping at the Farmer's Market, the way she did every Saturday morning, but with Nick stalking her like a wolf during mating season, she didn't dare. Finally she washed, rinsed, and stepped out of the shower, still contemplating her dilemma.

It had taken her months. She sighed, knowing the truth of the matter. It had taken years—several long and painful years—to finally get him out of her heart. How dare he come waltzing back into her life expecting her to be happy to see him? A light ringing sound caused her to hastily wrap a towel around her body and go into her bedroom.

"Hello?"

"Hey, girl."

Vicki sighed with relief; she'd come to expect every call to be Nick. "Hi, Angie."

"Are you going to the market today?" Angela said, the sound of a blender buzzing away in the background.

Vicki laughed to herself, grateful that some things remained the same. Angela was always cooking, trying new recipes, experimenting with foreign cuisine. It was her one and only hobby, and yet she was *still* a horrible cook.

"Yeah." Vicki surprised herself with the answer. "Why?"

"I need some strawberries for this strawberry pudding recipe. Can you pick up a pint or two? I'll pay you back."

"Sure, but my payment will be some of that delicious dish you're creating."

"You think you're funny, don't you?" Angela's culinary failures were well known to family and friends.

"Sorry." Vicki laughed. "I'll bring them by this afternoon. Just make sure that horny brother of yours is nowhere to be found."

"Okay, I'll tie him up in the basement. Is that good enough?"

"Works for me."

"Thanks, see you later." The statement was followed by a loud plopping sound. Angela's livid curses were the last thing Vicki heard before the line went dead.

Vicki laughed to herself, she was certain the noise had been Angela dropping her cordless phone into her pudding batter. She shook her head, wondering if this was the second or third phone Angela had lost to her cooking efforts. Vicki finally gave up. Given her friend's ineptitude in the kitchen, it certainly wouldn't be the last.

She dressed in a light pink summer dress, complete with big floppy straw hat and leather sandals. She dug out her large aluminum cart and left the house. Nick Wilcox had come to town, there was nothing she could do about that, but she stubbornly refused to live her life any differently because of it.

Vicki strolled along the boardwalk, her cinnamon-brown eyes perusing the rows and rows of fresh-picked vegetables and fruit, flowers in every variation, and other assorted knick-knacks. There was something about the Farmer's Market early Saturday morning that held energy like nothing she ever felt anywhere else.

The air was charged with energy. Multiple races, and multiple languages filtered over the crowd like a strange universal aria. Outdoor markets were one of the few places left where people still bartered for what they needed. The people themselves were worth the trip; every walk of life could be found on the boardwalk Saturday morning. It always amazed her how the area was brought to life with a few farm trailers and pick-up trucks.

She picked up a tomato and examined it carefully. She considered it thoughtfully, twisting her lips in contemplation. A fifty-cent tomato was no small purchase. It had to be weighed for value, pondered for its possible uses. Her eyes roamed over the rest of the tomatoes on the table, trying to find one a little less ripe. She started to put it down but held on to it a moment longer. What if someone else came along and picked it up before she decided? This may be her one chance to own *this* tomato.

Someone reached over her shoulder and handed the vendor one dollar. The vendor made change and gave it back to the person. Vicki's eyes trailed the large brown hand up his arm to his face. Her heart skipped a beat. From the first time he'd smiled at her on the playground twenty-five years ago to this moment, she'd never seen a more beautiful smile.

Nick chuckled. "I was afraid it would spoil before you decided."

Because his appearance had surprised her, Vicki had not been prepared, and found herself smiling in return. But she wiped it away and replaced it with a familiar scowl.

That's my girl, Nick thought. *Never give up without a fight.* "What a coincidence, meeting you here," he teased, fully enjoying the displeasure on her face. Nick was a firm believer that strong emotion of any kind indicated caring. Let her fume and sulk; he delighted in it. His greatest fear was imagining the day when he would see no emotion at all for him in her fiery eyes.

"Can't I even enjoy a day of shopping without you lurking around every corner?"

"Last time I checked the Farmer's Market was open to the public." He paused. "And I don't lurk."

"Whatever." She waved him off and started down the boardwalk, knowing it would not be so easy to get rid of him.

Nick walked along behind Vicki, pretending to study the trays of marigolds lined across the table like neat little floral troops. She toyed with some squash, picked up two large bell peppers, and placed them in a paper bag. She paid the vendor the one dollar and fifty cents required and moved along. She tried not to think about how nicely his black jeans fit, doing little to hide the sinewy muscles in his legs. She weighed two pounds of grapes and put them in a bag. She refused to think about the white T-shirt pulled tautly across his chest. Only his sunglasses hanging from the collar interrupted the expanse of stark whiteness. How could such a plain thing become provocative?

She paid the vendor for the grapes and moved on, watching Nick with her peripheral view. He was no more than a few paces behind, but now seemed to be truly interested in a table containing pre-packaged gift baskets.

She glanced discreetly back over her shoulder. The
basket he was holding seemed to contain a very large
bottle and an assortment of other smaller items. She
shook her head. All these fruits and veggies, leave it to
him to find the booze.

She continued toward the berries, seeing Nick pay the
man for his basket out the corner of her eye. She bought
two trays of strawberries, one for Angela and one for herself. She felt his eyes on her, and turned to see Nick smiling devilishly.

"You must have read my mind." He turned the basket
toward her.

Vicki could now clearly see the champagne sticker on
the bottle. Her mind flooded with memories. She turned
away so he wouldn't see her melancholy, remembering
the first time they'd shared strawberries and champagne.
It was the night he'd told her he loved her for the first
time. *What a joke,* she thought.

She decided to confront him, to tell him once again, as
she had several times already over the past few weeks, that
it wasn't gonna happen. *But this is Nick,* she thought.
When he set his sights on a goal, only God could stop him
from reaching it. And for some reason, after almost eight
years of separation, he'd decided he wanted her.

"Why are you doing this?"

"I told you, your mi—"

"No, Nick," she shouted, ignoring the stares of passersby.
"Why?"

"Keep your voice down," he hissed, conscious of every
face that turned in their direction.

She shook her head; he hadn't changed one bit. "Still
afraid I'm gonna embarrass you?"

The ever-present sparkle in his coal-black eyes seemed
to dim a bit. "That's not fair."

"Look at you," she said, stepping back from him. "You're handsome, successful, famous. Everything you wanted in life, you have it."

"Almost," he said. "I have everything but the one thing that matters most. You."

"Nick, you can have almost any woman you want," she pleaded.

"I want you." He lifted his eyebrow seductively. "Can I have you?"

"I said almost." She smiled, unable to fight his contagious good nature. "Look, we'll never be what we were, the past is the past."

"That's okay. I'm only interested in the future."

"What do you want from me?" Vicki knew Nick's stubbornness was what drove him. It had gotten him into one of the finest black colleges in the country, and on to an Ivy League university. It had propelled him through the ranks to become one of the top defense attorneys in the country at the age of thirty-six. But she needed to make him understand that stubbornness would not help him with this. Nothing would.

"Your friendship, that's all I want." His playful smile disappeared, and his face sobered. "For a quarter-century you were a part of my life. I just want my friend back."

"That's all?" she asked. Every message he'd sent, mentally and physically, over the past two months said he was looking for a lot more than that.

"That's all," he lied smoothly, holding his face solid and hoping she didn't read his eyes too well.

"Friends?" She studied him for several seconds, and nodded briskly. "Friends, I can do."

Every marathon begins with one step, he thought, and gave a short sigh of relief. They spent the next two hours shopping together. Nick forced himself to ignore the feel of her breast accidentally rubbing against his elbow as she reached past him to squeeze a peach. He fought not to pull her into his arms when she laughed at his story about his friend, Kevin, who had mistakenly hit on a drag queen in a club a few months ago. He tried not to think about the many times they'd made love, and the many times he hoped they would again.

As he helped her carry her bags back to her car, he hid the desire to kiss her good-bye. *No,* he reminded himself. They were friends, and that would have to be enough . . . for now.

"All rise."

Nick stood without thinking. His mind was completely occupied with thoughts of a tight-fitting forest-green skirt and matching silk blouse. Even with the four feet between them, he could smell her perfume wafting across the aisle.

Judge Scott settled behind the bench and called the courtroom to order. Nick didn't hear him. All his senses, including hearing, were focused on Vicki. Her stocking-clad coffee-brown legs were stretched out beneath the other table. Nick sighed, remembering how well they fit around his neck.

"Mr. Wilcox?"

Nick jumped, startled by the stern voice of the judge. "Yes, your honor?"

"It's your witness."

Nick stood and pulled himself together. "The defense calls Felix Olajywon."

The tall West Indian man stood in the back of the courtroom and strolled to the front. When he passed between the twin tables, he paused and turned his head in the direction of the prosecutor. Nick noticed the subtle movement and frowned, wondering what the man was doing.

Olajywon continued on and took his place on the stand, but in his wake Nick could see the look of horror on Vicki's face. Nick snapped his head around to look at his client, who was watching him with a look of confusion. He could feel the blood rushing to his bald head. Nick knew the type of man he was representing, and that his client kept company with some of the slimiest elements in the city of Chicago. Unfortunately, these were the types of thugs he was forced to call as *character* witnesses. But despite all that, he truly believed Tommy Morrison was innocent. He would not have represented him otherwise.

"Mr. Wilcox?" Judge Scott called again. He was losing his patience with the day-dreaming attorney.

"Yes, your honor."

Nick composed himself and moved toward the bench. He approached the large man who reclined in the hard-backed wooden chair on the stand. The man was still practically glaring at Vicki.

Nick eased in as close as possible to the witness, turning his back toward the jury. "If you touch her, I'll guarantee your boy never sees the light of day," he whispered, loud enough to be heard by Olajywon only.

The man's eyes widened, and he looked to his friend sitting behind the defense table. He didn't know what to make of the threat; this lawyer was supposed to be on their side.

Judge Scott saw Nick's lips moving, but wasn't sure what was said. He cocked an eyebrow. "Did you say something, Mr. Wilcox?"

"No, your honor," Nick lied. He turned to face the witness, his sharp, dark eyes silently reiterating his words.

Judge Scott frowned. *What is Wilcox up to?*

Tommy Morrison, sensing the unease between his attorney and Felix, sat up straight behind the table. From the troubled look on his former partner's face, he knew something was wrong.

Nick began to question the witness regarding the past activities of his client. He watched the man's behavior very carefully as Vicki cross-examined, but Olajywon was watching him as well. He was careful not to look directly at Vicki.

Nick chose to ignore the constant taps on his shoulder, not wanting to hear anything his client had to say. He would deal with him later.

Tommy Morrison sat stiff-backed, watching the gray metal door. He had no idea what had gone wrong in the courtroom. Only that after questioning his friend Felix, Mr. Wilcox had returned to the table with an angry scowl that remained in place the rest of the afternoon.

He knew calling Olajywon as a character witness was a risky move, but given his options, he had no choice. He'd spent the last year of his life in the company of murderers and thieves, certain that the monetary benefits outweighed the guilt on his heart. He'd been wrong. Terribly, irreversibly wrong. That mistake had cost him more than he could've imagined.

But after the death of his brother, Walter, he had honestly tried to change his life. He made a point of staying close to home, and began looking for a job. He wanted a life Walt would've been proud of, a second chance for both of them.

It worked, until he walked into a liquor store one horrible afternoon. He literally shivered, recalling the gruesome scene that now haunted his dreams. Seconds, mere seconds, was all it had taken to imprint the image on his mind forever. He'd only stopped by the store to buy some chewing gum. He was going on a job interview and wanted fresh breath. Instead, he pushed open the glass door and walked straight into hell.

There was blood everywhere . . . and the bodies, an elderly Arab man, and two young black men. Tommy swallowed hard, staring down at the body closest to the door. At first, he had not believed what he was seeing, but the light green eyes were all the proof he needed. The lifeless heap lying at his feet was his childhood friend, Benedict Brown. Or Benny, to those who knew him, and Tommy knew him well.

The other young man he didn't recognize, but the shop owner had been in the neighborhood for years. He'd always been friendly and fair. Tommy couldn't think of a single person who spoke ill of him; certainly, no one capable of a massacre such as this.

It took seconds to take in the scene and decide on what Tommy felt was the only course of action for a former gang member with a record. He ran, fled the store as fast as he could. But apparently not fast enough. There were witnesses. People who saw him, and had no problem describing him to the police. With his record, this arrest was his third strike. If he was convicted, he was going away for life. When the police knocked on his mother's front door, he knew his second chance was over.

Tommy had never been a religious person, but when he saw the famous attorney Nick Wilcox, his mother's distant cousin, pull up to his house as he was being taken away in a squad car, Tommy knew someone upstairs was looking out for him. Which brought him back to his present predicament and his attorney's strange behavior in court.

Finally, the door swung open. The guard cast Tommy a weary look and stepped aside. Nick's tall, muscular form nearly filled the doorway as he entered the small room. Tommy watched his attorney's eyes. He listened to the guard bolting the door, certain to the core of his soul that things were about to take a turn for the worst.

"Why are you looking at me like that, Mr. Wilcox?" Tommy asked. He knew without a doubt that the fact that Nick was standing inside the doorway instead of taking a seat across the table from him like always could not bode well for his future.

"You're going to have to find other representation. I plan to speak to the judge tomor—"

"What?" Tommy was out of his chair; his heart pounded against his chest.

Nick closed his eyes and took a deep breath. He was already fighting the urge to beat his client senseless. This little act of indignation wasn't helping. "Like I was saying, I'll speak to Judge Scott tomorrow morning and—"

"But why?" Tommy felt as if the room had darkened. "What'd I do?"

Nick crossed the room in three long strides and had the younger man by the collar. "Don't play innocent with me. I know what your boy is planning. If anybody touches her—"

"Touches who?"

"If you harm her in any way, you won't have to worry about life in prison. I'll kill you myself."

"What are you talking about? Harm who?"

The light tapping on the small, square glass window caused Nick to look around. The guard was signaling to him to back off. Nick kept his fist tightly clinched around the collar of his client.

The metal door cracked and the guard stuck his head inside. "Let him go, man. That scum's not worth your career."

In his current rage, it took several long seconds for reason to sink in. Nick released the man, more afraid of himself than his client. Nick turned and stormed out.

The guard looked at the face of the utterly baffled man left standing alone in the room. The inmate looked lost and confused; the guard couldn't help feeling sorry for him as he led him back to his empty cell.

When Vicki received the message regarding the meeting in Judge Scott's chambers, her first thought was that the judge had followed through on his threat to appoint new counsel, which she was beginning to think might not be a bad idea.

Vicki knew Nick was affecting her performance, and she didn't know what to do about her sweaty palms and throbbing headaches. When she entered the wood-paneled room and saw Nick looking like a beaten dog, she knew something far worse had happened.

His clothes were tousled, as if he'd slept in them. His normally clean-shaven face had a slight growth. She knew he'd not been home—his or anyone else's—from the look of him.

"Come in, Ms. Proctor," Judge Scott said, pulling on his robe. He'd arrived only minutes before. "Please, have a seat." He gestured to the chair beside Nick.

Vicki cast a sidelong glance at Nick. His eyes were trained on a small stain on the carpet. She knew he was intentionally avoiding eye contact with her, and that made her nerves stand on end. Nick Wilcox was a lot of things—cocky, arrogant, brilliant—but never timid.

"Mr. Wilcox has brought something to my attention," Judge Scott continued. "Something that I think you should be made aware of."

"What is it?" Vicki asked, looking pointedly at Nick. She willed him to look at her. She needed to see that ever-present glimmer of confidence in his dark eyes.

"He believes Mr. Morrison's associates were planning to harm you in some way," Judge Scott said.

Vicki's head swung around to Judge Scott, but what she saw was the sardonic smirk on the face of Felix Olajywon as he past her table, and the gun-firing movement he made with his index finger and thumb. She knew what he'd meant by it, but was unaware anyone else had seen it. She shook her head. When would she learn that nothing got by Nick?

"He's asked to be removed from the case, and that you be given the proper protection if you choose to stay with it."

Again she looked to Nick. "Did Tommy Morrison tell you this?"

"No, I saw what happened in the courtroom yesterday."

Vicki sat back in the chair, trying to absorb everything she'd been told. She felt as if the wind had been knocked out of her. Her mind was swimming with the possible outcomes of both staying with the case and walking away from it. And what about Nick? A discovery like this would be nothing less than a press feast. They would eat him alive.

She stood and walked over to the window. She stared out, thinking. The two men waited patiently, understanding that a bomb had been dropped on her and she needed time to digest it.

"Have you spoken to Morrison?" she finally asked.

"Yes," Nick answered, knowing instinctively that she was talking to him.

She turned to face him. "What did he have to say about it?

"What could he say?" Nick snapped defensively as he remembered the way he'd treated the man. He'd never lost his temper with a client, but the thought of that man or one of his goons touching Vicki had sent him over the edge.

"Nick," Vicki started, cautiously coming to stand beside his chair. "Is it possible that Olajywon is acting alone, that Morrison knew nothing of it?"

Nick was on his feet and looking at her as if she'd lost her mind. "The man wants you dead, and you're trying to defend him!"

"Hear me out." She glanced at Judge Scott, who had sat back in his chair and was listening with rapt attention. "I know you well enough to know you wouldn't have defended him if you didn't think he was innocent. Given what you know of him, do you really think he is involved with this?"

Nick slumped back down in the chair. "You said it yourself, Vicki, I'd defend the devil. Remember?"

Judge Scott's eyebrow cocked. *Where had that comment come from?*

"Nick, I trust your opinion. If you really think he was involved, I'll accept that. But if you're doing this out of anger, I think you owe it to yourself to reconsider. Remember why you took the case, and don't punish your client for the behavior of his associates."

Nick sat staring up at her, too stunned to speak.

"Your Honor, can we possibly have a short continuance to look into this?" she asked Judge Scott.

The elderly man was watching her in equal amazement. "Yes. Monday morning we'll meet again. Is eight A.M. okay?"

They both nodded.

"Until Monday."

Nick rushed through the revolving doors into the high-rise office building of his law firm while pulling on his suit jacket. He'd flown the red eye from Chicago to Little Rock to attend this very important meeting, and, glancing at his watch, he sighed in relief, realizing he would make it on time. The building was practically deserted on a Saturday morning, but that made it the perfect time to meet with this particular group of men.

He glanced at his watch again. Barely, but he would make it.

"You're cutting it close." Dorian Anderson, his friend and campaign manager, was headed straight for him. "What took you so long?" Dorian, equal in height but with a leaner build, fell into step with Nick's long strides.

"Didn't get out of court until almost six last night," Nick managed to get out while twisting and knotting his tie.

Dorian shook his head, still mystified as to how Nick, who'd moved to Chicago to reunite with his lost love, had found himself defending a petty thief accused of murder.

"Well, it doesn't matter." Dorian shrugged. "Long as you made it."

"Who's here?"

"Roland Maxwell, Samuel Blackton, Bane VanLouden and Pete Marlowe."

"All four?" The weight of power and money gathered

in his office right now should've been enough to physically tip the state of Arkansas.

"Apparently these gentlemen have big plans for you."

Nick ran a hand over his smooth head. He didn't for a minute underestimate the luck of having four of the heaviest hitters in Arkansas politics interested in sponsoring him in his bid for attorney general. Stopping outside his office door he turned to Dorian. "How do I look?"

Dorian ran a critical eye over the man he'd placed his bet on. He was certain that in a year Nick Wilcox would be the next attorney general and he, Dorian Anderson, would be right at his side.

"You look fine," Dorian said, and started to open the door.

"Wait," Nick spoke, laying his hand over the door's gold-plated emblem that read "Nicholas Wilcox, Attorney At Law." "Give me a minute."

The two men had met during their second year at Yale, and become fast friends. Dorian knew that one day a rare opportunity would knock on the door of Nicholas Wilcox. He just never imagined he would be a part of it.

Over the years, Dorian had discovered what few people knew. Nick's persona of cool aloofness was a shield, developed through years of self-imposed discipline. Beneath the man of conviction and confidence that he was famous for beat the heart of the chubby kid who was once the school bully's favorite target. He was now a bookworm disguised in the body of a jock, and it was at times like this that the timid boy inside would surface. Through necessity, Nick had become a master of suppression. A few minutes alone in a deserted hallway was all he ever needed to regain his typical self-possession.

He nodded. "I'm ready."

Dorian opened the door and led the way through the

small lobby area where on any given weekday, Shawn, Nick's assistant would be seated, and into a side office set up as a conference room. Because of the unusually small size of the room, it was sparsely decorated, with a medium-sized mahogany conference table surrounded by six leather chairs and small floral prints that lined the walls.

Four men, varying in age between fifty-eight and seventy-two, stood when Nick and Dorian entered, surveying their candidate. They each knew his strengths and weaknesses, and as a group they had already decided what to emphasize and what to conceal. They knew his habits, good and bad; all the sins of his past and his acts of charity as well.

They were the quartet the *Arkansas Times* had dubbed "The Fantastic Four," and they had in their combined power the ability to make men kings or paupers. After careful research and secret investigations, they'd unanimously decided to crown Nick Wilcox as the next attorney general. These four men knew more about Nick than members of his own family did. They would never have agreed to finance his campaign otherwise.

"Gentlemen, sorry to keep you waiting," Nick went around the table and shook each hand. "Please have a seat," he gestured, before taking the chair at the head of the table.

"Nick," Roland began, "Dorian was just telling us that you are commuting between Little Rock and Chicago. What's this about?"

Nick was not surprised that Roland, the leader of this small cartel, would be the first to speak. Nick studied the man carefully for several longs seconds before finally answering. "Yes, I am. It's a personal matter."

Roland Maxwell, at the age of sixty-five, was one of the most powerful men in the state of Arkansas, and it was he who'd first approached Nick with the idea of running for office. Nick knew that of the four men facing him, Roland was the one who needed to be convinced. The others would follow his lead.

"Personal, huh?" Roland lifted his arched white eyebrow. "Nick, how committed are you to this race?"

"Completely, of course."

Roland rubbed his chin. "We have a good five, maybe six months before this campaign gets underway. It seems to me this is the wrong time to decide to fly off to Chicago to handle your personal business."

Nick's full lips tightened into a straight line. The words were carefully chosen, but the message was clear. "Gentlemen." Nick made a point of looking at each of the men as he spoke. "Let me reassure you. Come November of next year, I will be the elected attorney general of the state of Arkansas. The issue in Chicago will be resolved long before."

"Why are you being secretive, Nick?" Sam Blackton, the only black man in the group, spoke. "Is this something that's going to come back and bite us in the ass?"

"No, no, I promise you. My reason for being in Chicago can only add to the campaign, not in any way damage it."

"Well, hell. If there's nothing to it, why not just say what it is?" Pete Marlowe, the weakest partner in the foursome, a good ol' boy whose roots extended well back to the Confederate South, was the only member of the group Nick had any doubts about. He was certain he was not Pete's first choice for candidate. But Nick had been dealing with the Pete Marlowes of the world his whole professional career, and this particular model was not especially threatening.

"Nick is securing his future bride," Dorian supplied with a smile. Unlike Nick, this group of men did indeed intimidate him. Dorian had been a campaign manager long enough to understand that these were very good men to have on your side in a race, but as good as these men were to their friends, they were equally unkind to their enemies.

Nick glared at Dorian, sitting across the table from him. He was going to have to have a talk with his campaign manager about his right to privacy. Contrary to the impression Roland was trying to convey, the campaign wasn't anywhere near to beginning. Nick planned to be married to Vicki and resettled in Little Rock long before the time came to announce his bid for attorney general.

As his wife, it was inevitable that Vicki would become a vital part of the campaign, and this group of sharks would investigate every inch of her past and present. Nick wasn't worried; Vicki was cleaner than Aunt Tilde's chitterlings. But what he didn't want was for them to begin their investigation of her now, before he'd had a chance to prepare her. And the less they knew about her until that time, the better.

"What's this?" Roland's bushy, gray brows drew together. "You're getting married? Why didn't you tell us about this? Who is she?"

Nick sighed. "There's nothing to tell yet. I haven't proposed." He cut a dark look at Dorian. "It's still very much up in the air. But as soon as I have something definite to tell you, I will."

"Well, who is she?" Bane VanLouden spoke for the first time. Bane was the youngest of the group at the age of fifty-eight. A man in prime condition, he could've easily passed for someone much younger. He was a newcomer to the state of Arkansas. Nick didn't know as much about Bane as he wished he did; the man's past was somewhat of an enigma. But whoever he was, he apparently had the right connections, or he wouldn't be sitting with this group of men.

"Victoria Proctor," Dorian piped up again. "She and Nick grew up together; she's an attorney as well. In fact, she's a prosecutor for the state of Illinois."

Oh, yes. Nick was practically seething. He was most definitely going to have to have a talk with Dorian.

"Well, now." Pete smiled. "Sounds promising."

"Like I said." Nick held up both hands in a useless gesture of holding back. He knew the floodgate had already been opened. They had all the information they needed to begin the data collection process. "Nothing has been settled."

Roland was studying Nick with intense scrutiny. "Indeed it does," he said, in response to Pete's comment. "Makes one wonder why you were hesitant to mention her, Nick."

Nick could hear the wheels churning in Roland's mind. He was thinking of all the reasons why such pertinent information would be held back. A candidate's wife who happened to be a former prosecutor could only be a plus to the campaign. Why hide her? He knew Roland would look into every facet of Vicki's life until he found the answer.

He gave his most winning smile and looked to each of the gentlemen. "The truth of the matter is, as handsome and charming as we all believe I am, there's still a chance the lady will say no."

The four men chuckled heartily, accepting the plausible explanation of male pride. It was an emotion they each understood well. Dorian breathed a sigh of relief and pulled out the files that had brought them together on this Saturday afternoon.

They spent the rest of the afternoon going over the various points of the issues Nick wanted to address, most of which were acceptable to the group, and a few they rejected in lieu of their own suggestions and interests.

In less than seven hours, Nick was on a return flight to Chicago, still dressed in the clothes he'd flown into Little Rock wearing. He reclined in the small airplane seat and fell asleep. His last thoughts were: How much longer could he keep up this exhausting pace? And how much longer must he wait to hold Vicki in his arms again?

CHAPTER FOUR

"Come on, Vicki. No rest for the wicked," Peaches called over her shoulder as she raced along the Grant Park jogging path at a steady pace.

"If I ever catch up to you . . ." Vicki huffed loudly. Every part of her body was aching. ". . . I'll show you wicked."

"You hate me now, but you'll love me when you can fit into that teal dress you bought last year. You know, the one with the tags still on it because you bought it two sizes too small?" Peaches spun around and ran backwards while taunting her friend.

Vicki stopped dead cold. "You went in my closet?!"

"Of course. But what were you thinking?" Peaches continued to tease, making sure she remained out of arm's reach. "Did you really think a couple of bowls of Special K was gonna make it happen? With those hips? Please!" Peaches laughed loudly as she turned and raced ahead.

"I'm gonna kill you." Vicki was feeling inspired. She sprinted to catch up.

By the time she did, they were both approaching the ice cream vendor, and all threats of violence became null and void against the soothing taste of the icy vanilla cream.

The two women sat across from each other on the park bench, the way they often had. Whenever one of them decided her gluteus maximus was spreading beyond control, the other was obligated to diet also. Luckily, neither had the fortitude to continue their dieting efforts for long. But still, tradition was tradition.

This time the instigator was a favorite pair of rapidly shrinking Capri pants, which were now a pile of dust rags in the cleaning bucket under Peaches's kitchen sink.

"What's the deal?" Peaches asked.

"What do you mean?" Vicki said, finishing her cone. She stood to stretch her legs on the bench.

"Don't play dumb with me. Give me the latest. What's going on with Nick?"

"Nothing." Vicki was now regretting her decision to tell Peaches, the most discerning person she knew, that her ex had returned and was proceeding to wreak havoc on her life. At the time she'd needed to vent, and even though Angela was her usual sounding board, somehow dogging Nick to his sister didn't seem right. She'd confided in Peaches. Peaches, who never let anything go until it had been examined, analyzed, and dissected to death.

"We've decided to put the past behind us and just be friends."

"Uh-huh," Peaches muttered into her cone. Even muffled, her agreement was less than convincing.

"What? You don't think we can be friends?"

Peaches studied Vicki carefully for several seconds before answering. "Just friends? No."

"Why not?"

"Come on, Vicki, I've seen pictures of the guy in the newspapers. He's gorgeous. Are you trying to tell me that every time you see him, you're not picturing him naked?"

Vicki bent in half under the guise of continuing her

stretches, but mostly to hide the flush of her face. As always, Peaches had hit the nail on the head.

How many times in the past few weeks had she looked at him across the courtroom remembering their lives together, *before* Andy Pallister came into it? The simple pleasures: reading the Sunday morning paper together, dining out at their favorite restaurant, the pleasure of making love.

She'd felt abashed with shame. While watching him present evidence to the jury—just yesterday—she'd had a vivid memory of him in the shower. She saw him reaching up to adjust the flow of the showerhead in their old apartment in Little Rock. She was standing next to him, watching him sing the chorus from Earth, Wind and Fire's "Reasons" in all his naked glory.

"See?" Peaches's twisted mouth screamed told-you-so. "You're thinking about him naked right now, aren't you?"

"So what? I may not be able to control my thoughts, but I can certainly control my actions." Vicki had decided long ago that denying any obvious truth with Peaches was like carrying an umbrella full of holes in a rainstorm: pointless.

"And how long do you think you're going to be able to control it? Not to mention the fact that I don't think he has any intention of controlling how he feels about you."

"Well, I guess it's up to me." Vicki realized the statement sounded weak even to her own ears.

Peaches tossed the last bit of her cone in her mouth and the napkin into the trash can beside the bench. "Well, if what you've told me is any example, I'd say your *control* is in for one heck of a fight."

Peaches was gone again, racing ahead. Vicki watched

her go, then followed behind at a less enthusiastic pace. Thanks to her friend's sobering words, and the ice cream cone, she was no longer in the mood for exercise. A few minutes later, Peaches had disappeared from sight and Vicki continued along at her snail's pace. She watched the children on the playground, while an elderly man was sitting on a bench feeding pigeons. The park was alive with typical Saturday afternoon activity.

Sensing someone else on the path, Vicki moved to the side to allow the runner by, her mind still distracted as she considered Peaches's warning. The hairs on the back of her neck stood on end, but instead of turning to look, she instinctively began to run again.

She knew. She just knew who was behind her, closing in on her. She pumped her legs at an accelerated rate, and after she was at top speed, she glanced back over her shoulder. Nick was almost beside her. She didn't look back again; she needed all her concentration to stay the few steps ahead of his much longer legs.

She ran like prey. Knowing, in some strange way, to the man behind her, she was precisely that. The target of his hunger. What was he doing here? And why was he chasing her? It didn't matter. One glance in his eyes was enough to confirm that she'd reacted in the only way she could. She fled him, as she'd fled eight years previously, and this time was proving as futile as the last.

The wind whipped against her face, and whatever sweat coated her body dried to her skin in the light breeze whisking past her. Her heart was pounding, her lungs pumping, and the heavy steps echoing to her right were getting louder and louder. Closer and closer.

A hand came around her waist, her feet came up off the ground, and she found her back pressed against a stone wall of flesh. His strong arms twisted her body, using her own momentum to propel her back into his arms. One of his strong legs slid between hers, forcing her to straddle it; his fingers curved around her waist. Her back slammed against a tree, and she found herself pinned between the hard bark of an ancient maple and the hard body of a very modern man. His body molded to hers shoulder to toe. His fingers dug into the tender skin at the base of her spine. His hot mouth clamped down on hers, and it had all seemed to happen in the blink of an eye.

The heart's reaction: *Damn. That was smooth.*

The brain's reaction: *How dare he!*

The brain won. She mustered all the indignation she could between gasps of air. "How dare—"

Her fury fell on deaf ears. Nick accepted the invitation of her open mouth and slid his tongue inside. He deepened the kiss, demanding her participation. Vicki turned her head left and right, trying to break away from his ravenous mouth. Lifting one hand from her waist, he cupped her chin tightly, holding her in place, as his tongue continued its assault.

Vicki's body begged her brain for surrender. But the mind refused to give in. Her tongue wanted to play with his; her fingers wanted to explore the width of his broad shoulders. Her breast pressed solidly against his hard chest. Her feminine self desperately wanted to respond to his very masculine enticement, but the danger to her heart was too great.

"Mmoop," she mumbled against his mouth.

He moaned with pleasure in return.

"Mmop mmick. Smmmop."

"Yes," he whispered against her throat. "That's it baby, give in to it."

She pushed at his shoulders. They were as strong and

solid as she remembered. "I said get off me, you jerk!" She pushed against him harder, but he barely moved.

He lifted his head enough to look into her face. His dark eyes seared her soul. She felt as if he were looking straight through her. "You don't really want me to stop, Vicki. Do you?"

The heart said: *Please, God, no. Don't stop.*

The brain said: *Shut up, heart.*

Vicki forced her back up against the tree, trying to put even a molecule of space between their bodies, and found there was not a molecule of air to spare.

"Let me go right now," she hissed. Her brown eyes were burning with an unspoken warning.

Nick's eyes twinkled with something wild, and for a few moments Vicki was unsure if he actually would let her go. Finally, he released his tight hold and stepped back from her. His chest was still rising and falling hard with his unspent lust.

Seeing him in his present state, Vicki understood what she'd done wrong. She'd run to deter him, and managed to arouse him even more than he already was. More wild thing than man at that moment, he was turned on by the chase.

"What do you think you're doing?"

Regaining his typical regal composure, he smiled and said, "Giving my wife a good morning kiss."

"I'm not your wife."

He shrugged his shoulder. "Maybe not officially." His bad-boy smile intensified. "But that's just paperwork."

Vicki turned to leave, but his arm came up against the tree to block her path. "You taste just as I remember." He tilted his head to the side and leaned forward until he was almost touching her collar bone. "Your scent is the same, too. I could track you across the world by your scent alone."

Her mouth twisted in disdain. "Is that a threat?"

"If you make it one. Plan on leaving Chicago soon?"

Realizing she wouldn't be set free anytime soon Vicki folded her arms over her chest. She leaned back against the tree, confident she could hold her own as long as he didn't touch her again. *Please, God, don't let him touch me again.* "Like I would tell you if I were planning to relocate."

Nick completely ignored the comment, and instead spent the time enjoying the sight of her somewhat clingy sweat suit. "I want to make love to you again so badly," he whispered almost breathlessly at the sight of her still-heaving bosom.

"We all have wants, Nick." She pushed his arm away. The conversation was getting too intense to remain his easy hostage.

"Why won't you even give me a chance?" He spoke to her retreating back.

Vicki paused long enough to respond. "What's the point?"

"The point is, I still love you, and you love me, and we fit, Vicki. We fit better than any two people I've ever met."

"We *used* to fit, Nick, in the past tense."

"And we can again. It's still there, I feel it." Taking her hand, he lifted it to his beating heart. "In here. And so do you."

"I'll admit that seeing you again after all these years has sparked a residue of what I used to feel, but that's all it is—a memory of what once was."

"What can be again."

"You can't relive the past, Nick."

"I told you, I'm interested in the future."

She reluctantly pulled her hand away from his chest. "My future does not include you."

Nick stood beneath the maple tree and watched her walk away. This was not the way it was supposed to go. He knew she missed him as much as he missed her. He'd apologized for the way things ended until he was blue in the face.

What was it? What was she holding in her heart against him? Nick knew—whatever it was—it was the key to bringing her back to him. Whatever it was, he needed to weed it out of her. And soon.

Nick sat in his jeep watching the small brick house with its neat lawn and picket fence. The only things missing were tiny gingerbread men sprinkled across the rooftop. Who would've guessed a thug like Tommy Morrison could've been raised in such a home. *Or,* Nick thought, *maybe it serves as a reminder that Tommy wasn't always a thug.*

It had been nothing but fate that brought him and the Morrison family together. Several weeks ago, while packing his jeep to leave for Chicago, his Aunt Tilde had come sauntering out with a cooler full of frozen fish she wanted delivered to her cousin Katie, who lived on the south side of Chicago. It had been years since the two women had seen each other, but they still kept in touch with phone calls and the occasional gift.

Nick went to Katie's first upon entering the city, anxious to be rid of the horrible smell he'd spent the past ten hours trapped with inside his jeep. He felt as if the smell of fish had permeated his skin, and it was a hot shower on his mind when he pulled up to the ensuing chaos.

As he arrived, Tommy was being led away in cuffs. The

young man's confused eyes passed briefly over Nick as he was shoved into the back of a squad car. His grief-stricken mother stood blurry-eyed in the doorway, help-less to do anything to protect her only remaining child.

Katie Morrison had seen Nick's timely arrival as a mir-acle. The day he'd arrived in court for the arraignment and found Vicki standing behind the table for the pros-ecution, Nick had had to agree.

He'd wondered how he would go about introducing himself back into Vicki's life, and found his answer in the words, "Nick Wilcox, representing the defendant."

Finally, he got out of his car and went to the door. He knocked a few times and waited patiently, knowing the elderly woman inside needed time to answer it.

"Who is it?" The weak sound of a woman's voice came from the other side of the door.

"Mrs. Morrison, it's Nick Wilcox, Tommy's attorney," Nick called loudly. He listened to the rattling of a chain and the sound of the deadbolt being released.

The first thing he saw was a beaming smile across a light brown face. Her salt-and-pepper hair was pulled back in two neat french braids that fell down her back. She was dressed in a colorful housedress, and the sleeves were pressed to perfection. As she opened her arms to embrace Nick, he smelled the faint odor of cooking grease on her.

Nick smiled as he accepted her warm welcome. Katie Morrison reminded him of his aunt, the two could've been sisters instead of the distant cousins they were.

"Nick, you don't have to be formal, sugar. We're family." She squeezed him tight. Nick knew she meant every word. She was that kind of genuine. Had she not been sincere, it would've been evident in everything from her eyes to her speech.

"Make yourself at home, I have to check on my pork chops." She scurried back toward the kitchen, her plastic-soled slippers making a scratching sound against the vinyl runner that ran the length of the house.

Nick practically fell into the worn sofa. The pretty sage-green cover hid its true age from the naked eye, but the body knew as soon as you sat down. His eyes perused the shelves lined with innumerable knick-knacks. *A life-time of collecting,* Nick thought.

After a few minutes she came back into the room, wiping her hands on her apron. "What brings you by, Nick?" she asked, settling into a chair across from him.

"Mrs. Morrison, I think—"

"Katie." She smiled. "If I've told you once, I've told you a thousand times. My name is Katie, not Mrs. Morrison," she teased.

Nick smiled in return. Her natural warmth and exuberance was making this far more difficult than he'd anticipated. "Katie, there's been a problem." His mind struggled to phrase the statement properly. Women like this bore the weight of their children's sins as if they were their own. If Tommy did have something to do with the threat made against Vicki, Nick knew this mother would bear the guilt for her son.

"Oh?" Her graying brows knitted in concern.

"A threat was made against the prosecutor on the case. I'm not sure if Tommy had anything to do with it or not." Nick sighed. If Tommy were a part of this, Nick would drop him like a bad habit, but feared what that would do to this woman, who'd already been through so much.

"Are you asking me a question, Nick?" she asked, sitting forward again. She could see the conflict in his heart as clearly as a cloud swirling above his head.

"Yes." He paused. "I guess I am. A friend of Tommy's

made a death threat against Vicki Proctor, the attorney prosecuting the case. We're not sure if this friend acted alone, or at Tommy's request. Katie, you've been honest with me about everything right from the start." Nick leaned forward and stared intensely into a pair of wise, old eyes. "I guess I'm asking you if you believe Tommy would go that far to avoid prison?"

Katie sat back in her comfortable chair again and closed her eyes. She stayed that way for so long Nick wondered if she'd fallen asleep.

As if coming out of a trance, she spoke. "When Tommy started running with that gang of his, he changed. My boy started doing things I didn't think he was capable of. Stealing, and—hurting people." Her voice trailed off. She shook her head. "Had you asked me that question a year ago, my answer may have been yes.

"When he pulled my Walt into it, my heart split in two. Both my boys living a life that wouldn't amount to anything but a prison cell or a headstone. I tried to wash my hands of them both, but how could I?" Her brown eyes pleaded with Nick. "How can any mother turn her back on her children, no matter what they may become?"

Nick's mind briefly wandered away to the pretty dark-skinned woman who haunted his dreams; he remembered little of her. He often wondered if she would be proud of him, of the man he had become. He often wondered what it would've been like to grow up in the shelter of her love.

"Katie, you're not responsible for what Tommy or Walter chose to do with their lives."

"Oh, yes, I am, Nick," she said. "God gave them to me, and what they became is based on the love I gave them."

Nick felt his stomach churning as he imagined what he must do. The case would not be dismissed. Tommy would find another attorney and start all over again, putting this poor woman through yet another hellish trial.

"Nick . . ." She slipped her hands into her oversized pockets. "The night Walt died, Tommy carried him home cradled like a baby in the crook of his arms. He laid him on that very couch." She motioned to where Nick was sitting. "Tommy slumped down on the floor beside his brother's lifeless body, and stayed there weeping until well after dawn."

Nick fought the urge to hop up off the couch. He had the uneasy feeling of sitting on a grave.

"That night I got down on my knees, and I thanked God." Her aged eyes bore into Nick. "I thanked him for not taking *both* my boys." She sighed heavily. "After that night, Tommy didn't run off with the gang anymore. And when they came here looking for him, he sent them away." She paused again and stood. Nick stood also, knowing the conversation was coming to an end.

"I don't know who killed those people, but it wasn't my Tommy. The night Walt was killed I lost a son, but I also got one back. Do you understand what I'm saying? The Tommy sitting in that prison cell is *not* the Tommy that ran with the gangs and hurt people, Nick. He's the one who sat on this floor and wept like a baby for his dead brother."

Nick looked deep into her clear brown eyes, and nodded. Both his mind and conscience were clear. He knew what he must do. He hugged Katie once more, walked out the front door of her storybook house, and drove straight to the law library. He had some work to catch up on.

***

A week had passed since Nick had returned to Judge Scott's chamber with his determination that Tommy Morrison was not involved in the threat, and that he would continue to defend his client. He'd suggested to both Vicki and Judge Scott that Vicki remove herself as the prosecutor, but she had refused.

The pair had argued loud and bitterly right there in the middle of Judge Scott's chamber, with the judge sitting and watching like a fascinated observer. Later, Vicki reflected on the mortifyingly high number of times she and Nick had completely lost all their professionalism and polish, choosing instead to act like a couple of unruly brats fighting over a lollipop.

Vicki had made a point of not speaking to Nick any more than absolutely necessary after that. She was determined that there would be no more drama between them, scenes that overshadowed the importance and seriousness of the case. A man's life was at stake, and their paltry problems would have to take a backseat.

Which was why, when Vicki arrived for her weekly Sunday morning brunch with Angela, she paused on the sidewalk. The sight of the familiar black Jeep Grand Cherokee in the driveway made her hesitate. What was he doing here? On a Sunday morning no less.

Carrying a tray of fresh-baked breakfast biscuits—her contribution to brunch—she went around to the side door of the small brick house. She was careful to step over the mud puddles formed by last night's rain showers. Her cream-colored slingbacks were brand new and matched her lace dress perfectly; she wasn't about to mess them up. She tapped on the screen door before pulling it open, and froze where she stood.

There sat Nick, lifting a spoon of grits to his mouth. He smiled, and she felt her knees knock. *If only he was as ugly as the dog he is,* she thought, *it would make this friend thing much easier.*

"Good morning." His welcoming smile slid into the devilish grin that was classic Nick. Vicki felt a chill run through her body. She'd lost her virginity to that grin.

"Good morning." She placed her tray of biscuits on the stove, and moved over to the coffeepot. "Where's Angie?"

He cut into a large slice of ham. "Still getting dressed."

Vicki noticed the assortment of foods on the stove, the pot of unburned grits, the perfectly cooked scrambled eggs and cooling slices of ham.

"You cooked?" Vicki asked, knowing Angela had never in her life prepared a meal this perfect. Nick, on the other hand, could've been a professional chef if he put his heart to it. Vicki always thought it was kind of unfair the way nature had divided that particular talent between the siblings.

He nodded, unable to speak with his mouth wrapped around a forkful of eggs.

Once she had that assurance, Vicki picked up a plate and piled it high with food. She sat down across the table from him and noticed his sage-colored linen suit, cream shirt, and matching tie behind the napkin tucked neatly at his collar. The tiny crucifix that hung around his neck, and his single diamond stud earring, were his only pieces of jewelry.

"Where are you going?" she asked, fearing she already knew the answer.

The sly grin floated across his lips again. "To church . . . with you."

"Church? You don't go to church! You *never* go to church." Vicki knew how panicked she sounded, but the terror in her heart was real. She couldn't have hid her fear if she wanted to.

Nick's eyebrows furrowed in concern, hoping she didn't begin to hyperventilate. He waited for her to regain control of her breathing before saying, "Like I told you, I've made some changes in my life." He cut off another slice of ham.

Before Vicki could respond, Angela came strolling in dressed in a double-breasted peach suit and a single strand of pearls. Her long black hair hung well past her shoulders. With her dark skin and sharp features, she was a very pretty female version of her brother.

"Good morning, Vicki."

"Good morning," Vicki said half-heartedly, wondering if it was too late to back out and go home. The thought of sitting in the crowded pews all morning with Nick's warm thigh pressed against hers was simply too much.

Angela watched the couple eating with undisguised envy, her nose assaulted by the wonderful smells coming from the stove. She fought to hide the tinge of annoyance she was feeling. No matter how she tried her grits always stuck to the pan.

Her wine-red lips twisted in frustration. "We better get going so we won't be late."

Vicki and Nick shared a knowing smile across the table.

"Okay, but let me have a couple of spoonfuls of your strawberry pudding before we go," Nick said, rising to put his plate in the dishwasher.

Angela's ear's perked up. "What?"

"Just a little, it was really good last night," he continued with his back to his sister.

"It's kind of early for pudding, don't you think?" Angela asked, not trusting the compliment.

"It's never too early for pudding." Nick reached overhead and pulled a bowl from the cabinet. By the time he turned around, Angela was standing behind him with the chilled bowl of pudding, holding it proudly.

"Want some, Vicki?" she asked, heaping several spoonfuls into the bowl.

"No, thanks." Vicki tried to hide her disgust. The strange orangish concoction showed no signs of anything resembling strawberries or pudding. "I'll make do with this." She shoveled another spoonful of warm, buttery grits into her mouth.

She watched Nick devour the dessert, taking large spoonfuls and swallowing without chewing. Most impressive of all, he managed to do it all with a smile. He even gave the occasional murmur of delight while his baby sister looked on proudly.

Vicki had never had more respect for him than she did at that moment. She knew that in the future, if anyone asked her to define love, this image would come to mind.

Despite Nick's presence, the service was enjoyable and left Vicki feeling rejuvenated for the upcoming week. As they stood in the reception line leading to the rear exit, Vicki could feel Nick's warmth immediately behind her. Although no part of his body was touching her, with the snail's pace at which the line was moving she knew she would be near to scorching before they reached the door.

Someone in the back accidentally pushed forward, causing a domino effect. Nick fell forward before catching his step. One hand came up to brace Vicki's elbow while the other rested at her waist.

"Excuse me," he whispered. Nick's hot breath was right at her ear, and Vicki was certain she was about to combust.

Images of their bodies entwined in lovemaking flooded her mind; the remembered feel of him, skin on skin, mouth to mouth. The pieces of nature's most perfect puzzle fitting together. Just as she began to savor his touch the connection was gone. She forced the images away, feeling guilty for having such thoughts. What was this man doing to her?

The feel of Reverend Campbell's hand on her arm startled her back to reality. "Sister Proctor, good to see you," he said, but his eyes were focused on Angela, two paces behind.

"Wonderful sermon, Reverend," Vicki said, and moved to stand beside him, waiting for Nick and Angela to come through the line.

"Well, who do we have here?" Reverend Campbell smiled at Nick.

"Reverend, this is my brother, Nicholas Wilcox."

Nick shook the man's hand firmly.

"Welcome, Brother Wilcox," Reverend Campbell said, and immediately shifted in Angela's direction. He took her hand between both of his. "Sister Wilcox, you're looking very lovely today." He glanced discreetly over her long form and returned to her face.

Nick didn't miss the appreciative gleam that twinkled in the reverend's hazel brown eyes. A look which caused Nick to study the minister a little closer. Taking note of his youthful appearance and the lack of a wedding ring eased his protective brotherly instincts. Still, he'd heard about disreputable ministers who used their female congregations as their own private harems.

Angela blushed. "Thank you, Reverend. Your sermon was uplifting, as always." She started to move away, feeling the line of parishioners crowding forward, but Reverend Campbell held her hand.

"Um, Sister Wilcox, if you have a few minutes, I'd like to speak to you in pri—"

"I'm sorry, Reverend," Angela interrupted. "I really have to hurry home. I think I left something on."

Nick's eyes grew to the size of quarters, and were only surpassed by Vicki's half-dollar stare. "Left what on?" Nick blurted out with absolutely no thought.

Angela turned and glared at her brother. "If I knew, I wouldn't have to rush home, would I?"

Nick's eyes narrowed. "Huh? That doesn't make any—"

"Please excuse us, Reverend," Angela smiled beautifully while pulling her hand free of the light grip. She shot Nick one last dirty look and nodded in the direction of the rear exit before moving that way with all the grace of a fleeing gazelle being chased by a tawny-eyed leopard.

"Well, Brother Wilcox, glad you could join us today." Reverend Campbell's eyes shot back to Angela for only a moment, but it was enough for Nick to see the disappointment beneath the mask of a polite smile. "I hope we'll be seeing more of you."

There was something there, Nick thought. *Something . . .* but he wasn't sure what. Nick knew from the conversation in the car on the way to the church that morning that the minister had been over the small parish for only a few months, brought in by a unanimous vote after their elderly pastor retired.

Nick shook the man's hand one final time and moved toward the door where Vicki and Angela were waiting. He made a mental note to ask Vicki about the new minister as soon as he could.

As the trio exited the building, their path was blocked by a heavy-set woman dressed in a bright turquoise evening gown, large feathered hat, and matching four-inch turquoise stilettos that seemed more suited to the

Ebony Fashion Fair than Sunday morning at the Starlight Baptist church.

"Well, just look what we have here." The woman beamed, her huge brown eyes taking in Nick's lean form with blatant interest. "Angela, you never said you had a brother." Her pearly white teeth were well taken care of and seemed to stretch from ear to ear, giving her features a mulish cast. Angela and Vicki exchanged a knowing expression that was none too friendly.

"Sister Verdell Thurman, my brother, Nick Wilcox." Angela begrudgingly made the introductions, seeing no way to avoid them without appearing rude.

"Not *the* Nick Wilcox?" Verdell's eyes seemed to double in size, and she heaved a breath that brought her already abundant bosom up several additional inches.

Try as he may, Nick couldn't help but notice how her pushed-up bust was now inches from his face, as she had sidled closer to him while speaking.

"Angela, you didn't say your brother was *the* Nick Wilcox."

"Seeing how she didn't tell you she had a brother, Verdell, I doubt she would've told you he was *the* Nick Wilcox," Vicki blurted out, each word dripping with sarcasm.

Sister Thurman only ignored her, and inched in closer to Nick. She howled over her shoulder, "Connie! Come and meet Angela's handsome brother."

Vicki hid the grin that appeared as Constance Thurman came into Nick's line of vision. The look of utter amazement on his face was not one Vicki would forget.

An almost exact replica of Verdell Thurman appeared from around the corner of the church. From what Nick could tell, the only visible difference between the sisters was that this version was cloaked in fuchsia instead of turquoise. It was the exact same style of dress, complete with matching fuchsia hat and stilettos.

"Well." She stopped a few feet from the group and beamed just like her sister, mulish expression and all. "Aren't you a handsome devil."

Nick smiled, albeit, a stiff, befuddled smile. He simply relied on instinct. The ability to hide his true emotions behind a mask of polite indifference was second nature.

"Angela, you didn't tell me you—"

"We've been through that," Verdell snapped, before glancing briefly in Vicki's direction.

"Brother Wilcox, will you be attending regularly?" Connie Thurman flanked Nick. Closing in opposite her twin, the two women had him fully trapped.

Nick looked directly at Vicki. "I really enjoyed the service today. I'm considering joining."

"Joining?" Vicki and Angela sounded in unison. He was certain of Vicki's reasons for concern, but surprised by his sister's reaction.

"Yes, joining," he reiterated.

"Oh, how wonderful," Verdell chirped in the high-pitched soprano voice that made her the pride and joy of the Starlight Trumpeters. "We can use some young blood around here."

"Oh, yes, indeed." Constance mimicked her sister's enthusiasm while her eyes took in Nick's muscular form. "Yes, indeed."

Vicki and Angela watched with muted laughter as the two women closed in on him like a pair of hungry jackals cornering their quarry.

"Angela, didn't you leave something on?" Nick hinted to his sister, sensing impending doom.

"No," Angela answered innocently. "Nothing's on."

"But inside the church, you just said—"

She smiled. "I was mistaken."

Nick's dark eyes darted to Vicki, not that he expected any compassion from that direction, but surprisingly that's where it came from.

"Verdell, can you give a message to Charles for me?" Vicki asked

Verdell didn't hear the question; her mind was too busy racing with whom to tell first. This handsome, obviously single, young man's arrival was most definitely food for the gossip mill. And Angela's brother to boot. It would be real interesting to see how things began to unravel in the next few weeks.

Everyone could see that Reverend Campbell had a thing for Angela Wilcox, although he'd been unable to do anything more that make the occasional shy advance. Only the object of his affection seemed to be ignorant to his intentions. But now, with a brother around, he would surely see how the reverend watched Angela with that lost puppy dog expression.

Not to mention those soulful looks Brother Wilcox kept giving Vicki Proctor. Oh yes, Verdell thought, things were about to get a lot more lively around Starlight.

"Verdell."

"Um, oh, oh—I'm sorry, were you speaking to me?"

"Yes, I was asking if you could tell Charles, the printer, that the rehearsal has to be changed this week, from Tuesday to Thursday."

"Oh, sure." Verdell leaned forward to say something to her sister.

"*Now*, Verdell," Vicki snapped.

The woman swung around and stared at Vicki in wounded silence.

"Before he prints the bulletins for the week," Vicki added, regaining her composure and smiling benignly.

She wasn't worried about Constance; she went where Verdell went. But getting rid of Verdell was like trying to pry a dog off his bone.

"All right," Verdell said stiffly. With a roll of her eyes in Vicki's direction, she turned to face Nick again. "Brother Wilcox, I look forward to seeing you real soon." With that, the two sisters released their prisoner and sauntered back into the church with all the haughtiness of a pair of proud peacocks.

Nick tugged at his sleeves, trying to straighten the creases caused by the women's tight grip. "Took you long enough," he hissed at Vicki.

"You're welcome." She turned and strutted away.

"And you." He turned on his sister. "How you gon' hang me out to dry like that?"

"Oh, quit your griping and come on." Angela turned and followed in Vicki's wake.

Nick let out a heavy, gusty breath of disgust and followed the two women back to his jeep. He considered driving away without them more than once. The only thing that stopped him was fear of the unknown. He knew what type of vengeance Angela was capable of alone, and he'd seen Vicki's wrath in its full brilliance. But together? Now that was a scary thought.

He hit the button to open the automated lock switch, and started the car while his passengers climbed in. They'd intentionally left him to the mercy of what he knew on sight were probably the worst gossips in the church. By next Sunday, word that *the* Nick Wilcox was planning to join the church would've spread throughout the congregation.

This was not at all the way he'd intended things to go. But things had not been going the way he'd intended since his arrival in Chicago. When last he spoke to Dorian, the race for attorney general was gearing up. Two other candidates, both of whom were personal acquaintances of Nick's, had already announced their intentions to run for office. By now, his courtship with Vicki was supposed to be in full bloom. And he most certainly was not supposed to be wrapped up in the middle of a murder trial. No, nothing was going according to plan at all. He was only happy that he'd allowed himself so much time for the wooing of Ms. Proctor. And, at the rate things were moving, he was going to need every bit of it.

CHAPTER FIVE

"Is anyone sitting here?"

Vicki was sitting alone at a small round table, staring out the cafeteria window at the passersby moving in the courtyard. Hearing the familiar voice, she sighed heavily. This man's uncanny ability to find her anywhere was really becoming annoying.

"Yes." She used her paper napkin to wipe her face and hands. For one hour per workday she was supposed to be free of Nick Wilcox. One hour. Was that too much to ask?

Nick stood holding his cafeteria tray containing a cellophane-wrapped sandwich, apple, and milk. He glanced at the three empty chairs surrounding Vicki, his mouth twisted in derision. "Who? Casper the ghost?"

"Still better company than you," she muttered.

He flopped his tray down on the table and fell into the chair next to her. "Scoot over." He intentionally crowded her, forcing her to move her chair over.

"Can't you take a hint?"

"Can't you stop being hateful?"

"I would, if you'd leave me alone."

"Sorry, baby, can't do that." He started unwrapping his

sandwich and prepared to eat. "Not until you admit you still love me."

"There are stalking laws, you know."

"You're so cute when you're ticked off."

Vicki turned to face him, once again struck dumb. And she'd been struck dumb a lot lately. All she could do was simply stare and shake her head. *The man must have some kind of mental illness.*

He cast a glance at her while cutting his sandwich in half. "You love me. I've had that love as long as I can remember. And no matter what you say, I can still see it." He nodded toward her. "There, in your eyes."

"You have got to be the most conceited man I've ever known."

"How could any man have your love and not be conceited?"

"I don't love you, Nick, and I'll be glad when this trial is over and you are out of my life for good." She cleared her trash from the table and piled it on her tray, preparing to leave.

Nick slumped back in his chair, stretching his long legs under the table, and watched her. "Do you remember back in seventh grade, Mr. . . . ." He popped his fingers trying to recall.

Vicki unwittingly took the bait. "Mr. Wortermocker," she supplied. "Seventh grade was Mr. Wortermocker."

"Right." Nick knew he could count on Vicki's exceptional memory. "Do you remember that day in Mr. Wortermocker's class when he was called away to the office, and Keshawn Thompson took the chance to jump on me?"

Vicki frowned, now certain that Nick was more than a little light on top. *Here we are in a crowded courthouse cafeteria, and he's recalling a butt-kicking he got in seventh grade.*

"Yes," she said hesitantly. "What about it?"

"Do you remember what happened later?"

Vicki wanted to pretend she didn't, but she did—clearly. And strangely enough, she was just curious enough about where this conversation was going to answer the question.

"Yes. Keshawn said you started it, and his friends backed him up. Even though the rest of us denied it, you were suspended for three days. Mr. Wortermocker never did like you."

"No," he said, finishing a bite of his sandwich. "Not that. I mean what happened to Keshawn later that day."

Vicki thought for a moment, before she felt a rush of blood to her face, remembering. "Yes. Somebody locked him in his own locker. He was in there for most of the afternoon before anyone found him."

Nick folded his arms across his chest, his lips twisted in a purely calculated smile. "You think I don't know how Keshawn ended up in his own locker?"

Vicki decided it was ridiculous to deny the childish prank of an outraged twelve-year-old girl. "How did you know?"

"I saw you."

"No, you didn't." She fought to hide the somewhat satisfied smile that came across her lips. She'd wanted to tell Nick when it happened. Back then, they'd shared everything. But he was already facing a suspension, and, knowing Miss Tilde, a belt-whipping as well. She'd decided he was better off not knowing. Now, even though it was twenty-odd years later, there was a strange sense of gratification in discovering he'd known all along.

"Um-hm." He sipped his milk. "Keshawn liked you. I saw you smiling at him and batting your eyelashes. I was angry. I thought—well, let's just say it was very comforting to watch you shove him inside and lock the door."

"Yeah." She smiled as her expression took on a far away look. "It did feel good."

"See, that proves it, " Nick stated. "You loved me." He bit into his sandwich again.

Vicki stood. Shifting her hips, she placed one hand at her waist. "All that proves is that Keshawn Thompson was a bully who deservedly got a dose of his own medicine."

Her cynicism didn't touch his resolve. "If that were true, you would've pushed him in that locker months before . . . like when he tied your ponytails in a knot."

Unable to dispute that simple truth, and not wanting to face the implications of the remark, she picked up her tray. "I don't even know why I'm talking to you about this. That was seventh grade, Nick. Seventh grade. We were kids. That was all before things changed." She looked down at the table, out the window, anywhere but at Nick. "That was long before a lot of things."

For a few fleeting moments, Nick thought, he was able to take her back in time with him. Back to a time when they'd been best friends, completely inseparable, each totally devoted to each other's happiness and protection as only best friends can be. For a few brief moments she'd lost the anger and disdain that characterized their current relationship, and remembered something good about him. But it was slipping away fast.

"Things always change, Vicki. Children grow up, beliefs and ideas change. The world is a constantly *changing* place. But love, Vicki . . ." he laid his hand on her arm, ". . . real love doesn't change."

Over the following weeks, Vicki randomly swung by Angela's unannounced. Nick had not been present on any of her visits, giving her hope that maybe he'd given up at least one of his ambush sites. She shook up her lunch routine as well, often eating at various restaurants in the area. If nothing else, Nick's presence had shown her how much a creature of habit she was. This was not a good inclination for a single woman to have, especially one who routinely put criminals in prison for a living.

Nick did continue to show up at Angela's on Sunday mornings ready for church services. And, true to his word, he'd even joined Starlight. Vicki had to admit his new devotion to his religion was impressive, but the cynic in her wondered about the real motivation behind his change of lifestyle.

Try as she may, she'd been unable to completely wipe away the memory of his kiss in the park. Or the recurring thought she'd had since—how right it felt, how good it felt to be in his arms again.

It was this thought she was dwelling on when she pulled up in front of the church at ten minutes to seven. She pulled a gospel CD from the disk player in the dashboard and returned it to its case. Tonight she would be teaching her small choir group an upbeat song from the album. As she entered the building almost everyone was already there.

"Hi, guys." She approached the front of the sanctuary where the huddle of thirty-somethings sat waiting for her. After murmurs of acknowledgement, they each returned to their private conversations, watching as their director set up for rehearsal. She turned the organ on so it could warm up, positioned the boom box on top, and distributed the music sheets.

Finally, after several minutes, Vicki turned to the group. "All right everyone, we are going to try something different tonight."

The group meandered into the choir stand. The

majority of the choir members usually came straight from work to the rehearsal, only a few had even stopped by their respective homes or had dinner. The overall sluggish nature of the group showed their lack of nourishment.

Vicki wasn't a bit concerned. She knew once the music started, the energy level would come without any help from her. She put the CD in the player and asked that everyone follow along on their sheet music. Soon enough, feet were tapping and heads were bobbing.

After guiding the four sections of the choir to the right note for their group, she did an a cappella rendition with the whole group. She had to stop and go to the organ twice; the altos kept losing their note. Soon the four-part choir of male and female voices was aligned in perfect harmony. Once she was confident that they all knew their parts, she settled down behind the organ and prepared to play along. Seven years of lessons had not been wasted. Finally, she turned the boom box off and signaled the group to begin. She guided them through the song, lifting her left hand in directorial guidance, and playing the organ with her right. Within forty-five minutes everyone knew the song. Feeling sure they would have it down before the rehearsal ended, Vicki paused for a snack break.

They were returning to the choir stands from the snack machines in the dining hall when Vicki heard someone enter at the back of the church. Turning to greet the late-comer, she felt her heart drop to her feet.

"Is that who I think it is?" Vicki heard someone whisper. She knew that rumors about Nick were already circulating throughout the church, one of which being that he was already pursuing a romantic interest in the church. In people's ignorance, much was said in her presence, no one imagining that staid Sister Proctor could possibly be the woman they spoke of.

"That's him, all right." This time Vicki recognized the voice as Sabrina Medley, her lead alto. Nick approached the front of the church with his recently discarded dark brown suit jacket crumpled in his large hands. The top button on his buttercup-yellow shirt was undone, and his matching tie hung loose around his neck. Even from a distance, Vicki could read fatigue in his every movement. His dark eyes were bloodshot with overuse. Despite his obvious weariness, he was smiling his magical smile, and Vicki felt every bone in her body quivering beneath her flesh. He wouldn't do this to her? Would he? *No, not even Nick is that cruel,* she decided.

He stopped only inches in front of her. "I've come to join the choir."

Vicki sighed heavily. Apparently he was indeed that cruel. "But you don't sing."

"How would you know?"

"Do you?"

"Don't know." He shrugged. "Never tried." His stance made it clear he was prepared to defend his presence. Nick had no intention of leaving regardless of how poorly he sang. The Lord's house was open to anyone, including those vocally challenged.

Over the past month, he'd tried desperately to give her some room, only seeing her as an opponent across a courtroom, and Sundays. She no longer ran in the park on Saturday afternoons or visited her usual eating haunts. Nor did she frequent the Farmer's Market on Saturday mornings. Nick knew these things because he'd spent several hours over the past couple of weeks, trying to bump into her with no luck. He knew instinctively that she was running scared, that he needed to back off, but he couldn't. He needed her like he needed air, and seeing her so rarely was like trying to breathe through a straw.

"Nick, don't do this," Vicki whispered, trying to ignore the intensely curious stares of the group in the choir stand.

"Don't do what?" he asked. "Lift my voice in praise?"

"This isn't about praise and you know it," she snapped, finding it hard to rein in her anger.

"Ah, Vicki." Sabrina was standing beside her now, staring up at Nick with large moonstruck eyes. "Aren't you going to introduce the newcomer?"

Seeing Vicki's hesitation, Nick extended his hand to the Sabrina. "Nick Wilcox." He smiled at the young woman, and when she smiled back he felt a flash of queasiness in the pit of his stomach. Nick had seen the look in Sabrina's eyes in other women's many times, most of which had gotten him in trouble.

He was honest in what he'd said to Vicki; he truly felt he was a changed man. Not the self-absorbed, egomaniac player he'd been eight years ago. He was a new man now, but the old one was still trying to get equal time. He'd been able to keep a tight leash on that old dog, promising him Vicki in return for his patience. But every once in a while a smile like the one on the face of the woman standing next to Vicki would cause the canine in him to raise his head.

"Welcome, Brother Wilcox." Sabrina pushed her way around Vicki and took Nick by the arm. "Everyone, welcome Brother Nick Wilcox." Sabrina introduced him to the choir as she led him up into the stand.

One by one the group came forward and introduced themselves. Most kept a second eye on their leader, surprised by the distress in Vicki's brown eyes and the obvious tension on her pretty face.

"Okay, everyone, a few more songs and we'll break for the evening." Vicki sighed in defeat and returned to the organ.

Nick cocked an eyebrow; he'd forgotten she played. He discreetly pulled his arm free of Sabrina's hold and tried to slide across the bench away from her, but Sabrina moved right along with him. Nick realized he'd made a mistake. He'd only allowed Sabrina to lead him into the choir stand because it was the easiest way to get past Vicki. But she obviously mistook it for an invitation, one he had no intention of extending.

At Vicki's signal, the group stood and began to rock back in forth in rhythm. One off-beat domino hindered the perfect swaying movement of the group. Vicki chuckled to herself. Nick had always been so good at most things; she'd allowed herself to forget the few things he stunk at—like dancing, for instance. She'd forgotten he had no rhythm, at least not vertically.

Vicki watched mercilessly for a while, as Brother Todd, the man on the other side of Nick, constantly pushed him back, trying to nudge him into sequence with the music. But as soon as Nick had the beat, he would fall out of step. Finally, seeing the trepidation and embarrassment in his face, Vicki stopped the music.

Across the stand their eyes connected. She silently offered him the opportunity to exit discreetly without greater embarrassment, but Nick stood his ground.

Vicki twisted her mouth in frustration, said a silent prayer for forgiveness, and chose a very up-tempo song for her next selection. She called out the single-word title and picked up the pace.

Everyone in the group recognized the music and mentally shifted gears, preparing for the rapidly changing vocal scales of the song. Everyone except Nick, who'd never heard it before. The group started rocking back and forth much faster than before. Nick was being bounced between Sabrina and Todd like a ping-pong ball.

Nick's wide shoulders were no match for the wave of movement around him, not to mention the additional humiliation of not knowing the lyrics. Given no other alternative, he bounced along as best he could and pretended to mouth the words. He made a mental note to swing by the music store tomorrow and pick up some gospel CDs. But for tonight, he would just have to suffer through it.

Vicki continued to play, thoroughly enjoying Nick's torment. She watched the water forming on his slick head and the confusion in his eyes, his large hands that seemed to be clapping two seconds too late, and his stiff, jerky movements. As her limber fingers glided across the keys, Vicki silently wondered what happened to Nick's rule to live by—number eight: *"Always be prepared."*

Vicki sat alone in the upscale restaurant waiting for her dinner companion to arrive. *"Real love doesn't change."* Try as she might to forget Nick's words, they continued to resound in her head.

"Hello, dear." Preston kissed the top of her head as he slid into the chair next to hers.

Vicki tried to conceal her guilt alarm, having been caught with her mind on a man other than the one with her right now. "Hello, Preston." She pretended to read the menu laying open before her. Vicki had discovered a long time ago that reading the menu fifteen times or more was favorable to listening to him prattle on about his elitist ideals.

"Sorry I'm late, I had an important meeting."

Vicki knew that was her cue. She was supposed to ask
with whom, giving him the opening he needed to begin
prattling on about the influential and powerful people
he rubbed shoulders with on a daily basis, and how helpless they would be without his legal guidance. But she
wasn't in the mood today, so she didn't ask.

A waiter appeared, as if by magic. "Are you folks ready?"
he asked with a smile. His pad and pen were ready.

"Yes," Preston began, "the lady will have—"

"Preston!" Vicki said, irritated by his presumptuous
behavior.

Preston looked at her as if she'd sprouted two heads.
Vicki understood why. Preston ordered for her all the
time, why would she be offended now?

The waiter, sensing the unease, spoke up. "I'll give you
a few more moments," he said before slipping away.

"What's wrong?" Preston asked.

"Nothing. I apologize. I'm tired, I guess. I haven't
really had any time to rest in the past few weeks."

Preston reached across the table and covered her
hand with his. "Well the Morrison case will soon be over,
and your life will be back to normal." He tactfully left it
at that, not wanting to remind her of the judge's recent
ruling that her DNA evidence was inadmissible. "Is there
anything I can do to help?"

Vicki was touched by the genuine concern in his eyes.
She didn't bother telling him that just that afternoon
Nick had completely discredited her eyewitness. Preston
had always showed little interest in her work. In fact, Preston Dawson showed little interest in anything that
wasn't centered on him. She had to admit she was a bit
surprised he even remembered the name of the defendant. Or, he might have read about it in the papers.
Actually, Vicki had made a point of saying very little to

him about this case, even less than normal. Preston knew some of her history with Nick, and the last thing she needed to deal with was another jealous man.

Although some part of her knew any show of possessiveness on Preston's part would be just that, a show. On the surface, their relationship appeared to be ideal—two people with similar interests and the same occupation, they always had much to discuss. They accompanied each other to their various social engagements and spent nights together doing the typical date stuff. But there had never been any emphatic declarations of love, or discussions of the distant future. They never spoke of what their children would look like, or good places to raise a family. And most importantly, neither questioned the other as to why they *didn't* discuss these things. Passionless and bland; for both parties, it was what they wanted.

Or was it? Vicki had been asking herself that a lot lately. "I'm sorry I snapped at you."

"It's okay, maybe once you get something to eat you'll feel better." He rubbed her hand once more and signaled for the waiter to return.

They each gave the man their individual orders, and discussed city gossip and politics while waiting for their food to arrive.

Vicki made an effort to remove the recurring images of Nick from her mind and concentrate on the man sitting across the table from her. Preston would be considered a handsome man by anyone's standards. His rich cocoa skin and large brown eyes always made her think of a basset hound. *Pleasant enough,* she thought. But Vicki knew if put up against Nick, Preston would wilt like a daisy up against a rose.

Which was amazing, considering her memories of the chubby little dark-skinned boy who'd teased her mercilessly on the playground. But she had to admit, the potential was always there, in his smile, and those twinkling midnight black eyes. Yes, the Nick she knew now was always inside the chubby little boy. He just needed some time in the cocoon.

"Wouldn't you agree?" Preston was speaking to her.

Vicki forced her mind back to the table, and tried to remember the last few words he'd said. "Absolutely," she answered, knowing the comment had had something to do with one of his coworkers named Griffin, and the man's constant competition with Preston for the most prestigious cases.

Finally the food arrived, and they were able to fill their mouths and skip the conversation altogether. After dinner, they returned to her apartment and did what they did most evenings. They lay together on Vicki's couch, curled beneath her favorite throw blanket, and watched TV until they both fell asleep. Vicki had dated Preston for almost a year, and decided after almost four months that he was probably gay. Truth of the matter was, she didn't really care. He was kind and safe, and she knew that in his own way he cared about her. Using the remote to turn off the TV, Vicki snuggled deeper into Preston's armpit, and yawned.

Despite his pursuit of her in every other domain, Nick had stayed away from her condominium. Vicki suspected that part of the reason was fear of finding her there with Preston doing something that could leave no doubt as to who was her mate, something she knew Nick didn't even want to imagine. Nick believed that her relationship with Preston was of a carnal nature—and yet, he *still* pursued her relentlessly. So what would he do if he knew the truth of the matter?

Vicki decided that if Nick wanted to think she was having a torrent of wild sex, let him. It was far safer to let the lie stand than for Nick to know the truth of the matter. For if he ever got wind of how long it had been since a man had touched her intimately, Vicki knew for certain that all bets would be off. Their pleasant truce and new platonic friendship would be over before it started.

CHAPTER SIX

Vicki hurried through the throng of people filing into the courtroom and made her way to the front. She'd had a hard time getting her car started that morning, and was forced to go back inside her condo to call AAA for a boost. When she returned and tried again, the car started right up. She said a silent prayer of thanks and assumed that the problem was nothing more than a cold battery. In too much of a hurry to question it further, she took the chance on driving to the courthouse and managed to make it without incident.

Scrambling through her leather bag, she pulled out the case files. She glanced at Nick across the aisle. He was huddled with his client, speaking rapidly, and the other man was listening closely and nodding in agreement. Since the accusation of Tommy Morrison's involvement with the threat against her had been dispelled, Nick had jumped back into the trial with zeal. He was still presenting his defense, but the case was drawing to a close. One look at the jury told Vicki he'd already presented enough doubt.

She winced when she remembered how he'd attacked the testimony of one of the arresting officers. The man's clear dislike of the defendant could not be interpreted as anything but bias. It left everyone in the courtroom wondering about Morrison's claim that he was punched in the face when the policeman pushed him into the back of his squad car. Even she was having a hard time believing the veteran officer, and with the jury hanging on Nick's every word as if he were some great sage predicting the future, Vicki knew things were not looking good for her.

She straightened her files, tucked her bag under the table, and was settling into her chair behind the when she noticed the scrap of paper. She assumed it was something left from the previous occupant, and was about to toss it in the wastebasket at the end of the table. Human curiosity got the best of her; she unfolded it, and immediately recognized the slanted writing.

V,

   We need to talk. Have dinner with me tonight at my place.
N

After scanning the upscale address, Vicki glanced across the aisle. Nick was smiling at her. *Does this nut really believe for one moment that I would be alone with him in his apartment?*

She lifted the scrap of paper, making sure Nick saw it. She crunched it into a tiny ball in the palm of her hands, and watched his smile disappear.

"All rise." The bailiff's deep baritone sliced into her thoughts. "The Honorable Judge Thomas Scott presiding."

The nerve of that man never ceases to amaze me. Vicki fumed. What did he think he was doing?! Did he really believe she would sleep with him after he'd once again humiliated her in court? Was she supposed to just let him blow through her life, taking both her winning verdict and her dignity?!

The time it took for Judge Scott to amble up into his seat gave her a chance to regain control of her erratic breathing. *Remember where you are,* she silently counseled herself. But still, all she could see through the haze of red clouding her brain were her small hands wrapped tightly around his thick neck, her fingers digging into his warm flesh.

No, think happy thoughts, her brain insisted.

Those are happy thoughts, her heart argued.

The next witness taking the stand interrupted her internal argument. She had to refocus, get her mind centered on the task at hand, which was defeating Nick in the only realm that mattered. She was certain Tommy Morrison was guilty as sin, and Nick was very close to putting the petty criminal turned murderer back on the streets.

As much as she would love to hurt Nick Wilcox in the physical sense, she would have to suspend her desires and hurt him in the only way she truly could. Here, in this place, which she knew was the only place that mattered to him. The courtroom was Nick's stage, where his light shone the brightest. Defeating him in court would hurt him more than physical injuries ever could.

The morning passed, and soon they recessed for lunch. Vicki grabbed her bag and charged for the door. She was close, only a few feet away from the double-door entrance, when she felt the familiar tight grip on her upper arm.

"Let me go, Nick."

Nick waited until the other occupants of the courtroom had cleared from around their immediate location before speaking. "Will I see you tonight?"

"No."

He frowned. "I don't understand why you're still angry. What did I do that was so bad?"

Vicki turned and looked up into his eyes filled with confusion. She was amazed, and even more hurt if that were possible. "You really don't know, do you?"

He hunched his shoulders. "No. I really don't. I knew when you left Arkansas you were angry, but I can't believe you're still holding a grudge after all this time."

She folded her arms across her chest. "Why do you think I left, Nick?"

He answered without hesitation. "Because I won the Pallister case."

"What?!"

His eyes widened at her emphatic question. Instinctively, he knew that was not the right answer and was too afraid to offer another. The pit beneath his feet was getting deeper and deeper.

"Betina Ramirez," Vicki hissed.

Nick's scrunched his thick eyebrows. "What?"

"Betina Ramirez. She's why I'm still angry."

Nick scanned his memory bank. "That crackhead you wanted to put on the witness stand?"

"*That crackhead* who witnessed the whole crime as it was taking place. *That crackhead* who saw your client enter the victim's apartment, who listened to their argument, who watched in horror and helplessness as Andy Pallister strangled his mistress with his bare hands. But you and the police, all you could see was a drug addict."

Nick sighed in frustration. They were supposed to be discussing dinner at his place, not some junkie from eight years ago. "Vicki, she was an unreliable witness and you know it."

"What I know is that if you'd opened your mind the tiniest bit . . ." She held her index finger and thumb centimeters apart to demonstrate. "She may never have had to take the stand."

Okay, Nick thought, *she's only getting angrier by the minute.* He gave her his most disarming smile. "I tell you what, have dinner with me tonight and we can discuss this further."

"You really must think I'm a fool."

"What are you saying? You'd have to be a fool to have dinner with me?"

"Yes."

"All this over some crack—witness from eight years ago, who may or may not have seen something? Who most likely imagined the whole thing? This is ridiculous, Vicki."

"You know, Nick, when you told me that you wanted to be friends again, I really believed you. But now I can see that like everything else that comes out of your mouth, that was a lie." She turned and stormed away.

Nick caught up with her as she neared one of the column-enclosed alcoves. He grabbed her around the waist and pulled her into the small space. He pinned her against the wall using his large body as a shield.

"Let me go." She squirmed against his rock-solid form and moved him not at all.

"*You* are going to listen to *me* for a change."

She continued to push against him, his tight hold remained in place and she soon realized she was only managing to exhaust herself. "Go to hell!"

"I would if you were there."

Vicki's eyes widened; she had no response.

"I love you, Vicki. I've made no bones about that. I want you so bad I ache for you." He pressed his lower body against her, and she felt the undeniable proof of his words. "But I never lied to you, and if all I can have is your friendship . . ." His mouth tightened in a determined line. "So be it."

"Do you honestly expect me to believe that crock? You're just trying to get me in bed."

The feel of her body against his and her unwillingness to listen to reason frustrated him beyond bearing. His control snapped. "Who says we need a bed?" Nick moved forward, pressing his body completely against her with all the points of interest touching.

Vicki's brain screamed for her to push back, but the woman in her wanted something else: the physical proximity of so much intense masculine energy, familiar and warm. No, he was hot, hotter than a furnace on a winter night. Her breathing was becoming labored; her heart was working overtime, lifting her bosom up even closer to his chest. With every deep breath, his powder blue silk tie threatened to slip into the cleavage of her low cut V-necked dress. And God help her, she was loving the close connection, coming within a hair's breadth of reaching out to him. Her mind swirled with conflicting emotions. How could she want a man she otherwise couldn't stand?

He ran the back of his large hand along her jawline, fingers touching her bottom lip, stroking, holding her spellbound with his ebony eyes. Two hearts in sync, racing, pounding. Every part of his being was charged and ready, remembering, wanting. He claimed her mouth as his hands claimed her body, roaming freely, exploring.

She was gasping, desperately trying to breathe. Feeling as if she were drowning beneath the onslaught of emotions his touch ignited. Vicki heard herself moan, and wondered where the sound came from. That's when she knew: Her treacherous body was actually reveling in this attack, responding to him without her mind's consent. Her physical self was ready and willing, and she had to put a stop to this.

She whimpered as his hands squeezed her buttocks, lifting her up to him. Pressing her hips to his, she felt the throbbing bulge straining against the front of his slacks pressing against her belly.

"No," she whispered between gulps of air. His mouth found its way behind her earlobe and down around her hairline. "Oh, no," she moaned mournfully. It was happening. Her double-crossing body was readying itself for him. She felt her lower belly warming, the hot liquid coming down in preparation for what it felt was inevitable.

He held her securely around the waist with one arm, while the other found its way between her legs and up her inner thigh to her center point. He felt it through her stockings, through her panties; he felt the fire building in the core of her being and he knew it was for him.

The sounds of voices in the distance sounded like an alarm in his head. Their temporary privacy was about to come to an end. He looked down at the luscious woman in his arms. Her head thrown back in pleasure, she clung to the lapels of his suit jacket. Her need showed clearly in her swollen mouth, warmed by his kiss, her panting body desperate with desire. *Oh, yes.* He gave a small smile. She was still his.

He heard the voices drawing nearer, but Vicki seemed to be oblivious to them. He felt her grinding hips still pushing up against his hand. She wanted completion; she needed to reach the top of the mountain, and he very much wanted to take her there. But the people in the hallway were too close, too damn close.

"No baby, not here," he whispered against her ear while settling her back on her own two feet. "Tonight, my place."

Vicki's mind was spinning. He released his hold on her,

and grabbed her arms again to steady her wobbly legs. The combination of his words and the light clicking sound of heels on the marble floor was enough to break the spell.

Vicki took one deep breath and pushed against his chest with both arms. Her mind whirled with confusion; she shook her head vehemently from side to side trying to reconcile her conflicting emotions. "I won't let you use me. I won't!"

"Use you?" he asked, genuinely stunned.

"If I were stupid enough to show up at your place tonight, is this what you were planning? To force yourself on me?"

"Force myself on you?!"

"Is there an echo in here?"

Nick took in her disheveled appearance with smug satisfaction. Her rust-colored dress was still twisted at the waist, her hair was tousled from his fingers, her lipstick was smeared from his kisses—and he'd never wanted her more in his life.

"Yeah, right, you were really fighting me off."

"Stay away from me, Nick." Her eyes pleaded. Her voice softened. "Please."

"I can't," he whispered. "You know how I feel about you. Hell, I moved cross-country to be near you. You think I can just turn that off because you *say* you don't feel the same?" He spun around, moving away from her. Vicki sighed in relief, not realizing she'd been holding her breath.

"Tell me, Vicki." He stood with his back to her. "If you don't feel the way I do, why does your body respond to me the way it does?"

She cupped her head in her hands. "I don't know."

Her words were muffled by her hands, and she shook her head, in confusion. "I don't know anything anymore."

"I can't make you admit you love me, Vicki." He turned to face her again. "But you can't expect me to stop trying."

The voices were upon them. Two voices, one a man and the other a woman, speaking in soothing tones. Vicki's instincts summarized the situation: an attorney trying to reassure her client. How many times had she herself spoken to an irate client in such tones? Nick waited until the couple passed to step out into the hallway.

The woman spun around. "Nick?"

"Veronica?" Nick pasted on his public servant smile and moved away from Vicki to give her time to correct her appearance. Not to mention, her still-aroused body was becoming unbearable to be near, and he feared what he might do if he stayed close to her.

Nick took Veronica's hand, and looked to her client expectantly.

"Nick Wilcox, my client, Mr. Yoshimoto. He's the CEO of Whitehall Financial. Mr. Yoshimoto, Nick Wilcox, the *second* best defense attorney I know," she teased. The two men shook hands.

"Nice to meet you, Mr. Wilcox." Yoshimoto carefully scrutinized Nick.

"The pleasure's all mine." Nick smiled stiffly under the intense stare.

"You've probably seen his picture in the papers," Veronica continued. "That pretty face has graced the cover of almost every news magazine imaginable."

Veronica didn't notice the woman still in the alcove behind Nick, but her client did. Yoshimoto waited before acknowledging the other woman, unsure if she wanted to be seen; she did not. Vicki tried to slip away unnoticed.

Nick's long arm reached out and caught her as she moved past him. Bringing her around in front of him, Nick introduced her.

"This is the prosecutor, Victoria Proctor. We're trying the Morrison case together. Vicki, this is Veronica Cole, an old friend of mine, and her client, Mr. Yoshimoto.

Mr. Yoshimoto looked from Vicki to Nick before offering his hand to Vicki.

Vicki shook his hand, and extended hers to Veronica.

Veronica stared down at the hand for a few seconds before turning to Nick. "Oh, yes, I read about that case in the local paper."

Nick smiled down at Vicki who was looking more and more uncomfortable by the moment. "She's giving me quite a run for my money."

She has a thing for Nick, Vicki thought, taking in the tall woman. Geared in famous names from head to toe, she looked as if she'd walked off the pages of *Vogue.* Her smile was pleasant enough, but there was something in her eyes that negated the effect.

"Nice to meet you, *both.*" Vicki tried to move away again, but Nick's strong fingers only tightened around her upper arms.

Veronica had been hoping to see Nick again before she left Chicago, thinking that two old friends in a strange city where neither knew anyone might be the setting needed to finally lure him into her bed. But try as she may, she found it impossible to dismiss the woman he held possessively.

Veronica took in Vicki's neat, professional appearance. Her rust-colored, V-necked belted dress accentuated her ample curves; her matching pumps complemented her well-toned calves, and her shoulder-length hair was pulled back and twisted up with a rust-colored clip that appeared to be slightly lopsided. Veronica's lips twisted in derision, taking in the smeared lipstick. It was apparent Nick had already found a bed partner.

Well, it doesn't matter, Veronica decided. This plump little woman could never compete with her ultra-svelte physique and cosmopolitan looks. Although Nick *was* holding on awfully tight, like he was almost afraid to let her go.

"Do I know you?" She finally acknowledged Vicki with something akin to hostility.

"I don't believe so," Vicki answered, wanting desperately to be away from this place, away from this man. *Why won't he let me go?* She could probably break free if she really tried, but it would cause a scene she'd much rather avoid.

"Maybe," Nick said. "She's originally from Arkansas. In fact, she worked for the prosecutor's office in Little Rock for . . ." He looked to Vicki for the answer.

"Five years," she volunteered. Vicki was beginning to feel extremely awkward. She could taste Veronica's dislike as if it was something palpable in the air. She could feel Nick's hunger like a current shooting through his hand into her arm. And she could sense Yoshimoto's offenses radiating from him. *The man is guilty,* she thought. It was a ridiculous notion, considering she didn't even know what crime he was being charged with. But she was certain. He wore his culpability like a cloak, and any experienced attorney would know it.

With a flurry of hair-tossing and synthetic laughter, Veronica was too caught up in trying to serenade Nick to notice the color of the sky. But Mr. Yoshimoto saw every action and reaction, the ones both voluntary and non. Vicki watched his dark eyes dart back and forth; she could see his brain analyzing the situation.

"Sorry, but I've really got to go." Vicki pulled again,

and this time Nick released her. Apparently, he wanted a scene no more than she did.

"About that issue we were discussing . . ." He gave Vicki a meaningful look.

"As far as I'm concerned, it's settled."

"I'll see you . . . later?" He hinted at his dinner invitation for that evening.

Vicki misunderstood the question, believing he spoke of later in the day, as in back in the courtroom after lunch. "Of course. Good-bye." Vicki moved away as fast as her three-inch heels would allow.

Yoshimoto turned to the other two. "Veronica, I'll meet you in the cafeteria."

"Okay, I'll be right there." Veronica smiled, doing a poor job of hiding her disgust. The man was guilty as sin; she'd known it when she accepted the case. But the evidence against him was circumstantial, and she was sure she could get him off and collect a fat fee in the process. She'd never anticipated his attitude, never imagined he'd behave as he did. He made no secret of his obvious disdain for the American legal system and went as far as to tell the judge that she had no authority over him. His arrogance was obvious; the jury was aching to punish him.

The only bit of luck had been his final acceptance of the prosecutor's plea bargain earlier that morning. He would be hit with a hefty fee that he could easily afford, but all the other charges would be dropped. And now that she'd found Nick again, Veronica thought, the day was getting better and better. Maybe her last weekend in Chicago wouldn't be boring after all.

"Nice to meet you, Mr. Wilcox." Yoshimoto took one long last look at Nick before he turned and walked away.

Nick watched the man go and wondered what that

calculating look was about. The man was obviously sizing him up, but why?

Lost in thought, Yoshimoto turned a corner and walked directly into a clerk loaded down with files. The young woman lost her balance and her files slipped through her tight hold, falling in disarray all over the marble floor.

"Hey, why don't you watch where you're going." The woman was petite, but she glared up at him like a prize-fighter. Yoshimoto watched as she squatted to pick up her files. He snarled down at her, thinking how easy it would be to snap her twig of a neck between his fingers. She had no idea to whom she was speaking in such an offensive tone, no idea that she was dancing with death.

Returning to his train of thought, he continued on his way to the cafeteria without so much as a apology. So, *that* was the infamous Nicholas Wilcox. Like everyone else in the city of Chicago, Yoshimoto had been following the trial of Tommy Morrison in the papers and television news programs. But unlike everyone else, he had a vested interest in the outcome. He was one of only three people who knew for certain that Tommy Morrison was innocent. The other two were Tommy Morrison, of course, and the hitman whom Yoshimoto had tasked with the killing of Benedict Brown.

He pursed his lips remembering the details. The assassin had been careless, killing the store clerk and another innocent bystander. But, in the end, the Brown man was dead and that was all that really mattered. Hearing some of the sensation surrounding the case, he had looked into the background of Nick Wilcox, and discovered a natural showman with a scientific mind.

At the beginning of the trial, he'd believed that Morrison would be convicted in a fairly short amount of time, given that there were witnesses to his fleeing the scene, a lucky coincidence for the real murderer. But, over the course of the past few weeks, Nick Wilcox had seemingly done the impossible, and presented the jury with enough reasonable doubt to make them pause. Some analysts were even saying there was a good chance Morrison would be acquitted. Not that it mattered to Yoshimoto one way or the other; there was no way he could be tied to the case.

He had used one of the newest members of his secret organization, a beginner who wanted to prove himself. But given his carelessness, he had not done a very good job of that. He would have to deal with the man when he returned home. To show him the error of his ways. If they allowed that type of shabby work to go unpunished, he and his associates would've been exposed long ago.

Yoshimoto turned the corner to go into the cafeteria. The cool air had a septic odor that drowned out the smell of the already unappealing food. It almost turned his stomach, but he continued nonetheless. He pasted on a pleasant smile and nodded to the occasional passerby. Yoshimoto watched as one woman, apparently recognizing him, nudged the man beside her and pointed in his direction. He nodded in greeting to the couple, and watched their bewildered expression turn to awe. *Idiots,* he thought, *the lot of them.* But they would never know how he felt about them. It was essential that they never knew how he felt about them.

Vicki stood in the long cafeteria line surveying the multitudes of cellophane-covered offerings. She craned her neck to see what was on the hot side. For some reason she was starving. Her cell phone sounded with the usual musical tone and her shoulder bag vibrated. Digging down into her large purse, she put her fingers on the phone with her first attempt.

"Hello?" The cafeteria line started moving again. Vicki cradled the phone with her shoulder and lifted her tray. "I'm okay. Just a little hot under the collar, that's all."

Vicki moved along behind the tall man in front of her, never noticing the woman directly behind who was straining to hear her conversation.

"How did you guess?" Vicki chuckled.

The woman behind her leaned forward.

"Girl, you wouldn't believe what he tried to pull. He had the nerve to invite me over for dinner tonight."

Veronica was trying to hear the words of the person on the other end, but it was impossible.

"Please." Vicki's shouted response caused the man in front of her to frown at her over his shoulder. She lowered her voice. "Are you crazy? Peaches, trust me, the kind of cooking he's talking about doing is not done in the kitchen."

Veronica strained to hear to no avail.

Vicki laughed. "You are bad. Okay, I'll give you that. But it's not *usually* done in the kitchen." Vicki was lost in her conversation with her friend; she didn't notice that she had progressed to the front of the line. The man in front of her was the only person standing between her and the cashier.

"Hey, I've got to go, but I'll call you later after I'm out of court for the day."

Veronica was so frustrated, she was tempted to snatch the phone away and hear for herself.

Vicki shook her head emphatically. "No, I won't consider

it. This man has my head turned around as it is. The last thing I need to do is to give him any more ammunition."

Vicki was silent for a long time. Veronica moved closer until they were almost touching. She was dying to know what the friend "Peaches" had to say. Based on Vicki's comments, she knew the woman on the other end of the phone was encouraging her to go to Nick's for dinner.

"No. No, Peaches," Vicki shook her head as if her friend could see her. "I can't. You don't understand what it was like getting over him. I can't go through that again."

Vicki fell silent, and Veronica was dying of curiosity. Not being able to hear what encouraging words were being offered, she was fearful that it would be enough to change Vicki's mind.

Finally Vicki spoke again. "Yeah, I know. But I'm not going and that's that."

Vicki listened to Peaches while the man in front of her cashed out. "Okay, I'll talk to you later. Bye." Vicki hung up the phone, paid for her Caesar salad and Pepsi, and moved away, never realizing the intense scrutiny and palpable animosity of the woman who still stood at the register shooting silent daggers into her back.

Nick stood over his kitchen sink rinsing the pasta, when the doorbell rang. He cursed under his breath; she was early. Luckily, he'd started cooking as soon as he got home. The sauce was ready and the wine was chilling on ice. The salad was cooling in the fridge, and the kitchen was filled with the scent of freshly baked bread.

He'd considered doing something much more extravagant for their first night back together, but Vicki had never been one for showy displays. He kept it simple. She could never resist his spaghetti, and tonight he needed every advantage he could muster. That included the chocolate chip cheesecake—her favorite dessert—that sat cooling on the countertop.

"I'll be right there," he called, shaking the pasta to keep it from sticking to the cooker before setting it in the sink to finish draining. Wiping his hands on the kitchen towel, he tossed it over his shoulder and headed for the front door. He took one final glance around his elegantly decorated living room, frowning at the few remaining unpacked boxes standing in the corner. They took away from the ambience of seduction he'd carefully created, but if all went right tonight he might never have to unpack them.

After almost three months in the Windy City, his plans were finally coming to fruition. In a few moments Vicki would be in his apartment, and, in a few hours . . . in his bed.

He was so certain of his success when he shopped for this dinner, he'd also purchased all the makings for a big breakfast. He smiled, remembering Vicki's healthy appetite after lovemaking. Yes, things were finally going the way they were supposed to.

He ignored the second knock, taking a moment to find the remote and turn on the stereo. The melodic sounds of India Arie's "Brown Skin" floated out across the room. He smiled again. Perfect.

Turning, he swung the door open wide, and with a grand gesture motioned to the room at large. "Welcome to my humble abode."

"Nice."

What is she doing here? "Veronica?"

She entered the room, taking in the buff-colored leather sofa and matching wing chairs, the frosted glass tables, and matching elongated stereo system station.

Sparsely decorated with earth tone–colored pieces of African art from various regions, his preference for the Masai people was unmistakable. The large room was designed to be both the living and dining area and had a very Spartan feel to it. Even to a stranger, the masculine presence which permeated the walls gave evidence of its occupant.

She paused in the center of the room, and turned in a circle. "Very nice."

Nick, who still stood holding the door open in stunned disbelief, finally spoke. "What are you doing here?" He recovered his senses enough to realize what a nightmare this situation could easily become. He glanced back out into the hallway to be sure it was empty before closing the door. Whatever Veronica wanted could wait until Monday morning. Right now, she had to go—and fast.

Veronica tilted her head to the side and smiled. "Oooh, I love India Arie." She headed in the direction of the stereo.

Nick scanned his memory, trying to recall when he'd given her his address and why. It didn't matter now. Nothing mattered now, except that she had to go—and fast.

"Uh, Veronica . . ." He crossed the room at lightning speed and plucked the CD case she was reading out of her hand. "I'm expecting company. I'm sorry, but I'm going to have to ask you to leave." He hustled her in the direction of the door.

She dug in her heels and braced herself. "She's not coming."

Nick skidded to a stop and released his hold on her. "What?"

"The little chubette from the courthouse. I assume that's who you were expecting." She cast a nasty smirk over her shoulder. "I heard her tell her friend she wasn't coming."

Nick's mind was racing. Was Vicki really serious about that Preston person? *No.* Nick shook off the possibility. Earlier that day, in that alcove, she'd responded to his touch like a nymph. Whatever was between her and that guy, it was definitely not passion.

The sound of a woman clearing her throat brought him back to the present and his uninvited guest. Veronica turned to face him. She slid her hands up his chest and over his shoulders. "She's not coming, Nick," she whispered close to his ear, "but I'm here."

His mind said she had one hell of a nerve inviting herself, nevertheless his instincts told him to tread lightly. He forced himself to remember that Veronica was a citizen of Arkansas, a very *influential* citizen of Arkansas. With the election coming up, that was not someone he could afford to ostracize. He pasted on a smile. "So, after hearing that she was not coming, you decided to take up the invitation?"

"Why not?" she asked, without shame.

Nick fought the urge to shake his head in disgust. The sista was fine and successful; who would've suspected she was pathetic enough to do something like this?

There was a time, Nick thought ruefully. Long ago, this would have been the kind of prey the ol' dog in him hunted. DND's he called them, Damn Near Desperate. Easy pickings during his player days, but that was then— and this was now.

He considered letting her stay for all of a minute. Someone had to eat all that food. But the thought was overridden by his desperate need to be alone. He needed to think.

"Veronica, I'm flattered," he said, with his typical easy

charm. "Really, I am. But I don't think this is such a good idea."

Veronica's smile fell. "Why not?"

"Occasionally we have to work together, and I wouldn't want things to be awkward."

"But you work with her, too. Are you expecting me to believe you'd prefer that countrified thing over this?" She ran her long fingers over her slim body, outlining her smooth lines. "She can't compete with this."

Nick took in her long form with a critical eye. Veronica was very pretty, but her superficial looks, created with the aide of Maybelline and Vidal Sassoon, were no match for Vicki's more wholesome beauty. Vicki was purely an Ivory soap kind of girl. She needed no accompaniments to accentuate what nature had given her. And Nick knew firsthand that she was as lovely at six A.M. as she was at six P.M.

He twisted his mouth in consideration. Veronica's prostrate form may be good for measuring straight lines, but she had none of the sensual hills and alluring valleys that he loved on Vicki. He decided, after careful consideration, Veronica was right; there was no competition.

He sighed, realizing Veronica was not going to make this easy. "Yes," he continued, refusing to abandon diplomacy just yet. "But Vicki and I used to be involved years ago. My relationship with her is different. Truly, I am flatter—"

With her building rage, her lovely countenance had taken on a hideous appearance. "Flattered my ass." Her hands went to her pelvis bones and her fair complexion turned blood red. "Are you telling me that I got dressed up . . ." She gestured to the neatly tailored after-five suit. "And drove all the way across town for nothing?"

Nick stepped back, stunned by her venomous response.

She was acting as if he were trying to cancel a date at the last minute, and they both knew she was never invited to begin with. This was a side of Veronica Nick would never have imagined. She always seemed together, but this was definitely not the super-composed woman he thought he knew.

"Veronica, I think you'd better leave."

"Why?" She whined. "I told you, she's not coming! Why not share the evening with me?"

Nick was getting the eerie sensation that Veronica may have a lot more problems than anyone really knew. This situation did not warrant such an unusually strong and passionate reaction.

"What the hell is going on, Nick? You flirt with me. You touched my hair. Don't act like you don't remember."

"I was being friendly."

"Friendly my—"

"You need to watch your mouth." How could he not have seen this crazy side of Veronica before? This woman was truly unstable.

"You were obviously expecting *someone* for dinner. Why not me?"

"Veronica, you can either leave on your own . . ." He gestured to the door. "Or with my help. But one way or the other, you're leaving. Now."

"Why, you sorry son-of-a—"

"Oh! Hold up! Hold up!" Nick put up a hand to still her tirade. "I'm truly sorry for any misunderstanding, since you obviously feel I've misled you somehow. But that does not give you the right to stand up in my house and call me out of name."

Her lips twisted in disdain. "Bitch," she finished. She began again. "You sorry son-of—"

"Get out." He grabbed her by the arm and propelled

her toward the door. "I was trying to spare your feelings, but bump that. You want to play nasty, fine. Take your scrawny little butt home, or wherever it is bats go to sleep."

Nick opened the door and pushed her through it. Veronica spun on her heels and stared in amazement as the door slammed closed in her face.

"You're gonna regret this, Nick. You hear me." She banged on the dead-bolted door. "Nobody treats me like this. Nobody! You hear me, Nick Wilcox?"

Nick lay against the door wondering how a day that started well had ended so badly. Finally, the banging against the door ceased, and Nick listened to the sound of her heels sloshing against the plush hallway carpeting as she stormed away. He imagined her pushing the elevator call button, and standing there—still in a rage—until the electronic doors opened and carried her back down to the street and back to her own life.

Her idle threats meant nothing to him; what did bother him was the fact that a woman who obviously had some serious mental problems was allowed to practice law. But what could he do about it without proof? Nothing. Deciding that, he turned his attention to another woman, and the considerable trouble he'd gone through setting the stage for what could've been the most romantic night of their lives. The first night of the rest of their lives. What a waste.

Once he accepted the death of that dream, he turned his attentions to the only thing left. What next?

CHAPTER SEVEN

Vicki sat, wringing her hands, waiting for the judge to read the verdict. She cast a sidelong glance at Nick to see how he was handling the wait. Of course, he looked calm as a summer day. His client, on the other hand, bit nervously at his fingernails.

"Will the defendant please rise." Judge Scott's creased face gave no hint as to the words written on the piece of paper in his hand. Vicki watched as both Nick and Tommy stood tall.

"We, the jury, find the defendant, Thomas Morrison, not guilty."

Tommy almost fell when his body weakened with relief. Nick braced the man's shoulders to steady him. The courtroom exploded with activity as reporters charged through the doors, rushing to get to their individual newsrooms. The crowd of onlookers, who'd only moments before sat still as stone statues, erupted in a flurry of opinions, now openly discussing the case. The room became loud and disorderly. Judge Scott was forced to pound his wooden gavel to regain control.

"Mr. Morrison, you are free to go."

Nick dared to cast a brief glance in Vicki's direction. She looked as dejected as he knew she would. He wanted to say something, but had no words to comfort her. He wanted to tell her she'd fought like a champion, but he knew how shallow the words would sound. The best he could do was to leave her alone, and let her come to that conclusion on her own in a few days, when the taste of defeat wasn't so fresh.

He packed his leather attaché and turned to leave. The Morrison family's reverent "thank yous" interrupted him. He graciously accepted the pats on the backs from strangers and friends alike. He knew the morning's papers would sing his praises as the hero of the hour, having saved an innocent man from a sentence of death.

He weaved his way through the crowd of reporters and spectators and out into the light of the day. He didn't once look back to find Vicki in the crowd of exiting spectators. He simply couldn't bear it.

He hurried toward his car, pulling mercilessly at his tie. In the distance, he heard someone calling congratulations to him, on his *win*. He waved and smiled in acknowledgement, but inside he certainly didn't feel like a winner. In fact, he was almost certain he'd lost something instead.

"The Morrison trial is over?"

Nick looked up, startled by the sound of someone entering his office unannounced. His brows scrunched in irritation, but he hid the expression from Dorian, who stood leaning against the door jam.

"Um-hum," Nick muttered, returning his attention to the deposition laid before him. He hated being interrupted while he worked, and that was in the best of circumstances. But now, with trying to divide his attention between two states, his thriving law practice in Little Rock and his fruitless pursuit of Vicki in Chicago, time had become a precious commodity.

He'd taken another midnight flight from Chicago to Little Rock, and planned to spend the next few days getting caught up on the paperwork that Shawn had neatly stacked on the corner of his desk. His four young associates could manage most of the incoming cases, but some of the more influential clients insisted Nick handle their business personally. Nor did anyone on his staff mention the firm's financial concerns, they simply set them aside until whenever Nick had time for them.

When he'd decided to pursue Vicki, Nick had delegated his various responsibilities to each of his underlings. He told only those closest to him of his temporary relocation to Chicago, fearing how the press could misconstrue it during the upcoming election.

With Dorian acting as the office manager in his absence, things were running smoothly in the office, and as far as his clients were concerned, it was business as usual.

"I see Shawn brought you those files we discussed. As you can see, word is already spreading about your plans to run in next year's election. Several of those . . ." Dorian motioned to the stack of post-it message sheets, "are potential campaign contributors who want to meet with you. Take a look and let me know which ones you can work into your current schedule."

"I will, but I've got a lot to get done this weekend." Nick cast a quick glance over the stacks of files spread around the office. Everywhere he looked there were books, manila folders, and loose papers. "I'll have to let you know later."

"Okay." Dorian stood in the doorway for several awkward seconds. He sensed Nick's exhaustion and felt the need to say something, but was unsure as to whether or not he should.

When Nick had laid out this plan, Dorian thought it was insane. Who chases down a woman they dated eight years prior to ask her to marry? What if she's already with someone? What if she never wants to see you again? At the time, Nick had assured him these were trivial problems at best. But now, three months later, the cost of his efforts were taking their toll. He looked like a man at war, and, from the bags under his eyes, he was losing.

"Well . . . okay. I'll let you get back to work."

"Okay," Nick muttered, never taking his eyes off the papers before him. Several seconds later, he still felt the other man's presence. "Is there something else, Dorian?"

"No."

"Okay, I'll see you later."

"Okay."

Nick waited. Finally, he put his pen down and leaned back in his chair. "Come on in, Dorian."

Dorian smiled and strolled across the room with wary eagerness. He took the seat across from the desk, and reclined. "How are you doing?"

"I'm fi—"

"No, I mean how are you *really* doing?"

Nick studied his friend for several long minutes before running both his hands over his smooth head. He sighed and leaned forward. "To tell you the truth, I'm tired as hell."

"You look it."

"Trust me, I feel it."

"Not to be nosy, but are you making any headway. I mean have you . . . you know."

Nick snorted in disgust. "I can't even get her to my apartment for dinner. She hates me, I mean really hates me. I didn't understand that when I went up there. I thought she was just a little mad. But she is so far past mad, it's not even funny."

"Then why don't you come home? If you're that keen on getting married, there are dozens of women right here in Arkansas who'd give their left arm for a guy like you."

Nick smiled. "Are you flirting with me, Dorian?"

Dorian chuckled. "Sorry, man, you're not my type."

Nick's smile faded as a frown creased his brow. He was remembering the defeated look in Vicki's eyes when the judge had announced the verdict in the Morrison case. His mind flashed back to that fateful day eight years ago, when a different judge had handed down the verdict in the Pallister case. She'd had that same look of despair and betrayal then. How could he have forgotten that look?

He'd gone in search of her, hoping to right the wrong, to repair the damage his greed and ambition had wrought on their life-long relationship. And all he'd done was cause her more pain, more hurt.

Dorian leaned forward in the chair, bracing his forearms on his thighs. "What's next?"

"You got me." Nick shrugged. "I've known this woman as long as I've known myself. I had her love before I had chest hair. We used to finish each other's sentences, and now—it's like I don't know anything about her. I can't say or do anything right. And even if I could, she's so angry she'd never hear it."

"I can see she means a lot to you."

"She means *everything* to me."

Dorian stood to leave. "Well then, the only advice I can give to you, my brother, is don't give up."

Nick shook his head; his lips set in a determined line. "I don't plan to."

***

Vicki could feel Nick's eyes on her. She felt it as intensely as if he were reaching across the table to touch her. She ignored him, choosing to focus instead on the lesser of two evils: Angela's cooking. She took a stab at the lump of off-white substance, which she could only assume started out as rice. She swallowed hard and opened her mouth to force down the goo.

She felt another pair of eyes on her, and turned to her left. Kevin, one of Angela's crewmen and the person for whom Vicki believed this nightmare was being con-cocted, was watching her closely. He studied her with the unwavering scrutiny of someone watching a car crash. You see it coming, and yet you can do nothing to stop it. Vicki smiled, in an attempt to reassure the man. The sar-donic twist of his mouth said he wasn't buying it.

"Here we are," Angela said in a singsong voice as she glided into the room carrying a covered platter.

Vicki was afraid. Very, very afraid. One quick glance in Kevin's direction and Vicki knew she was not alone in her fear. They'd already had three courses—three horrible, excruciatingly tasteless courses. What form of torture could Angela possibly have under the cover on that platter?

Nick was reclining comfortably in the dinette chair directly across from Vicki. A lifelong veteran of Angela's culinary fare, his cast-iron stomach had seen it all. Like an experienced gambler, he knew when to hold 'em— and when to fold 'em. Right now, he was nursing his second glass of a very fine tasting cabernet. Of course, certain wines enhanced the flavors of foods, but she wondered if there were any that hid the flavors instead.

Vicki chanced a glance across the table and found her-self trapped by Nick's seductive dark pools. Caught like a deer in headlights, she felt paralyzed by his hypnotic stare. His mouth spread into that infamous Nick Wilcox grin, and his eyes darted in the direction of the platter. Vicki felt her fear intensify. What did Nick know about the mystery platter?

She tried to ignore him, which proved harder than she thought. Kevin was in actuality sitting nearer to her, but it was Nick's familiar, subtle cologne that was drifting into her nose. And that intense heat of his. He always radiated with some internal fire that seem to inflame whatever area he occupied, no matter how large the space.

"What's that?" Staring at the covered platter, Kevin's trembling voice revealed his terror.

Angela smiled at him. "Lemon meringue pie," she announced proudly, and lifted the cover to reveal a yellow, oval shaped blob in an oven-warped pan.

Vicki stared at the platter and silently shook her head. Luckily, Angela's back was to her, for she would never want to hurt her friend's feelings. She knew, like Nick and probably Kevin, that Angela had spent most of the day preparing this meal. It always amazed Vicki how anyone who tried so hard could always manage to get it wrong.

"I'm full," Kevin said, in a not too believable tone.

Angela's brilliant smile deflated. "You love lemon meringue pie," she said, before collecting a few discarded plates and retreating to the kitchen.

Kevin watched Angela disappear through the doorway before speaking. "Yeah, she's right." Kevin spoke to no one in particular, "I love lemon meringue pie . . ." He pointed at the platter. "That thing is *not* lemon meringue pie."

Nick sat up in his seat and glared at the other man. "Hey, man," he warned. "Watch yourself."

As Angela breezed back into the room, Kevin paused, considering the deadly tone of Nick's words. He wasn't a coward by any standards, but he had to feel some respect for the man trying to defend his sister's undefendable cooking.

Kevin had heard the rumors about Angela's cooking from some of the other guys, but he'd simply chosen not to believe it. And even if he had believed it, he probably would've come anyway. To Kevin's way of thinking, when the sexiest foreman alive invites you to dinner, you accept. Never did he imagine regretting the decision the way he was regretting it right now.

What baffled him most of all was that he knew he wasn't the only one near to nauseated. Angela's brother and girl-friend kept right on eating the slop and going on about how good it was. Kevin couldn't bring himself to do it, and besides, Angela Wilcox had the toughest skin of any woman he'd ever met. He could tell her the truth, right?

Out of some perverse curiosity, Vicki attempted to cut into the glob knowing that as a life-long friend she was at least obligated to taste it. When she attempted to lift her slice onto her plate it poured over the knife like thick syrup.

"Oh, Vicki, don't eat that. That's for Kevin." Angela gestured over her shoulder as she started toward the kitchen with another pile of dishes. "I've got something special for you."

In her fascination with the lemon meringue pie, Vicki had never noticed Nick leaving and returning to the room. But now he was standing at her elbow with a second platter. Vicki could see a tan creation with black spots through the glass cake dish.

As Nick set the platter down beside Vicki, he smiled at her again. His full lips were only inches from her cheek; his fierce heat was searing her. Surely that was why she was breaking a sweat, why her pink silk cowl-neck blouse was beginning to cling.

Vicki stared through the glass, trying desperately to identify the thing inside. An eerie suspicion crept up her spine, and she realized Nick was watching her with more than a little interest. She quirked an eyebrow at him. What was he up to?

"I reminded Angela of how much you love chocolate chip cheesecake," Nick said, in answer to her unasked question.

Cheesecake? That thing was suppose to be cheesecake? How could anyone, even Angela, do that to perfectly good cheesecake ingredients? Oh, the poor thing. It was a disgrace to its kind. Vicki silently mourned its unnatural death. She mourned what it could've been and what it would never be. And to think, Nick had encouraged this disaster!

"Eat up." Nick smiled, and returned to his seat across the table.

Vicki knew she was trapped. Everyone who knew her knew that cheesecake—any kind of cheesecake—was her favorite. But definitely, chocolate chip ranked highest on that list. How could she explain not eating it to Angela?

Angela breezed back into the room, completely oblivious to the varying degrees of fear her cooking had instilled in her guests. "Dig in," she beamed at Kevin, motioning to the yellow blob.

Kevin looked to Vicki, then Nick, and knew immediately he was on his own. "No thanks," he said, with as much aplomb as he could manage.

"What do you mean?" Angela asked. "You love lemon meringue pie."

He smiled. "Really, I'm full." Her face fell, and it tugged at his heart. "Really," Kevin rubbed his well-toned stomach, evidence of his years working as a construction carpenter.

Angela glanced around the table as if taking in the partially eaten dishes for the first time. Most of the platters and bowls still contained the largest portion of the foods she'd cooked. Angela's crestfallen expression transformed to one of pure indignation as the truth of the situation dawned on her.

She shot a glare at Vicki. "Don't you want some cheesecake, Vicki?"

Vicki swallowed hard, realizing it was times like this that friendships were made and lost. "Sure." Vicki removed the glass cover and began to cut the cheesecake. She refused to look at Nick, knowing she would see nothing but smug satisfaction.

In the meantime, Angela sat glaring across the table at her guest of honor. She had spent hours in the kitchen preparing this meal. It was one of the best she'd ever done and he had the audacity to complain? Okay, the lemon meringue was a little warped, but at least it hadn't exploded like the last one. *And what was Vicki's problem?* Angela thought, feeling particularly proud of her cheesecake. It was almost lump free.

"Are you full or you just don't like my cooking?" Angela asked Kevin, her arched brow raised in silent challenge.

"Both." Kevin shook his head. "Angela, I can't do this." His fork clattered to the table. "This . . ." Kevin gestured to the table in general, looking for the proper epithet. "This stinks."

Nick started to intervene, but Angela cut him off with the wave of a hand and was instantly on her feet. "What did you say?"

Kevin threw down his napkin and followed her lead. "Angela, you're gorgeous, and funny, and kind, and probably the best foreman I've ever worked for. But your cooking stinks."

"Maybe you've been eating your own cooking for so long you don't recognize gourmet cuisine."

Kevin eyes widened in amazement as he stared at the woman across the table. "You have got to be joking? Right?" Kevin looked frantically from Vicki to Nick in desperation. They were both watching the interaction with something akin to panic. He was alone in his declaration. "They know it as well as I do, they just won't say it. Your cooking stinks!" He scooped up a blob of the yellow goo. "Stinks, stinks, stinks!"

"Your palate isn't sophisticated enough to appreciate good food."

"Oh, I can appreciate good food, *when I taste it.*" He looked once more to Vicki and Nick; still there was no help forthcoming. They both loved her, they'd sit here and eat this crap until their stomachs exploded.

But she was just his boss, Kevin thought, his exceptionally pretty boss. But even that couldn't cover the gross aftertaste in his mouth right now. Maybe he'd have to find another job come Monday morning, maybe not. But either way, he couldn't do this any longer.

"Good night, everybody." Kevin turned and walked toward the front door. He paused at the entrance of the dining room. Without turning to face Angela, he asked, "Do I need to show up Monday or not?"

"Of course," she snapped. "Luckily, your lack of taste doesn't affect your carpentry skills."

With that, Kevin walked through the entrance and out the front door.

"I knew I shouldn't have invited him." Angela scuttled up a handful of dishes, ranting and raving about unsophisticated ingrates all the while. Carrying the load of dishes, she stormed out of the room, completely forgetting her two remaining guests.

Vicki waited until Angela had cleared the doorway. "You jerk!" she hissed across the table to Nick. "How could you do this?" Using her fork, she poked the piece of cheesecake on her plate.

"She asked for suggestions for a second dessert." He shrugged his shoulders. "It was as good as any."

"And as to that . . ." She wagged her index finger in indignation. "Why didn't you help her with this meal? You knew she was inviting another guest."

He leaned forward, struggling to keep his voice low. "I tried. She said she didn't want any help."

Vicki sighed; that did indeed sound just like Angela. For some unfathomable reason, she couldn't accept that fate had gifted her with absolutely no skills in the kitchen. "Well, I guess another one bites the dust."

Nick shook his head and began clearing the remaining dishes. "He wasn't right for her, anyway."

"How would you know?"

His dark eyes locked in on hers again. He stared at her keenly, and Vicki felt as if he were staring right through her, reading her most hidden thoughts, her most secret desires.

"When two people are right for each other, they feel it. A magnetic pull, one to the other. Even if it's not something they want to feel, something they try to resist." He smiled in his special way. "In their hearts, they know they belong together. And it's only a matter a time before they find their way into each other's arms. "

Vicki watched the large man storm through her office entry and slam the door shut in his wake. "I can't believe Morrison got off. He was at the scene of the crime within minutes of it occurring. How could anyone with half a brain think that was a coincidence?"

Vicki leaned back in her chair and studied her boss. She knew his remarks were not directed at her. Ellis was always emotional about a loss, but he never blamed his prosecutors. His attitude was that he hired the best staff possible, and if they couldn't get a conviction it simply couldn't be done. But that never stopped his tirades.

Vicki stretched and yawned as he continued to rage against the system, against idiotic jurors and low-life defense attorneys. She'd expected this visit; now she only hoped he'd finish up soon so she could return to her work.

He finally ended with his usual vow to "get the guy sooner or later." He turned and started back the way he came; he stopped inside the door and turned to Vicki. "You did a hell of a job, Proctor, don't doubt it."

"Thanks, Ellis," Vicki said, picking up her pen to return to her work.

"We'll get the guy, don't you worry. Eventually, we will get him." Ellis stormed out of the office, once again slamming the door behind him.

Vicki only shook her head and continued scribbling notes. She had not the heart nor mind to tell Ellis that, by the end of the trial, the very effective Nick Wilcox had even her doubting the evidence. She could never have told Ellis that thanks to Nick's emphatic closing remarks she had begun to have . . . questions.

She had to wonder if any man like Morrison, with his previous criminal history and gang association—if he truly *were* innocent, would the police, or Ellis, or anyone familiar with criminal behavior patterns believe it? If he was simply in the wrong place at the wrong time, given his past, did he stand a chance of a fair trial? The answer she concluded was always the same: a loud, definitive no.

Sometimes it seemed to her as if the system was

designed to convict men like Tommy Morrison, guilty or innocent. But, unfortunately for Ellis, Tommy Morrison had a secret weapon, an equalizer.

Vicki shook off the thoughts, choosing not to dwell on the fact that had the circumstances been different, she very well may have sent an innocent man to his death.

Nick sat on the back pew of the church sanctuary with his headset over his ears. Thanks to Sabrina, he now had a collection of the more popular songs chosen by the illustrious choir director of the Starlight Trumpeters.

Like every other aspect of his life, Nick attacked the task of learning the long list of spiritual hymns with a zealous intensity. *Angela had been right about one thing,* Nick thought, *he did not accept failure well.* Not well at all. And he knew Ms. Proctor would be all too happy to see him fail in this particular endeavor.

He knew if he set his mind to it, he could learn the songs to the point of sounding like an actual choir member, and by joining the church he ensured himself more time with Vicki. What he had not expected was the additional pleasures he would derive from it.

Chicago was a strange town to him, and outside of Angela and Vicki, he knew very few people. But the new friends he'd made in the church were beginning to fill that void. He found himself playing basketball on Saturday afternoon with a few of the men from the choir, men of varying ages and occupations whose only common bond was their shared experiences as black men. Experiences only another black man could understand. They discussed their lives, and checked each other's behavior with the kind of candid honesty only a basketball court could afford. They bolstered each other up when life's burdens felt heavy.

He began volunteering to visit hospitals on Sunday afternoon with the Mission Society, a small group of older women who each in their own way reminded him of the women of his childhood. Women like his Aunt Tilde, who'd stepped in and raised him and Angela when their parents were killed in a car crash. And women like Vicki's mom, Maude, who'd single-handedly run a small commercial chicken farm while simultaneously raising three children. And, even more recently, women like Katie Morrison. Women who cherished their children with a love that defied words.

These women represented the strength and backbone of the black community, and were a diligent presence that the younger generations took for granted far too much. After a lifetime of watching them in action, Nick understood that these ladies were not used to asking for help. What they needed done, they did themselves.

That's why, when they went out on their missionary work, Nick tried to be there to carry the heavy boxes and set up the tables and equipment. His reward was to spend the afternoon basking in the generous warmth of grand-motherly love. He'd joined Starlight Baptist Church to get closer to Vicki, and had inadvertently found a lot more.

He sat tapping his pen against the back of the pew in front of him, totally caught up in the music in his ears. He'd arrived almost an hour before the scheduled rehearsal time and knew the building was practically deserted. That's why, when he felt a hand on his shoulder, it nearly caused him to jump up off the bench.

"Didn't mean to scare you, Brother Wilcox." Reverend Campbell smiled and offered his hand.

Nick accepted and returned the smile. "Sorry, Reverend, I was caught up in the music. I didn't hear you come in."

"Gospel?"

Nick shrugged self-consciously. "I thought I would try to catch up with everyone else."

Reverend Campbell nodded thoughtfully, "Sister Proctor can be a bit demanding, can't she?"

Nick's mouth twisted in mock severity. "You don't know the half of it."

Reverend Campbell smiled. "I think I might."

Nick tilted his head and studied the man closely. *What was that supposed to mean?* Nick thought, wondering for the first time if his feelings for Vicki were so obvious to everyone.

"How do you like our little church?" Reverend Campbell gestured to the sanctuary at large.

"I'm enjoying myself very much. It was kind of awkward moving to a new city and not knowing anyone, but I find myself making friends."

"That's good. I'm glad to hear our parish is making you feel at home. But at least you are not here all alone. I mean, you have your sister."

Nick smiled to himself, wondering if the good reverend knew how transparent his own affection for Angela was. "That's true, I do have Angela."

"How is she?" Reverend Campbell tried to sound only mildly interested. It didn't work. "I noticed she wasn't in church last Sunday."

"No, she had to work." Nick watched the other man closely. "Sometimes in her line of work, she has deadlines to meet, which means working weekends."

"Yes, I'm sure," Reverend Campbell said. The disappointment was clear in his voice. "Well, tell her hello for

me when you see her." He smiled once more and turned
to walk away.

"I will," Nick said. "Uh, Reverend Campbell . . ."

Reverend Campbell stopped and turned.

"Why not tell her yourself?"

"I beg your pardon?"

"Sunday afternoon she always cooks a big dinner for
myself and Sister Proctor. I was thinking maybe you
would like to join us this Sunday?"

Reverend Campbell's eyes lit up. "I would love to, if
you don't think Sister Wilcox would mind the unexpected guest?"

"Oh no." Nick waved away the concern. "She loves
cooking for guests."

"Well all right, I'll be there."

"Six o'clock. Do you need directions?"

"No, I'm sure we have her address on file. I'll get it from
there." He smiled again. "I'll see you Sunday at six." He
turned and walked away with a lighter spring in his step.

Nick returned to his place on the pew to await the
arrival of the rest of the choir. He replaced his headset
and turned on the music. He knew what he'd just done
was a risky venture, but he had a feeling about the good
reverend. Maybe . . . just maybe.

The man seemed to be genuinely interested in Angela,
and if that were the case, it was time they found out how
deep his affections ran. And there was no better way to
test it than to expose him to Angela's cooking.

CHAPTER EIGHT

Vicki believed that once she put the Morrison case behind her she would see less and less of Nick. But, as fate would have it, the opposite seemed to be occurring. Despite her attempts to shake up her routine, she soon discovered Nick hadn't lied about his tracking capabilities. Her love for the Farmer's Market made it impossible to stay away for long, and as soon as she popped up there, so did Nick. Instead of being put out by his presence, she was finding it more than comfortable these days.

He seemed to have given up on his attempts to seduce her, choosing instead to be the friend he'd promised he could be. Much to her surprise, Vicki found she was not adverse to the occasional Saturday afternoon matinee with him, or a few hours in the local coffee shop on a rainy evening, finding it very easy to relax in the presence of someone who knew so much about her.

With potluck brunches and monstrous dinners at Angela's, interrupted only by morning services at Starlight, they spent most of the entire day together on Sundays. Vicki even extended an invitation more than once for him to run with her and Peaches in the park. Of course, with

Nick's obvious charm and Peaches's inclination to flirt, the pair found little use for her during their outings. Vicki felt no animosity, knowing on some level that they were both simply doing what came naturally to them. Vicki knew Peaches flirted as a matter of breathing, and despite his preoccupation with her friend, Vicki still found Nick's hungry eyes on her when he thought she wasn't looking.

But despite the obvious attraction that still existed, Nick somehow managed to keep his feelings to himself, a fact for which Vicki was extremely grateful. It took all her combined energy to keep up the façade of disinterest, but she was simply too afraid of what would happen if Nick sensed her true affection for him. Despite their unspoken truce, she knew she could never let Nick know how much she enjoyed his company, knowing instinctively that if he did they would be back to square one. Hunter and prey.

Vicki reclined in her desk chair, surfing the Web, and as always found herself distracted by everything except what she'd come to shop for. She was currently looking at hourglasses like the many that lined the shelves of her bedroom. It was a hobby she'd taken up during high school and had maintained over the years.

The phone rang. Vicki glanced at her desk clock and wondered who would be calling her at 1:08 A.M. "Hello?"

"Hey, gorgeous." Nick's seductive voice floated over the line.

Her heart rate sped up; she paused to regroup before speaking. "Hi, Nick."

"What'cha doing?" he asked, as if calling someone's house in the middle of the night was perfectly acceptable behavior.

"Do you know what time it is?"

"Yes. Do you?" he teased.

"Too late for you to be calling my house." She tried to sound angry, but a slight chuckle slipped through.

"Why? You're obviously awake."

"What do you want?"

"To talk to a friend. I couldn't sleep."

She frowned. Very few things interrupted Nick's sleep. That list included end-of-the-world disasters and bricks falling on his head. *Oh yes,* she thought, feeling the butterflies in her stomach, there was one other thing that could keep him awake.

"What are you doing?" he asked again.

"Surfing the Web." She bit her lip to concentrate. No matter what, she could not let the conversation go in *that* direction.

"Looking for antique hourglasses?" he teased.

"As a matter of fact . . ." she laughed as her words trailed off, remembering that most of the ones she already owned came from him in the form of gifts over the years.

"You're pretty much an expert on the subject. Have any Web sites to suggest?" she asked with a chuckle.

"You're joking, but if you want I could give you a few hints. Those things aren't easy to find, but there are a few more reliable sites."

Vicki realized she'd never considered the time it took to find all those glasses over the years. "No, thanks. I was really researching for a gift for Big Mama."

"Oh, yeah, her birthday is coming up. What is she now? Ninety-three or ninety-four?"

Vicki was reminded of just how much they knew about each other. Having been friends since grade school, they'd been a part of each other for all the important events in a person's life. Nicky and Vicki. Growing up, how often had they been called by the phrase as if they were one being?

"Try one hundred."

"Whoa. I never would've guessed that."

"Neither does anyone else who's ever met her."

"Are you going home to celebrate it?"

"I'm not sure yet."

"I thought you were the volunteer party planner?"

"More like appointed party planner, and I am. I just have to see what's in my savings account."

"If you need a loan, let me know."

She smiled into the phone. "And what type of interest would you charge on a loan, Mr. Wilcox?"

"That depends on what you have to offer as collateral, Ms. Proctor." His voice dripped with suggestion. Vicki's heart sped up. What was she doing? This was the conversation she *didn't* want to have.

"I never congratulated you on your selection of Sunday dinner guest. I can't believe Reverend Campbell managed to choke down one of Angela's meals and leave with a smile."

"I'm sure he probably ran home and sucked down a bottle of Pepto Bismol, but I really didn't think he would insult her."

"You were right. He really does like her, you know. I don't know why she won't show an interest."

"I don't know if you remember, but our dad was a minister."

"Oh, yeah, that's right. I forgot about that. Seems to me that would make her more open to dating a minister."

"Just the opposite. My Poppa was a good man, but he was strict with us, and even more with Mama. He had to be. A whole congregation was looking to him to set an example."

"And his woman, too."

"You got it. Mama had to do everything right, or it became the talk of the church."

"And Angela has a problem with that?"

"You may not have noticed, but my sister tends to have a mind of her own."

Vicki laughed. "Really? Angela—stubborn? No way."

"She always said she would live her life her own way."

"And that doesn't include being a preacher's wife?"

"You got it."

"Humph, we'll see."

"Wanna place wagers?"

"Nick!"

"Just kidding." He laughed. "So, what've you got planned for tomorrow?"

"A day trip."

"Where to?"

"Detroit. There's an antique doll dealer there who has an original Lil' Souls rag doll. I remember Big Mama talking about the one she had as a child. I thought it would be nice to get it for her birthday."

"That's a great idea. But watch yourself with those antique dealers, some of those guys are hustlers."

"Takes one to know one."

"That's cold-blooded," he said, but Vicki could hear the smile in his voice. "Can I come?"

She hesitated. "Uh, it's going to be an all day trip."

"That's okay, I've got nothing going on here." Nick was happy Vicki couldn't see his frown. She'd never accepted his explanation for moving to Chicago solely to be closer to her. Now that she was finally opening up to him, he didn't want to scare her off by telling her that his entire schedule was at her disposal. "Can I?"

She sighed. Even if she said no, he probably would

not accept that as an answer. "Sure. I'll pick you up at five-thirty, and Nick . . ."

"Yeah?"

"Don't make me wait."

He smiled into the phone. "Never."

True to his word, Nick was ready promptly at five-thirty, and, after stopping at a fast food restaurant for breakfast, they set out on east ninety-four for the five-hour drive to Detroit. They spent the time singing along with the radio and playing car travel games.

Lately, their life-long friendship seemed to be falling back into place as if it had never been severed. Neither acknowledged the easy camaraderie they shared; the feeling was too pleasant, and neither wanted to ruin it.

Crunching on a cookie from the snack stash, Vicki was glancing around the area as she drove down the highway, which was strangely deserted for a Saturday morning.

"I spy with my little eye, something . . ." She glanced around again. "Green and tall and living."

Nick twisted his mouth and looked at her with disgust. He did not even bother to sit up in his seat.

"What?" she asked.

"You can't spy a tree. There's thousands of them between here and Detroit. It could be any one of them."

"Exactly." She laughed, seeing the unfairness of the game but not caring one bit. He always considered himself smarter than she, let him prove it. "Which one—"

The statement was cut short by a loud popping sound before the car's engine began losing its momentum. Vicki guided the car onto the service drive and out of the main flow of traffic until it finally came to a complete stop.

"What happened?" Nick sat up. Smoke began to drift up from beneath the hood.

"I don't know." Vicki looked perplexed. "It was running fine all week."

An alarm went off in Nick's head. "And the week before that?"

Vicki looked away guiltily.

Nick shook his head. "I can't believe you got us out here in the middle of nowhere in an unreliable car. I don't suppose you took it in to a mechanic to find out what the problem is?"

"I was planning to," she whined.

"Pop the hood," he said, before giving her a look of utter exasperation and moving to get out the car.

Vicki reached down, pulled the lever, and watched as Nick lifted the hood. "What is it?" she called out of the window. Her question received no answer. She opened the door to get out, but Nick came around and stopped her.

"Got your cell phone?"

"Yes, why?"

"We need to call for a tow." He sighed heavily. "This thing is not going anywhere on its own."

Two hours later, they stood at the counter of Al's Auto Repair waiting while Al, himself, wrote up the repair requisition. A younger man, wearing navy blue work pants and a light blue shirt with the Al's logo smeared with car grease, came through the door that led to the garage. He whispered something in Al's ear; Al turned his head and whispered something in return. The younger man nodded, and without acknowledging Nick or Vicki returned to the repair portion of the garage.

"Sorry, folks, but it looks like we used our last radiator

for that model car an hour ago. We're going to have to wait for the part."

"Well, how long will that take?" Vicki asked.

"We expect a shipment in the morning."

"Morning?" Vicki and Nick's simultaneous responses caused Al to take a step back from the counter.

"Sorry." Al hunched his shoulder with little regard. "It's the best I can do." With that, he turned and walked back into the manager's office behind the counter.

"What now?" Vicki already knew the answer. There was only one thing they could do at this point. Wait.

"Do you know of a hotel in the area?" Nick called to Al in the office.

He came back out of the office taking a bite of a half-eaten sandwich. "The closest thing to a hotel is a truck stop about half a mile up the rode." He glanced at Vicki, taking in her silk jogging suit and name-brand running shoes, and Nick's neatly pressed jeans, polo pullover, leather loafers, and designer sunglasses. "Probably nothing you folks are used to but it's the only one in the area."

Nick and Vicki looked at each other in silent understanding. A young black couple at a truck stop in a hick town? Not if they could help it.

"How about car rental agencies?" Vicki asked.

"Sorry, nothing around here. At least, not that I know of."

Nick asked, "How far is the next city?"

"Kalamazoo's another hundred miles."

"A hundred miles?" Vicki didn't mean to whine, but this was all getting to be a bit much.

Nick set his lips in a determined line. He nodded his thanks to Al and turned to Vicki. "Well, looks like it's the truck stop."

"Wait right here." Al motioned. "I'll get one of my

men to drive you up there. Wouldn't want the lady to ruin her pretty shoes on that nasty dirt road." Al smiled for the first time, showing the many gaps in his teeth.

The driver dropped them off at the motel almost fifteen minutes later. At Nick's insistence, they booked a single room. Vicki wasn't comfortable with the idea of sharing a room with him, but he'd explained in no uncertain terms that she *would not* be sleeping alone in a strange motel.

To their mutual surprise and delight, the room turned out to be relatively clean and neat. Two double beds were covered with almost new, plainly adorned comforters. The carpeting was worn, but looked fairly clean. The bathroom was modern and fully equipped with an ample supply of towels, not to mention a few unexpected amenities, such as complimentary toothpaste and four new toothbrushes. The room also came with a modern 25" TV/DVD combo and cable.

"This is not so bad." Nick called to Vicki from the bathroom.

"No, I guess not," Vicki said, her eyes repeatedly drawn back to the two beds. *I can do this,* she silently encouraged herself. *I can share a room with him without sharing his bed. I think I can, I think I can.*

"Did you say something?" Nick asked, poking his head out of the bathroom.

"No." She picked up a take-out menu from a local pizzeria. "Want something to eat?"

"Maybe later," he called back. "Right now, I think I'm gonna get a shower."

Such a simple statement, and yet it flooded Vicki's mind with licentious thoughts. She called the pizzeria and ordered a deluxe with extra cheese before turning on the TV. She repeatedly turned up the volume, trying to drown out the sounds of the shower running. She flipped the channels, but nothing caught her attention. All she could see were images of Nick's beautiful male physique standing beneath an onslaught of water.

The shower stopped. Was he going to redress, or simply come strutting out with a towel wrapped around him. No, he wouldn't. Would he?

Lord have mercy, Vicki thought, as her heart pounded against her chest. Nick was rubbing his face and bald head with one towel and another was firmly wrapped around his midsection. It did nothing to conceal the well-toned shape of his thighs and buttocks, his flat stomach rising up to distended pecks, stretching out to muscular arms corded with brawny power. His dark skin created a striking contrast against the stark whiteness of the towel.

He lowered the towel from his face and smiled. "You should get a shower, the water feels great."

"Um, no thanks, maybe later. I ordered pizza."

Nick crossed the room, the faint scent of soap wafting in his trail. He flopped down on the other bed, reared back on the pillows, and crossed his legs. "What'cha watching?" he asked, being forced by his position to speak to her back.

Vicki continued to surf channels, refusing to turn in his direction. "Can't find anything interesting."

"Humph," Nick muttered, rubbing his chin. It was taking all his self-control to fight the urge to jump up and kick his heels. Tonight was the night. Nick knew it as surely as he knew his own name. He'd never expected this twist of fate, not when Vicki picked him up that morning at his front door, not when the car had broken down, not even when they'd booked the double-occupancy room. Not until a few moments ago, when he crossed her path and saw the look of raw lust in her eyes. He was just surprised the towel around his waist hadn't spontaneously combusted. She wanted him, almost as much as he wanted her.

He had not planned this rendezvous. There were no scented candles or romantic music, but there was Vicki with an ill-concealed hunger for the passion he could give her. And there was the fact that Nick Wilcox hadn't gotten where he was by passing up golden opportunities.

Her hair was pulled up and clipped, which seemed to be her favorite style. Nick thought it was an improvement over the tight bun she'd always worn when they were together. He studied the smooth slope of her rounded shoulders, the line of her back coming down and dipping into the small hollow, flaring out again to her full hips and thighs.

"Vicki?"

"Hum?" She still refused to look at him, instead focusing all her attention on the "Cheers" rerun playing on the TV.

"You should get a shower." His deep voice became even huskier. "It's really soothing."

Vicki felt her whole body stiffen in realization that the second part of that statement had come from a much closer proximity than the first.

"You're tense," he whispered from just behind her.

Vicki gasped, feeling his hot breath against her ear. He'd crossed the distance between them with the stealth of a panther. She felt his large hands coming over her shoulders and beginning to squeeze her tight muscles. She fought the urge to lean back into the massage.

Nick silently cautioned himself. She was ready, but he could feel her hesitation in every knotted shoulder muscle. "Why don't you lay back and relax, and let me—"

Vicki shot up off the bed like a rocket launching. "You know, I think I will get that shower now." She turned, and with a few long strides reached the bathroom. "Let me know when the pizza gets here." She closed the door, and a few seconds later Nick heard the lock catch.

Nick's memory replayed those few seconds before her disappearing act. When she stood looking down at him, he'd seen the smoldering passion she fought desperately. But he'd seen other things as well, things he'd not expected to see. There was fear; not the kind incited by unwanted emotions, but a more genuine feral terror. And even more disturbing than that, the most damning emotion of all, mistrust.

He waited. The pizza arrived, he paid for it, tipped the driver, and continued to wait. He waited until he could stand to wait no longer. He walked over and pressed his forehead against the door. She was so close, only inches away. Her sex-starved body was separated from him by only a few inches of wood. He needed her; she needed him, too. What was she running away from?

"Vicki?" Nick tapped on the door. "Baby, talk to me."

She chuckled nervously. "What do you mean? I'm trying to get a shower."

"You've been in there forty-five minutes, and I've yet to hear the water running." He waited several tense seconds, assuming she was mustering the courage to face him. But instead of seeing the door open, he heard the shower water starting. "Vicki, you can't stay in there forever. We need to talk about this. I can't believe you're still angry about a case you lost eight years ago. It's ridiculous."

The water stopped and the door flew open. "Ridiculous? Two women lost their lives and their murderer went free because of you. You, Nick. And you have the nerve to talk about ridiculous?

"*Two* women? What are you talking about? Andy

Pallister was only accused of murdering one woman, his mistress, Jan Holsten."

Her brown eyes gleamed with copper fire. "Yes, you're right." Her lips twisted in a nasty snarl. "He was only accused of murdering one woman, because he didn't kill the second one until *after* he was acquitted."

Nick shook his head, trying in a vain attempt to shake loose the whirling confusion. "I don't under—"

"Betina Ramirez."

Nick threw up his hands in frustration. "We're back to that crack—"

"He killed her, Nick."

"What?"

"Andy Pallister killed her."

Nick stood staring in dumbfounded silence. No. It wasn't true. It couldn't be true. He had not released a murderer back on society. It couldn't be true.

Vicki pushed past him. She sat down on the first bed she came to and covered her face with her hands. She'd promised herself she would never speak of this to him. Even after all these years, the hurt was still too intense, the anger too extreme. Remembering it all made her want to charge at him with protracted claws and tear his gorgeous face off.

He came and knelt before her. "I understand you're angry," he began. "But if I'm to understand this, you're going to have to start at the beginning."

All the blood drained from Vicki's face. Time stopped. Her mouth fell open and she sat gaping at this man who'd once meant more than oxygen to her. The few seconds that passed could've been an eternity.

In an uncontrollable urge and by a will of its own, she watched as her open palm connected with the skin of his cheek. The snapping noise was punctuated by the twist of his head. He turned to face her again, and the fury that consumed her was unlike any emotion she'd ever felt. It was righteous vengeance incarnate.

"Now?! Now you want to hear me. Now!" Her small hands balled into tight fist as she pounded against his bare chest. "Now! It means nothing *now!* She's dead. Dead, Nick. Because of you." Unable to still the flood any longer, the tears poured down her face. Nick's tight flesh felt like granite beneath her hands, but still she pounded away. "You wouldn't listen to me." She screamed with all the rage she'd held for the past eight years. "He was a murderer. I tried to tell you. God knows, I did! But you wouldn't listen."

If what she was saying was true . . . Nick tried to think back, to remember everything he could about the suave politician who'd charmed the state of Arkansas. At the time he'd believed Andy Pallister was a victim of the media machine. A hero made villain by the newspapers and news channels. But what if none of that were true? What if he'd defended and released a man who'd not only murdered once, but twice?

Finally, when it seemed as if the beating would never end he reached up and grabbed both her wrists. "Sssh," he cooed, pulling her off the bed and against his chest.

Vicki had exhausted herself, and offered little fight against his embrace. She lay silently, in seeming compliance, against his solid form. There was little evidence of it in her calm countenance, but Nick was well aware that a volcano continued to boil beneath the surface.

With a heavy sigh, she began the story he'd refused to hear all those years ago. "Jan Holsten and Betina Ramirez were best friends, had been for years. But when Jan got involved with Pallister, he forbade her to see Betina. Apparently, he didn't approve of his mistress keeping company with a crack addict. Betina said that many times when she and Jan met in secret, Jan would be covered in blue and purple bruises, but she always had some lame excuse ready to explain it. Betina was in the apartment the day of the murder; she heard Pallister come in. And, knowing he would punish Jan for her being there, she hid in a closet. She heard the whole argument, the whole thing from start to finish. He accused Jan of cheating on him. Jan denied it vehemently, and apparently this only enraged him more."

Vicki took a deep breath, as though the rest of the story required a refortification. She continued. "He beat her, Nick. You saw the autopsy reports. And had you not been clouded by your own prejudices you would've considered that most brutal deaths are at the hands of people the victim knows, not some anonymous burglar. After Pallister was arrested, Betina came to me. She had tried to give her story to the police, but no one would listen. I tried to help her as much as I could. But, as the prosecutor, there was only so much I could do without looking like I had a personal vendetta against him.

"After your client was acquitted, Betina went to the police again and again trying to make them listen. But of course, nothing came of it. After all, he'd been acquitted. I helped her schedule a press conference; she'd hoped maybe one of the newspapers or television news programs would be interested enough to look into it. Jan Holsten was her best friend and she'd watched her being brutally murdered. All she wanted was for the truth to come out.

"Nick . . . she never lived to hold the press conference. There was a little noise made about her death—very little. Andy Pallister was never suspected."

"Why didn't I hear about any of this?"

She sneered. "You had already moved on to find the next feather in your cap. The Andy Pallister trial had given you what you wanted, Nick—fame, and the beginnings of fortune."

Nick held Vicki tight against him trying to take in everything he'd heard. Once again he searched his mind for clues, and found them. He remembered the twisted snarl Pallister had given him the one and only time Nick had bothered to mention the prosecutor's surprise witness. Pallister had assured him the woman was nothing more than a junkie trying to stir up trouble in hopes of selling her story to the tabloids. The explanation was plausible, and Nick accepted it without hesitation. He proceeded to thoroughly discredit Betina Ramirez.

Vicki never even bothered to put her on the witness stand, knowing that Nick would parade every bit of dirt he'd discovered about the woman before the jury. For him, that had been the end of it. And now he'd learn that, for Vicki, it had only been the beginning.

He rested his chin on top of her head. "I'm sorry," he whispered. His plea was not only for the woman in his arms, but also for the woman whose life he'd failed to save. "I'm so sorry."

Vicki looked up at him, her usually clear brown eyes glistening with unshed tears had darkened to almost midnight black. Her face became expressionless. With one hard jerk she pulled herself free and stood. "Sorry can't bring back the dead." Her voice was barely above a whisper, but the danger written in every word was undeniable.

Nick craned his neck to look up at her, and found her glaring down at him with menace. She turned and made her way back to the bathroom, closing the door, and this time it was only seconds before the sound of running water was heard.

Nick felt a cold that had nothing to do with the temperature in the room and his partially nude appearance; it had everything to do with the deep sense of dread swelling up inside him. He felt as if he were dying. In fact, he was almost certain his heart had stopped beating inside his chest. The reality of what had happened eight years ago fell on him like a blanket covering all the lies he'd convinced himself of since.

For the second time in his thirty-six years, Nick Wilcox felt like a failure. And once again, his failure was directly tied to the woman he loved.

He ran both his large hands over his bald head before covering his face. "Damn," he whispered between his fingers. The one word spoke volumes. It was an admission of guilt; it was an apology; and he knew that for Vicki it was too little, too late.

Several minutes later, Nick turned off the TV and crawled into the second bed. He lay with his arms folded beneath his head, staring up into the blackness, listening to the sound of running water that continued to flow without end. He listened to the sound of the wind whipping around outside the motel window, a warning of the storm to follow.

But not even a tidal wave could remove the stain of blood he now felt covering his hands. After an unknown amount of time, the rain began, building into the torrential downpour the wind had promised, drowning out the sounds of the mechanical waterfall in the bathroom. Nick felt the driblets of water sliding down the sides of his face long before he recognized what had caused it. His very soul had been fractured. And for the first time since he'd come back into her life, Nick realized how futile were his attempts to win Vicki back. How could he expect her to forgive him when he'd violated the most basic principle of a relationship? *Believe in me as I believe in you,* that's all she'd asked of him. He'd failed her, choosing to believe a stranger instead.

He closed his eyes and let the peace of unconsciousness wash over him, until he became oblivious even to the storm raging outside their cocoon world. Or the one raging within his mind.

CHAPTER NINE

Nick stood leaning against the windowsill with his arms crossed over his chest watching her sleep. The rain outside had stopped, but the downpour of guilt and remorse inside him still persisted.

He'd slept for a few hours. Long enough for Vicki to have finished her shower and fallen asleep in the bed opposite him. She slept in her underclothes. Nick could see the strap of her pink bra peeking at him over the edge of the blanket. She looked peaceful in her deep slumber. But he was wide-awake, and his whole body ached for her.

Despite his self-condemnation, despite her obvious— and now he understood—justified feeling of contempt toward him, he still needed her, maybe now more than ever. Only she could heal the hurt inside him, only she could stop the emotional bloodletting he felt in his very soul.

He moved before he had time to reconsider. Before his mind could catch up with his heart and remind him that she despised him. Before he remembered how horribly he'd failed her.

Dropping his towel, he bent his knee and crawled across the bed. Lifting the covering, he aligned his body to hers. He lowered his heavy form with the greatest of ease.

Vicki's eyes opened immediately, causing Nick to wonder if she was really asleep to begin with. She stared up at the man lying on top of her; nothing in her eyes reflected surprise at waking to find him there.

Bracing himself above her, Nick studied her face as well as he could in the dark room. *What was she thinking? What was she feeling?* A beam of light stole through the slit in the curtains, resonating the faintest trace of moondust across their bodies. Nick reached up and cupped her head in his hands, rubbing her temples with his index fingers. He had no idea what he was doing. He most certainly had no inclination of how welcome his attention was. Would she knee him in the groin and throw him off? Or would she open her mouth, part her legs, and welcome him into her body? It could go either way.

He buried his head and whispered, "I'm sorry," against her neck. Never had he spoken more hollow words, but they were the only ones he had to offer. The only atonement he could give.

"I know, Nick." She rested her chin on his shoulder. "But that changes nothing." Vicki's arms came up and wrapped around his neck of their own volition. Her robust thighs parted, allowing Nick to sink into the crevice of her body. Her calves wrapped around his and her hold on him tightened.

Nick had known it, had felt it instinctively. She needed him as much as he needed her. But here was the physical evidence of that need; she clung to him like a drowning woman to a life raft. They were separated by the tiniest, thinnest pieces of satin material Nick had ever felt. It was the only thing standing between him and paradise; how easily it could be removed. But instead, he made one of the hardest decisions of his life. He chose to do nothing. The next move would have to be hers.

Vicki lay wrapped around this man she still loved too much. She silently asked herself the same questions she'd asked a thousand times. How did they end up here? How did everything go wrong? And why after all this time was she still powerless to resist him? How did he always know what to say, what to do, to break her down?

Her voice broke the silence. "Loving you is like trying to love a tornado, Nick. You're so destructive you can tear my life to shreds in a matter of minutes, and yet I seem to be uncontrollably drawn into you. No matter how I fight it, I can't get free. And the worst part is that as I'm being pulled into you, I'm still awed by you, even though I know without a doubt that you will destroy me."

"I would never hurt you on purpose."

"Nor does a tornado choose to destroy, it just does what's in its nature to do."

"Vicki, I know it's hard for you to believe this, but really, I'm not that man anymore."

Vicki hugged him tighter. Her precious Nicky; he truly believed he could change that easily. The idea was as preposterous as a lion waking up one morning and deciding to become a vegetarian. Even if the heart is willing, the mind and the body are simply not able.

Nick wouldn't be Nick if he gave up that predatory instinct that made him the attorney—no, correction: It made him the *man* he was. Those characteristics were what she admired about him, but they were also what she despised. She feared one day that all-consuming passion of his would lead to his downfall.

He lifted his head to look into her eyes. "I realize now

how I hurt you by not believing you. But I swear, baby, I'm a different man now. I've changed, Vicki, truly I have."

She stroked his face. "No, you haven't, Nick, but it's okay." She lifted her head to touch her lips to his. He returned the kiss, prying her mouth open with his tongue. Exploring, roaming, tasting. She was everything he remembered. He began sliding the strap of her satiny bra down her arm, kissing every inch of skin exposed by the movement as he went. "You're so sweet, Vicki." He shifted between her legs as the throbbing of his manhood became uncomfortable. "So very sweet," Nick whispered, again returning to her mouth. His fingers slipped around her back and unhooked her bra with one tiny flick of his wrist.

She felt strong hands simultaneously closing around both her breasts. His hot mouth closed around one, while his thumb continually strummed the other with expert precision. Vicki felts arrows of desire shooting from her breasts to the center of her body. She arched her back, lifting herself up to his mouth; her whole body was alive with the intensity of its craving. Vicki took two deep breaths to fight off the increasing speed of her heart. She bit her lip to stifle the moan caused by hands sliding along the sides of her body, over the soft roundness of her stomach and her well-toned thighs. His fingers spread over every inch of her visible skin. Slipping under her, around the curve of her full bottom and into the valley of her lower back. He kissed her through the thin fabric of her underwear. Even through the thin cloth the warmth of his mouth was undeniable.

Nick shimmied up her body, coming to rest in the crook of her neck. Vicki lay paralyzed, unaware she was holding her breath until he lifted her hair off her neck and kissed behind her ear. Choosing that spot was proof of his familiarity with her being. Because only a lover who knew her well, a lover like Nick, would know about that extremely sensitive spot. It was the secret combination that unlocked the vault of her desire.

He lowered his head and suckled at her breast like a hungry babe. Vicki's body arched in a perfect bow at the feel of his hot mouth closing around her nipple. He suckled hungrily before taking her between his teeth. His hand eagerly squeezed and prodded the other breast, preparing it for a similar fate. Rolling his tongue along the underside, around, and over the top until he reached the dark brown peak; taking it whole, drawing it into his mouth with agonizing slowness until Vicki cried out. He shifted to repeated the torture.

In the beginning, Vicki had told herself that she could let him have her body, but not her heart. Now she realized how ludicrous it was to believe she could retain control over either, once he claimed her. Even as she fought to stone her heart against him, her body recognized him for who he was. He was the man who'd given her her first tastes of passion all those years ago. He'd set the standard for love, teaching her to want things she'd never wanted, to feel things she'd never known she was capable of feeling. And regardless of whatever lie she was able to convince her mind of, her body recognized its mentor.

Almost hesitantly, he kissed a trail down the length of her body. Her whole being shivered with the thrilling sensation of tiny kisses, strategically placed for maximum effect. He came to rest between her thighs and pillowed his head on her stomach.

"I know it probably means nothing now, but I never knew about any of that." Nick's normally baritone voice was hoarse with lust and regret. "I really thought he was innocent."

"I know." She ran fingers over his smooth head. She

began shifting beneath him, squirming under the weight of his large frame. Not because he was too heavy, but because he was too masculine, too much of a reminder of what she'd been denied. And as he'd already proven again and again, her body would open to him even if her mind refused.

No, her brain screamed. *Don't do this. Remember what he did to you the last time? Save yourself!* In a fit of panic, she lifted her arms to push him off. But his strong arms came up to cover hers, holding her in place almost as if he'd expected this change of heart. In reassurance, he kissed her forehead, her cheeks, her chin. It didn't take long to change her mind. He nibbled at her lobe and behind her ear; she felt her body relaxing, and all attempts at escape were forgotten. A few feathery kisses in dangerously close proximity to her mouth, and it opened to him. His tongue was deep inside, drinking her in. Without conscious thought, she wrapped both arms and legs around him and was responding to his kiss with enthusiasm. She shook her head, trying desperately to reconcile body and mind, but it was pointless. Her love-starved body was beyond her mind's reason.

Holding both breasts, his tongue ran from tip to tip, and soon her taut nipples were wet and glistening with the evidence of his attention. He leaned back on his forearms, watching her face. He knew she was fighting what she was feeling. Her head swung from side to side; her mouth opened to form silent words. She appeared to be in utter misery, and Nick intended to show no mercy.

He bent his head to take her whole breast into his mouth once again, and her agonizing cry of pleasure was his reward. Even as she whimpered no, she pressed herself into his mouth, and wrapped her legs tighter around his torso.

Nick's mouth was exploring and reacquainting itself with an old friend as he felt her pushing up against him, clawing at the bed as she thrashed about. Her need was on her with a vengeance; a need festered by weeks and weeks of expectation.

This was destiny, pure and simple. Somewhere in the back of her mind, Vicki had known from the beginning, from the first moment she'd seen him enter that courtroom on that fateful day. She'd known that it was just a matter of time before she would find herself here. Beneath him, around him, one with him.

She felt the bed shift as he lifted himself. Her underwear slid down her legs, and he was over her again, flesh against flesh, his hardness against her softness. His warm breath in her ear telling her in no uncertain terms that it was only the power of his will holding him back at this point.

Reaching down between their bodies, she closed her fingers around him and heard his sharp gasp of air as his whole being stilled. He seemed frozen in time as her fingers explored him. The sensation was always confusing, Vicki thought, that something so flinty hard and rigid could be covered in silk. His penis throbbed in her hand as she stroked the length of him.

"Come into me, Nick," she pleaded, as every ounce of her own willpower slipped away, "I want you inside me." Her hands circled around his lower back and over his buttocks, releasing him from the hypnotic spell.

"I know baby, I know." He comforted her with words, while he struggled to find a condom in his wallet.

Even as his hands pulled the crushed wrapper from his wallet, he knew it was no good. *How long had it been in there?* he thought to himself. He hadn't been with a woman in over a year, and his last few girlfriends had always provided their own protection.

He tore open the wrapper anyway, even while saying a silent prayer that it would still be usable. Somehow, he knew God wasn't going to grant this particular wish. As the dried-up piece of plastic peeled away from the cellophane, his suspicion was confirmed.

With painful clarity, he surmised the situation, running through the facts and possible outcomes in his head at mind-boggling speed. He touched her, feeling her throbbing wet readiness on his fingers, and swallowed hard.

Vicki, still with her eyes closed and oblivious to the situation, subconsciously lifted her hips to him, waiting for him to enter her—and he considered it. *This is Vicki after all,* Nick thought, his soon-to-be-wife, even if she didn't know it. Worst case, she would get pregnant, and Nick saw nothing wrong with that at all. In fact, the thought of Vicki carrying his baby was more an argument *for* rather than against.

But she would hate him for what she would see as nothing less than blackmail. A baby would be a bond stronger than marriage. And even though they'd talked about it, years ago, he had no idea how she felt about having children now.

"Hurry, Nick," she moaned, still clawing at the bed while her pelvis pumped against his busy fingers. He rubbed her protruding nub and felt her body stiffening. *She's there,* Nick thought.

Without another thought, he lay flat against the bed, lifted her legs over his shoulders, and took her in his mouth. Her body exploded. She bucked hard, crying out in absolute rapture. And he held her, feasting on her honeyed nectar until her wild bucking became tiny rhythmic shudders, until finally stillness. Perfect, sated stillness.

Nick cursed under his breath, feeling the twitching
motion of his ungratified sex. He cursed again as his
spilled seed dampened the floral bedsheets. He held her
hips, feeling her body settle down beneath him. Sometimes, Nick thought, life could be so damn unfair.

As Vicki floated back down to earth, her mind was
spinning in bewilderment. Why didn't he? Noticing the
discarded condom carelessly cast to the far corner of the
bed, she understood.

"Not to sound ungrateful, but why didn't you do it,
and just pull away before it was too late?" Her whispered
words shattered the tranquility of the moment.

He lay with his head on her stomach for several long
seconds, almost afraid to confess the truth. But this was
Vicki, and he wouldn't lie to her. He would hurt her no
more. "Because I wouldn't have pulled away."

Vicki considered his words and the implied meaning.
The only answer she could muster was a muted, "Oh."
Nothing else was said about it.

By noon, a driver sent by Al picked them up from the
motel. They were on the rode back to Chicago by one-
thirty. Neither spoke of the night before.

Nick was too afraid he would hear her denounce what
they'd shared with deep regret and vow it would never
happen again. He knew she was still uncertain, and that
uncertainty was dangling by such a thin thread that the
slightest push could lock her into position either way. He
would bide his time, pretend that nothing untoward had
happened, and hope that in time she would accept their
reunion as a fact.

Vicki drove in brooding silence, her reticence brought
on by a much plainer motive. Having spent those few

hours of absolute bliss in Nick's arms, able to recall every wonderful moment in vivid detail, Vicki knew she would never again be satisfied with the staid, ho-hum, and agreeably platonic relationship she shared with Preston.

When Nick returned to her life almost three months ago, he'd declared that she belonged to him. She'd laughed in his face and told him he was insane. And now, every prediction he'd foretold had come to pass. She did *still* love him. Nothing felt as right as being in his arms.

She wondered how she was supposed to return to her bland existence and give up the possibility of ever feeling him inside her, of knowing the fulfillment of love that only they could create together. She knew she wouldn't. She couldn't. But what galled her the most was that Nick had known it all along.

Vicki realized she had to accept the truth; there was no one for her but Nick. She could now acknowledge this reality to herself, and silently eat a few barrels of crow, but she refused to open her mouth and give him the opportunity to say told-you-so.

CHAPTER TEN

Nick glared at Vicki across the choir stand. "What do you mean move back another row? You've already moved me back twice. I'm the only one back here."

"Please, Brother Wilcox, just move back. You're drowning out the tenors," Vicki pleaded patiently. She fought the urge to point out that he was also drowning the altos, sopranos, his fellow basses, *and* the organ.

Nick took a deep breath and moved back—yet another row. Two more and he would be in the rafters, alone. "Is this better?" he asked, his jaw flexing with tension and embarrassment.

Two miles from the back door would be even better, Vicki thought, but wisely held her tongue. "Thank you." She smiled. "All right everyone, from the top." She motioned with her hand and the choir began in harmony.

Nick's ear-shattering baritone was still audible, but Vicki had reduced the effects as much as possible. His naturally low-pitched bass voice seemed to drop three octaves when he sang. If one could call the noise emanating from his throat *singing*.

The sound of the front door opening caused Vicki to look

around as Reverend Campbell came into the sanctuary. Shaking off pellets of rain from his all-weather coat, he waved in greeting to the choir before heading in the direction of his office.

The group continued rehearsing three more songs in preparation for Sunday. The choir as a whole had been more than gracious to their newest member, despite his glaringly obvious handicaps. And, as difficult as it was for Vicki to fathom, Nick actually seemed to be enjoying himself, despite his undesirable positioning.

After a short prayer, the group was dismissed. Some members hurried out the front door to get home to their families; others stood around in smaller groups making plans for the evening.

Nick watched Vicki move to collect a light windbreaker jacket. The torrential rains of late had only been tempered by the gusty winds. It was pouring rain outside, even as the small assembly moved about inside the warm building.

Nick briefly took in her thin, black, straight skirt and cream blouse. It was standard uniform for the choir. But Nick couldn't help thinking it was too cold for her to be dressed flimsily. She didn't even have an umbrella. He would have to give her his, he decided. He'd come too far to lose her to pneumonia.

He was stepping down out of the choir stand when he felt a tug on his sleeve. He turned to find himself facing Sister Sabrina Medley. She smiled, and Nick felt a sharp pain of discomfiture. The woman's feelings for him were written in every line of her face.

He'd done nothing to encourage it and yet they seemed to continue to grow with every meeting. He knew he would have to put a stop to it, and soon. The last thing he needed was for Vicki to believe he was seducing her choir members. But as to how to stop it he was clueless. All the obvious attempts had failed. He shuddered, remembering the nightmare scene he'd recently experienced with Veronica. He most definitely had to put an end to this infatuation.

Sabrina's hold on his arm tightened. "Some of us are going out to dinner. Would you like to join us?"

Nick smiled. "No, thank you, maybe another time." He spotted Vicki. She already had her jacket on and was moving toward the rear of he church. "Please, excuse me."

He started to move away, but Sister Medley held his sleeve. "It's a little Italian restaurant on the south side. I think you'd really like it." She smiled seductively.

Nick sighed. This was the problem. He'd tell her no in the clearest of terms, and she would persist. He only hoped it wouldn't come to a bad end one day.

"No, but thanks again." He turned in time to see Vicki disappear through the doors. He moved faster, hoping to catch up with her in the parking lot.

Since their road trip, Vicki had kept him at arm's length. He'd asked her over for dinner, and she'd repeatedly refused. He'd found more than one excuse to come to her house, but she was never available. They still interacted in the way of casual friends, but the budding intimacy was at a standstill.

They still ran in the park with Peaches, still dined at Angela's once a week, and spent their Saturday mornings roaming the lanes of the Farmer's Market. But Vicki made a special point of avoiding any real intimate contact. Their arms no longer brushed when they were standing in close proximity; she no longer reached over him to pick the breadbasket up off the table. How he missed those appetizing glimpses of cleavage. In fact, as best he could determine, there seemed to be some type of one-foot rule regarding the distance to maintain at all times. No matter how he maneuvered to spend time alone with her, she worked just as hard to avoid it. He was feeling more frustrated now than he had before they'd made love.

He opened the door just as her little blue car disappeared around the corner of the building. He felt his heart sink. This was *not* the way it was supposed to work out. Not at all. By now, he was supposed to be firmly entrenched in her heart and bed. They were supposed to together. Together. And well underway in the planning of their wedding.

"Excuse me, Brother Wilcox, can I speak to you a moment?"

Nick was startled by the sound of Reverend Campbell behind him. He turned and smiled, taking the other man's hand. Since their dinner at Angela's, Nick's opinion of the young minister had gone up several notches.

As much as Nick loved his baby sister, he knew first hand that it took a brave heart to choke down her cooking while exclaiming how thick and rich her lumpy half-cooked mashed potatoes were. Or how succulent her over-cooked roast was. But even the good reverend had been stumped by Angela's version of sweet peas, which she'd unfortunately cooked to the point of puréeing. Instead of commenting on the sweetness of her sweet peas, he'd made some vague reference to the nutritional value of green vegetables, never admitting that he was uncertain as to *what* green vegetable he was being served. All the while Angela beamed with the pride of Julia Child.

"Yes, Reverend, what can I do for you?" Nick followed Reverend Campbell back into the building with a heavy sigh. Vicki had slipped through his fingers once again; he could only hope she'd make it home without catching a chill in the rain.

Reverend Campbell glanced back over his shoulder at the few remaining stragglers, most involved in their own conversations, but a few were watching the two men.

"Please, come into my office for a moment. This won't take long." He gestured in the direction of the open door.

Nick took a seat across from the large wood desk. The lawyer in him scanned the sprinkling of picture frames sitting on one corner and made an assessment. A couple of the frames contained a large group of people of varying ages who all resembled Reverend Gabriel Campbell. The largest frame was of a bowling league, and Gabriel stood in the middle holding up a trophy. There were a scattering of others photos, but none contained anything that resembled a love interest.

Nick knew he was wrong for being skeptical of the man, who'd been nothing but decent and honorable. But this man obviously had his eyes on Angela, and, minister or not, Nick wanted to be certain he wasn't out to use her.

"What can I do for you?" Nick asked.

"Well . . ." Gabriel glanced up, and Nick realized he was hesitant to state what was on his mind. "First of all, thank you for inviting me to dinner the other week."

Nick smiled. "No, actually, I want to thank you for your kindness. I know my sister's cooking can be a bit different, but she puts her heart into every dish."

Gabriel smiled in return. "I know that. I could see how proud she was of her effort." His hazel eyes took on a far away look. "She's beautiful always, but even more when she's beaming with pride. Her smile—" Gabriel stopped abruptly, realizing how close he'd come to blathering his feelings. "Uh—yes, well, that's what I wanted to speak to you about."

"Her smile?" Nick teased. It was shocking that this

An Important Message From The ARABESQUE Publisher

Dear Arabesque Reader,

I invite you to join the club! The Arabesque book club delivers four novels each month right to your front door! It's easy, and you will never miss a romance by one of our award-winning authors!

With upcoming novels featuring strong, sexy women, and African-American heroes that are charming, loving and true… you won't want to miss a single release. Our authors fill each page with exceptional dialogue, exciting plot twists, and enough sizzling romance to keep you riveted until the satisfying end! To receive novels by bestselling authors such as Gwynne Forster, Janice Sims, Angela Winters and others, I encourage you to join now!

Read about the men we love… in the pages of Arabesque!

Linda Gill
PUBLISHER, ARABESQUE ROMANCE NOVELS

P.S. Watch out for the next Summer Series **"Ports Of Call"** *that will take you to the exotic locales of Venice, Fiji, the Caribbean and Ghana! You won't need a passport to travel, just collect all four novels to enjoy romance around the world! For more details, visit us at www.BET.com.*

A SPECIAL "THANK YOU" FROM ARABESQUE JUST FOR YOU!

Send this card back and you'll receive 4 FREE Arabesque Novels— a $25.96 value—absolutely FREE!

The introductory 4 Arabesque Romance books are yours FREE (plus $1.99 shipping & handling). If you wish to continue to receive 4 books every month, do nothing. Each month, we will send you 4 New Arabesque Romance Novels for your free examination. If you wish to keep them, pay just $18* (plus, $1.99 shipping & handling). If you decide not to continue, you owe nothing!

- Send no money now.
- Never an obligation.
- Books delivered to your door!

We hope that after receiving your FREE books you'll want to remain an Arabesque subscriber, but the choice is yours! So why not take advantage of this Arabesque offer, with no risk of any kind. You'll be glad you did!

In fact, we're so sure you will love your Arabesque novels, that we will send you an Arabesque Tote Bag FREE with your first paid shipment.

* PRICES SUBJECT TO CHANGE.

YOU'LL GET 4 SELECT ROMANCES PLUS THIS FABULOUS TOTE BAG!

ARABESQUE

THE "THANK YOU" GIFT INCLUDES:

- 4 books absolutely FREE (plus $1.99 for shipping and handling).
- A FREE newsletter, *Arabesque Romance News*, filled with author interviews, book previews, special offers, and more!
- No risks or obligations. You're free to cancel whenever you wish with no questions asked.

FREE TOTE BAG CERTIFICATE

Yes! Please send me 4 FREE Arabesque novels (plus $1.99 for shipping & handling). I am under no obligation to purchase any books, as explained on the back of this card. Send my free tote bag after my first regular paid shipment.

NAME _____

ADDRESS _____ APT. _____

CITY _____ STATE _____ ZIP _____

TELEPHONE ( ) _____

E-MAIL _____

SIGNATURE _____

Offer limited to one per household and not valid to current subscribers. All orders subject to approval. Terms, offer, & price subject to change. Tote bags available while supplies last.

Thank You!

AN085A

Accepting the four introductory books for FREE (plus $1.99 to offset the cost of shipping & handling) places you under no obligation to buy anything. You may keep the books and return the shipping statement marked "cancelled". If you do not cancel, about a month later we will send 4 additional Arabesque novels, and you will be billed the preferred subscriber's price of just $4.50 per title. That's $18.00* for all 4 books for a savings of almost 30% off the cover price (Plus $1.99 for shipping and handling). You may cancel at any time, but if you choose to continue, every month we'll send you 4 more books, which you may either purchase at the preferred discount price. . . or return to us and cancel your subscription.

* PRICES SUBJECT TO CHANGE

THE ARABESQUE ROMANCE CLUB: HERE'S HOW IT WORKS

THE ARABESQUE ROMANCE BOOK CLUB
P.O. BOX 5214
CLIFTON NJ 07015-5214

PLACE
STAMP
HERE

man, who spoke eloquently before hundreds of people, became a stuttering schoolboy at the mention of Angela.

Gabriel chuckled, thankful for Nick's easy manner. "No—well, not *just* her smile. I hope this doesn't make you uncomfortable, but I'm sure you have noticed I have an interest in Sister Wilcox, a very strong interest. I was wondering, if maybe, you would be willing to give me a little guidance."

Nick sat up, coming to attention. This conversation was taking an unpleasant turn. What was this man asking of him? Tips on how to *mack* his baby sister?

"What kind of guidance?"

Gabriel held up his hand in understanding. "I know you're her brother and probably wouldn't feel comfortable discussing her personal life with someone you barely know, but—"

"You're right, I wouldn't. I'm sorry, Reverend, but anything you want to know about Angela you're going to have to ask Angela."

Gabriel's face fell. The hopeful gleam in his hazel eyes vanished. "I just felt—if I knew a little more—could answer a couple of questions, I might stand a better—I mean, that I might . . ." Gabriel sighed in frustration. "Never mind. I understand."

Nick felt like a heel. He'd seen the spark of interest flare between Angela and Gabriel, and had taken the initiative of inviting the young minister to dinner to evaluate his intentions. And the man had proven himself ten times over. He was not only willing to suck down the gruel, he'd had the decency to pretend to enjoy it. Risking indigestion rather than hurt Angela's feelings, proving in no uncertain terms that his feelings were genuine. All Gabriel was asking for was a little information. Something to help him in his quest to win the heart of the woman he desired.

Nick sat back in the chair and studied him. He finally determined to help the seemingly kind, intelligent, and shy preacher claim his prize. Nick knew his decision was probably influenced by his own experience as a man who understood the difficulties and frustrations of trying to love a woman who simply wouldn't act right. With that thought, he pasted on his winning smile and said, "What did you want to ask me?"

"Vicki, darling, please hand me a towel." Preston's cocoa-brown arm reached around the floral shower curtain, his hand grasping at thin air.

Vicki rolled her eyes angrily before reaching beneath the bathroom sink counter to get a fresh towel. She considered using it to suffocate him, but simply handed it over instead.

She leaned against the counter with her arms folded across her chest. She'd had almost thirty minutes to calm down, and was still fuming. Of all the audacious, pompous, arrogant things Preston had down in their one-year relationship, this one took the cake.

Never before had she come home and found him in her apartment. How dare he use the key she'd given him for *emergencies only* to take this kind of liberty? What if she'd had company?

Visions of Nick sprawled naked across her bed raced through her mind, heating her body. But surely that wasn't what she meant by company? Was it? *No*, she determined. It was just damn irritating that Preston would let himself in without an invitation. Didn't she have some right to privacy?

"How was your rehearsal?" he asked, calling from behind the curtain,

"Fine." She answered in one-syllable words, as she had done from the moment she entered the apartment.

Anyone who knew her well would've picked up on the underlying anger, and the fact that Preston seemed heedless of it bothered her even more. *Nick would've noticed,* her heart whispered.

Preston stepped out of the tub and continued drying himself. "Well, my day was atrocious," he offered, sensing she would not ask.

As he continued to dry his body, Vicki couldn't help the mental comparison her mind was making. Where Preston was soft, Nick was hard as solid granite. Well-built would've been an understatement; Nick was more . . . sculpted. Molded, like a fine marble statue. One of those built by the ancient Greeks based upon what they believed the body of a god should look like. *Yeah,* she smiled, *one of those statues.* That was Nick.

". . . and I said, 'Hey pal, what do you think you're doing?'"

Huh? Vicki bit her lip, realizing she'd not been following the conversation. Preston glanced in her direction; something like awareness flashed in his eyes. He wrapped the towel around his waist, and it sagged. Images of Nick walking toward her across the motel room, the white towel wrapped snuggly around his taut mid-section sent a shiver up her spine. No, Preston definitely was not Nick.

"What's going on, Vicki?" Preston stood with his legs spread, his arms akimbo. Vicki thought the effect might have been more intimidating without the saggy towel dipping below his pudgy stomach.

Feeling guilty for her train of thought, she went on the offensive. "What are you doing here, Preston?"

He tweaked her cheeks. "Can't I visit my honey?"

Vicki pursed her lips. "It would've been nice if your honey knew you were coming."

"Hey now, what's this frowny face about? Did I do something wrong?"

Vicki turned and walked out of the bathroom. *Did I do something wrong?* His question reverberated in her head. *No,* she thought, *but I have, in letting this relationship continue this long.*

He followed her out, studying her black skirt and cream blouse, and wondering why didn't she wear earth tones more; they suited her complexion much better than tedious blacks and whites.

"Honey, what's wrong?" He reached forward and took her hand.

"Preston, please come into the living room with me. We need to talk."

Preston's expression went blank. "All right," he said, hesitantly.

Once they were seated, Vicki tried to stall by offering him something to eat or drink; her guilt over what she was about to do overriding her anger at coming home and finding him in her house. As to that . . .

"Preston, you never did say what you were doing here." Something else occurred to her. "And why were you taking a shower here?"

Preston's face went from blank to pure alarm. "I—I came to see you, and I was feeling—dirty. No. Wait. That's not what I meant. I mean I was feeling a little— unclean. I wanted to see you. Is that wrong?"

Vicki stood. She felt her personality shifting gears. Vicki the woman was taking a back seat to Prosecutor Proctor. What was going on here?

Those few seconds seem to be all Preston needed to

gather his wits. "I'm sorry about that. I felt like you were accusing me of something."

"Humph." Vicki turned and walked to the window. If he thought he was getting off that easily, he had another thought coming. "Tell me about this atrocious day you had."

Preston seemed to hesitate for a moment before answering. "Well, I stayed late to try to get some work done. You know I've been working on this really nasty class action suit against Abeco, involving food poisoning. Anyway, I was in the office, I thought alone, and who do you think I see flittering around the file room?"

Vicki listened, trying to pick up on the unspoken story. Most witnesses said no more than they had to. If you wanted the whole truth to anything, a good attorney knew you must always listen for the unspoken story. 1) He was working late. Nothing unusual there; he often worked late into the evening. 2) He was working on the Abeco case. She knew that was thrown in to impress her, the way he always threw around his clients names to impress her. 3) Griffin was there. Griffin was his nemesis; the two men always seemed to be vying for the same high profile cases. And they seemed to share the same inflated opinion of their own importance. Actually, for two men who despised each other, they had a lot in common.

"Looking over his shoulder, I see he's going through the Abeco files," Preston continued, oblivious to Vicki's careful evaluation of his every word. "And I said, 'Hey pal, what do you think you're doing?'"

Vicki nodded; now the conversation in the bathroom was making sense. Okay. 4) He caught Griffin going through his files. That explains why he was angry.

"Needless to say, I'm exhausted and just want to rest," he concluded, and reached to pick up the remote control.

That's it? Vicki recalculated. His story was missing some elemental pieces. "Well, what did you do when you discovered he was rifling through your files?"

Preston sat up with all the indignation he could muster. "I gave that sorry jackass a piece of my mind!"

Vicki blinked once, twice. *That's it?* Did she miss something? "That's it?" she voiced her thought out loud.

Preston slumped back on the couch. "Well, what did you expect me to do, honey? He works there too, and the files are for the use of all the attorneys."

"You didn't question his reason for looking through your case files? Or confront him in any way?"

"Fist fighting is for men of little intellect."

Vicki's mouth twisted sarcastically, "I'd like to see you try using your intellect in a back alley off Fifteenth Street."

"Vicki, really, I think there's a big difference between a low-life thug who'd accost someone in an alley, and a man of Griffin's class and sophistication."

Beep, beep, beep. Vicki's radar went off. There it was: the missing piece of the puzzle. Despite all his ranting to the opposite, some part of Preston admired Griffin. She wasn't sure what it meant, but a sneaky suspicion was creeping up her spine.

"That's true." She decided to test her theory. "A handsome man like Griffin would never be caught anywhere near the vicinity of Fifteenth."

"Never," Preston whispered dreamily, as he closed his eyes and relaxed into the couch.

Vicki came to stand over him, and waited. It may take a few minutes, but she knew eventually he'd see the grievous error he'd made.

Sure enough, within a few seconds his eyes popped open and he sat straight up. "I didn't mean—that is to say—" Preston looked up into her clear brown eyes and knew it was pointless to lie. "Aw, hell." He fell back against the couch again.

Strange as it was, this moment was not what he'd expected it to be. He thought he would be riddled with guilt and shame. But instead, he felt a sense of relief, of a heavy burden being lifted from his shoulders.

Vicki could see the turmoil in his face, and she felt pity. She cared for Preston, but theirs was no deep, passion-heated love affair. She sat down beside him, compelled not by the girlfriend in her, but simply by the friendship they'd shared over the past year. She wanted to comfort him.

She took his hand between hers. "It's okay. I've always known there was something wrong with our relationship, I just didn't know what it was. But tell me, Preston, did you know, when we got together?"

Overwhelming relief at her easy acceptance was like a miracle. He sat up and clamped onto her entwined fingers. "I didn't, Vicki, I swear it. In fact, I didn't know until today. I mean—I've always had . . . feelings for him. I didn't understand what they were until today. I think he was as surprised as I was. I never set out to hurt you, Vicki. You've got to believe that if nothing else."

Vicki felt a small bit of disappointment, more than any type of hurt. Compared to the devastation that washed over her life when she left Nick, this was nothing.

"I came here because I wanted to talk to you about what had happened," he continued. "And when I got here, I realized you were the *last* person I could talk to. I was confused . . . I still am."

Seeing the thin coating of water forming in his eyes, Vicki pulled him into an embrace. "It's okay." She pulled back and smiled at him. "You've got some thinking to do, some decisions to make. I think you need to talk to Griffin more than me."

Preston smiled back, even as one of the newly formed tears spilled onto his smooth cocoa-brown cheek. "You're terrific, you know that?" He hugged her fiercely.

"So I've been told," she teased.

Preston wiped his eyes and cast a hesitant glance in her direction. "Vicki, I know you said I should talk to Griffin right now, but I think I just want some time alone with my own thoughts, to try to sort things out. Can I stay here for a while with you, maybe order a pizza and watch a movie?"

She smiled back, feeling an unexpected sense of relief herself. "Sure, I'll go order the pizza and you find something good on TV." Vicki stood and turned away from the couch; she paused. "Preston."

"Yes?" he called over his shoulder, already heavily embroiled in channel surfing.

"Don't enter my house uninvited again. Got it?

He smiled to himself. "Got it."

With that, Vicki strolled down the hall to her bedroom. A silly smile kept playing across her face, and she hadn't the faintest idea of why. *You know why,* her heart said.

She didn't envy the soul-searching Preston would be forced to do over the next few days, but she knew they would at least be able to retain their friendship. A friendship that she truly valued, and now she knew that that had been the only thing keeping her from breaking up with him.

This little discovery had given her the best of both worlds. She could keep her friendship with Preston, and leave the door to love open for Nick. *Life is strange,* she thought happily, as she dialed the number for the pizzeria.

CHAPTER ELEVEN

Decked out in a Chicago Bulls jersey, Bulls cap, and giant red finger, Vicki followed Nick—dressed in equally fanatical attire—through the masses that crowded the stadium and out into the night air. "I still don't understand," she whined.

Pointing at his Jeep, Nick pressed the alarm OFF button on his key ring, and flashed a wry grin over his shoulder. "If you don't by now you never will. I should've known it was hopeless trying to teach *you* about basketball."

She feigned hurt. "What's that supposed to mean?"

"He held the passenger door open for her and smiled. "That for all your rare charm and beauty, the ability to understand sports *just ain't* one of 'em."

She climbed inside and began fastening her seatbelt. "Maybe if I had a better tutor . . ." She let her words trail off with a grin.

Nick ran his finger along her blue-jean clad thigh. "I'm the only tutor you need." He matched her smile with his own. "I'll teach you everything you need to know."

Vicki fought the urge to shiver at his touch. "Well, get me home, professor. I've got an early flight tomorrow."

Nick secured the door and came back around to the driver's side. Vicki used the time to calm her nerves. Why did his touch effect her like that? And how much longer would she be able to hold to her request for time?

Shortly after Preston's revelation, Vicki had invited Nick out to dinner at a restaurant, not trusting herself to give her little speech with any kind of earnestness in either of their homes. She'd explained to Nick that she was no longer averse to the idea of a relationship, but that she needed some time.

She needed to be sure what she felt was truly love and not momentary lust. He'd assured her that it was not lust, but agreed to the time requirement. Over the past few weeks he'd been more than understanding. They spent most evenings together, and all of their weekends.

Nick still had not spoken of his plans to return to Arkansas with her as his new bride. Or his intention to run for attorney general next November. It wasn't that he was hiding it from her, there just had not been the proper opportunity to introduce the topic. He was sure once he had a ring on her finger the rest would be easy.

When they pulled up in front of her condo, they sat in the car and talked for a while. She never invited him in; he never asked. If time was what was needed to make her his forever, he thought, a few more lonely nights was a small price to pay.

"When will you be back?" he asked, knowing that the much-anticipated birthday bash for Big Mama, Vicki's grandmother, was finally coming to fulfillment. Vicki had made all the arrangements; everything was in place. Now all she needed to do was go home and help her mother prepare for the many expected guests.

"I'm taking two weeks of my vacation time. How about you?" she asked. Vicki thought it was a strange coincidence that Nick was returning to Little Rock during the same period of time. He'd only been in town for a few months, and that brought up another question. One that he'd yet to give her a straight answer on. "Nick?"

Nick sensed the question before it was asked. He'd been able to dodge the bullet without having to lie to her. And if he wanted to keep his perfect record it meant exiting the vehicle immediately. He opened his door, pretending not to hear her call his name. He circled and opened her door.

He effected a low bow and made a grand gesture. "My lady, the red carpet awaits you."

The combined effects of uncommon gallantry and that devastating smile of his worked their magic. All thoughts of questioning him as to his employer slipped away.

She stepped out and dipped into a curtsy. "Why, thank you, sir." She glanced at the empty sidewalk leading to her concrete stairs. She shook her head at their little act, wondering at this man who could make her feel silly, sensual, and happy at the same time.

With a swift kiss on her lips he returned to his jeep and waited while she entered the house. Nick knew it was only a matter of time before she finally cornered him with questions about his employment. If he told her about his law firm that kept him running back and forth between Chicago and Little Rock, she'd ask why he didn't relocate the firm to Chicago. And that would open the door on all those *other* questions he wasn't ready to answer yet.

He planned to return to Little Rock during the time she was in Hope. Without her there was no reason for him to remain in Chicago. And, according to Dorian, questions were beginning to be raised about his absence. Questions he didn't need right now. Well, at least this time when he returned it would be with the prospect that soon, very soon, he wouldn't be returning alone.

Nick hit the snooze button on his alarm clock, but felt no hurry to rise. He lay staring at the ceiling of his Little Rock apartment with his arms folded beneath his head.

He was thinking about Vicki, and that she was less than two hours away by car. How easy it would be to drive down to Hope and pay her a surprise visit.

He sighed, knowing it wouldn't happen today. One of his largest clients had scheduled a lunch meeting with him to review their annual financial statements. This was something any one of his subordinates could handle, but this client insisted that only Nick handle their files. And his firm was compensated greatly to ensure the exclusive service.

He wondered briefly if the office of attorney general would hold many similar such requirements and restrictions? It was a moot question. He knew it would. Politics is politics, be it the halls of a Little Rock law firm or the halls of Congress.

The only real difference was the scope in which he worked. As attorney general he could go after some of the dirty heavy hitters he'd known about for years but been unable to do anything about through a single legal firm. And as attorney general he would have the entire state of Arkansas behind him, and all the available resources that went with it. Nick had played the game long enough to know how to win. And he knew in that position he could make Vicki proud.

Where did that thought come from? Did he want to make Vicki proud? Had that subconsciously been a part of the decision process in choosing to run? His private musing was interrupted by the sound of the telephone ringing.

"Hello," he answered sluggishly.

"Morning, sugar."

Nick smiled into the phone. "Hi, Aunt Tilde."

"Did I wake you?"

"No, just gave me a great way to start my morning," he said, while sitting up in the bed. He and his Aunt Tilde had always been close. Hearing the long pause before she spoke again set off a small alarm in his head.

"I need to ask a favor."

Nick became alert. In the twenty-five years since Matilda Howell's baby sister Carmen and her husband Malcolm had died in an auto accident and she'd taken in their two orphaned children, Nick had never once heard his aunt ask a favor of anyone.

"Anything. What do you need?"

"A lawyer."

Nick fell silent trying to understand what she meant. "You mean as in *legal representation*?"

"I'm afraid so."

"Why?"

"I've gotten myself into somewhat of a mess down here, and I need some help getting out of it." Something about her voice troubled him. Nick looked at the clock on the nightstand.

"I've got a meeting this afternoon, but I'll be there this evening." His long legs were already sliding to the floor. "But first, why don't you explain the situation?"

"I would much rather talk to you face to face."

"Okay. I'll be there as soon as I can."

"Thank you, Nick. I knew I could count on you," she said, sounding like her normally chipper self again.

Nick hung up the phone and began his day, all the

while wondering what use his elderly, peace-loving aunt could have for a lawyer?

Vicki sat astride her horse, Silent Thunder, and looked out over the vast expanse of green meadow that had been the only home she'd known for the first eighteen years of her life.

This was the place that formed the foundation of her being, her belief in some unknown all-encompassing universal design. This was where the need to be a part of that greater plan had been born. She'd known what she wanted to do with her life long before she had a name for the occupation.

"Tck, tck." She clicked her tongue, at the same time squeezing her knees against the sides of the mare. The animal began moving forward in response to the motion, but at the ripe old age of thirty, Silent Thunder was now more *silent* than *thunder.* But Vicki didn't mind; this was her horse, her baby, and had been since Vicki had witnessed her arrival into the world all those years ago. Vicki had grown into a strong woman in those thirty years, and, given the advancing age process of animals, Silent Thunder had grown beyond that in the same amount of time.

Vicki squeezed her knees again, and Silent Thunder's trot became a steady gait. Even though it had been almost a year since the pair had ridden together, they fell into perfect sync, the way only old friends could. Vicki continued to survey the land before her, and considered the things she'd spoken with her family about only that morning.

Everything was in place for Big Mama's one-hundredth–birthday gala. All that was missing was Big Mama herself, and Vicki would climb the steep mountainside, which was only accessible by horseback, first thing in the morning to retrieve her. Now she should've been free to relax and enjoy the feeling of being mellowed by the serene environment and the unique blessing of still having her grandmother with her after a century of living.

But instead, she was dealing with the knowledge that her mother was seriously considering selling their family farm. The only home Vicki and her two siblings, Carl and Rhonda, had ever known. They'd all agreed over breakfast that the decision was their mother's, but the three had cast each other hesitant looks, knowing the loss would be greater than just a source of income.

Three generations of Foresters and Proctors had grown up on the farm and profited from the chickens and eggs that were raised there. All three members of the last generation had chosen other paths, leaving only their mother and her small group of workers to manage the place. This was why, ultimately, the three children had left the final decision up to their mother. None of them wanted the responsibility.

Vicki knew it was selfish, but she loved what she did, and had no desire to abandon law for the alternative of breeding chickens. As for her siblings, she knew the primary problem with both was simple and the same: They were lazy.

After the death of her much-beloved husband Carl Senior, twenty years prior, Maude Proctor had turned all her attention to the only evidence of their love and their life together: their three children, and the business they'd worked side by side to build.

Maude managed to completely spoil two of her three children and double the annual profits of the small farm at the same time.

Vicki, being the eldest, was spared. And that was only because Maude was forced to call upon her from time to time to assist in the care of the other two, which naturally developed a more selfless and mature person.

With a small-business loan from her parents, and the help of a small group of devoted farm hands, Maude had managed to take a mediocre chicken farm and turn it into one of the quickest growing farms in Arkansas. Unfortunately, the growth of Proctor Farm had become stifled by the infiltration of large corporate-owned farms in the area, but Maude had held her own and continued to grow at a steady pace.

Only Vicki knew how hard it was for her mother to meet their monthly payroll and still maintain the high standards set by her grandfather two generations ago. Neither Carl Junior nor Rhonda had taken more than a passing interest in the accounting side of the farm, in as much as it provided them a source of income during tight financial times in their lives. Vicki understood her mother's reasons for considering selling, but it didn't make the idea any less easy to stomach.

Vicki and Silent Thunder cleared the small mound that separated Proctor land from the Howell's Farm, which belonged to Nick and Angela's maternal family. The farm was where the young orphans had come to live with their Aunt all those years ago, and, in turn, became the only place the siblings would ever think of as home. Vicki couldn't help imagining how different her life would've been if fate had never brought Nick to her small corner of the world. Nick had affected many of her choices in life in one way or another. Had she not met him, would she be the same woman now?

Vicki brought the horse to a halt and sat looking over the smaller farm. It had been almost a full week since she'd said good-bye to Nick at the airport in Chicago. She'd attempted to call him, but remembered he was in

Little Rock this week, and she did not have the phone number there. She felt it strange and annoying that he'd made no effort to contact her. Her mother's phone number had been the same for over ten years; he *did* have her number. It left her to wonder if, in the face of her request for time and now her absence, he'd finally accepted defeat. But even as she told herself that, she found it hard to believe. Nick Wilcox had never in his life given up easily.

Preston had opened up to Vicki and tried to explain to her that what he was feeling for Griffin seemed to simply come out of nowhere and run him down like a Mack truck. Vicki didn't bother explaining to Preston that she understood that feeling all too well.

She had initially asked Nick for time to be sure what they were feeling was more than momentary lust. He'd not only complied, he'd been downright chaste in his behavior toward her. But Vicki feared with Nick's undeniable appeal and far too many enticing memories, once she returned to Chicago that they wouldn't remain *just* friends for long. She knew once their relationship reached that plane she would be lost forever. Even now, remembering the feel of his hot mouth between her legs was enough to heat that region of her body to throbbing.

Sensing the change in her companion, Silent Thunder snickered. The sound was enough to free Vicki of the web of seduction that Nick had managed to tangle in her brain. Vicki patted the animal's warm neck and made a mental note to visit Ms. Tilde before returning to Chicago. She turned the horse in the direction of the lake and took off at a light gallop. Again, for what felt like the *gazillioneth* time, she silently wondered what Nick would advise his aunt to do about the land developer who was trying to buy up every tract of land in a fifty-mile radius.

"Hello?"

"Angie, it's me."

"Hey, it's about time you called. What's up?" Angela relaxed, hearing the sound of her brother's voice. She'd been anxiously awaiting this call for what felt like forever. Nick had called her shortly after his ambiguous conversation with Aunt Tilde to basically put her on standby mode, unsure of what the situation would be in Hope when he arrived.

Having never married or had a family of her own, her sister's children had been the closest things Matilda Howell had to offspring. And their love for her was equally strong. Once apprised of the situation, Angela had been as shocked as Nick that Aunt Tilde would have any use for a lawyer, and couldn't begin to imagine what the cryptic call had been about. Nick had promised to call her as soon as he arrived in Hope, but that was two days ago.

Nick began with a sigh. "Apparently, there's a surveyor for a land development company who's been coming around trying to buy the farm."

"Aunt Tilde would never sell that farm."

"You know that and I know that, but apparently the surveyor thought he could change her mind."

Angela knew her aunt as well as Nick, everything from her huge heart full of love to her fire-hot temper, and she knew without hearing it said which end of her personality the surveyor had come in contact with.

"What happened?"

"Aunt Tilde told him to stop coming around." Nick paused for a moment. "He wouldn't listen."

"What did she do, Nick?" Angela asked hesitantly, finding it hard to hide the anxiety in her voice.

"She took a couple of shots at him," Nick answered flatly.

Angela gasped. "Oh, no."

"Luckily, she didn't actually hit him, but she was arrested."

"Oh, no." The two words were all Angela could manage in her current state of shock. She didn't know what she'd expected to hear when Nick finally called, but this most certainly wasn't it.

"I was able to post bail and bring her home. Angie, she's probably going to have to stand trial, the way things look now."

"What are we going to do?"

"Well, there's no reason for you to come home yet, but I'll keep you updated and let you know if things change."

"I'm having some problems with my electricians; they're threatening to strike. I really can't leave right now, but I'll be there as soon as I can. Is there anything I can do from here?"

Nick thought for a moment about how angry his aunt had been when he'd posted her bail and brought her home the previous day. She'd pulled against the officer who escorted her out of her cell, calling him every vile name under the sun. Nick saw the look of relief on the faces of the other officers, many of whom had received their own tongue-lashings over the past two days of her incarceration. They all appeared very happy to turn her over into the custody of her nephew.

And even now, after having a hot bath and a full night of sleep in her own bed, she was still fuming, and not regretting her decision for one moment. Nick knew if this thing went to trial, his aunt would be as unruly and vocal in a court of law as she had been in the police precinct. In her mind, she'd acted completely within her rights to ward off trespassers, and probably would not hesitate to tell the judge and jury as much.

"Yeah, there's something you can do from there."

"What?" Angela asked, eager to help in any way she could.

"You can pray this thing doesn't go to trial."

Angela hung up the phone and leaned against the small, mahogany side table. Aunt Tilde arrested? That was far worse than anything she had imagined. She sighed in relief. At least Nick was there with her, and right now he would be far more useful to their aunt than she would.

"Is something wrong?" A male voice spoke from the dining room doorway.

Angela fought the urge to smile, remembering her dinner guest. She straightened her shoulders before turning to face him. "Oh, no, just family business."

Gabriel scanned the concern in her dark eyes, but held his peace. Obviously something had upset her, but he would not pry. Nick had told him how greedily Angela guarded her privacy, and that invading what she perceived as *her space* would be a fatal error. Remembering that tutelage he attempted to change the subject.

"That apple turnover was delicious." He smiled and held up his empty bowl. "Can I have seconds?"

The brilliant smile that flashed across her face was worth eating ten bowls of the tasteless apple mush, Gabriel decided. She was beautiful, intelligent, proud, and strong. A modern-day Cleopatra. And if he remained diligent, she could be *his* Cleopatra. So what if she couldn't cook? They would just have to eat out—a lot.

"Sure." She moved past him toward the kitchen, "I'll be right back with the tray." As Angela pushed open the door leading into the kitchen, she thought: *Finally a man who can appreciate good food.*

Vicki looked in every direction before unbuttoning her shirt. It was late, and the lake was close to deserted. She was alone. By the time she slid her pants down her thighs, she felt completely comfortable. Once she was naked, she went screeching into the icy cold water, unable to remember when she'd felt more alive.

The cool lake felt like a heavenly raiment around her naked body. She turned onto her back and floated, holding her head barely above water. She stared up at the beautiful stars shining overhead as they easily lit up the dark night. After her body had become adjusted to the cool temperatures, she turned over and began swimming back and forth along the length of the small pond, her body warming even more from the exertion.

She lulled in the water, listening to the sounds of the night forest around her, the crickets chirping in the distance, the faint sound of leaves bristling in the wind. It was an unusually warm night for Arkansas in spring, and that had been the lure that brought her here, just as it had done often when she was a child.

Many nights she'd met Nick here, but that was before puberty struck like a dreaded mutation that changed everything. Once she became conscious of the changes in her body, she avoided her late night swims with her best friend. Once Nick became conscious of the changes, she stopped the swims altogether. But tonight was like any one of those nights before puberty, when the only care she'd had was what her mother would pack in her lunch box the next day. She'd forgotten how good it felt to have a few moments of life with absolutely no worries.

She swam and swam until her limbs began to ache, unsure of how long she'd been out there. Reluctant to leave the solitude, she turned over and dog paddled in the water. Something about the evening air began to change, and she started hearing strange noises around her. Vicki decided she'd had enough and swam back toward the bank. Coming close to the shore, she saw something that caused her to freeze in the water. The new warmth coursing through her disappeared, leaving her feeling cold and clammy.

"Don't stop on my account." Nick was smiling sinfully, as he stood with one leg propped on a large boulder near the edge of the pond.

Dressed in a pair of snug-fitting jeans, a button-up plaid shirt, and ancient-looking cowboy boots, this very relaxed-looking Nick was no less tantalizing than the sophisticated metropolitan counterpart. Vicki wondered very briefly if the image before her, looking too good to be real, was in fact that.

Nick mistook her hesitation for shyness and began looking around the bank of the pond. He found the pile of clothes neatly folded on another nearby boulder. "Oh, you want these?" he asked, holding the pile up.

Her eyes narrowed as she watched him lift up her light blue silk panties and rub them against his cheek. Vicki realized that she was indeed dealing with the real McCoy. A vision would never be so crass.

"What are you doing here?" she finally managed to get out.

"Apparently we had the same idea, but Aunt Tilde asked me to feed the hogs at the last minute."

"In Hope, Nick. What are you doing back in Hope?"

He was now carefully examining her matching light blue under-wire bra. "Doesn't this metal thing hurt?"

"Answer me. Why are you here?" she asked, treading water and getting colder by the second. She wasn't sure if the shock she was feeling was from seeing Nick or the cooling water.

"Aunt Tilde needed me," he said, before offering up the stack of clothes again. "You look cold. Here're your clothes. Come and get 'em. "

"Put my clothes down and leave, Nicholas," she commanded, hoping to sound forceful enough to intimidate him.

Given the playful laughter that immediately followed the comment, she knew she had failed. After all, he held all the cards. Not only did he have the distinct advantage of being fully dressed, he was also in possession of the only clothes available to her within half a mile.

"Can't do that." Unfolding each individual item, he laid her garments out in a neat row along the grassy embankment: her highly starched blue jeans, her lavender peasant blouse, her white bobby socks, and undergarments.

Holding her dark brown riding boots in his lap, he sat down beside his handiwork looking prepared to wait all night if necessary. "Come on out." He smiled. "It's nothing I haven't seen before."

At that moment Vicki wished with all her might that looks could kill. If it were possible, Nick would've been reduced to nothing more than cinders by now. But instead, he was still there, sitting and waiting, looking oh-so-smug and self-satisfied. How in the world could she love this man?

"Nicholas, leave now."

His face sobered in determination. "Nope."

"I swear I could strangle your neck right now."

His smile returned. "By all means, please try. But you'd have to come out of the water, now wouldn't you?"

"God, how I hate you."

"If I believed that for one second, I'd leave you alone forever. But you don't, and we both know it."

"Nicholas Andre Wilcox, go away."

"Nope."

"If you had one shred of decency—"

"I don't. So that's a moot point."

"Nicholas, if you don't—" Vicki began to choke and gag as her open mouth filled with water. Soon, she was flinging her arms around in the water, struggling to breathe.

Without hesitation Nick was on his feet and in the water. With ten powerful strokes he reached her, lifting her slipping head above the water. Scooping one muscular arm under her breast he held her tight and began moving back toward the shore. His strokes were long and fast, but with only one arm it took longer to return than it had to reach her.

Without thought, Vicki had wrapped her convulsing body around his arm, holding to him like the life raft he'd become. She continued to choke and gasp, trying desperately to suck in enough air to breathe. Finally they reached the shore. Nick set her down on the beach and prepared to administer CPR when he noticed the water still gurgling in her mouth.

Turning her on her side, he pounded on her back and let the pond water pour out of her mouth. Soon she was pulling in large gulps of air and breathing again.

Nick sat her upright, bracing her against his shoulder

to look down into her face. "Are you okay?" he asked, watching her clear brown eyes for dilated pupils. He slumped in relief to see her black pupils focused firmly on him.

"Yes," she choked out, bending her cough-wracked body in half. "Yes, I'm fine."

"Are you sure?" Nick sat her up against her will. His eyebrows furrowed in concern, he wiped the water droplets back away from her face. Vicki allowed herself to be examined by him; she hadn't the strength to fight him if she'd wanted to.

Once he was assured of her well-being, he pulled her wet, naked body against his coarse cotton shirt. The drenched material was clinging to his strong chest and provided little barrier between the two bodies. Nick held her, and rocked her in his arms.

Soon, the choking stopped altogether, and her breathing returned to normal. Both seemed to have forgotten she was completely naked and cuddled in his arms. All Nick could think of was the perfect serenity of the moment, and Vicki was reveling in the feeling of safety she found in his strong arms.

Once her breathing had returned to normal, Nick turned her to face him. "Don't scare me like that." He held her arms tight and squeezed her against him once more. *I can't lose you.*

Vicki settled against his chest without resistance, but the look of horror she'd seen on his face was not a look she would ever forget. Soon she felt the tiny kisses on the top of her head, her cheek, and her neck. Everywhere but her lips, as if he were intentionally avoiding them. Vicki felt a bed of grass beneath her naked body and viewed a blanket of stars above. She sensed his intention before seeing his large shadow looming over her; hands were on her breasts, kneading, squeezing, and teasing. She closed her eyes, and gave in to the sensation of his warm lips on her icy cold flesh.

"You have beautiful breasts, Vicki. Have I ever told you that?"

The feel of his warm hands on her chilled flesh seemed to make her mute. He continued to toy with her, running his index finger over one large mound of flesh; feather-light touches hardened her peaks. Vicki gasped and arched her back into the caress as his fingers moved worshipfully into the low valley between the mounds. Vicki wondered how she could have forgotten how good this felt?

Without warning, the strong hands with the gentle touch disappeared, and the internal warmth that had begun to spread through her body quickly retreated. After waiting several long seconds, hoping his touch would return, Vicki finally opened her eyes to find Nick sitting beside her. His legs were drawn up to his chest and his arms rested on his knees. He was staring out across the water, seemingly lost in his own thoughts.

Nick tossed a rock out across the lake and spoke in a voice devoid of all warm sensuality. "Are you sure you're okay?"

The businesslike tone of his voice shattered the moment. Vicki propped herself up on her elbows and stared at his broad back, willing him to turn and look at her; he never did. Remembering her nakedness, she felt her cheeks flush with embarrassment. She scrambled to sit up and tried to cover herself with her small blouse.

"Yes, I'm fine," she said, and paused. "Thank you."

A heavy silence fell over the land, the air charged with unspoken declarations. Vicki looked out over the picturesque scenery and wondered what had happened to the children who used to play here. Several feet away, dangling from a decrepit weeping willow, a tire swing hung in perfect stillness, completely useless in their grown-up world. When had everything become complicated? When had their lives become full of serious pursuits, intricate plans, and mundane concerns?

"How long are you staying in Hope?" Vicki asked.

He shrugged. "Not sure, depends on how long Aunt Tilde needs me." Nick knew his aunt would be mortified if he shared her recent incarceration with anyone, even the Proctors, her closest neighbors. The two families had been more like extensions of each other rather than just neighbors over the years. As much as he wanted to talk to Vicki about it, he had to respect his aunt's right to privacy.

"Big Mama's birthday party is Saturday." She hesitated before asking, "Are you coming?"

Nick thought about it a moment. "Maybe I shouldn't. It's been years since I've seen her, and she wasn't exactly *nice* to me the last time."

"Don't be ridiculous, she's not *nice* to anyone," Vicki added with a laugh. "She tends to say what's on her mind, and most folks can't handle that." She was unsure why she felt the need to persist in this. "I know Mama will be happy to see you. And Rhonda and Carl came home for the celebration, not to mention every Proctor or Forester in a hundred-mile radius will be there. The *Little Rock Chronicle* is even sending a reporter to cover it."

"Is she still living in that shack up in the hills?"

"Yes." Vicki sighed heavily remembering the long trek across steep mountain terrain she had waiting for her in the morning. Her grandmother, at the age of one hundred, still lived on her own, deep in the hills in the tiny cabin where she and her ten siblings had been born and raised. "I'm going to pick her up tomorrow."

Nick spoke without thought. "I'll go with you."

Vicki hesitated for several seconds before responding. "Okay, but if you don't mind, I'd like to get an early start. Lord knows, I don't want to be caught up on the mountain at night."

Nick chuckled, "I hear you," he rubbed his hands together to shake the loose dirt from his still-damp palms. He got to his feet with an ease that shouldn't have been natural for such a tall man. "As for the party, I'll think about it." He offered his hand and helped Vicki to stand.

They stood staring into each other's eyes and far beyond, deeper down into the other's soul. Their hands were still locked tightly together; Nick understood the invitation written on her face. A look of hunger and need reflected in her lovely doe-brown eyes. That was in direct response to the longing she saw in his own eyes.

Vicki stood before him in all her naked splendor, blatant desire radiating from every pore of her coffee-brown skin. To say the moment was perfect would've been an understatement. This was what he'd wanted for as long as he could remember.

He chuckled; he couldn't help it. The irony of the situation was cruel.

"What's so funny?" She smiled, feeling Nick's contagious laughter.

"Life," he answered, with a wry twist of his mouth.

Vicki just stared with crinkled brows. *Life?* She opened her mouth to say something more, but before she could he interrupted.

"How did you get here?" he asked, seeing no obvious modes of transportation available.

"Silent Thunder's grazing beyond that ridge." She nodded to the left, still holding tight to her small blouse. It did little to conceal anything, but gave a small sense of security. Now that they were standing, she was far more aware of her vulnerability.

"Silent Thunder?" He smiled. "I thought she would've been dead by now."

"Bite your tongue." She laughed, amazed that she could stand there bare as a baby and joke with him, considering everything that had happened.

"I'll go get her, you get dressed," Nick took one more look at Vicki.

Her clothes were damp from her body, her shoulder-length hair had curled, and the thin sheen of water on her face gave her flawless skin a glistening effect. Yes, Nick thought again before walking away, it was a perfect moment. But this moment had come at the risk of almost losing her, and he couldn't forget that.

The memory of her arms tossing above her head, the look of desperation he'd glimpsed right before she began to go under; he knew he'd never been more terrified in his life. And now what she was offering him was gratitude, nothing more. Of that he was also certain. And as easy as it would've been to take her right there under a perfect moonlit sky, he didn't want making love to her to be an act of compensation. He wanted it to be an act of love. He'd waited too long for her complete surrender and now knew he would settle for nothing less.

Vicki watched him go, certain at any moment he would change his mind and return to her. He never did.

She dressed and waited, looking back out over the small pond. Still feeling a bit damp, her mind and body had not yet fully recovered from her near brush with death. She wrapped her arms around her waist to ward off the chills, both internal and external.

Her mind was scrambled in confusion. For three months Nick had chased her from one end of Chicago to the other. She'd held her ground and refused him . . . to a point. But when they found themselves back at one of their childhood haunts, she'd offered herself to him, and he'd turned her away. What did that mean? Had her constant refusal to commit to him caused him to truly lose interest? Was their second chance over before it ever truly began?

CHAPTER TWELVE

"Um, um, um!" Nick wiped his mouth with the linen napkin. "Aunt Tilde, you've done it again." He smiled and rubbed his flat stomach, now completely filled with all his favorite breakfast foods. After almost two months of his own cooking and a few sprinklings of Angela's nightmare meals, Nick found it more than a little satisfying to stretch out his long legs under his aunt's table once more.

The older spinster sister of his much younger mother was more than grateful to oblige, and had been from the moment they'd arrived on her doorstep almost twenty years ago. Matilda, being the oldest of her five siblings, and the only one without a family of her own, had taken both Nick and Angela in and raised them with all the loving care she would've given her own. The two children, having lost both their parents in a tragic auto accident, went through a very natural adjustment period in which they rejected almost everything Matilda offered, including her love.

But persistence won out and eventually they accepted her into their hearts. Matilda had always made sure they understood she had no intention of replacing their mother, and often went out of her way to keep Carmen's memory alive for them. During their first week in her home, she combed through her attic and dug out as many pictures of her sister as she could find, and within days they were framed and lining the walls of the farmhouse. Many nights she put them both to bed with stories of their mother's exploits, both as a child and as a young woman.

One of their favorite stories, repeatedly requested over the years, was how their parents met. It was the story of Malcolm Wilcox's determination to win the heart of a woman who'd sworn she'd never marry the son of a minister. Her great complaint was that they were just too "holier than thou," and she had no intention of spending her life married to a saint.

Being the wild child who enjoyed nothing more than the occasional evening spent in a well-stocked party joint, everyone accepted Carmen's stoic pledge. Everyone except Malcolm, who persisted in attempting to court the beautiful farmer's daughter. Matilda had been witness to every bit of her sister's stubborn determination and often cruel rejection of the young man, certain like everyone else that Malcolm was fighting a losing battle.

In the end, many would say the devil lost to an angel's smile, a smile his son would inherit. The couple was finally united in marriage, and before long Nick was on his way into the world. The wild child had been tamed into a loving wife and eagerly expectant mother.

Nick often found himself thinking of that story regarding Gabriel's pursuit of Angela, and as inspiration for his own current attempt to capture a beautiful black butterfly.

"Got any room for more?" Matilda smiled, removing the empty plates from the table.

Nick had made plans to meet Vicki to head up the

mountain at ten A.M. He looked at his watch.It was nine thirty-five. Nick pulled his belt loose, unsnapped his pants, and smiled up into the crinkled, loving face. "I'll make room."

The phone rang as she was scooping another heaping pile of hashbrowns onto his plate. Reaching over her shoulder, Tilde took it from the base on the wall. "Hello?" Her normally cheerful voice turned to ice within seconds. "No. No. And no. Don't call me anymore!"

Before she could slam the phone down, Nick grabbed her wrist. "Let me." His commanding tone was in direct opposition to her hostility.

She pushed the phone into his chest and stormed out of the room, waving her hands wildly and mumbling to herself.

Nick took a deep breath before putting his mouth to the receiver. "Hello, my name is Nick Wilcox, Ms. Howell's attorney. Who am I speaking with?"

"Did you say Nick Wilcox?" The male voice on the other end asked in surprise.

Nick called forth his most imposing tone, assuming the other party recognized his name, and the reputation that went along with it. "Yes."

His one-word answer was met with dead silence.

"And who am I speaking to?"

"My name is Dale Sanders, and I'm the attorney for Mr. Plummer, the plaintiff in this case." The man paused. When Nick said nothing, he continued. "I also represent Alpha Development, Mr. Plummer's employer, and the ones on whose behalf Mr. Plummer was acting when he visited the Howell's farm in an attempt to conduct a survey. I'm calling because my client has decided to drop the charges against Ms. Howell. Had I known she retained counsel I would've contacted you directly, Mr.

Wilcox, but as of our last meeting I was under the impression she had no representation."

"I'm her nephew. I live in Little Rock, but was out of town at the time of the arrest. May I ask why your client has decided to drop the charges?"

"Well, Mr. Plummer understands that Ms. Howell is an elderly woman who lives alone, and after careful consideration he's decided that, given the situation, her actions were understandable. No harm was done, and Alpha Development has pretty much commissioned me to make this problem go away."

Nick pursed his lips; this was way too easy. "Well, that is very generous of both your client and his employer."

"Of course, given this turn of events, and the fact that my client is still very interested in the Howell's land we would like to resume negotiations with her regarding her thirteen-acre tract."

Here's the rub, Nick thought. "I didn't realize there were any negotiations pending. It was my understanding that Ms. Howell had already rejected your offer."

"Well, all that happened some time ago, and given the newest set of circumstances, we were hoping maybe she would be willing to reconsider."

"And if she refuses?"

Dale Sanders paused. He was well aware of who he had on the other end of the line. Nick Wilcox was considered one of the shrewdest, sharpest attorneys around, and playing games with him was like teasing a lion with a steak. If you weren't careful you could become the meal.

He knew that whether he chose to speak frankly or tried to hide the truth behind a subtle threat, Nick Wilcox would hear the message loud and clear. But his opinion of the messenger would be the most affected, Dale thought, remembering a tidbit of gossip he'd heard years ago about Nick's high opinion of one of his law professors who always spoke bluntly to his students.

"I think we both know that this offer would not even be on the table if Alpha Development did not believe this act of compassion would be reciprocated."

Now it was Nick's turn to pause. He appreciated the other man's frank speech, although he was perfectly prepared to meet a lie with a lie and play the game as long as necessary. He preferred the truth; it kept things simple.

"Yes, I'm sure it wouldn't be."

Dale Sanders sighed heavily, knowing a stalemate when he heard it. "Will you at least make the offer to your client?"

"Of course. But I need to warn you, Mr. Sanders, my client is prepared to take this all the way to trial."

"If you're half as good as they say, Mr. Wilcox, I don't believe it will come to that."

Rhonda Forester's frailty was a sham. Her once robust full-figured form was now reduced to a shell of its former self, but the lifelong nickname of Big Mama had stuck. Even slumped, her unusual height was still evident, but her once sturdy frame was now brittle and weak, the result of a century of living. At first glance, anyone could still see traces of a startling beauty; her walk and movements still belied a natural grace and elegance. But that's all anyone would've seen at first glance, a remnant of what once was.

On closer observation, with one look into her light brown eyes, they would've known their first impression to be a falsehood. They would've seen a sharpness of mind, and high intelligence that had nothing to do with timidity and meekness. They would've seen an avid curiosity that bordered on mischief. They would've seen the very lively, very exuberant woman that resided inside the husk. And at the ripe age of almost one hundred she could still sit on a horse as well as a woman one-quarter her age.

She sat in her favorite rocker on her front porch, her small, battered suitcase sitting at her side, and watched the approaching riders. She'd been expecting her grand-daughter, but not the man who rode at her side.

Vicki waved in greeting as she pulled to a halt at the end of the gravel walkway. She dismounted and headed to the porch, completely forgetting that she was not alone. Her only thought was for the woman on the porch; the image was synonymous with happy childhood memories. Careful not to hurt her, she embraced her grandmother in a tight hug.

"Oh, I've missed you." Vicki smiled and kissed her silky cheek.

"I thought you forgot all about me, since I never hear from you. I may live in the hills, but I do have a tele-phone, you know," Big Mama teased.

Feeling properly chastised, Vicki bowed her head. "I know. I've been busy with work." She noticed movement in her peripheral vision, reminding her that Nick was with her. "Big Mama, I don't know if you remember—"

"I remember him." Big Mama's brown eyes ran over Nick in quick assessment. "That Wilcox boy you were always running off with."

Vicki looked away to hide her blush. "Uh, yes, that's him."

Something instinctive told Nick not to get within arm's reach of her; he simply nodded his head from his position at the bottom of the stairs. "Good to see, you

Big Mama," he tried his most winning Colgate smile on her. The twist of her mouth told him she was not impressed.

"Looks like you've moved up in the world." Her tone could not be mistaken as anything but sarcastic.

Nick knew what he looked like in worn jeans, an old FU jersey, and well-seasoned riding boots. When Aunt Tilde beckoned him home from Little Rock, he'd packed in a hurry, excluding all his typical casual wear. That morning his options had been some of his old college clothes packed away in Aunt Tilde's attic, one of his tailor-made suits, or a pair of his expensive designer jeans and a silk shirt. The trail to the top of the mountain consisted of riding over rocky terrain, through a forest heavily strewn with large low-hanging trees, and across fields of tall bushlike grass. Needless to say his choice in attire was obvious.

To someone who had not seen him in ten years, he looked like some kind of college campus hobo. The last time this woman had seen him, he'd been a young man struggling to pay his way through college with part-time jobs and government grants. Dressed as he was, he still looked like that young man. He *did not* look like he'd moved up in the world, and they all knew it.

Nick sighed. He knew the old woman didn't like him, never had, although he never understood why. But the two-hour ride alongside Vicki to get here was worth whatever caustic remarks she could dish out. He only regretted that he and Vicki would not be returning alone.

He noticed her bag. "Looks like you're ready to go." He tried again with one of his winning smiles.

"You're a sharp one, aren't you?" she muttered, struggled to her feet, and smoothed out her housedress.

Nick felt his jaw tighten. He'd been taught to respect

his elders, but this particular *elder* was beginning to try his patience. And they'd just arrived; they still had a two-hour ride back down the mountain. He took the suitcase Vicki handed to him, and went to strap it onto his saddle with the bungy cord they'd brought along.

They took an hour to eat the small lunch of potted-meat sandwiches, chips, and milk Big Mama had prepared for Vicki—a lunch which she begrudgingly extended to include Nick. Afterward, the trio worked together to clean up the kitchen and close up the little shack. It wasn't long before they were set to leave.

Big Mama allowed Nick to help her up into the saddle in front of Vicki. Nick and his stallion, Wicked Ways, were larger and sturdier than Vicki and Silent Thunder. Nick considered offering to carry Big Mama in front of him, knowing he could give her more stability, but he was certain she would've refused, and, knowing her, none to politely. He said nothing, just saddled up and led the way out of the yard at a trot.

Vicki followed behind horse and rider, and even at their leisurely pace, the small group crossed the open prairie quickly. With the reins held loosely in his hands, Nick guided the rust-colored stallion in the direction of the path leading down the mountain.

The horse responded to the subtle body gestures of the man who was more than comfortable atop such a great beast. Concentrating on their every step, both were fully aware of all the dangers, such as unseen pot ditches and startled rattlers, hiding in the high grass.

Vicki felt her heart pounding in her chest, watching Nick's broad shoulders and shifting hips. He rode well; he always had, despite his obsession with his career and obvious preference for the more cosmopolitan setting of cities like Little Rock and Chicago. He set an easy pace for which Vicki was grateful. She was in absolutely no hurry to return to the ensuing chaos of her mother's decision to sell the farm.

When Maude had announced it over breakfast that morning, Carl Junior went ballistic, and Rhonda had dropped her head into her hands and began to wail like a dying calf. Vicki wondered where all this emotion was when her mother was struggling to run the farm on her own, or even when she'd sought their opinions on what to do about the offer. Vicki and her mother had met each other's eyes over the table of mourners, and both simply shook their heads in exasperation.

Unfortunately, Maude realized her mistake in over indulging her two youngest children far too late to change it, but their tears no longer affected her. She'd made her decision, and she planned to stand by it.

But now that resoluteness had become Vicki's undoing. Over the years, both her siblings had come to the conclusion that Vicki was always to be their plan B. When Rhonda's car broke down and her credit was too bad to buy a new one, she called Vicki to co-sign. When Carl's latest ex-girlfriend broke up with him by moving out and taking every stitch of furniture he owned while he was at work, he called Vicki for a loan to refurnish. And now that their mother was planning to sell their childhood home, they both felt it was up to Vicki to talk her out of it.

Vicki had spent most of her early morning trying to convince them she had no say in the matter. Their mother had decided, and that was all their was to it. When they continued to persist, refusing to accept her answer, she'd thrown up her hands and walked out. She knew the moment she walked back through the door it would all begin again.

"Hey there!"

Vicki's head spun around at the faint call. She looked out across the meadow at the only farm in the area, and spotted the older man standing on his tractor waving his hands frantically over his head. Vicki pulled Silent Thunder up alongside Nick, who'd already brought Wicked Ways to a halt.

Realizing he'd gotten their attention, Hank Durant climbed back into the seat of the tractor and drove across the field toward them. Neither of the horses were startled, both having been raised around farm equipment.

"Hey there." Hank Durant waved again, as he got closer. "I thought my eyes were playing tricks on me." His brown weather-beaten face was evidence of the amount of time he spent in the sun. His callused hands were evidence of his life as a farmer. "Nicky Wilcox! As I live and breathe." His brown eyes beamed with surprise. "And little Vicki Proctor!" He wasn't as surprised to see the third member of their group; being neighbors they saw each other often. "Howdy, Big Mama. Headed down to Maude's for your birthday party?"

Big Mama smiled. "Hey there, Hank. You're coming to the party, aren't you?"

Nick noticed the exchange with a bit of annoyance. Where was her "You're a sharp one, aren't you," when Hank Durant stated the obvious?

"Oh, I'll be there." Hank smiled again. "Although I'm not inclined to leave my land unattended with these land developers snooping around."

That comment gained both Nick and Vicki's full attention.

"The developers have come this far up the mountain?" Nick asked.

"Oh yeah." Hank nodded his head feverently. "They

seem to be after every parcel of land around these parts." He scratched behind his ear. "Though can't say what they would plan to do with it. Most of this land's not good for anything but farming. Too unlevel."

"Have you decided if you're selling or not?" Vicki asked.

Hank's easy smile disappeared. "Ain't no decision to make. I can't sell this land. It was bought with the blood and sweat of my great-granddaddy. Can't put a price on that."

Seeing the confusion on her granddaughter's face, Big Mama leaned away to get a better look at her. "Don't you remember the story, Vicki?"

Vicki hunched her shoulders in shame, knowing instinctively that the story was important and she *should* remember, but she did not. "Afraid not," she confessed. She was even more embarrassed when Nick spoke up. Apparently he did remember the story.

"In 1889, a group of freed slaves came out here from Tennessee. Using their small savings and what they could scrape together, they bought the land from a railroad company that discovered they could not build through such rocky terrain. They divided the land among them and began farming it, in the process creating a flourishing community of businesses and farms."

"That was until the local whites found out who it was that bought this land from the railroad company." Hank Durant continued where Nick left off. "They come through burning down almost every building in town in 1894. But the farmers rebuilt, fortifying the buildings with brick and stone. The white settlers came back again, and burned the town in 1903. But that was the last time, because the farmers had scraped together enough money to hire a handful of gunslingers to deal with the problem."

Hank Durant shook his head in memory of what he'd been told.

Vicki waited for someone to continue. When no one did, she asked, "What happened?"

Nick's deep voice was heavy with some unidentifiable emotion. "It was a bloodbath, but in the end . . . most of the farms and businesses were still standing."

Vicki felt her breath catch in her throat, as a shocking thought hit her. "Big Mama, that was the year you were born."

"We've held on to this land for over a hundred years, Vicki." Big Mama cast her eyes out across the open fields. "We wouldn't give it up then, and we won't give it up now."

Vicki felt torn, hearing the history behind this land, and knowing her own mother's intentions to sell her portion. She wondered if she should say something about her mother's decision to Big Mama before they reached the bottom of the mountain.

Nick looked skyward. "Vicki, it's getting late. We should be going."

She nodded in agreement. "It was good seeing you again, Hank." Vicki smiled.

"You too. And you too, Nick." Hank Durant smiled again. "Have you kids jumped the broom, yet?"

Vicki's coffee-brown complexion turned beet red. "Uh, no—no, we haven't"

Nick smiled. "Not yet, Hank, but you will be invited to the wedding."

Hank nodded his good-bye to Big Mama before turning his tractor around. He headed back across the field, completely unaware of the uncomfortable situation he'd left behind. Everyone in the area knew of the childhood friends turned sweethearts; in such a tight-knit community it was hard to keep something like that secret. Hank, along with many others always thought the couple would eventually get married; it was something that had always been assumed. And apparently, it was something that still was.

Before long the pair of horses came to a pass that made it impossible to continue on side by side, forcing Vicki to fall back, but she was still able to keep Nick and Wicked Ways well in sight. Big Mama broke their companionable silence by speaking her thought.

"I wonder what that reporter is going to write about me in his paper." She sounded like a woman half her age, and her eyes twinkled with anticipation. "Never been written about in the newspaper before."

Vicki smiled at her obvious enthusiasm. "Well, I'm sure whatever he writes will be nothing but praise. You have every right to feel proud, Big Mama. Turning one hundred is no small thing, you know. "

"I know." Big Mama frowned. "But I wish you all would stop trying to give me credit for something God did."

"Yes, ma'am." Vicki bit her lip to keep from chuckling. *Leave it to Big Mama,* Vicki thought. *Try to give her a compliment, and she takes it as an insult. No wonder Nick thinks she doesn't like him.* The thought brought him to the forefront of her mind. Her head came up in time to see him disappear around a bend several feet ahead.

Having grown up here, both Vicki and Nick knew the mountain like the back of their hands, as did their horses. Even if night fell before they reached the bottom, there was no way they could get lost.

As if reading her thoughts, Big Mama spoke. "Heard that Wilcox boy moved to Chicago."

Vicki wasn't sure if that was a statement or a question; either way she had no intention of answering. She was certain as to where her secluded grandmother would've gleaned that information: her matchmaking daughter.

"Who told you that, Mama?"

Big Mama shrugged. "People talk, in town, church. A body can't help but hear things."

Nice try, Vicki thought. She was still certain the information had come from her mother. No one was more pleased than Maude with Nick's attempts to resurrect their long-dead love affair. Vicki decided to let the subject drop. Maybe if she were lucky, Big Mama would, too. She was not lucky.

"Did you know he was planning to move there?"

"Nope." Vicki shifted in her saddle, the sun was beginning to dip below the horizon. "Look, here comes the sunset." Vicki tried to distract her grandmother's attention away from the present topic, but knew it would probably be easier to wrestle a bone away from a hungry dog.

"Wonder why Chicago of all cities?" Big Mama asked the question, not expecting an honest answer, but she got one anyway in her granddaughter's guilty body language.

"Don't know." Vicki contrived to sound disinterested.

Vicki listened attentively for her grandmother to continue her inquisition, but all she received was a faint "humph" sound after a while. Vicki knew that wordless expression was probably more potent that any words she could've said.

"Looks like we're going to have fair weather for your party." Vicki continued her vain attempts at redirection.

After several awkward moments, Big Mama finally said, "Looks like the cold weather's finally past. But all this rain lately ain't good for my aches." Big Mama looked out across the hazy salmon-colored sky. "In fact, looks like rain's coming now. Be here before nightfall."

Vicki looked up and didn't see a raincloud in the

sky, but she didn't doubt Big Mama for a minute. Her grandmother was always right about those kinds of things. A stillness settled over the air, almost in answer to her prediction.

Vicki listened to the evening sounds of birds chirping, and fallen leaves rustling as a nearby squirrel skittered across a pile and up to its treetop home. Both women watched in silent camaraderie, enjoying a late spring evening as the sun began its descent.

"Don't like it at all," Big Mama muttered.

Vicki frowned in confusion. *Are we still talking about the weather?* Intuitively, she knew they weren't, and could only pray that the statement was in reference to something other than the Wilcox boy and his move to Chicago.

"What's that?" Vicki asked.

"This whole thing of Maude selling the farm. My Rufus is probably flipping over in his grave at the thought of any part of this land being sold."

Vicki sighed in relief. She had still been debating whether or not to mention her mother's decision to her grandmother, but apparently Big Mama already knew.

"With no one to help manage the business, it's been hard on her all these years since daddy died." Vicki offered her own reasoning. "Trying to pay the hands and keep the quality up to standard is almost impossible with the type of steep competition in these parts. I don't like it anymore than anyone else, but I understand it." She paused to stifle a yawn. "Mama's doing what she feels is best, Big Mama. It's her decision. And there's really nothing any of us can say about it."

Big Mama shook her head. "Still don't like it," she muttered, but her tone was much more resigned. "Well, least she ain't signed no papers yet, there's still time to change her mind."

Good luck, Vicki thought, but held her tongue. She realized the next bend in the road would be the last before they reached the bottom. They were almost home. She was beginning to believe foolishly that her grandmother would let her get away this one time without intruding on her personal life.

"Found you a man yet?"

Vicki frowned at the back of her grandmother's head. Big Mama knew about Preston, but she never took the relationship seriously. Vicki wondered briefly if in her infinite wisdom, her grandmother had seen the handwriting on the wall.

"I broke up with Preston," she offered by way of an excuse. It didn't work.

"Not that pansy, I mean a real man. One who *likes* women."

"Wish someone would've told me," Vicki muttered.

Ignoring the remark, Big Mama stayed on point. "Well?"

Vicki gave the same answer she'd given to the same question for the past two years. "No, ma'am, I haven't found a man yet."

"Humph." Big Mama glanced at her granddaughter over her shoulder. "Well, you'd better find you one." She swung back around in her awkward seat. "Before that Wilcox boy gets his hooks into you."

Vicki shook her head. Would Big Mama ever acknowledge Nick by his given name? For some unknown reason, he'd been the Wilcox boy for almost twenty-five years. Maybe one day she'd have the nerve to ask her grandmother what it was about Nick that offended her.

"Nick and I are friends." *For now,* Vicki thought. It was best not to mention that.

Big Mama swung around again, and studied Vicki like a two-headed beast. "Child, have you lost your mind?"

Vicki's eyes widened at the unfounded accusation. What had she said wrong?

"That boy ain't no more interested in your friendship than your Aunt Freda is heaven bound. And you'd best not fool yourself into believing that." She wagged an index finger. "Else you'll find yourself flat on your back." She huffed loudly. "With his *friendship* rutting away at you."

"Big Mama!"

"I speak the truth, child, and you best not forget it."

Vicki simply closed her gaping mouth. She had no answer for that, and was sure her grandmother didn't expect one. As far as the older woman was concerned, what she'd said was nothing more than sound advice. But Vicki knew Big Mama had simply given voice to an image Vicki had been toying with all morning. Truthfully, the image had been with her since the night before at the lake. Her mind was spinning with vivid memories of loving Nick. Images that had been coming to her more often than not, lately.

Nick had made no secret about what he wanted, and considering what had almost happened in the motel and again at the lake, Vicki was beginning to wonder if it was different from what she wanted. She knew for certain that she and Nick would never again be the couple they once were: two people who complemented and completed each other. But there was nothing to say they couldn't provide each other with a little physical comfort, was there?

Vicki gave rein to Silent Thunder, who, sensing home, had picked up the pace of her slow canter. They rounded the last bend and the Proctor farm came into view, along with Nick who was now galloping out across the open field.

Wicked Ways's long legs were stretched out, and his red mane was blowing in the wind. Vicki sighed with desire at the image. Nick and his Wicked Ways . . . how well they went together.

Vicki shook her head and smiled, before leaning forward to peck her grandmother on the cheek. *Rutting friendship,* she thought. *Leave it to Big Mama.*

CHAPTER THIRTEEN

Nick picked up the second heavy wooden box and lugged it across the room, while his aunt stood with her hands on her hips directing his efforts.

"That's it, sugar. Put it right over there." Tilde smiled and turned away, already moving on to the next dust-covered box.

"What do you have in there, anyway?" Nick asked, settling the large crate in place and using the back of his forearm to wipe away the sweat forming on his smooth head.

When his aunt asked him to help her with a small project in the attic, he had no idea it would turn into this all-day all-out moving effort.

"Oh, just some old dishes and such," she called over her shoulder.

Her head was already buried in the next large crate.

The sounds of Marvin Gaye's "What's Going On" drifted in through the only window in the confined space. While his aunt was busy scrounging around in the bottom of the crate, Nick leaned his long body out the window to get some air. He rested his forearms on the sill, enjoying the cool breeze on his hot skin, and checked out the party across the meadow. From his vantage point, the many guests looked like a horde of colorful ants descending on a picnic.

"It looks like a pretty large turnout for Big Mama's birthday bash," he said.

Tilde froze, her head still buried in the box. "Were you invited?" she asked.

"Yeah," he answered offhandedly. A gust of wind breezed over his bald head and felt like heaven.

Matilda Howell and Maude Forester-Proctor had grown up together, and, as a result, so had their children. Tilde had been one of the first names on the invitation list for this celebration, and her absence would be noticed. But she'd much rather field questions about her absence from the party than try to explain the brand new worry lines around her eyes, or the uncontrollable nervous shaking of her hands.

She would've been horrified to think that any of the neighbors and friends she'd known all her life were aware of her legal troubles. She chose instead to stay away until she felt she had her fears more in hand.

"Don't let me keep you, Nick. Go on to the party." Tilde tried to hide the sadness in her voice, but Nick heard it loud and clear.

This woman was the closest thing he had to a mother, and the bond was just as strong. He knew this whole attic project was to keep her mind off the recent events. He also knew his presence provided some small measure of comfort. To leave her alone with just her thoughts and worries for company was far too cruel to imagine.

"No, I'm not going." He chuckled. "I've always gotten the distinct impression that Big Mama doesn't particularly care for me."

The box she was exploring muffled Tilde's laughter. "She thinks you're a whoremonger."

Nick swung around. "What?"

Tilde stood straight, still trembling with laughter. "She told me herself, back when you and Vicki first took up together. She said she was sorry to see Vicki settle for a whoremonger." She hunched her shoulders. "Sorry Nick, but those were her words, not mine."

"I hope you defended me," he said, with nothing less than pure indignation.

Tilde leaned back against the box, still smiling. "No offense, Nick, but in those days that description of you wasn't that far off the mark."

"Aunt Tilde." Nick felt himself growing heated with embarrassment. "How can you say that?" He asked the question, knowing full well the answer.

Somewhere between high school and college, Nick, the roly-poly bookworm and favorite target of the school bully, had sprouted into Nick, the well-built handsome playboy and star running back. Unfortunately, his ego had not been prepared for the change. Sometimes he wondered if that was why his heart would settle for nothing less than Vicki now. She was the one woman who'd known and loved both Nicks.

"Okay, I may have done a little to deserve it, but still . . ." He turned back to the window and continued to spy on the party below. He wondered briefly how Vicki had put up with him during that time. Even to his tainted memory, his exploits seemed like the actions of another man. Actions that the man he was now simply could not justify or understand.

He'd had everything: scholastic success, which was something he'd always valued, and popularity, which was something he'd always craved. And Vicki's love, which

was something he'd always taken for granted. Unfortunately, somewhere along the line, popularity came to be
all that mattered.

"Do you want all those old files, or should I toss them
out?" Tilde asked, once again buried waist-deep in a
large crate. Her arm was extended as she pointed to the
corner, where boxes and boxes of Nick's old case files
were stacked, forgotten and neglected with the passage
of time.

Nick strolled over and began sorting through them.
Each box contained rows of manila folders, each stuffed
with everything from witness reports to evidentiary find-
ings. He came across boxes labeled "*State of Arkansas v.
Andy Pallister*". He could still hear Vicki's resounding con-
demnation that first day of the Morrison trial. "*Innocent,
huh? Would that be the Andy Pallister kind of innocent?*"

The *State of Arkansas v. Andy Pallister* had been the case
that put Nick Wilcox on the map. It had also been the
wedge that tore Vicki from his side. Vicki, who'd always
stood by him, had announced that she could not stand
by and let him set a murderer free. Although he was unaware of what he was doing at the time; still, through his
own stubborn ignorance, that was what he'd done.

Nick had graduated from Yale summa cum laude, and
as such was given his choice of offers from some of the
most well-respected law firms in the country. He'd
known on some level that his place was with Vicki. He
decided to take a junior associate position with a prestigious firm in downtown Little Rock, knowing Vicki had
began working in the Little Rock prosecutor's office that
previous summer.

They had quickly reunited, falling back into their
unique rhythm of friends and lovers as if they'd never
been apart.

He frowned, remembering that reunion had been a lot easier than this last one. Vicki was finishing up her five-year internship in the prosecutor's office, when the case of *Arkansas v. Pallister* had been unceremoniously dropped in her lap. For her, the task of prosecuting the politician accused of hiring a hitman to murder his mistress was nothing more than a matter of doing the job. Nick remembered her coming home to their small apartment many nights and telling him about how the whole case gave her a strange, uneasy feeling, almost from the moment she began reviewing the crime scene evidence.

She had become sick while looking over the crime scene photos, and was soon convinced that what she was studying was the work of a deranged mind bent on revenge. The barbaric manner in which Jan Holsten had been butchered showed none of the cold-blooded aloofness typical of a professional assassin, or the perfunctory behavior of a housebreaker, which was the scenario offered by the defense.

Vicki became convinced that Andy Pallister was not only guilty of planning his mistress's untimely death, she was certain he'd done the deed himself, and told Nick as much over breakfast the same morning he'd first read about the case in the newspaper.

Nick had been laboring on at his firm, biding his time and waiting for opportunity to knock. And when it did, he had recognized it immediately for what it was. He'd known almost instinctively that this trial, with its high profile defendant and nationwide media coverage, had the potential to launch his career into the big leagues in a way few things could. This case had *star-maker* written all over it.

When he learned that his firm was to represent Andy Pallister, he'd chalked it up to divine intervention and began to campaign for a seat on the defense team with a zealousness that would've shamed Johnnie Cochran. He won that seat, and easily moved into the position of lead counsel.

Early on in the trial, Vicki had come to him with what she described at the time as a gut feeling. Something she felt was stronger than physical evidence, something she knew could touch their lives. Nick, of course, in all his customary arrogance had blown off her real fears as absurd paranoia.

He'd tried to convince her that her fear lay in the fact that they were squaring off against each other in court for the first time, and that having opposing sides of the same occupation, they were bound to face this sort of a dilemma at one time or another.

She'd fought him tooth and nail, begged and pleaded with him to drop the case, since he had a choice in the matter and she did not. But Nick could taste the success that would come with this sort of public victory, and the lure was simply too powerful. In the end he'd won, what he now knew to be the most empty and shallow victory of his life.

Brought back to the present by his aunt's repeated request, he answered, "No, don't throw them away. I'll take them back to Chicago with me."

"Suit yourself." Tilde was now rummaging through stacks of old catalogs and magazines. She paused for a moment, unable to hide her bone-deep apprehension any longer. "Nick?"

"Yes?" he answered through clenched teeth, while bending to pick up one of the heavy boxes.

"Am I going to go jail?"

Nick turned toward his aunt and could clearly see the terror she'd tried valiantly to hide. It was all there. For one brief, fleeting moment, every ounce of her unspoken fear was written on her face.

Putting the box back down on the floor, he walked over to his aunt. The closer he came, the more she was forced to tilt her head to keep their eye contact, until finally he stood before her. He wrapped his long arms around her and pulled her close, resting his chin on the top of her head.

"No, Auntie, you are *not* going to jail." He sighed. "Not as long as I have breath in me."

"Carl, baby, be a dear and bring Big Mama a can of be—" Settled comfortably in her favorite lounger, she cast a look over her shoulder for her youngest daughter. "Beer," she whispered to her grandson, once she was sure the coast was clear.

Carl Junior smiled. "Big Mama, you know you shouldn't be drinking beer at your age." He patted her wrinkled hand lovingly, and shook his head.

Her deceptively humble expression turned sour with disappointment. "Boy, you as bad as your mama."

"We love you and want to keep you with us a while longer, Big Mama. That's all." Her granddaughter and namesake passed within a few feet of the pair and caught the drift of the conversation.

"Don't you go trying to lecture me too, Rhonda Jean," Big Mama called over her shoulder. "I remember a time you both would've heeded me without pause."

The back screen door swung open, and Vicki, carrying a large aluminum pan, braced her back against it, while Maude came through carrying another large pan.

The two women moved through the throng of laughing and dancing people. They skirted around the small stand where the blues band was playing toward the long banquet tables near the two large barrel-style grills. Vicki maneuvered her way through the crowd of family and friends, passing a smile here and a word of welcome there, amazed to spot faces she hadn't seen since she was a child.

On the edge of the crowd a white man was hunkered down in an awkward squatting position. His 35-mm camera was slung carelessly around his neck, lens pressed firmly to his face, while his flash bulb lit with quick succession in his effort to capture every memorable moment.

Maude, having much on her mind, inadvertently ignored most of the guests, but for a taste of Maude's famous barbecue, the crowd was willing to accept her rude behavior. Anyone who'd every tasted Maude's barbecue knew by the smoke oozing from the duel grills, and the inviting aroma emitting from it, that it would be well worth the wait.

"There's my Vicki," Big Mama said, holding her arms open to her eldest grandchild. "You still love me, don't you, baby?"

Vicki went into the arms eagerly, and squeezed her tightly. "You know I love you with all my heart." She leaned back to look into her grandmother's triumphant face. "But I will not give you a beer." She watched the look of victory fade.

"Maude," Big Mama huffed. "What have you done to turn Vicki against me?"

"Nothing, Mama." Maude came up to join the group, wiping her sauce-stained hands on her apron. "I didn't have to do anything. You forgot who pays your medical bills, didn't you?"

Big Mama huffed once more to hide her embarrassment. She had truly forgotten that Vicki paid for her health coverage and prescriptions, which meant all her medical correspondence went to Vicki's Chicago address. In fact, all her bills went to that address, since her granddaughter had been handling her financial affairs for the past several years. She smiled to herself, thinking how nice it was having a lawyer for a granddaughter.

Loud, raunchy laughter coming from the other side of the large yard told everyone cousin Freda had arrived. The younger Rhonda edged off from the group and disappeared into the house. Carl ducked around the tables and disappeared into the large group. Leaving only Vicki, who stood staring at her mother in horror.

"You invited her?"

"Now, Vicki." Maude tried to summon her most soothing motherly voice. But it did little good. Her eldest daughter's eyes had already turned to copper fire.

Vicki looked down at her grandmother in bewilderment. Everyone knew there was no love lost between Big Mama and her oldest daughter, Freda.

As if reading her thoughts, Big Mama held up her hands. "Don't blame me, I didn't invite the heffa."

Freda Forester was a one-woman wrecking crew, boisterous and bawdy to the extreme. And, as sure as the sun rose in the east, wherever she went, trouble would follow. Vicki had planned for this party to be a nice little *dignified* family gathering to celebrate a century of living. But Freda's presence almost assuredly promised the opposite.

"Maude!" The high pitch screeching reached across the vast field. "Maude, where are you?" Maude sighed in frustration; she'd sent Freda an invitation because Tyrell, her nephew, said his mother would be out of town for the next three weeks. In an act of diplomacy, Maude had sent the invitation, expecting Freda to find it upon her return.

"I didn't actually expect her to come." Maude tried in vain to defend her actions to her mother and daughter.

The crowd parted to reveal a stout woman covered in a neon yellow jumpsuit. Her bright burnt-orange hair and gaudy jewelry were the perfect accents to the outfit. She stopped occasionally to exchange hugs and kisses with those members of the family who didn't know her well enough to despise her, and a few who did but didn't have the guts to say it.

Stepping carefully across the turf in her three-inch neon-yellow heels, she reached the small group. Freda noted the scowls on the faces of her mother and niece; her sister was the only one who pretended to be happy to see her.

"My. My. My." She reared back with her chubby hands fisted at her midsection. Being perfectly round, she didn't really have a waist to speak of, Vicki thought, noticing the gesture.

With a scowl and the rolling of her eyes in Vicki's direction, she turned to her younger sister. "Maude, you done gone all out, girl."

Freda knew Vicki was the one who planned the party, but hell would freeze over before she'd give her any credit for it. Her eyes cut to the guest of honor, resting comfortably in her lounger and looking every bit the queen of the Nile.

"Happy birthday, Mama." Freda nodded curtly, and handed over the small, colorfully decorated box cradled in the crook of her right arm.

Big Mama cocked an eyebrow at the gift before finally accepting it. "Thank you, Freda," she muttered begrudgingly.

Freda moved to stand between her sister and niece in a possessive way. Freda had always believed that Vicki and Big Mama were cut from the same cloth, and both pieces distrusted her instinctively. Of all the family, only Maude had showed her kindness with any consistency. She always believed it was because Maude was the baby of the family, and far too young to remember some of Freda's more colorful exploits. To Maude, she'd simply been Big Sister.

Knowing about the party, but also knowing she wouldn't be invited, Freda had gone to Arizona to visit with some old friends. Unfortunately, she managed to wear out her welcome almost a week ahead of schedule. Arriving back home, she'd found the invitation to the centennial bash, and in truth, Freda was as dumbfounded as everyone else as to why Maude had decided to invite her. She knew how much the family dreaded her presence, and that unified disdain had almost kept her away. Almost.

She'd finally decided she couldn't resist the opportunity to stir up some trouble, especially in light of her newest acquaintance.

The thought brought her attention back to the man, who was still trying to plow his way through the barrage of dancing bodies and laughing people. Finally, he emerged looking flustered and out of place in his turquoise-blue polo shirt, khaki Dockers, and white skin. He was as out of place as a fish on land in the sea of brown faces, and the clearly written disdain on his face wasn't helping matters one bit.

Maude was the first to speak to the stranger. "What are you doing here, Mr. Sanders?" she asked, recognizing the attorney who'd paid a visit to her last month on behalf of the land development company. But regardless of her decision to do business with him, she was not at all comfortable with having the stranger intrude on a family gathering.

"Mrs. Proctor, how nice to see you again." He smiled. Something about the youngest woman standing in the small circle of females was ringing a bell in his head, but he couldn't place her.

He turned to Big Mama and offered a small, neatly wrapped package. "Mrs. Forester, allow me to congratulate you on a century of living on behalf of Alpha Development. May you have many more birthdays to come."

Big Mama accepted the gift with hesitation. Both Maude's confused expression and Vicki's tense body language were telling her the man was not invited, nor was he welcomed, and the fact that he'd arrived with Freda was an automatic point against him.

"Maude, I hope you don't mind my bringing an unannounced guest." Freda tried to sound apologetic, but her underlying excitement was slipping through. "Mr. Sanders and I were right in the middle of discussions when I noticed the time. Seeing he's a business acquaintance of us both, I saw no harm in bringing him."

"Oh?" Maude asked, fighting a queasy feeling that was settling in the bottom of her stomach. The pieces were beginning to add up in her head, and she was not happy with the total.

Dale Sanders felt a shiver of dread run down his spine as he stood silently listening to the bold-faced lie. The woman had called him at his office and *specifically* invited him. In fact, she even drove the two hours to Little Rock to pick him up, all the while implying that Maude had extended the invitation. Listening to her, and sensing the tension in the small group, he was now wondering what kind of game was being played, and more importantly, what his part was in it.

Maude considered the worst possibility, and decided even Freda couldn't be that low-down. *Could she?* Glancing at Vicki and Big Mama, who both stood as still as statues, she thought they seemed to be bracing themselves for whatever would come out of Freda's mouth next. And what did come out shocked everyone there.

"Me and Mr. Sanders were discussing the cottage land." Freda never took her eyes off her mother while she spoke.

"Why would you be discussing *my* cottage?" Big Mama's dark eyes were shooting daggers at Freda and Dale Sanders in turn.

"He's made me a considerable offer for my half of the land," Freda said, with savage satisfaction.

Maude gasped; Vicki simply shook her head. They both knew how important that land was to their family, their heritage. They both knew how important that piece of land was to Big Mama.

Rhonda Forester sat looking up at her daughter in stone silence for several seconds, and the full impact of the conversation sank into her brain. Her daughter had been conniving almost from the moment she'd come into the world. She'd hurt almost everyone who'd been close to her in one way or another. Her talent for wreaking havoc was second only to her twisted hatred of those who shared her blood. But this time she had gone to far.

Big Mama lifted her frail form up out of the lounge chair. The wrath of fury that burned in her dark brown eyes was enough to have given Lucifer the shivers.

As if in response to the guest of honor's dark mood, the music stopped and most everyone turned to see what had tainted the cheerful countenance of the family matriarch.

With one hand planted firmly on her hip and the

other stretched out to her daughter, she spoke in a voice too calm for the words. "Listen to me carefully, Freda Mae, if you sell one acre of that land I will cut out your black heart."

Fully expecting the attack, Freda had come equipped to fight. "Papa left half of that land to me. I know you think it's all yours, but it's not."

"I'll say it once again, since you didn't seem to hear me—"

"Oh, I heard you all right." Freda was fuming by now. "And I'll do whatever I damn well please with my share of it."

"Freda, you're trying my patience," Big Mama said, between clenched teeth. Her index finger wagged on the wind.

"You can hold on to your portion and treat it like some kind of shrine if you want, Mama, but I plan to sell mine and enjoy the money while I still can."

Freda turned to storm away. Remembering the man she'd brought and used as nothing more than a pawn, she said, "Mr. Sanders, are you coming?"

Dale Sanders stood rooted to the spot. The passionate and cruel words spoken between the two women still hung in the air. He cast a pleading look in Maude's direction, trying to apologize with his eyes, but she refused to look at him. He looked toward the younger woman, the one who looked familiar, and realized he'd never even been introduced to her. She fairly glared at him.

Finally, he looked at the elderly woman standing in the middle of the other two, looking every bit like the enraged family sovereign that she was, his token offering still dangling from her left hand. She'd greeted him with wary hesitation and curiosity; now her brown eyes held anger and a promise of retribution. Despite her small size, her indomitable spirit was evident, and Dale Sanders knew he'd made a formidable enemy this day. Without another word he turned on his heels and followed Freda out.

He'd come believing that such an appearance would strengthen his relationship with Maude Proctor, along with the other farmers in the small community he'd been assigned to solicit for the purchase of their land. It was supposed to be a good faith gesture.

He made a mental note to be careful in his future dealings with Freda Forester. The woman was a proven liar, and whatever game she was playing could jeopardize the entire project.

Vicki sat on the cushioned seat of the large bay kitchen window that looked out over the back field, waiting for the receptionist to connect her with Ellis's office. From where she sat she could see Big Mama hanging sheets on the clothesline, even though Maude had a dryer in the laundry room.

When Vicki questioned her grandmother, she was told, "You can't buy spring freshness in a box, Vicki." Big Mama's answer was in regard to the fabric softener sheets Vicki and her mother routinely used. But, of course, Big Mama thought any woman who didn't make her own bread from scratch was lazy.

Maude had locked herself in her office, trying to get the farm's monthly payroll done by the end of the day.

Vicki wondered briefly which woman she was more like: the homemaker who managed to raise eight children on a farmer's income, or the enterprising businesswoman who struggled every day to keep her family business afloat.

She decided it didn't matter; to be compared to either would be a great compliment.

"Ellis here." The gruff voice reverberated through the receiver.

"Hi, Ellis, it's Vicki."

"Hey, champ, when you coming home?"

"That's why I'm calling. I have a family emergency I need to see to before I leave. I wanted to request an extension on my vacation time."

"Sorry to hear that. Anything I can do?"

"No, it's a financial matter."

"Well, still, if there's anything I can do, let me know. As for the extension, how much longer are you needing?"

Vicki smiled, knowing there weren't a lot of bosses who would've heard the words "financial matter" and still offered help. "If you could give me a few more weeks, I'd appreciate it."

"Consider it done. By the way, thought you would like to know we have another lead on your last case. Seems one of the victims, Benedict Brown, had some enemies no one knew about until recently."

"Oh?"

"Yeah, some pretty powerful enemies, but nothing I want to discuss over the phone. I'll tell you all about it when you get back. I hate to admit it, but it looks like Morrison may be innocent after all."

"Hmm," Vicki wanted to know more, but she knew Ellis was too paranoid to say more over an *unsecure* phone line. "Okay, I'll keep in touch and let you know when to expect me back. Thanks, Ellis."

"No problem, champ. Get back as soon as you can, we can use your insight with this new investigation."

Vicki hung up the phone and went about her day. Try as she may, she couldn't seem to shake the blue funk that covered the beautiful spring afternoon. Damning questions kept replaying in her head, questions that shook the foundation of her confidence.

Had she almost sent an innocent man to prison for life? Could her judgment have been clouded by her desire to defeat Nick? Or, worst of all . . . was Nick simply a better attorney than she was?

CHAPTER FOURTEEN

"Hello?"

"Hey, Angie, it's me." Nick sighed and slumped down in the kitchen chair.

"It's about time you called. I've been going crazy here alone."

"Sorry, I've been busy."

"Is there going to be a trial?"

"I still don't know. The plaintiff is offering to drop the charges, but only if Aunt Tilde considers their offer to buy the farm."

"Nick, she'll never do that."

"I know, but there may still be a way out of this without a trial."

"How?"

"I haven't worked out the details yet, but I'll let you know as soon as I do."

"Nick—you can't—I mean, she can't—"

"I know, Angie."

"You've got to fix this, Nick."

He sighed again. "I know."

After exchanging good-byes with his sister, Nick

returned his attention to his laptop computer. Running through one electronic case file after another, he was trying to find a precedent-setting case in which the defendant acted with violence to defend his or her home.

He'd found a few, but they all used a defense that involved the overtone of mental illness, and even with those few cases the defendant was found guilty at least fifty percent of the time. The ones that were dismissed were usually able to prove the defendant felt some type of immediate threat. Not simply because the plaintiff was being hardheaded and needed to be taught a lesson, which was the explanation his aunt had given to justify her extreme behavior.

Nick considered meeting with the surveyor and his attorney without his aunt present to see if a reasonable agreement could be arranged, but he knew his *client* would never go for it. The ringing phone interrupted his thoughts.

"Hello?"

"Hi, Nick." Vicki fought to control her nerves. His voice always did things to her, but given the nature of this particular call they were affected even more.

Recognizing the voice, Nick smiled into the phone. He'd been caught up in his aunt's defense, and hadn't seen nor spoken to her in the week since they'd escorted Big Mama down the mountain. "Just the person I wanted to talk to."

"Hold that thought, you may not think so after you hear why I'm calling."

"It would take a lot to change that opinion."

"Well . . . hear me out first." She tried to sound lighthearted. It didn't work.

Nick sat up in his chair, now fully attentive. "What's up?"

"I need your help."

"With what?"

"I think there is something fishy going on with this land development business."

"Fishy how?"

"Well, first of all, I want you to know I'm aware of Aunt Tilde's arrest."

Nick shook his head. He should've guessed news like that couldn't stay secret in such a small community. "I would've told you, it's just she—"

"No, no, I understand. I said that to say it's not the only such situation."

"What do you mean?"

"Well, Freda came to Big Mama's birthday party and announced her intention to sell her portion of the cottage land."

"You mean the cottage? As in Big Mama's cottage?"

"Yes, I've also heard that the bank foreclosed on the Williamson farm, and the Bookers had a mysterious fire that burned down their horse stable, killing four of their best breeders. I don't know Nick, I can't believe this rash of disasters is all coincidence."

"Me either."

"I've began my own private investigation, and I consider myself a more than capable attorney, but—"

"You are," Nick interjected.

"Thanks." She brushed off the compliment and continued. "But, I feel like I'm really in over my head with this. I mean, who knows how many other situations there are? I feel like I may have touched the tip of the iceberg. I could use another legal mind if you can spare the time."

Nick stared down at the open files on his computer. He really needed to focus all his attention on Aunt Tilde's defense, but what if this was all tied in somehow?

Of course, the most obvious difference between the

situations Vicki described and his aunt's was that the others were accidental, while his aunt had intentionally taken a shot at an innocent man. But what if the solution they found could help his aunt as well as the other farmers? And what if he stopped pretending that he wouldn't use any and every excuse to spend time with Vicki? *Say yes, and be done with it.*

"Nick?"

"Sorry, I was thinking." He tapped his bottom lip. "How many of the farmers have you talked to?"

"About five. I still need to talk to the Durants, the Crowders . . . I don't know, maybe six or seven. Truthfully, I can't remember all the families hidden up on that mountain."

"You're not alone."

"Will you help me?"

"Do you remember where the old fishing cabin is? On the other side of the lake?"

"Yeah, I think so."

"Meet me there in thirty minutes. We'll use it as our headquarters while we collect the farmers' depositions and gather our information. If there is something other than bad luck at work here, we'll figure it out."

Vicki sighed in relief. "Thanks, Nick, see you soon."

Nick hung up the phone and closed his laptop. He was beginning to feel as if there was something sinister about this whole thing. Why would a land development company go to such extremes to purchase or steal land that was good for nothing but farming?

Trying to build large complexes of any kind on hilly land would never work, for the same reason the railroad could not be built on it—it wasn't level. If Alpha Development did not want the mountain and surrounding

boroughs for the purpose of developing the land . . .
then for what?

Vicki opened her eyes to pitch-blackness. She glanced
toward her bedroom window, but the pink dawn light
was nowhere to be found. The clock on the nightstand
read five thirty-four. She turned over again, trying to
find a more comfortable position; nothing worked. After
several minutes of lying in the fetal position, she realized
sleep was nothing more than a fond memory.

She'd spent most of the night tossing and turning, bits
and pieces of a strange dream littered across her dozing
brain, but nothing solid, and certainly not enough to
fully disclose the dream to her conscious self. All she
could remember was that it had something to do with
Nick and doors, and on the outskirts of her mind she was
aware of a choice that had to be made. But she wasn't
sure if she were the one to make the choice or Nick. She
scratched at her kerchief and stood to stretch. There was
really no point in driving herself crazy trying to remember a dream that probably meant nothing anyway.

She padded to the kitchen to start a pot of coffee, and
noticed there was already a half-empty carafe sitting on
the warmer. She smiled and poured herself a cup before
heading to the front door. As expected, it was open to
the screen. She cracked it and stepped out onto the
front porch. Seeing the woman sitting in the swing was
not surprising. As far back as Vicki could remember, her
grandmother always rose well before sunup.

"Morning, Big Mama," Vicki said, with a hug and kiss.

"Morning, baby." Big Mama returned the affection
with one arm, while the other held the partially filled
cup of coffee off to the side, out of harm's way. She sat

rocking, her long thin legs dangling inches above the floor.

Vicki settled on the top step of the wooden porch and inhaled a deep breath of the pure country air. How she had missed this simple life.

"Days should be getting longer by now," Big Mama said, taking a sip of her coffee and watching Vicki over the rim.

"Hmm," Vicki muttered in agreement, taking a sip from her own mug. "I'm glad the bad weather held off long enough for us to have your party outdoors."

"Me too." Big Mama chuckled. "Maude would've been fit to be tied if she'd had all those people traipsing through her house."

"That she would've," Vicki agreed with a smile. "That she would've."

"By the way, thank you. Everything was really nice."

Vicki smiled to herself at the warmth and appreciation in her grandmother's words. The party preparations had consumed most of her free time for the past few months, not to mention the headaches—no, intense migraines—that had been caused by having to deal closely with her extended family. But somehow hearing those few heartfelt words made it all worthwhile.

"You're welcome, and you deserved every bit of the fanfare."

Big Mama stared into her cup, but Vicki knew she was seeing more than the small portion of coffee remaining. "Not everyone shares your opinion, I'm afraid."

Vicki knew who the everyone in question was. "Freda's crazy. Her opinion doesn't count." She smiled in an attempt to bolster her grandmother's downtrodden spirit.

A smile of gratitude flashed across Big Mama's face. "I

can't help wondering where I went wrong with that child."

"You didn't," Vicki insisted. "Freda is . . . Freda. She's selfish, Big Mama, always has been."

"You know," Big Mama began, her kindly brown eyes taking on a faraway look, "raising eight children on a farmer's income, we didn't always have a lot to give any one of our children. But we tried to be fair, and that's why we gave them each equal parts of the land. We never told them what to do with it. We hoped they'd use it to live on, like Maude and your daddy Carl did. But all we asked of any of them was not to sell that mountaintop, the cottage land."

Vicki felt she had to have an answer to the question that had been plaguing her since the party. "Big Mama, why did you give Freda the cottage? I mean of all your children, why entrust the most precious piece of land to *Freda?*"

Big Mama smiled at Vicki's obvious disdain and confusion. Her granddaughter had an intuition that could rival a wild animal's. She'd known almost from the time she could stand upright that her Aunt Freda was a snake, even if her mother, Maude, couldn't see the truth of her own sister. Almost from infancy, Vicki had done nothing to hide her dislike. She'd cried when the woman tried to hold her, and refused to toddle across the floor on her wobbly baby legs when Freda called.

Upon reaching maturity, Vicki discovered that everything she'd instinctively believed about her aunt was true. She watched, as time and again Freda manipulated and used her sister, just as she did her other six siblings. But Maude was the only one of the seven brothers and sisters who continued to allow the woman to come around her family. Something Vicki never understood . . . until her own sister and brother were born. Now she understood completely. Sometimes you love them, sometimes you hate them, but family is always family.

"When Rufus made his will, the children were all still very young, but Freda was the oldest." Big Mama frowned thoughtfully. "Freda was always a problem child, but we both believed it was something she would grow out of." Taking a final sip of her coffee, she shrugged. "If we would've known then what we know now . . ." Big Mama let her words trail off.

As always, Vicki was in perfect sync with her thoughts. She nodded in understanding. No more needed to be said.

They both heard the sound of hoofbeats before they saw the horse and rider appear over the bluff separating the Howell and Forester lands. As if Nick brought it with him, the shadow of a sunrise appeared directly behind him on the horizon.

Vicki stood to get a better look. "What's Nick doing here so early?" She shielded her eyes as she watched the horse shake his head playfully while he came loping out across the prairie. Completely at ease, neither man nor horse seemed in any great rush. It was still early dawn on what promised to be a lovely spring day, and the pair seemed to be on a leisurely tramp.

"Uh, Vicki," Big Mama called from behind her.

"Yes?" Vicki continued to watch the rider gallop toward them, thinking how much Nick looked like a hero out of an old western movie.

"I'm sure he's probably seen you in less, but it's still not proper to greet guests in your nightclothes."

Vicki looked down at the sheer gown clinging to her in various places. She screeched, turned, and ran back into the house. She spun back around at the entrance, and opened her mouth to speak.

Big Mama put up her hand. "Don't worry, I'm sure he and I can get along for the few minutes it takes you to get dressed."

Vicki wasn't as confident. She dressed hurriedly in a pair of blue jeans and a pullover sweater. Snatching off her headscarf, she brushed through her straight hair and pinned it up with a clip. Not even bothering with shoes and socks, she raced back out to the porch.

Nick sat on the back of Wicked Ways watching the woman on the porch. The woman on the porch was watching him with the same intense scrutiny. Neither said a word. Vicki shook her head. Was this Big Mama's idea of getting along?

Spotting her, Nick's face broke into a smile. "Morning, gorgeous."

"Morning." She fought the urge to glance at Big Mama, knowing that remark would not go unnoticed. "What are you doing here this early?"

Nick's brows crunched in confusion, then he glanced at his watch. "We did agree on six A.M., right?"

"Oh, no." They had agreed to meet at six to climb the mountain and finish up their depositions. There were still three families they needed to interview to confirm their suspicions. After that it would be a matter of putting the information together in the proper format and presenting their case.

"Give me a few more minutes to get ready." She turned to leave and paused, "Would you like a cup of coffee?"

Nick glanced back at Big Mama who was still watching him. He knew Vicki was offering him a way to get away from her disapproving grandmother. He thought about staying right where he was and continuing to exchange glares with the woman.

He needed to let her know that, like it or not, he had

no intention of going anywhere. Vicki was his, and no one, not even a cantankerous old woman, was going to keep him away from her. As if in answer to his silent vow, Big Mama arched one eyebrow in challenge.

"Well, maybe just one cup," Nick said, sliding down from his horse. He followed Vicki back into the house. One day, Nick thought, he was going to have to stand up to that woman and let her know that he was here to stay. But apparently, today was not the day.

By four in the afternoon, the pair was descending back down the mountainside, and what they had discovered in one day put everything they'd *thought* they knew in a tailspin.

In under two weeks, they had interviewed each of the farmers, researched Alpha Development, and reviewed the ownership records at the land office in downtown Little Rock. Both had been convinced almost from the outset that whatever Alpha Development wanted with the land, it was not for the purpose of building modern strip malls or high-rise apartments. Given the uniquely unsuitable geological makeup, neither could speculate as to what use the land could have other than farming. And what few reasons they could discern as possibilities were definitely not worth the extent the mega-corporation had gone to in trying to get their hands on it. But thanks to Ted Crowder, they now had an answer to their most pressing question.

They pulled their horses to a halt on the gravel road in front of the small fishing cabin. It sat by the small lake that had once been a prime spot for bass fishing for previous generations of Howells and Foresters. Over the years the fish population of the lake had dwindled to nothing, leaving the once-thriving fishing pond as nothing more than a swimming hole. Now it was the central command base for team Wilcox-Proctor. Swept out and wiped down, the rickety wood table had been replaced with two rectangular folding tables. The grimy walls were dusted and covered with tack boards and post-it notes.

The ancient bunkbeds were too large to remove; instead, the mattresses were aired and beaten. Equipped with electricity and running water, the only other amenities to be found were a dorm-sized refrigerator, now filled with soda and snacks, and a portable radio on the window ledge, a ledge that was now littered with stacks of paper.

As children, the pair had scoured every inch of the land and spent many days in and around the cabin. It often provided convenient cover when an unexpected storm would crop up, and over the past several days, it had provided another kind of refuge.

Inside the small cabin, Vicki felt they both had been somehow miraculously transported back in time. Back to the time when they thought in sync and shared a passion for injustice.

She'd watched Nick's jaw tense and flex in anger as John Booker, or "Bo" as he was lovingly referred to by friends and family, told them about the fire that had been set in his barn. He showed Nick the gasoline canister he'd found in back, and related the terror his family had experienced trying to rescue four of their best breeders, horses whose stud services fed and clothed the large family. But, more importantly, animals that they'd cared for and loved. And, in the end, they were forced to stand by helplessly and watch them die.

Nick was forced to shake his head in wonderment as Paul Williamson told him how the bank he'd done business with for the past forty years decided to fore-close on his farm because of a payment that was eigh-teen days past due. Paul was an elderly man; he and his wife, Ethel, had both been born and raised on the mountain. They'd raised their own family there. Like many of the small community, it was the only home they had known. The land had been in Paul's family for generations, and fully paid for many years ago. But the couple had refinanced in order to send their two youngest boys to college, hoping as all par-ents do, to give their children the best possible chance in life. And now, as a result, they were about to be set off their land and left with no place to go.

Vicki was more grateful with each passing day for whatever instinct had led her to call Nick. She accepted that both she and Nick knew the law equally well, but Nick had a cunning mind that far surpassed anything in her experiences as a prosecutor. To Vicki, having Nick with her was almost as if she had one of the high-priced, plush office–type corporation lawyers working on their side. Nick thought like them, plotted like them, con-nived like them because he was one of them. But for all their stratagizing and digging about, neither he nor Vicki had been prepared for what they would actually find.

Tossing her jacket across the small stool that sat in the far corner, Vicki flopped down on the bottom bunk. As a girl, she'd spent most of her time on horseback, but her sore body was reminding her that it had been a long time since she was a girl.

"What now?" Vicki asked, rubbing the back of her neck.

After depositing the leather saddlebag containing several manila files and the remnants of lunch, Nick grabbed a soda out of the refrigerator and propped himself against one of the folding tables. "Truthfully, I don't know. This is no longer a *legal* matter, per se. If Alpha succeeds in forcing these people off their land and swoops in to buy it up, there's really nothing we can do. It's all lawful."

"Well, what if we make it publicly known?"

Nick cocked an eyebrow. "Are you kidding me? Do you know what kind of madhouse it would be around here? No, that's exchanging one monster for another."

"Well, we'll have to band together and refuse—"

"Vicki, come on," he interrupted, exasperation heavy in his voice. "Refusing is not going to do any good. Look at what it's gotten us: Bo's barn up in flames, and the Williamsons cast off their land. And God knows what's next. No, refusing is not the answer."

Feeling more helpless than she had in years, Vicki threw up her hands. "Well, what would you suggest?"

Nick rubbed his chin. "I don't know. Not yet, anyway."

Vicki lay back and stretched out. "Well, when you come up with something, please let me know."

Nick watched her stretch, experiencing the same familiar throbbing in his lower region that he always experienced when watching her do . . . anything. It had been almost impossible to conceal the constant state of arousal he'd been in for the past two weeks.

The somewhat romantic seclusion of the cabin had not been lost on him either. Their investigation had forced them to spend a great deal of time together, and for Nick it had seemed like old times.

This was the life he'd been craving since the moment she'd walked out the front door of their small Little Rock apartment eight years ago. The life he'd been actively pursuing for the past three months, since he'd moved to Chicago to renew their acquaintance. A life he was beginning to suspect he would never have again, given her animosity and hesitation. But the past two weeks alone in the isolated cabin had been like a year in heaven.

Her sharp barbs had become gentle persuasions; her snarls had turned to smiles, and she touched him. Nothing intentionally sexual, even though the result had been nothing less than stimulating. But little touches: a hand on his shoulder, a playful jab to his ribs, a caress on his cheek. Like a great glacier that had somehow drifted into the path of sunlight, she was melting.

She'd thrown her heart behind this investigation. He watched as she held Ethel Williamson in her arms and cried with the woman as if absorbing her pain. Her eyes had burned with fury at the destruction left in the wake of the intentional fire that burned down the Booker's barn. There were other incidents, but none on as large a scale and with such encompassing devastation. They'd known the day they left the Bookers that whatever Alpha Development wanted with the mountain, they were willing to do just about anything to get it.

Over the years apart, when Nick would remember Vicki, it was always her most obvious charms that he'd recall: her full breasts and rounded hips, her sexy smile and seductive bedroom eyes. Now he wondered how he could've forgotten her endless compassion, which was the very thing that caused her to became a lawyer. Or her fierce determination to fight for what was right, which was what caused her to become such a *good* lawyer. Or her absolute intolerance for injustice, which was what finally drove her away from him. All these parts made up the Vicki he loved, the strong life partner that he desired, and the loving mother who would bear and raise his children. As he watched her now, his mouth twisted in disgust, realizing that in his ignorance he'd almost lost all that. All for the love of stardom and money.

"Is this how you felt?"

"What do you mean?"

"The Pallister trial, when you were trying to help Betina Ramirez, did you feel this helpless?"

Vicki sat up and looked at him. She needed to see him to know that his question was a quest for true understanding and not just his idea of a poor joke. One look in his eyes and she knew. "Yes, as a matter of fact, it did feel a lot like this."

"I can't apologize enough, Vicki. I really didn't know."

"You were a different person and those were different times."

"Would you say the new Nick is an improvement?"

"Very much so."

Nick stared down at his riding boots. Vicki thought his train of thought had moved on. She lay back down. Old and rusty it may be, but to her sore back, the saggy mattress felt wonderful.

"How?"

She sat up again. "What?"

"You said the new Nick is an improvement. How?"

Vicki first thought he was joking, until she noticed the earnest expression in his black eyes. He was genuinely curious, and Vicki knew that she could crush him with a few well-chosen words. And that was something she would never do, but she wouldn't lie to him, either.

She stood and crossed the room. Reaching up, she cradled his face between her palms. "Nick, you are the most passionate, the most self-driven man I have ever met. But you are also ruthless in the pursuit of what you want. Not to mention arrogant, egotistical, and completely self-absorbed."

"Is there a point to all of this?" he asked dryly.

"Yes." She smiled. "These are the qualities that make you—you. Baby, those things are the *essence* of Nick Wilcox."

Nick dropped his head, letting it slip through her small hands. She sounded certain, sure of herself. He knew that she was, and worse, he knew that she was right. How could he possibly change the core of his being? Not that he was even sure he wanted to.

"But . . ." she began again.

Nick couldn't have moved it he'd wanted to. He needed to hear what would come after that "but." He waited.

"You're also the most kindhearted, most loving, most righteous brother I know."

Nick lifted his head to see if her eyes were as sincere as her words. They were. He felt a miracle swirling in the air above his head. He said a silent prayer, asking God to bring it down on him. Could it be? Was this forgiveness he was hearing?

Vicki lifted her body to his and slid her arms around his neck. "My problem is, I love you. All of you." She lay her head against his chest. "All of your passion, all of your unjustified conceit." She smiled to herself, knowing it wasn't unjustified at all.

Nick didn't trust his ears. He pulled her away from him to study her eyes, trying to read the message behind her words. He smiled in that heart-stopping way of his. "And you see this as a problem?"

"Yes." Her smile faded. "You are who you are, Nick, and I know in my gut that one day you're going to hurt me again. Even though I am absolutely certain it'll probably destroy me, I can't seem to help loving you."

He frowned in confusion. "I thought you said I was new and improved?"

She laughed. "You are, in one way. Eight years ago you didn't know what mattered most to you, and I believe now you do."

"You?"

She nodded. "Us."

He held her at arm's length, trying to understand what she was saying. "If you know how much you mean to me, if you know you mean more than anything to me, what makes you think I'll hurt you again one day?"

She turned and walked away, stopping at the large bay window that overlooked the lake. "Nick, have you ever heard the story of the eagle and the scorpion?"

Nick rubbed his bald head, not sure he understood. "What are you talking about?"

She held up her hand. "Hear me out."

He leaned back against the table and prepared to listen.

"One day a scorpion came to a river and needed to cross. Being that he could not swim, he pleaded with an eagle flying overhead to carry him across. The eagle graciously agreed, and carried the scorpion across the water on her back. Once they had almost reached the other side, the scorpion stung the eagle, causing her to plummet to the earth in a dying heap.

"Before she died, the eagle asked the scorpion, 'Why would you bite me when I was trying to help you? I gave you safe passage over the water, and you rewarded me with death. Why?' The scorpion looked guiltily at what he had done, and answered her, 'although I am grateful for safe passage, I cannot help what you are or what I am. You are an eagle and I am a scorpion. I was doing—'"

"What is in my nature." Nick finished. He stood and

crossed the room, coming to stand behind her. He wrapped his arms around her waist and pulled her back against him. "Regardless of whatever else you may think of me, never . . . never." Nick took a deep breath to calm his boiling blood. "Never believe that it is *in my nature* to hurt you."

She turned in his arms and, coming up on her toes, she touched her lips to his in a brief and tender kiss. "Not hurt me precisely, Nick, but to win—at all costs."

He squeezed her tight, pressing her body to his chest. When he lowered his head to hers this time, the kiss was not brief, nor was it gentle. It was hard and demanding, and when his tongue forced its way into her mouth, it was devastating.

Wrapping her arms around his neck, Vicki responded in kind, simply helpless against the love she felt for him. She felt his large hands cupping her bottom, lifting her up against the hard bulge of his jeans. His warm mouth pressed on hers, gliding along her cheek, jawbone, and neck. She felt his hot tongue flick at the sensitive spot behind her ear, and she was falling, falling, unable to stop the tidal wave of desperate hunger flowing in her veins. It was frantic, and urgent, and completely undeniable.

She was partially aware of being dragged across the room, of her cotton plaid shirt being unbuttoned. Her bra strap slid down her shoulder, and his large hand was there on her breasts, and in the valley between, sliding down her stomach in search of her belt buckle.

"Ouch."

Her eyes popped open to see Nick rubbing his smooth, dark head. "What's wrong?"

"Damn bunkbeds." He griped in pain, but when he looked down at her partially nude figure cradled in his arms, his smile returned. "Now, where was I?"

She smiled in return. "We were on our way to paradise."

He kissed her neck, and slid her pliable body beneath his on the saggy mattress. "In that case, by all means, " he whispered against her flesh, "let me take you there." His mouth closing around her breast felt like fire. Her back arched, and the noise that escaped her mouth could be described as nothing other than a shout of applause.

She heard more than felt her belt buckle coming undone. Nick lifted her, roughly pulling off her jeans. He whispered in her ear, "I'm sorry baby, I don't mean to rush, but I need you so bad. I feel like I'm going to die if I don't get inside you right now."

The urgency she read in his lust-filled eyes matched her own. It was as real as the feel of his bare, throbbing penis against her belly. His hand was between her legs, rubbing and stroking with expertise, compelling her body to make ready for his entry. Her thighs fell apart in answer to his demand.

His large frame loomed above her open body for mere seconds and he began to enter her. Abruptly, he stopped, frozen in place by his sheer determination to go no further. The veins in his neck stood up against his mahogany skin. His mouth formed a tight line of resolve.

Vicki opened her eyes to this silent battle. "What's wrong?" she asked breathlessly.

"Condoms," he hissed between his teeth. "Hang on."

She shook her head in surrender. "It doesn't matter." She lifted her hips, forcing him deeper inside her.

He yelped. Vicki giggled, not believing he'd actually yelped like a puppy.

"It's not funny," he hissed again. "I don't want you to hate me if you get pregnant."

Vicki lifted her body, touching him in every place she

could. She took his face between her hands again and looked directly into his eyes.

"I'm yours, Nick. It doesn't matter if I get pregnant, because I'm yours. I can't fight you anymore. Please, make love to me. And whatever comes of this union can be nothing but a blessing."

Nick's eyebrows furrowed as if he could not understand the language she spoke. "Hang on." With a strength he was unaware he possessed, Nick pulled free of her hold.

Vicki sighed, accepting that this was something he felt he must do. Before long he was there again, strong arms encircling her, warm flesh against hers, hard organ sliding into the folds of her womanhood. He moved into her slowly, gently.

Using her left leg, she hooked it under his knee and broke his foothold. Nick fell into her body, deep into the center of her being, buried in the core of her womanhood, and further beyond, into the recesses of her soul.

Born of an innate knowledge as old as man, his body began to move in her, long expansive strokes that became short, powerful thrusts. Holding tight to her shoulders, fighting some ridiculous fear that she would disappear from beneath him, he pressed his mouth to hers in a hard, possessive kiss. He needed to own her, to brand her as his forever. Mimicking the actions of his body with his tongue, he exploded inside her, and soon after Vicki followed him over the edge.

Two hours and four orgasms later, they lay in each other's arms watching the twinkling of stars in the night sky through the bare window.

This is the way it's supposed to be, Nick thought. *This is the way it should've always been.* And now that he had her back, despite her doubts about him, he was going to make sure that this was the way it would stay.

"You accept that you are mine?" he whispered into her hair. "That we belong together?"

She nodded in defeat.

"And . . . will you marry me?"

"Yes." She yawned and nodded again, knowing she could give no other answer.

Nick smiled. He was feeling so good that he decided to push his luck. "Vicki?"

"Hmm?" she muttered sleepily.

"Told you so."

She turned over in his arms and snuggled deeper into his chest. "Jackass," she whispered before drifting off to sleep.

CHAPTER FIFTEEN

"Hello?"

"Hey, Angie, it's me."

"What's going on there? Have you and Vicki found anything interesting?"

Nick chuckled. "That's an understatement."

"Really? What?"

"Well, thanks to Ted Crowder, we now know what Alpha Development wants is not on the land, it's *in* the land."

"What that's supposed to mean?"

"It's a long story. I'll explain when you get here. I was calling to find out when your flight is arriving tomorrow. I don't want to have to hear your big mouth for being late."

"Yeah, yeah, just make sure you're there. Flight one twenty-four from Chicago at four-forty-three P.M."

Nick repeated the information as he wrote it down in his palm pilot. "That's good, you'll be here in time for the meeting."

"What meeting?"

"Vicki and I are holding an assembly meeting here tomorrow to talk to all the farmers at once. To make everyone abreast of what's happening and what our options are."

"I don't know what you and Vicki have been up to, but it sounds productive."

Nick was remembering the previous night, and the night before that, and the night before that. He and Vicki had been lovers for almost a week now. The little fishing cabin turned headquarters was now a love nest.

They spent their days with their heads huddled together in debate regarding the investigation, and their nights with their bodies huddled together in a completely different kind of interchange.

"We are making progress. The meeting is not until eight. You'll be here in time to hear everything that's revealed."

The doorbell ringing drew Angela's attention. "Got to go, my date is here. I'll see you tomorrow evening."

"Hold up. Did you say date?"

"Yes, now—good-bye."

"Don't you hang up on me, Angela Marie."

The doorbell rang again. "Nick, I've got to go."

"Who's the lucky guy?" he teased.

She was silent. The doorbell rang again.

"I hope it's not that Kevin guy. He was a real jerk."

"No," she said. "It's not Kevin."

"Oh," Nick drawled. His smile widened as he realized the good preacher must be making progress. "Okay, I'll see you tomorrow."

Nick could not see Angela's eyebrows scrunched in concern, but he heard it in her voice. "What was that 'oh' about?"

"Nothing, just an 'oh'."

The doorbell rang again.

"You better get that." Nick smiled into the phone. "And by the way, tell Gabriel hello for me."

With that, Nick hung up the phone, certain that on the other end a string of obscenities unfit for Christian ears was being let loose into the receiver. He shook his head as he walked out of Tilde's country-style kitchen. He wondered if Reverend Gabriel Campbell really knew what he was getting into.

"Nick." Maude Proctor wrapped herself around the waist of the much taller man. "It's good to see you."

"How are you, Mrs. Proctor?" Nick smiled down at the woman who'd been like a second mother for most of his youth. Looking in her face, he could clearly see Vicki in twenty years. It was nice to know she would still be a beautiful woman.

"Sorry I haven't visited you and Tilde since you've been back, but with Mama's birthday, and this and that regarding the business, there's always one crisis or another. "

Nick held up his hand to halt the apology. "No, I'm the one who should apologize, not only for not visiting, but for monopolizing Vicki's time since she's been home." Nick felt no need to mention that the thought of coming face to face with Big Mama again was the real reason he avoided her house. "I know you don't get to see her much, and with this investigation she's been with me most of the time she's been here."

"Well, that I don't mind at all. I'm just pleased you two seemed to have found a answer to the troubles we've been having." She paused. "You have found an answer, haven't you?"

"We think so," he said with a nod.

The small crowd gathered in Matilda Howell's barn parted to allow Vicki and her grandmother through. Vicki led the older woman to one of the metal folding chairs in the front row, and after she lowered herself into the chair, Vicki spread a small colorful quilt across her lap.

He watched as Big Mama touched her granddaughter's cheek lovingly before Vicki turned to join him.

"Are we ready?" she asked upon approaching.

Nick scanned the group and nodded.

"Where's Angela?" Vicki looked around for her friend.

"She's in the house helping Aunt Tilde with the refreshments. But let's not wait any longer." Nick clapped his hands loudly over his head. "All right everyone, please take a seat, we've got a lot to discuss and we need to get this meeting underway."

Standing at the back of the group, John Booker spoke first. "What's this all about, Nick?"

"Hang on, Bo, we'll get to that. Please take a seat for now."

The group settled in, and Nick stood up on the makeshift platform he'd fashioned from hay bales. "Now, I know you all are wondering why we asked you here today, but before we get to that, with a show of hands, how many of you have spoken to the Alpha Development representative this week?"

No hands went up in the air. Nick nodded. *The less contact the better,* he thought. The last thing he wanted was for Alpha Development to know they'd discovered the truth of their scheme. Less time for the land developers to change their strategy meant more time for the farmers to develop their own.

"We know you all have been through a lot," Vicki began, before accepting Nick's hand and stepping up on the platform beside him. "But take comfort in knowing you're not alone. Alpha Development has harassed us all in one way or another in the past few weeks."

A wave of surprised mutterings went through the

crowd; people turned to their neighbors in private discussions and questions. Nick could see the meeting was about to get out of hand; he clapped again to regain everyone's attention.

Nick's deep voice carried over the group. "Up until now, we've thought they were after the land, but now we know better. Ted . . ." Nick gestured to a middle-aged man sitting in the front. "Will you explain to everyone what you told me and Vicki."

Ted Crowder snatched a piece of straw out of one of the hay bales and hopped up to stand beside Nick and Vicki.

"Howdy, y'all," he called, and waved to the gathering. The greeting was returned with enthusiasm.

Bo stood again. "What's this all about, Ted?"

Nick shook his head, during his time away he'd forgotten that John Booker had little patience with anything but horses. "Now, Bo, I said we'd get to that. Let Ted speak."

Bo hesitantly sat back down and prepared to listen.

"How many of you know the story of the lost mine?" Ted began. He heard a few grumbled mutters but nothing more. "Well, my daddy and granddaddy both knew the story inside and out, and told it to me often when I was a child. Apparently, in 1869, during the gold rush, a miner named Hubert Woods supposedly found a few nuggets of gold near here. At the time, these parts were still pretty much uninhabited, except for the Indians.

"According to the story, he made a map outlining the mountain and the lake, and where he found the nuggets, before going into Little Rock to test his nuggets and stake his claim. Turns out, the gold was real, but his map was useless. Y'all know how much of this land is covered in mountains, lakes, and pine trees." The crowd laughed. "Well, poor fellow could never find his way back. Legend says, after a few years he finally gave up ever finding it again, but stories of lost gold mines grew from there"

"Hell, Ted," Hank Durant called out. "That's a tall tale. Ain't no lost mine around these parts, and you know it."

Ted scratched at his head. "Maybe. . . maybe not, but Dale Sanders, that land development fellow, thought so, and he said as much."

"Why would he say something like that to you?" someone else called out. "I mean if he thinks the mine is around here, why tell you before he gets the land?"

"Well, the fellow's been coming around a lot lately and we've become somewhat friendly. He's a nice enough fellow, and I can't blame him for the folks he works for. Last time he came around, I offered him a touch of my homemade brew." Ted smiled. "Apparently it worked as some sort of truth potion on him. He confessed all sorts of things about that corporation. Like the fact that the man who's been surveying has been secretly looking for signs of the gold."

"Are you trying to tell us that this big corporation is trying to run us out of our homes for some gold mine that don't even exist?" Paul Williams stood with his arms akimbo. "Sorry, Ted, I find that too hard to believe."

A combination of noise and movement broke out as the group of confused farmers tried to make sense of such an outrageous claim.

Nick, who'd stepped down from the platform, now stepped up it again. "I know it all seems a bit much to believe," Nick looked out over the group, "But think about it. You've all said yourselves, you can't imagine what a company like that could want with this land. It's not good for anything but farming."

Ethel Williamson stood off to the side. "But Nick, it

don't make sense. There's got to be at least twenty families represented here. Why would they uproot all these families for something that might not even be real?"

Nick's dark eyes watched the elderly lady. Her confusion was real, as was everyone else's gathered there. And Nick was dumbfounded as to how to explain.

How could he tell them? What words could he use to lessen the impact of the truth? How could he explain that to a billion-dollar corporation they were not *families*, just numbers on a paper. How to make them understand that companies like Alpha had no qualms about uprooting generations of people for the mere possibility of what they could gain. They would empty the mountain of all life, human and otherwise—even destroy it if they had to. Once they were satisfied nothing was there, they would move on to the next conquest without a care for the ruin they'd left in their wake. Corporations like Alpha Development were like great carnivorous beasts, without conscience, ravaging anything and everything in pursuit of what they wanted.

These folks, who cared only for the people they loved and the land that provided them sustenance, could never grasp that type of ravenousness disregard. These kinsmen of spirit and mind, whose means were as pure and natural as their ends, could never contemplate that kind of evil. They took from the land what they needed to survive, and gave back just as much. No, Nick thought with pained regret, this small assembly of friends and neighbors, many of whom had never been beyond the edge of Hope, could never understand such unquenchable greed.

"I would like to say something." Vicki touched Nick's shoulder, before turning to the crowd. "When I was a child, all I could think about was getting off this mountain. I used to daydream about the world outside of this community, the hustle and bustle of big city life, all the money I could make. The expensive clothes and big expensive homes I would own. I thought about it so much, that I became obsessed with it. It really became *all* I could think about."

The crowd had become completely motionless in anticipation. Somehow they knew a revelation was to follow. And they each wanted to hear what it would be.

Vicki gestured to the crowd. "But being here with you all, I realize none of that matters. When I'm here, I understand that clothes go out of style, but your heritage last forever. Superficial things like cars and big houses, those things mean nothing when compared to history and family. Our ancestors understood that a hundred years ago. That's why they sacrificed everything they had to make sure we had a piece of this land. They died so that we could have that right, but to those who value money above all else, none of that means anything."

She moved to stand between Nick and Ted, wrapping her arms around both their waists. "That's why it's up to us to protect it. It doesn't matter why they want it, or what they plan to do with it, *we* can't let them have it."

"But what can we do, Vicki?" Bo stood up again. "When I wouldn't agree to sell, you see what they did to me."

"We believe we have a solution," Nick said. "This land has a unique history, being settled by freed slaves, and the descendants of those people are still tilling the land a hundred years a later. We can't stop them from wanting this land, but I do believe we can place it out of reach."

"We want to petition the National Trust to have the mountain declared a historic preserve," Vicki continued. "But we will need the support of everyone in this room. Are you with us?"

The loud supportive utterance throughout the room

was the closest they would get to a yes, Vicki thought. They were still doubtful, but resolved.

"All right," Nick said. "Vicki and I will get started on the process, and we'll be visiting with each of you in the next week. Thank you all for coming."

"Everyone, there are refreshments over here." Tilde motioned the group to the table she and Angela had sat up. The crowd began making their way in that direction, breaking off into small groups to discuss what they had been told, and some simply meeting in fellowship after being parted from their friends, given their isolated lives.

Vicki looked up at Nick standing beside her. "What do you think?"

He hunched his shoulders, knowing they still had a long haul, and declaring the mountain a historic preservation would do nothing to help his aunt's situation. Nor would it rebuild Bo's barn, or stop the foreclosure on the Williamsons'. If anything, it would anger Alpha Development into following through on their threats. But if they were successful, they could at least stop any more damage to the land, and the families on it.

Vicki watched the worry lines forming on Nick's smooth forehead, and the tight set of his mouth. She smiled to herself. This was the man she'd fallen in love with so many years ago. His care and concern for this small group went against every monetary motivation he could have. In fact, his presence here was in no way profitable. Not to mention he was probably making an enemy of Alpha Development. In short, he was risking his name and reputation to defend what could well be a losing cause. She hugged his waist tightly. Yes, she thought, her old Nick was back.

"Big Mama," Vicki called to her grandmother. "Are

you ready to go back inside?" She bent her arm to help the older woman rise.

Before Big Mama could answer, Angela touched her elbow. "Vicki, can I talk to you?"

"Vicki was about to put her off until later, but Big Mama interrupted with a wave of her thin fingers. "Go on about your business, child. The Wilcox boy can take me back inside." Nick's eyebrows went up, and Vicki's mouth fell open.

"You mean Nick?" Vicki asked, thinking that maybe Big Mama had gotten the Wilcox boy mixed up with someone else.

"If he don't mind?" She cast a threatening look in Nick's direction.

Nick understood clearly that the question was not a question, but he answered it anyway. "Uh, sure, not at all."

He moved to help the woman to her feet. She weighed little more than a feather. He cast one more befuddled look in the direction of Vicki and Angela before guiding her out through the crowd.

Vicki watched in fear as Angela fiddled with the tea-kettle. All that was required was two tea bags and a pot of hot water, she thought. Even Angela couldn't mess that up, right? Somehow her reasoning brought no comfort.

"I know what I am about to say may put me in the dog-house with Nick, but I feel if I don't speak up we may lose a great opportunity." Angela turned to Vicki, wringing her hands nervously.

Sensing the other woman's genuine anxiety, Vicki reached out her hand. "What is it?"

Angela accepted the gesture of friendship and comfort,

took the hand, and sat beside Vicki. She'd been wrestling with this nonstop for the past thirty minutes, and she needed to speak her mind before she lost her nerve.

"Well, when you and Nick mentioned the plan to petition for protection from the government, this idea popped into my head."

"What idea?"

"Why not get the press involved?"

"That would be great, but why would they bother? I mean, a bunch of black farmers petitioning to preserve their land isn't groundbreaking news."

"No," Angela said, and looked away. "But if a favored candidate in the race for attorney general was fighting on the side of that small group of farmers, it would become groundbreaking news. Especially if it is the childhood home of that candidate."

Vicki shook her head. "Angela, what are you talking about?"

"Vicki, Nick is planning to run for Arkansas attorney general in the next election. He was afraid of how you would take it; he wasn't going to tell you until after you were married. I know it's not my place to tell you, but I thought you should know that as soon as you're married, he plans to move you guys back to Little Rock and begin his campaign."

Vicki was too stunned to speak. Things begin to click in her head: snippets of conversations, and things she'd heard. The reporter she'd heard asking the question outside the courthouse during the Morrison trial, and the fact that Nick would never tell her anything about his career plans or where he was working since he moved to Chicago.

As if reading her thoughts, Angela answered her next question. "He only moved to Chicago to get you back.

He's been flying back and forth between Chicago and Little Rock like crazy, trying to be with you and maintain business as usual at his law firm."

The high-pitched whistle of the teakettle sounded, momentarily breaking the tension in the air. Angela jumped up to pour the water into the waiting mugs.

"I know how out of bounds I am here." Her voice dropped. "And I'm pretty sure Nick will hate me for a while, but I couldn't let this perfect opportunity pass us by."

After taking a deep breath to fortify herself, Vicki was finally able to speak. "I'm sorry for any rift this may cause between you and Nick, but I am thankful you told me. "

Angela returned to the table with the mugs, and the two women sipped in silence for a while, before Vicki spoke. "I'll call the press in the morning, try to round up some interest." She started to sip and paused. "Angela, thanks again." She reached across the table and squeezed her friend's hand. Then silence fell again, each woman lost to her own thoughts.

Even though she still felt she'd done the right thing, Angela wondered if in doing so, she'd cause her only sibling to turn away from her. Vicki was wondering if she'd already fallen too deep back in love with Nick to pull herself out again. *Who are you kidding?* her heart whispered, *You were never out to begin with.* He'd charmed her with a smile on a school playground twenty-five years ago, and had ruled her heart for most of her adult life.

What if she had been forewarned, given some type of mystical guidance that would've revealed to her what he was about all those years ago, shown her what her fate would hold? Some magical fortune-teller could've looked into a crystal ball and told Vicki she was destined to love a man whose lust for power would always dominate him. Even if this person would've called him by name, and foretold a lifetime of phenomenal highs and devastating lows, would she still have chosen to follow her destiny? Of course she would've, she thought, as sadness filled her heart. She loved him—completely. The good, the bad, and the deceitful; there was simply no way out of it.

"Nope, no paprika." Vicki stood on her tiptoes to see to the back of the cabinet.

Big Mama shook her head before pounding her small fist into the ball of dough. "I swear, I don't see how Maude manages to cook anything in this kitchen. She has none of the essential ingredients. Plain ol' everyday seasonings, is that too much to ask?" The elderly woman cast her eyes at Angela, who sat with a notepad, as studious as a schoolgirl eager to please her new teacher. "Put paprika down on that list, child. Ain't no use in you not cooking it the right way."

Angela, who'd been diligently writing the recipe to prepare Big Mama's famous smoked salmon, scribbled "paprika" on her notepad. Vicki shook her head and returned to seasoning her fish. *If Big Mama only knew,* Vicki thought, *no amount of paprika in the world could save a salmon once Angela got her hands on it.*

Vicki finished with the few pieces of fish she was preparing, and placed the pan in the refrigerator to allow the herbs to soak into the meat. She turned and walked to the bay window. She saw the drops of water on the glass before she noticed the rain shower muddying the ground.

"It's raining," she called to the women.

Big Mama nodded appreciatively. "Rain is good. Washes away the filth of the earth," she muttered.

"Speaking of filth." Vicki chuckled. "What are we going to do about Aunt Freda?"

Big Mama hunched her shoulders, but never stopped pounding away at her dough. "Ain't much we can do. I can't change your granddaddy's will, but at least now she can't sell the land. So she'll do what she always does. Go somewhere and sit down until she finds another way to stir up trouble."

"I wish there was some way to get rid of her once and for all."

"She's family, Vicki. We're stuck with her."

Angela watched in amazement as a one-hundred-year-old woman beat the ball of bread dough repeatedly, for what seemed like several minutes. "Big Mama, is all that really necessary?" Angela asked. "It seems a bit excessive."

Big Mama paused in her battering of the white blob that would eventually be raisin bread, and cocked one eyebrow in indignation. "I've heard about your cooking, child. And it seems to me you can use all the advice you can get. But if you feel you can do better, by all means, go right ahead." She wiped her hands on her apron, and stood with her palms braced against her thin hips.

Angela blinked wildly and looked to Vicki for help. Vicki stared out the window; the rain had become extremely fascinating.

"You think you can do better?" Big Mama glared at her protégé.

Angela swallowed hard. "No ma'am."

Big Mama nodded in satisfaction and returned her attention to the dough. Angela and Vicki exchanged a look of shared fear. Apparently, Vicki thought, Angela wasn't the only one who took her love of cooking to the extreme.

"As for you missy, what you gonna do about Nicholas?"

Nicholas? Vicki raised her eyebrow and looked back over her shoulder. Nick's selfless efforts at saving the mountain had apparently endeared him to Big Mama. At least he'd moved up from "the Wilcox boy."

"What do you mean, what am I gonna do?" Vicki did not want to have this conversation, not with anybody, and most certainly not with Big Mama.

"I figured since he's always trailing in behind you like a stallion after a mare, you'd do the right thing. Me and your mama didn't raise you to be a tramp, Vicki."

Vicki closed her eyes and shook her head, grateful that Angela was the only witness to her humiliation. "I told you before, Big Mama, we're friends." Vicki cast a side-glance at Angela, who was looking as guilt-ridden as always. Lately, every time Nick's name was mentioned, Angela's face would take on a look of bereavement. Vicki knew her friend regretted exposing her brother's plans.

After insisting it would never happen again, somehow, Vicki realized, she'd fallen right back into the same trap. She knew what Nick was about, had always known what Nick was about. Fame and fortune at the cost of all else. Yet, when he'd looked at her with those dark gypsy eyes and seductive smile, declaring he'd changed, she'd been the first one to want to believe him.

"You young women give your love away like it means nothing." Big Mama was still ranting. "And you can't rightly blame the men. Why buy the cow when you can get the milk for free? At least Nicholas wants to marry you, and it's not like you're getting any younger, you know."

Vicki swung around and glared at this woman she'd known and loved all her life. "Grandmother."

Big Mama froze in place, her fist buried in the ball of dough. Her granddaughter stood glaring at her with tight fist and a ramrod-straight back, but it was the one word answer that told her she'd over stepped her boundaries. She could remember being "grandmother" only twice before, and neither time was good.

A hush fell over the kitchen, as Big Mama returned to her dough, Angela doodled on her notepad, and Vicki returned to her place of contemplation. Staring out the window, she turned her thoughts inward. As much as she hated to admit it, Big Mama's question needed to be answered, for herself if for no one else. What was she going to do about Nick?

Eight years ago, Vicki had been asking herself that same question. She'd doubted her strength to walk away from him, and shortly after proved she could. Now she was doubting if she had the strength to trust him again; she wondered what proof Nick could offer to convince her.

A teary-eyed Angela confessed to her brother what she'd done, but before he could react, Vicki had already put the wheels of the media machine in motion. Angela's only consolation regarding her betrayal was that her assumption that Nick's name alone would be enough to gain the attention of the media was confirmed.

Within forty-eight hours the mountain was clamoring with news crews interviewing the farmers, and elbowing for pictures and interviews with the dashing candidate for attorney general. Nick was in his element, as always when in the spotlight, knowing who to acknowledge and who to ignore. If charm was a gift, then Nicholas Wilcox surely had been blessed.

Before long, the spotlight had shifted from a simple human-interest story to an in-depth investigation into the business practices of Alpha Development. In light of the negative publicity, the charges against Aunt Tilde were dropped in an attempt to save face, and the

Williamsons were given an extension on their loan. Nothing could be done for the Bookers, but by the end of the week, everyone felt assured that no more threats would be made.

Most of the farmers had returned to lives with some sense of normalcy as their petition for historic status was pending in Little Rock. Everything that could be done had been done. And now they were left with nothing to do but wait.

The day Vicki planned to return to Chicago, she finished the last of her packing and went in search of her mother. She stopped an approaching stockman to inquire as to where she could be. The man pointed to the small feed shed Maude had converted into an office space a few years back. Vicki thanked him, and turned in the direction of the shed.

Maude Proctor was sorting through a stack of unpaid invoices and tapping her pen to her bottom lip when her daughter entered her office. "What a nice surprise." She smiled, sitting back in her wood swivel chair. Her small bifocals sat low on her nose.

"I got all my packing done, and have a few minutes to spare before I have to leave for the airport."

"Did you talk to Big Mama?"

"Yes. I'm glad she's decided to stay here with you for a while. It makes me uncomfortable to think about her being up in the cabin all by herself."

"Me too," Maude said. "Hopefully, I can convince her to stay on for good. But you know how she is, stubborn to the core."

"Mama." Vicki sat forward in her chair, "I know you were planning to sell the farm, and now Nick and I have made that impossible. I just—"

"Don't." Maude shook her head. "I was looking for the coward's way out, and I'm glad you stopped me."

"It's not cowardly to want rest, Mama."

Maude shrugged. "Maybe not, but your daddy worked too hard to build this business up for me to toss it away like that." She popped her fingers.

Vicki leaned forward and touched her arm. "I know how hard it is on you, trying to do it all alone."

She sighed heavily. "I won't lie to you, my daughter, there are days . . . and nights when I sorely miss your father. He was always the one who would talk me out of these foolish ideas that occasionally come to me." She smiled. "I guess now that task falls to you."

"You're not foolish, Mama."

Maude chuckled. "See, you sound just like him.

Vicki stood and crossed behind the desk to hug her mother. "You're *not* foolish, just tired of doing it all." She leaned back and frowned at her mother in a way that reminded Maude of her deceased husband.

But it wasn't Carl Proctor standing before her, it was his daughter. A daughter so like him in character and strength. A strength Maude had often felt lacking in herself.

"You probably never would've considered selling, would you?"

Vicki hunched her shoulders. "I don't know, but I'm glad I didn't have to make that decision."

"Sometimes you remind me of your father." Maude finally spoke her thoughts aloud.

Vicki chuckled. "That's funny, everyone says I look more like you."

"Yes, you look like me, but you're *like* him. He was a good man, so strong and sure of himself. I could truly use some of that self-assurance right about now. I don't know how I'm going to keep this business afloat the way things are going."

Vicki bowed her head. "I miss him too, Mama."

"But you would never fall apart like I did. You always seemed confident." She cast a side glance at Vicki. "Nick's got that same kind of confidence. I guess that's why you two have always been friends. You're so much alike."

Vicki could see where this conversation was going. "Don't start with one of your Nick-fests. I'm really not in the mood to listen to you sing his song."

Maude crossed her arms over her chest. "I don't know what you're talking about. I was just stating an observation. And handsome, too."

"Mama," Vicki warned. "Stop it." Vicki turned and headed for the doorway.

"Okay, okay." Maude put up her hands in surrender. "Vicki?"

"Yes?"

"Despite my attempt to sell, I am proud, you know. Of this land, its history, our heritage. But most of all, I'm proud of you. I wanted you to know that."

Vicki returned to the desk and wrapped her mother in another tight embrace. "I know, Mama. I know." The two women fell silent for several long minutes, enjoying the warmth of the moment. The faint smells of fresh daisies and cow manure wafted on the air. Both as familiar as life itself; both smelled of home.

A gentle rapping on the door caused them to look in that direction and see Nick enter the small shed. "Hello, Mrs. Proctor." Nick smiled with all the ardor of a ten-year-old with a crush. He'd always thought Maude Proctor an incredible woman. And her daughter was definitely living up to the legacy.

"Nick. Speak of the devil." Maude teased her daughter. "We were just talking about you. Please come on in."

"Uh, thank you, but I was wondering if I could have a word with Vicki alone."

Maude started to rise. "Sure, just let me collect some of my work, I can take it in the house."

Vicki stopped her. "No." She cut a dark look in Nick's direction. "*We'll* leave."

She swept past Nick in a whirlwind. In her anger, she'd forgotten to say good-bye to her mother. She poked her head back in the cabin. "I'll stop in to say good-bye before I leave."

Maude nodded to her daughter and smiled at Nick. "You do the same."

Nick returned the smile. "I will." He followed Vicki out of the small shed and across the farm to the grazing pasture. He stood beside her, while she leaned against the wood fence. He waited several tense minutes, until it became clear she would not be the first to speak.

After the assembly a week ago, the media frenzy had descended upon them almost immediately, giving them little time alone. And when they were alone they were usually discussing the petition.

This was the first time Nick had been able to speak with her regarding her conversation with Angela. Truth was, he was almost afraid to bring it up, but she was planning to return to Chicago today, and he needed to know where they stood. He took notice of the fire in her copper eyes and the snarl on her lips. He felt a heavy weight in his stomach. Even angry, she was beautiful.

"So?"

"So what?" Vicki snapped, and cast a sidelong glance at his classic profile. His sharp nose and chiseled chin were softened by full lips. *Such delicious full lips,* Vicki thought painfully. Why did he have to have such delicious lips?

"Are we still getting married, or did Angela ruin my chances?"

"Don't blame this on Angela. If you'd told me yourself, she would not have had to. *You* made this mess."

His mouth twisted in doubt. "Maybe."

"What do you mean *maybe?* This is my life we're talking about, Nick. You can't go making a random decision and assume I'll go along with it."

"My decision to run for attorney general is not random. I put a lot of thought in it."

"Yeah, like you always do. Thought for how it will benefit you and to hell with the rest of us."

"You may find this hard to believe but I'm not doing this for me, I'm doing this for—"

"Don't even go there, Nick." She stalked several feet away and swung back to face him. "Déjà vu, Nick. I've heard this all before."

"It's true."

Vicki stalked back across the green field until she stood directly in front of him. Staring up into his eyes, she seemed surprised by what she saw. "You really believe that, don't you?"

He sighed in heavy defeat. "It's true." He hated his voice for cracking at so critical a moment. But his heart was bleeding, and there was simply no way he could hide it.

She took up her position at the wooden fence once more, looking out over the empty meadow. "All I want to know is why?"

"Why what?"

"Why do you want to be attorney general? Is it the prestige? The chance to use it as a political stepping-stone?"

He turned her to face him. "Is that what you think?"

he huffed loudly. "Of course it is. It would never occur to you that I may want to make a difference for the people around here."

"It occurred to me. It just didn't fit with what I know about you."

"What's that supposed to mean?"

"Doing something for the greater good is not in *your* best interest."

Nick stood to his full height of six feet, two inches and glared down at her with resentment. "You really have a low opinion of me, don't you?"

She returned his anger with her own. "Have you given me any reason not to?"

"I was planning to tell you."

When?! After I said 'I do'?"

The answer to the question was yes, but Nick's instincts told him it was the wrong answer. "Where do we stand, Vicki?"

The question hung in the air unanswered.

Nick felt completely lost. A man who was renowned for always having the right words, was speechless. He'd managed his life with the precision of a military general, and his greatest battle was about to be lost with one simple misstep. Not even a lie precisely, just words left unsaid.

In truth, he didn't blame Angela. He couldn't blame Angela. Vicki was right, he should have told her. But would she have married him? Now he would never know.

"I still love you, Vicki. I always have, and I always will. I still want to marry you." He waited for a response. None came, so he continued. "We belong together, you know it as well as I. Don't fool yourself." He took her chin between his thumb and forefinger, and forced her to look up at him. "Nothing will ever feel as right as you and me."

She jerked her head to the side to pull free of his grip.

The last thing she wanted was for him to see the water forming in her eyes. His words were breaking her already bruised heart. Her mouth remained set in a tight line. He would never know what it was costing her to stay silent. Vicki vowed he would never see her shed another tear on his behalf.

Nick had the feeling of holding a crushed butterfly in his hand. Beautiful, fragile, and easily destroyed. He leaned over and placed a gentle kiss on the top of her head.

"When you make up your mind about us, you know where to find me." With that parting statement, he walked away.

Vicki stood like stone until the air around her became completely still again. She heard faint laughter coming from the direction of the stable. Nick must've run into one of the stockmen. They all knew him; he was as familiar a presence around the farm as Vicki herself. She listened to the distant sounds of snorting and harness reins jingling.

She turned in time to see Nick kicking Wicked Ways into a full gallop. Unable to hold them back any longer, two eager tears began their path down her face as she watched Nick ride out of her life.

CHAPTER SIXTEEN

"So, Nick," Pete Marlowe started to speak while motioning for the waiter at the same time. "Is it safe to assume your *personal* business in Chicago is taken care of?"

Nick glared at the older man's profile as Pete gave his drink order to the young waiter. Nick did not like the illicit tone he'd used to emphasize the word "personal." Nor did he like watching as the man downed his fourth martini in twenty minutes, or the condescending way he spoke in general. No, Nick decided, there wasn't much to like about Pete Marlowe.

"Yes." Nick wiped his mouth, thinking that if he could manage to keep his conversation with the man to a minimum, the luncheon would pass quickly.

"Glad to hear it," Pete muttered while cutting into his porterhouse steak. "Time is winding down, and we are going into the trenches soon. We need to know your concentration is on the task at hand, Nick, not focused on some piece of—"

"Pete," Nick thought it best to cut the man off before he said something that would get him beat down in the middle of this expensive and very posh restaurant. "What is this all about?"

Pete's blue eyes sparkled maliciously for all of five seconds before he managed to pull his contempt back behind his carefully constructed façade. Nick was not fooled. The quartet may have done their research on Nick Wilcox before choosing to sponsor him in his bid for attorney general, but Nick had also done his homework.

He knew that Pete probably had fought against the other three when they'd decided on him, a black man, as *their* man. He knew that beneath that expensive suit and friendly demeanor was a legacy of hate that was probably making this luncheon as difficult for him as it was for Nick. But unfortunately, Nick also knew that the quartet was a quartet, and not a trio. Which meant if he wanted the backing of this small group of powerful men, that meant accepting Pete Marlowe as well.

"A friendly reminder." Pete shoved another bite of steak into his mouth, his eyes gleaming in secret understanding. "We need to know where your loyalties lie." He continued speaking with a mouthful of steak. Nick had to look away before the vision of half-chewed beef rolling around in his mouth nauseated him. "You can't go into this race half-cocked, Nick. It's all or nothing for us as well as yourself." His grease-smeared lips formed a deceptively pleasant smile. "We're behind you one-hundred percent, and we need to know you also have our best interests at heart."

"Have I done something to make you believe that I do not have your best interests at heart?" Now more than ever, Nick was certain this was not a friendly reminder of the upcoming race. This man had something on his mind, and Nick was ready for him to get to the point. Now, before his proximity became intolerable.

"No." Pete shook his head. "At least not intentionally. I don't believe you would do anything to any one of us, knowingly."

Nick was losing his appetite. He pushed his plate forward and rested his forearms on the edge of the table. "Okay. Let's talk about something I may have done *unknowingly.*"

The waiter arrived with the fourth martini, and Pete immediately took a sip, which became a gulp. Nick wondered briefly if his benefactor had a drinking problem.

"Nick, I understand your need to help *your* people." Pete made a gesture with his hand. "But a little word of advice."

Nick's eyes narrowed; his arms folded across his chest. *This should be good,* he thought. "What word would that be, Pete?"

"Before you go racing off to rescue the villagers from the dragon, make sure the dragon's not your friend."

Nick had had enough of this lunch, this man, and his ridiculous analogies. It was time to end it. "What the hell are you talking about, Pete?"

Pete's passive expression became rock hard. "I'm a stockholder in Alpha Development. A *majority* stockholder."

"Ah, I see." Nick was fighting the urge to grin. So that was what this was all about.

Pete's mouth twisted in a snarl, "That's all you have to say?"

Nick wiped his mouth with the linen napkin. "What would you have me say, Pete?" He swallowed another spoonful of cheese and broccoli soup. "That I'm sorry?" He shook his head. "Well, I won't say I'm sorry for something I'm not. I'm not sorry for helping my family and friends save their homes from a corporation that, first of all, misrepresented their objective. And second, used immoral if not illegal means of obtaining that objective."

Pete was doing a poor job of hiding his outrage. His nose was flaring like a rabid bull, his face was flushed to a hot pink, his lips were tightened into a bloodless white line. He half-lifted his heavy form over the table, and he glared at Nick in open hatred. "You listen here. The only reason you're in this race is because me and my friends thought you might be capable of something. But, just like we found you, we can lose you. We have a lot of time invested in you. I personally have a lot of money riding on you. Money, I might add, that comes from that *immoral* corporation. Before you go getting up on that high horse of yours, you'd best keep that in mind."

Nick sat staring at the man for several seconds. With lighting speed, he reached across the table and grabbed Pete by his tan silk tie and jerked him down until the two men were nose to nose. "Now *you* listen to me. If you ever get in my face again, you'll find out what I am capable of. You and your friends can take your money, your time, and your backing and shove them up your—"

"Sir, please."

Nick drew a breath and turned to glare at the young waiter who stood beside their table. The sheer horror reflected in his eyes caused Nick to pause. One conciliatory glance around the crowded restaurant let him know that his private conversation was private no longer. Nick released Pete who was still frozen in shock, and stormed out of the restaurant without another word.

Several hours later as he lay restlessly in bed, Nick was still trying to understand how he'd gotten himself in this predicament. *I can't believe I lost Vicki over this damn race.*

Less than one year ago, he was embarking on an impressive and ambitious plan: to gain the top legal seat in the state and win back the woman he loved. Now, after assaulting Pete Marlowe, and effectively killing any chance he had of running in the upcoming attorney general race, he lay alone in his empty bed.

He didn't regret how he'd handled Marlowe; he'd only wished he'd gotten in one good punch before the waiter showed up. Maybe he would never be the attorney general for the state of Arkansas, he thought, but it would be far worse to never be the man he believed he was capable of being. The man Vicki wanted him to be.

Nick had always been driven by the more enterprising parts of his personality, everything from bringing home the best possible report card to scoring the winning touchdown. He'd come into the world with an innate desire to be the best in anything he chose.

He understood and accepted it as part of his character, for it had always been a part of him. But not until eight years ago had his ambition overridden his better judgement, a mistake that had cost him more than he could've imagined losing at the time. It had not only cost him his relationship with Vicki, but now he knew it had cost a woman her life.

And now, once again, he had let his ambition come between them. Nick had tried to reason with himself, to justify his reasons for not telling Vicki about his intentions to run. But in the end, he could not deny the truth. He hadn't told her because he feared she would not approve. And he hadn't wanted to admit that his participation in the race would not have been swayed by her opinions, just as his participation in the Andy Pallister case eight years ago had not been swayed by her opinions. His corporeal aspirations had left him at the mercy of men like Pete Marlowe. Men who could give all and take it away like pagan gods.

"My ambition," he huffed loudly. What was his ambition doing for him on nights like tonight, when all he needed was to lose himself in Vicki? His battered ego severely needed the kind of healing that could only be found between her well-toned thighs and perfectly formed breasts that fit in his palms like they were molded to them. What he needed was convalescence in the form of tender kisses.

He shifted beneath his covers, realizing his body was responding to his thoughts. The memory of her mouth opening to him so willingly. Vicki's kiss. He sighed. After everything that had happened between them, it was easy to forget it all started with two best friends sharing their first kiss behind Carl Proctor's '79 Cadillac Seville.

Had he lost her for good? There was a time, shortly after he'd moved to Chicago, when he'd thought so for sure. But he'd managed to win her back, to remind her of what she felt for him. Somehow, he knew she would try to push those feelings deeper down inside her this time, to make herself completely immune to him, if possible.

So, what are you going to do about it? His conscience scorned him. *Sit by like a wimp and let her push you out of her life? Out of her heart?*

His jaw set in a determined line as Nick decided it was time to apply rule number four of the Nick Wilcox rules to live by: *The circus is not over until the tent comes down.* He glanced down at the full erection poorly hidden beneath the thin sheet, and chuckled out loud. *Okay*, he thought, *not exactly a circus tent, but the analogy would still stand.*

Vicki peeked from behind the curtain once more. He was still there. Across the street, standing beneath a tree, the shadow of a man was silhouetted against the night. She moved along the wall until she reached the cordless phone sitting on the round nightstand beside her bed. Picking it up, she dialed 911 and waited for the operator.

"911, what's the emergency?" came the feminine voice on the other end.

"Hello, my name is Vicki Proctor and I am an assistant prosecutor for the city of Chicago. There is a man watching my house right now, and I believe he was the defendant in a recent case I tried."

"Is the man there right now?" the operator asked.

Vicki took a deep breath to control her frustration. "Didn't I just say he was?"

"Do you know the man's name?"

"Will you *please* send a patrol car?"

"Ma'am, I understand you're upset, but I need to get some information first."

"His name is Tommy Morrison."

"Did you say, Bobby?"

"Tommy. As in Thomas."

"One moment, ma'am."

Vicki breathed a sigh of relief. Finally, help was on the way.

"Ma'am?"

"Yes?"

"Did you say you recognize the person?"

"Of course I recognize him. I tried to send him to jail! There were threats made against me during the trial. Please, please send a patrol car."

Vicki jumped at the sound of a hard bumping sound near her front door. She scanned the room, and the only thing she saw with any weight to it was her brass lamp.

"Ma'am, are you still there?"

Ignoring the operator, Vicki unplugged the lamp,

and, cradling the phone in her shoulder, moved in the general direction of the sound. "I think he is trying to get in the house. Please, send a car *now.*"

"One moment," the operator said with disinterest.

Vickie clicked off the phone, and dropped it; since it was serving absolutely no purpose.

Now free to hold the lamp with both hands, she moved out of her bedroom and along the walls toward the front door. The bumping sound came again; this time it was louder, and immediately followed by a tapping sound. *Knocking?* Vicki thought. The tapping sound came again, it was definitely knocking.

Why would someone who wanted to kill her knock on her front door?

She eased closer, still gripping her lamp close to her chest. She swallowed once and steadied her voice. "Who is it?"

"Ms. Proctor," the young man called through the door. "It's Tommy Morrison. Please, don't be afraid. I don't wanna hurt you. It's just—I remembered something important and I didn't know who to tell it to. I know you think I killed those people, but I didn't, I swear it. And I thought what I know could help you find the real killer."

Vicki watched him through the peephole the whole time he spoke. He displayed none of the obvious behavior of a criminal. No looking around for witnesses, no menacing stare at the door, just a frightened young man.

Vicki wondered briefly if she had lost her mind to be considering what she did next. She cracked the door an inch and peeked out at the man. "I'll give you one minute to talk, and I'm calling the police." Vicki thought there was no need for him to know there was a chance they were already on the way. In case he did turn out to be the killer.

"Remember in court I told you that I recognized one of the victims?"

"Yes, Benedict Brown."

"Yeah, well, I remembered something Benny told me. He was in love, see—with a Japanese girl, but her people weren't cool with it. Her dating a black man, and all."

"Okay." Vicki shrugged. "What does that have to do with anything?"

"I remember Benny saying her ol' man was hooked up with some real heavy hitters. You know, Mafia types. Benny was kinda scared, but said he wasn't going to let no one come between him and Hoshiko. Hoshiko, that was his girl."

"Get to the point."

"Well, I remember Benny asked me to take him to pick her up once. I took him, and didn't think anything of it, until I saw the girl crawling out an upstairs window. Benny said that if her dad caught them together, he would kill him. That's what he said, those actual words. He would kill him."

Vicki cast a casual glance up and down the street, looking for a patrol car. The street was clear.

Tommy continued. "She crawled out the window and down this white ladder thing and come running to the car. She hopped in, and we took off. But before I drove away, I saw a man standing in a downstairs window. He was standing back a little, but I have really good eyes, and I managed to get a look at him. He stood right there the whole while. He saw everything. I told Benny, but he thought I imagined it. He said if Hoshiko's dad had seen them, he probably would've come out of the house with a shotgun."

"What does any of this have to do with the trial?"

"Well, I remembered seeing you and Mr. Wilcox talking to Hoshiko's father in the hallway at the courthouse.

He was with some lady." He popped his fingers trying to find a way to describe the woman. "She was a red bone, real tall, real pretty." He nodded, believing that was a sufficient description. And as it turned out, it was: the description brought up the crystal-clear image of Nick's friend, Veronica.

Vicki tried to recall the man with her, but was unable.

"You think Hoshiko's father had something to do with the convenience store robbery?"

"See, that's just the thing. I don't think this was no robbery. I mean," he said, "I committed a couple of liquor store robberies when I was in the gang, and we never left a mess like that. And one glance and I knew that no one had touched the cash drawer. It didn't even look like anyone tried to open it."

"Okay, let's say the angry father killed Benny Brown. What about those other two people?"

Tommy shrugged at the one eye peeking through the crack. "I can't even tell you. None of it may mean anything. But I wanted you to know."

Vicki nodded, her mind already considering this new information. "You better get going. I called 911 before I knew you just wanted to talk, and the police may ride by here to check."

Tommy nodded, already in motion. "Thanks for hearing me out. And tell Mr. Wilcox thanks, too."

Vicki closed and locked the door. Tommy was already acquitted; what could he possibly gain by coming here tonight? And if this mysterious Hoshiko and her father were involved, no one would've suspected him. Even taking bigotry into account, Vicki still found it hard to believe a man could die simply because of whom he chose to love.

Before she knew it, she had picked up the phone

again, and called Ellis. She left a brief message telling him that he may want to look into Benny Brown's love life, and the little information Tommy had given her. She stopped short of telling where she acquired her information.

Vicki was tempted to pick up the phone and call Nick. The phone was in her hand by the time she managed to talk herself out of it. His client was acquitted, there was no reason to call him with news regarding a closed case.

She moved toward her bedroom to return her lamp to its position on her nightstand. Truth was, she wanted to hear his voice. It had been almost two weeks since her return from Hope, and both her body and heart were experiencing withdrawal. Her only consolation was that she was almost certain that Nick was just as miserable.

Vicki looked up at the sound of tapping on her office door. She smiled. "Come on in, Ellis."

Ellis's ever-present scowl was firmly in place. "You were right." He crossed the room in a few strides. "Yoshimoto is dirty. We are still following the paper trail, but it appears he's chosen the typical ways to hide his illegal activities. Third-party entities and dummy corporations." He made a dismissive gesture with his hands. "But that kind of stuff is always easy enough to dissimulate. I expect we'll have enough to arrest him by the end of the week."

Vicki sat back in her chair. "Do we have enough evidence to connect him to the murder of those three people in the liquor store?"

Ellis shrugged. "Sorry, kid, I know you really want him for the Brown hit, but I'd be happier if we can catch him on tax fraud. This guy has enough money to hire a legal army to fight off a murder conviction. He's well-liked by the public at large, and I'm not sure how receptive a jury would be to the idea of him being involved in a bloodbath like that. But tax evasion is a lot more believable, and when the IRS gets finished with him, he'll be ruined financially."

Vicki crossed her arms over her chest, her lips pursed tightly. "He can't get away with it, Ellis. I almost sent an innocent man to prison because of him. He played us for fools." She shook her head. "If you won't help me, I'll investigate the murder by myself."

Ellis put up both his hands defensively. "Hold on, champ."

He rubbed his chin and considered her. Proctor was one of his best prosecutors, and she put her best into every case without allowing herself to get personally involved. For her to make a statement like that said how much it meant to her.

His mind flashed back to late August, 1975. His mouth twisted; that case still left a bad taste in his mouth. Ellis understood better than anyone the guilt associated with trying an innocent man. It was too late to do anything about that case, but this situation could still be righted.

"We'll start with the daughter, Hoshiko. Talk to some of her friends, see who knew of her romance with Brown."

Vicki breathed a sigh of relief. "Thanks, Ellis."

Ellis, who was always uncomfortable with emotional displays, inched toward the door. "No problem, champ. I'll let you know as soon as we track down the daughter." With that statement, he disappeared through the doorway and merged into the traffic of the crowded hallway.

Vicki relaxed now that she had Ellis's support. She meant what she'd told him. If left with no alternative, she would've conducted her own investigation. She couldn't shake the feeling of being dirty, ever since she'd discovered how well their office had been manipulated by Yoshimoto. He'd used the resources of the prosecutor's office, which meant he had used her, and one way or the other he was going down.

CHAPTER SEVENTEEN

Vicki looked at her watch again. She'd promised Peaches she would be by her side when the doors to the art gallery opened, but she was detained at the beauty saloon. The noisy chatter of people filled the air as she rounded the corner to the entrance of the gallery, easing her guilt a little. People were only now beginning to file into the gallery. She wasn't late after all.

The sun was beginning to set, and the rush-hour traffic of Michigan Avenue was still bumper-to-bumper, the bright headlights adding ambience to the bustling city avenue. Waiting for the crowd to thin a bit, she turned toward the setting sun, reveling in the brilliant oranges and yellows. She always loved this time of day, when the world was settling in for the night.

"Beautiful." A deep voice directly over her left shoulder startled her.

Vicki turned to find Nick standing a few inches from her, dressed to perfection in a black tuxedo. The last time she'd seen him, he was dressed in cowboy boots and blue jeans and had looked just as delicious. His smile twinkled almost as much as the diamond in his ear.

The surprising vision was like a balm to her troubled soul. Vicki fought the temptation to reach out and touch him, to confirm that he was flesh and blood and not a phantom conjured by desire.

"What—what, are you doing here?"

His smile deepened. "This is the night of Peaches's debut, isn't it?"

Regaining her composure, Vicki folded her arms across her chest. "What's that got to do with you?"

"She invited me."

Vicki felt her fingers curling into a fist. Oh, how she wanted to knock that self-satisfied smirk off his face. She turned and began moving toward the doors, in an obvious attempt to put as much distance between them as possible.

Nick started to follow right away. He paused, deciding to take a few seconds and enjoy the view. Vicki's strapless, black knit dress was hugging her in all the right places, from breast to thigh. He loved her body, even though she'd always been self-conscious of her wide hips and full breast. Some men would call her thick; he simply called her fine as hell.

Her shoulder-length hair was crimped and pulled up in a way that gave the effect of a jet-black cascading waterfall poured over her right shoulder. Tiny onyx stones surrounded by diamonds hung from her ears and neck. Sheer stockings that showed off her well-toned coffee calves, and black sling-back pumps were the perfect accent.

Fascinated by the jiggle of her behind as she maneuvered her way through the crowd, he almost lost sight of her. He hurried to the doorway, and given his formidable height and size, the crowd parted easily. Taking her by the elbow, Nick guided her through the crowd.

Once they were safely inside, Vicki jerked her arm

away from his grip. "Still trying to push me around I see," she snapped, before storming off across the room.

Nick chuckled to himself. Vicki was so busy making her dramatic exit, she never noticed Peaches making a beeline in their direction.

"Where is she going?" Peaches asked in confusion, as she came to a stop in front of Nick.

"I don't know," Nick muttered, before turning his attention to the woman in front of him. Over the course of the few months he'd lived in Chicago, Vicki's friend had also become his. Despite her odd appearance, he'd come to learn that Peaches had a sharp, inquisitive mind and a forthright nature that had shamed him more than once.

Peaches stood no more than five feet, even in the large platform heels she wore almost constantly. Dressed in a tangerine silk smock and matching pants that suited her petite form, the evidence of her eccentric artistic personality was her long, strawberry-blond locks. But, like everything else about Peaches, they suited her perfectly.

When Nick had first met her, he'd been bothered by the sight of a white woman wearing locks. In his ignorance, he'd felt it was something akin to mocking. Peaches had put him in his place, explaining the history behind hair locking and the fact that many cultures other than just those of African descent practiced the custom. She cited recorded instances of locking as a Jewish tradition as far back as the days of Moses.

Peaches grabbed the tall man in a surprisingly strong embrace, but given her small status she barely reached his waist. "I'm so happy you could make it."

Nick laughed, thinking how much she reminded him of some kind of tiny Rastafarian fairy. He returned the hug, and whispered, "Congratulations," over her head.

"Don't congratulate me yet, I haven't sold anything."

Peaches took a sip from the glass of champagne she held.

"But the doors just opened," Nick defended staunchly.

"See, *that's* why I like you. I tried to tell Vicki how terrific you are, but she refuses to hear it." She took another sip of champagne, grinning at Nick over the rim, "In fact, I'm kinda surprised to see you here tonight. I got the impression you haven't, uh . . . been around."

"I told you I would come, didn't I?"

She hunched her shoulders. "Yes, but—"

Nick placed his finger over her lips; he had no desire to hear her voice his own concerns. "You underestimated me, Peaches. Believe me," he said, before taking a glass of champagne off a passing tray, "this thing is nowhere near over, yet."

She smiled and touched his arm. "Well, I wish you the best. She deserves some happiness, Nick." Peaches's smile faded, and her small face took on an ominous cast. Her light blue eyes bored into him for several uncomfortable seconds, before finally she said, "If you hurt her again, I'll kill you." With that dire warning, she turned and walked away.

Nick tried to chuckle and laugh it off, but it didn't work. *What could that tiny woman do to me?* he thought. "I ain't afraid of her," he muttered under his breath, frowning.

Peaches was a struggling artist who, after years of paying her dues, had finally come into her glory. She was the current darling of the Chicago cultural scene. But something inside Nick told him not to be fooled. Vicki had already filled him in on her background; he knew she'd come up the hard way, and people like that never forgot their street instincts. But since he had neither intention nor desire to hurt Vicki, the threat was null and void. Shaking off the chill of her words, he began to take in his surroundings.

He found himself standing in the middle of the large white room. The walls around him were lined with rows and rows of colorfully decorated prints. Rich, vibrant colors lit the room like magic. He chuckled to himself, realizing the patrons were as colorfully decorated as the prints on the wall. He spotted Vicki across the room. Peaches had joined her, and they both stood staring up at a black-and-white print that resembled a tornado gone mad. Peaches was making gestures with her hands. Nick assumed she was explaining the inspiration for the painting.

Several minutes later, Nick found himself studying another black-and-white print with straight lines and neat angles, titled "Rage," when he sensed the atmosphere in the room change. The tone of conversation shifted; people moved into smaller groups, some openly pointing to the large entourage that had just entered.

Someone important had arrived. Nick knew the feeling well, having himself been the center of such attention a few times. He watched Peaches as she hurried across the room in her large platforms, elbowing her way through the throng.

The crowd near the door opened up, and there in the middle stood a small Asian man. Given his features, Nick guessed he was Japanese. In her heels, Peaches stood eye to eye with the man. She was laughing overly loudly at something the man had said. Nick knew that laugh. That was the you-have-money-I-need-money laugh. The man was probably a collector, and, given Peaches's comical behavior, probably one with deep pockets.

He looked back across the room, and found Vicki standing alone. When he'd guided her into the gallery earlier, she'd smelled so good. He had wanted to bend and kiss her neck, but knew she'd go ballistic. He watched her turn and discreetly search the crowd until her eyes locked with his. She looked away, but not soon enough. Nick felt his chest swelling with satisfaction.

He started to cross the room to her before realizing she *expected* him to chase after her, to follow her around the room like a puppy on a leash. *No,* he decided, *a man's got to have some pride.* Instead, he turned and began exploring the artwork.

Nick came to a halt before one of the larger prints. It looked like a large peacock tail or maybe a rainbow, but either way the colors were almost alive. He was so enthralled by the painting, he never noticed the man who came to stand beside him.

"Do you like this one?"

Nick cocked his eyebrow in curiosity, before answering the question. "Yes, it seems to speak to me."

"Yes, Ms. Peaches has shown signs of remarkable talent in her latest collection. I am pleased with her progress." The man stood with his hands behind his back, studying the picture in earnest.

Nick narrowed his eyes. Something about the man was familiar, but he couldn't place it.

The man extended his hand, "Allow me to introduce myself. My name is Yoshimoto."

Nick took the extended hand. "Have we met before?"

"Briefly. In the courthouse. I believe you were representing the Morrison man."

It clicked. "Oh, yes. Veronica Cole's client. How nice to see you again."

"The pleasure is mine." Yoshimoto gave a slight bow. "Please forgive me for approaching you in this venue." Yoshimoto gestured to the gallery at large. "But I have a business proposition I would like to discuss with you at your earliest convenience."

"A business proposition?"

"Yes, you see . . ." Yoshimoto cast a brief look around to confirm that they were alone. "I find I am in need of someone with your unique skills."

Nick smiled. "I take it you mean the skills of a defense attorney, and not those of an art connoisseur."

Yoshimoto chuckled. "You are correct, sir." He reached into his jacket pocket, pulled out a business card, and offered it to Nick.

"I will be out of town on business the rest of week, but I would like to talk with you when I return, if that is possible."

Nick read the card. It said nothing more than his name, his company, his title as CEO, and the usual list of accessible numbers. In fact, the only discerning characteristic on the plain white card was a small, unusual symbol in the upper left corner. It appeared to be a full-blood red moon, with a large scimitar-style sword slicing straight through the center. "Regarding?"

"It's a complicated matter. Please come and see me. No need to schedule an appointment, I will make myself available to you." Yoshimoto bowed before he turned and walked away as if the matter had been settled.

Nick stood looking at the card. He knew the statement regarding his availability was intended as a compliment, but something about the small man bothered him. Over the years, Nick had learned to trust his instincts completely. The one time in his life he had not listened to them, he'd lost Vicki. Right now, his instincts were telling him Yoshimoto's *business* was nothing he should get involved in.

Nick tucked the card in his jacket, thinking he would

probably never use it, and returned to studying the unusual pictures. Each one seemed designed to appeal to a different emotion. The thought that all this beauty could've been created by Peaches was almost unbelievable. He found himself once again standing before the brightly colored canvas. What was it about this picture that drew him?

He felt someone tug on his arm, and looked down to see that Peaches had reattached herself to him. She was smiling up at him in her usual adoring way, seeming to completely forget her threats of violence earlier.

"I see you've picked one of my favorites. I call it 'Rapture.'" She beamed.

Nick nodded, thinking the name suited it far better than "Peacock," which is what he had been calling it. "It's beautiful." He studied the picture carefully, wishing he had something intellectual and authoritative to say. He remembered something Yoshimoto had said, and decided to mimic him. "It shows signs of talent."

Peaches dropped his arm. "Oh?"

"Yes, I'm pleased with your progress."

"Oh, really?"

The way her blond eyebrows came together over her crinkled nose should've told him to shut up. But for some godforsaken reason, he kept right on talking.

"Yes, it's a great improvement." He nervously took a sip of his champagne and made a mental note to go to the bookstore tomorrow and pick up a couple of books on art. This was getting ridiculous.

Peaches twisted her lips in annoyance. "How would you know how much of an *improvement* it is when you've never seen any of my other work?"

Uh oh, he thought.

She gestured wildly with her hands. "I mean, maybe

there is something I don't know. Maybe you work as an art critic for the *Times* to supplement your income as an attorney. Or maybe you have this *extensive* knowledge from all the fine art you've seen in courtrooms."

Nick was dumbfounded; he noticed people beginning to crowd around the irate artist and the object of her scorn.

"No, Peaches, you misunder—"

"I understand just fine. Everyone has an opinion, I understand that better than most. But I don't expect people I consider to be my friends to insult me at my own show." She shook her head, turned, and stormed away.

Nick was still standing in the same spot, in complete shock, when he heard snickering nearby. He turned to see Vicki standing beside him.

"Looks like you've lost a fan." She was grinning with pure gratification.

"She's crazy," Nick said blandly, still staring in the direction Peaches had fled.

Vicki hunched her shoulders. "She's an artist," she said, as if that explained everything. Taking a bit of the crabmeat appetizer in her hand, she took the opportunity to study Nick while he was still distracted by Peaches's bizarre behavior.

She hated to admit how much she had missed him, but she had missed him terribly. Being here, beside him again, it was taking everything inside her not to wrap herself around his large frame. How many times over the past few weeks had dreamed of reconciling with him. All she had to say were three little words: *I forgive you.*

"She'll get over it, she's just nervous about the show. She's sensitive about her work."

"No kidding," he said, with an insincere laugh. Truth was, the last thing he wanted was to hurt Peaches, and he was still unsure how to make it up to her. But even that dilemma could not distract from the realization that Vicki had come to him on her own.

They both started at the sound of Peaches's too-loud laughter floating across the air. Vicki realized that Peaches had rejoined Yoshimoto. Watching him with Nick earlier, and now Peaches, gave Vicki a queasy feeling in the bottom of her stomach, almost as if he were making a point of insinuating himself into the lives of the people she cared about.

"Do you know that man talking to Peaches?" she asked.

Nick shook her head. "Not personally, but he introduced himself. His name is Yoshimoto." Nick tilted his head to the side. "In fact, we met him together at the courthouse a while ago."

Vicki was watching the man with an intense scrutiny. "I saw him give you something," she said suspiciously. "What was it?"

Nick frowned in confusion. "A business card. He wants to talk to me about a legal matter."

Vicki huffed. "I bet he does."

"Vicki, what's going on? Do you know Yoshimoto?"

"I know enough."

Nick heard the undercurrent of emotion in the statement. "Okay, what's this about?"

"Don't trust him, Nick."

"Why?" Nick silently wondered what was she *not* saying.

She hunched her small shoulders. "A feeling."

Nick studied her face; there was more here than simply "a feeling."

Vicki sensed Nick watching her, and knew that he would not let the matter drop. "Just something about him bothers me," she said, her eyes firmly trained on Yoshimoto and Peaches on the other side of the room.

She wanted to say more, to tell Nick about the investigation, but her professional obligations stilled her tongue.

"You know something about that man. What is it?"

Vicki took another sip of champagne. "He's sinister."

"Sinister?" Nick looked at the man again, as if expecting to see a pair of horns hidden in his short, black hair, or maybe a long, red tail flapping behind him.

"Just don't trust him," Vicki said, again with much conviction.

Nick could see the genuine concern and something akin to fear in her amber eyes. He placed his hand on her upper arm, and the brief contact was enough to send that familiar spark of electricity coursing through her body. Nick felt it too, but feared if he showed his reaction she would pull back.

"I'll accept that answer for now. But eventually, I expect you to tell me what's really going on here."

Vicki looked directly into his eyes. "I will."

She looked at the man across the room again, wondering if that well-dressed businessman with his magnetic personality and love of fine art could truly be a cold-blooded murderer.

In an unspoken truce, Nick and Vicki began touring the gallery together. Vicki, being one of Peaches closest friends, was able to give Nick some tidbit of information about almost every image on display.

Nick filled her in on all the happenings in Hope, from the time she'd left to the end of the following week when he'd returned to Little Rock, including Big Mama's attempt to teach Angela to make angel food cake. According to Nick, it was the first time he'd ever heard Big Mama curse. Unfortunately, no one realized Angela's feelings had been hurt until she informed Aunt Tilde she was returning to Chicago several days ahead of schedule.

"Oh, that's awful." Vicki cupped her mouth in mock horror. When in truth, she was fighting the urge to laugh out loud. The image of Angela and her grandmother locking horns over a bowl of cake batter was comical.

Nick's dark eyes twinkled with humor. He could see the smile peeking out from between her fingers. "It's okay. Big Mama gave me the recipe and a heartfelt apology to pass along to her. Angela's probably hunched over a bowl right now, with a blender in one hand and a wooden spoon in the other."

Vicki frowned in concern. "Do you think she will ever give up on her dreams of becoming a world-renowned chef?"

Nick huffed. "At this point, I think she would be happy with anything short of poisoning her family and friends."

Before either of them realized it, two hours had passed, some of the time spent in discussion with other patrons, and some in private discussion. After saying their good-byes to Peaches, Nick walked Vicki out to the parking lot.

On the way through the large glass entrance, Nick cast one last look at the Asian man with Peaches. He also took one final glance at "Rapture," still hanging serenely on the wall. He stared at it so long, Vicki finally tugged on his sleeve.

"What's wrong?"

"Nothing." He smiled down on her. "It's beautiful, I want to remember it."

Vicki cast a glance at "Rapture," and hunched her shoulders. It looked like an advertisement for crayons to her.

Nick walked as slow as he could, trying to prolong

their time together. But they reached the parking lot sooner than he would've liked. His mind scrambled for excuses to remain in her company. "Wanna grab something to eat?" Nick asked, when they had almost reached Vicki's car.

She looked up into his dark eyes to see if the invitation was an innocent as it sounded. Of course it wasn't. His eyes held the look of a leopard hunting a herd of gazelles, and she was the weak, little wounded one. "Why do you look at me like that?" she asked.

"Like what?"

"Like I'm the *something* you wanna grab and eat."

The smile on his face was pure sin.

"Don't answer that," she yelled, covering his mouth with her hand. She gasped in surprise to realize she was flirting with him.

Brain's reaction: *Cut it out!*

Heart's reaction: *I can't help it!*

"What's wrong?" Nick asked in concern, after noticing the look of horror on her face.

"Nothing," she muttered, and picked up the pace. The sooner she was away from this man the better.

"So?" he asked, as they reached her car.

"So?" she echoed in confusion.

"Dinner?"

"I don't think that's such a good idea, Nick," she said, digging around in her purse for her keys.

"Why not? We're friends, aren't we?" Nick asked innocently. He glanced at his watch. "Three whole hours together and I haven't once asked you to marry me." He smiled seductively, his dark eyes twinkling with mischief that directly contradicted his words.

Vicki felt his warmth. Somehow he'd drawn nearer to her, without actually moving. Her right eyebrow shot up.

Something about the way he said "friends" always made it sound like a dirty word. "Well, yes, I suppose."

"Two friends having dinner. What's wrong with that?"

Standing there in the moonlight, Vicki could see his intention written all over his body. Despite the whole *friend* charade, he hadn't given up one inch of his intention of getting her back.

Their gazes locked; Nick leaned forward.

"I—I can't—I can't find my, uh—" The statement was lost in her mouth, as Nick's lips met hers. Her arms came up around his neck and her lips parted beneath his. His taste was like water in the desert. And she drank him in with all the desperation of a dying woman.

Nick was the first to pull back, breaking her loose hold on his neck. "Keys" he whispered, as his full lips feathered across hers.

Vicki's eyes floated opened, and she found herself staring up into his lust-filled eyes. "Huh?"

"Your keys. You were saying you couldn't find your keys."

Vicki frowned. He was smiling.

The faint sound of a car alarm being deactivated in the distance was enough to break the spell. Vicki took one deep breath, then dived into her purse with a renewed enthusiasm. She had to get away from this man, before he made her completely lose her already weak resolve.

"I found this great little restaurant over by Navy Pier."

"No," she snapped. Taking a deep breath, she said, "No, I think it's best I go on home." She sighed in relief when her fingers finally rubbed over her keys in the bottom of her purse. She unlocked and opened the door. "Thanks anyway." She hurriedly climbed inside. "Maybe some other time." She slammed the door shut, stuck her key in the ignition, and turned it.

The sound that emitted from her hood was something similar to a whale dying. Nick fought to hide the smile forming on his lips. He stood outside her locked door with his arms folded over his chest. Vicki took another deep breath and tried again. The whale cry was even louder. She laid her head against the steering wheel in defeat.

She rolled down the window. "I'm tempted to call Al and give him a piece of my mind."

Nick couldn't hold his laughter any longer. "Before you file a lawsuit, pop the hood. This may be a completely separate problem." Nick looked under the hood, but found none of the obvious problems. Given that his mechanical inclinations were limited at best, he offered the only help he could. "Looks like I'm going to have to give you a lift."

Vicki calculated the possibilities. She could call for a tow truck and sit in the dark, empty parking lot for an hour or more waiting for its arrival, or she could accept a ride from Nick. That meant twenty minutes locked in a car, with him smelling like bliss and looking like heaven. She made a decision.

"No thanks, I'll wait for a tow."

Nick looked at her in disbelief. "You're kidding right? It's Saturday night, it will take at least an hour for a truck to respond to your call. And you can't get it fixed tonight, even if you get it towed into a garage. Let me take you home, and we'll come back for it in the morning."

Vicki bit her bottom lip. It really was ridiculous to sit in a deserted parking lot when she could be in her safe, warm home. "Okay."

Fifteen minutes later, they pulled in front of Vicki's condo. "Thanks," Vicki said as she opened the car door.

Nick grabbed her arm and stilled her. "Vicki?"

Vicki felt her heart began to beat rapidly beneath her skin. His heat was reaching out to her, pulling her back to him. She knew what he was going to say before he spoke the words. She didn't want to hear it, and yet, she already knew what her answer would be.

"Yes?"

"Can I come in."

Vicki tried to lie to herself. She tried to form the word no. She tried to tell herself that if he had not shown up at the gallery tonight, she would've gotten over him eventually. *Why did he have to come here?* she thought, fighting back the tears forming in her eyes. *Why did he have to come to Chicago? Why did he have to come back into my life? Why? Why?*

She was still pondering those questions when she felt Nick rubbing his large hand over her thigh. "Yes," Vicki whispered, before departing from the car.

Nick tried to hide his shock. He'd hoped for that answer—prayed for it—but accepted the possibility that she may not feel the same about him.

Despite his efforts to control his unruly body, he felt the familiar quiver in his loins as he watched Vicki stand, her black dress tightening around her perfectly rounded buttocks, pulling snug at her waist.

He followed her into the house in silence, fearing a single word or touch could change her mind. He struggled to keep his arms at his side. Nick expected her to stop in the living room and maybe offer food or drink. He expected her to make idle conversation, and in her nervousness try to stall for time. He expected a little bit of meaningful dialogue, and maybe she would even give him a chance to make his peace. He expected a lot of things, but certainly not what happened next.

Without once looking back, she strolled right into her bedroom, and stopped when she stood at the foot of her bed. She turned to Nick and smiled. His eyebrows rose as he smiled in return.

He watched her small hands slip beneath his jacket, sliding it off his shoulders. Rising up on her tiptoes, she hesitantly touched her lips to his. Nick needed no further encouragement. Wrapping her up in his strong embrace, he deepened the kiss she began, while his hands roamed her knit-clad body.

Vicki felt his heart pounding now that he was holding her. His tongue was hungrily probing her mouth.

"You're mine," he muttered against her mouth.

She nodded in answer, not wanting to sever the connection of their lips.

He pulled her to the side of bed with him, never allowing their bodies to separate, arms and legs entwined as they tumbled down. Nick felt her small hands rubbing him in places that caused him to moan, and groping him in urgent need. He tugged at her dress, frantically working to pull the zipper down her back. Vicki helped in every way she could, shifting to help the smooth fabric slide away more easily. Her need was voracious, and Nick intended to feed it until she was drenched in satisfaction.

His mouth pulled away from hers long enough to taste her cheek, her neck. Once he'd removed their clothing, and quickly donned a condom, he buried his head in her skin. She arched her body as he burrowed into the valley between her breasts.

His large hand gently removed her stockings. Seductively, he released each garter, and Vicki felt the slither of fine silk as it ran over her skin. He covered her body, running his hands along her outline, over her smooth skin, tasting her, suckling her.

His groin was pounding in rhythm with his heart. His breathing was labored, but he paused; he needed to be sure. He lifted enough to look down into her face. "What does this mean?" he asked with jagged breath.

Vicki was oblivious to sound; all that mattered was the warm, heavy weight cupped between her legs. The thumping she felt there, in that place where they would connect in the most intimate way, and the firm, muscled arms that now braced her pliant body. Nothing beyond that registered.

"Vicki?" Nick tried to reach her again. "What does this mean?"

She opened her eyes and looked into his. She was overwhelmed by the impure thoughts she saw reflected there. He was in as bad a way as she. How could he still be forming coherent thoughts when she was close to insanity?

"Isn't it obvious? I love you." She kissed his throat, his ear, his bald head, anything she could reach from her confined position. She would do whatever it took to make those lustful thoughts of his a reality. She parted her thighs even further, and as sure as the sun rises, Nick sank farther into the hollow of her body.

He groaned loudly. The veins in his neck were standing on end, his lips tight in concentration. But still he needed to be sure. "I have to know this is not just sex." Nick held himself over her. "Are you saying you love me enough to spend your life with me?

Vicki was frustrated beyond all comprehension. How could it be that her entire body was purring like a kitten and this man wanted conversation? Was he that immune to what she was feeling? Of course, she was saying she wanted to be with him for life. How could he not know it? Regardless of his doubts, she was not about to discuss it now.

Desperate times called for desperate measures. Holding on to his shoulders for balance, she parted her thighs and pushed her body up against him. The gesture gave life to the intense heat radiating from the center of their bodies. Her sex organ parted like petals of a flower beneath his fully erect and painfully throbbing penis; she was opening in welcome invitation.

Nick felt the damp folds of cloven lips and all apprehension disappeared. He was once again caught up in the tumultuous storm of emotion along with her. Cupping her bottom in his large hands, he lifted her up and plunged deep.

Several hours later, Vicki's eyes opened to the image of blurry red fire, which soon collated into the numbers of the digital clock on her nightstand. It was two forty-six A.M. Her mouth twisted into a crooked smile as she remembered the night before. She felt cool. Nick was stealing the covers again.

She turned over with the intention of recapturing her fair share, when the feel and sound of her hand scraping across her pillowcase caused her to lift her left hand to the light. The dark silhouette of a diamond solitaire sparkled in the moonlight. Vicki recognized it. It was the engagement ring Nick had given her when he'd first proposed, almost a decade earlier.

"Back where it belongs." His deep voice shattered the silence.

Vicki lifted her head and saw the shadowed figure at the end of the bed. He sat cross-legged, watching her.

"I'm surprised you held on to it this long," Vicki choked out. She was overcome by such strong emotions she could barely speak.

"I had to," he whispered before crawling across the bed toward her. "Giving up the ring would've been giving up the hope that you would be mine again. I couldn't do that."

Vicki smiled at the looming figure hovering inches above her. "Well, now you don't have to."

He smiled seductively. "Just make sure you don't take it off again. Promise me, Vicki." His full lips grazed hers.

"I promise," she whispered, parted her lips to his, and sealed the promise with a kiss.

CHAPTER EIGHTEEN

Early the next morning, Nick drove Vicki back to the gallery parking lot and waited with her until the tow truck came. After returning her home to await a call from the garage, Nick returned to his own apartment and began unpacking.

He'd arrived back in town barely in time to dress and attend the art show last night. His luggage still stood unattended near the front door. He picked up the two large leather bags and headed for the bedroom, when the doorbell chimed. He tilted his head and went to answer it. Nobody knew he was back in town except for Vicki and Peaches, and Vicki had no transportation. He opened the door to a brown wall, edged by white fingers on each side.

"Can I help you?"

"Are you Nick Wilcox?" A garbled voice called from the other side of the brown wall.

"Yes."

"I have a delivery for you." The wall shifted to the left, revealing a small man behind it. His clipboard with pen was clamped firmly between his teeth. Nick signed and helped the man guide the large, thin object into the room. After showing the courier out he returned to his package. A small note attached to the brown wrapper read:

Mr. Wilcox,
  Please accept this small token of my esteem in the hopes that we may do business together soon.

                                                    Yoshimoto

Nick unwrapped the parcel and was flabbergasted by what he found beneath the plain brown wrapper. It was the painting he'd admired the other night, the one Peaches had called "Rapture." *This is Yoshimoto's idea of a small token?* Nick had seen the price tag on the painting while he was considering purchasing it for himself; there was nothing small about it.

The picture grabbed and held his attention in the same way it had the night before. But this time, Nick saw even more in the colors. Shadows beneath the outlines that he didn't notice in the flattering lighting of the gallery were clearly visible now in the light of day streaming into his large open windows. He was sure this was the kind of lighting Peaches had used to paint in. He could almost feel the jubilation in the bold strokes, feel her happiness transcending the canvas.

Nick had no intention of doing business with Yoshimoto, and knew he should return the picture. But something inside him really wanted to keep it.

The phone rang, and Nick found it hard to turn away from the picture long enough to answer it. He was beginning to understand how people could get passionate about art.

"Hello?"

"Howdy, Nick," Roland Maxwell's Arkansas twang came through the line loud and clear.

Nick felt his jaw tightening. After his disastrous luncheon with Pete Marlowe he'd made no attempts to contact the quartet, certain that Pete would give his own account of what had happened and subsequently ruin any chances Nick had with the foursome.

"Hello, Roland," Nick returned in icy tones.

"I spoke with Pete this morning. He told me what happened between you two."

Roland's voice was stern and controlled some hidden emotion, but Nick was pretty sure the emotion was anger. Anger that they had wasted almost a full year on a man who would treat one of them with little regard. Anger that now they would have to start all over with another candidate.

Nick held his breath, wondering if Roland was calling simply to curse him and tell him that the quartet's support was officially gone, or if this call was to inform him of something far worse. Something Nick had considered since he walked out of the restaurant over a week ago and left Peter Marlow looking mortified and humiliated.

Nick knew these men had the power to destroy his law practice—even his career in Arkansas—and maybe beyond. The question was would they use that power, or simply cut their losses and walk away?

"Oh, really?"

"Yes. Needless to say, I'm disappointed."

"I'm sure you are," he muttered.

"I'm sure you are as well, Nick, and this puts me in a awkward position, probably one of the hardest things I ever had to do."

Here it comes, Nick thought. He braced himself.

"If I had known Pete was involved with a company like

Alpha I would've gotten rid of him long ago. Unfortunately, he had the good sense to register his shares through a dummy corporation. I've known about Alpha Development's dirty dealings for years. We would never have invited him into our group had we known he was involved with such an organization. I guess, in a way, I have you to thank for that. He was so angry about what happened with you he just blurted it out. By the time he realized his mistake, it was too late."

Nick's mouth fell open in amazement. "Are you saying Pete Marlow is no longer a part of the quartet?"

"Hell, no!"

Nick sat down in the nearest chair. This was not what he expected to hear. "Not to be rude, Roland, but why are you calling me?"

"Well, to apologize of course," Roland said, as if the answer should be obvious. "I want to make sure that SOB hasn't done anything to jeopardize our relationship with you. You do understand, Nick, that lunch meeting was not on behalf of our group. I knew nothing of it until he called to spout off about how you treated him." He chuckled. "Kinda wished I would've been there. Did you really pull him across the table by his tie, Nick?"

Nick fought to hide a smile. "Not completely across the table."

Roland laughed. "I'll be damned. Good to know our man has some fire in his britches."

Nick rubbed his bald head; this was not what he expected at all. He'd given up all hopes of running in the next election. And now, to learn that his chances were as good as ever . . .

He should've been ecstatic. He should've been overjoyed, but all he really felt was a small sense of relief that his firm was safe from the machinations of powerful men.

The attorney general's race, something that had once been so incredibly important to him, now meant very little. In fact, next to loving Vicki . . . it meant nothing.

The two men spent a few more minutes discussing Nick's plans for the next few weeks, and his impending nuptials, before Nick hung up and returned to his painting.

He stood staring at the canvas for a long time before deciding. What was the harm in meeting with Yoshimoto? For such an extravagant gift, he at least owed the man that much. He could hear him out, and decide if it was something that he wanted to be involved in. Talking was not enough to commit him to anything, right?

It took some time, but he finally convinced himself that he could keep the painting and his integrity as well. Ignoring the irksome tug of his conscience, he turned his attention to finding the most appropriate place to hang his new prize.

"Where's Nick?" Peaches asked, her arms swinging back and forth at her sides.

Vicki had driven by a bridal shop earlier in the week, and seen her dream dress in the window. It was the only one left and she bought it on the spot. Problem was, it was one dress size smaller than what she actually wore. Once again, she and Peaches were on the park trail. This time they decided to start with walking, and work their way up to running.

Vicki hunched her shoulders. "I'm not sure. He hopped out of bed at the crack of dawn, muttered something about appointments, and disappeared before I had my first cup of coffee."

"Oh." Peaches tried to hide her disappointment. It

had been a full week since her show, and she wanted to apologize to him for the way she'd lost it that night.

As if reading her thoughts, Vicki smiled. "Don't sweat it. Nick has pretty tough skin. I'm sure he's already forgotten how you chewed him up and spit him out."

"I hope so. I was so wound up. My first show, and I guess I was a little nervous."

"How did you do? Did you sell anything after we left?"

"I did pretty good actually. A few of my series prints, and of course Yoshimoto made a few purchases."

Vicki took the opening to ask Peaches about the man. "Peaches, how much do you know about Yoshimoto?"

"What do you mean?"

"His business, or background, anything you could tell me would help."

"Well, I know that without his support I probably would be a lot thinner," she laughed. "But in all truth, he does make me a bit . . . uncomfortable sometimes. Nothing specific, just a feeling I get when I look into his eyes. It's freaky."

"Really?"

Peaches took a deep breath. "Can we stop now?"

Vicki guided her over to a bench, hidden beneath a large oak tree. "But what do you know about his business?"

Peaches flopped down on the bench, and continued. "Not much. He's some kind of corporate bigwig. Japanese by birth, I think he stills lives there and keeps a small penthouse locally for his visits. Lots and lots of mullah, if you know what I mean. But beyond that, not much. Why all the questions?"

Vicki shrugged. "Some things I've heard about him recently have me concerned."

"Really? What kind of things?"

Vicki considered her friend for a moment, deciding on how much to say. She trusted Peaches implicitly, but considering the man in question was Peaches's greatest patron, she wondered if she should mention that he possibly had Mafia connections.

"Just . . . things," Vicki's answer was pure evasion.

Peaches cast a sideways glance. Vicki never discussed impending investigations, but it didn't take a rocket scientist to figure out Yoshimoto must be in some sort of legal trouble. She decided to let the subject drop, which was fine with Vicki.

She didn't want to create unnecessary fear in Peaches about her number one patron. But still, the voice in the back of her brain said the situation warranted some type of warning. "Peaches, be careful when dealing with him."

Peaches's blue eyes widened in surprise. She knew there was a lot Vicki was not telling her, but what she did say confirmed what Peaches already suspected. There was something not right about Yoshimoto. "Don't worry." Peaches smiled. "I can take care of myself."

Gabriel took a deep breath before forcing down another spoonful of collard greens, struggling to keep a neutral expression until the bitter substance finally, mercifully, slid down his throat. Once he was certain the experience was over, he dared to make eye contact with the woman sitting across from him. Angela's expression conveyed everything that was hopeful anticipation. He smiled in satisfaction. Angela returned the smile.

Her full lips turned up at the corner in almost smug self-assurance. Gabriel could almost feel the vindication radiating off her. As if, after so many years of hearing her culinary efforts demeaned, she finally had someone on her side. And on her side, Gabriel was perfectly happy to be.

Her dark brown eyes and alluring smile were the top tiers of her multi-layered beauty. Gabriel felt a strange aftertaste in his mouth, something on his tongue. He rubbed his tongue against the roof of his mouth trying to identify it. When he finally did, it took everything in him not to bolt from the table in disgust. Dirt. There was still dirt in the greens.

Angela was now engrossed in cutting into her over-cooked roast. Gabriel wondered briefly if he should say something. He looked to the other dinner guests and surmised that they were too caught up in scowling across the table at each other to notice if there was a whole dirt mound mixed in with the dinner. Angela glanced up and caught his eye again. She smiled *that* smile, the one that melted him from the inside out. *What's a little dirt?* Gabriel thought. Anyway, the damage was done. He re-filled his spoon and began the process, mentally calculating that he had about three more spoonfuls to go.

Vicki and Nick were engaged in their own private battle; piercing gazes were being shot back and forth across the table at lightening speed. Angela could feel the tension radiating back and forth like a ping-pong ball. Under the guise of cutting up her meat, Angela was busy trying to think of a way to defuse the situation before these two embarrassed her in front of Gabriel.

This was one of the best meals she'd ever cooked, and now that she had someone who appreciated her cooking, she wasn't about to let Nick and Vicki's dramatics scare him away. She was about to say something she hoped was witty and interesting enough to break the standoff, when the fireworks erupted.

"You know, I really wish you would stop glaring at me like that," Nick said before reaching to take a sip of wine.

Vicki sat back and folded her arms across her chest. "Sorry, I've never seen a real live *sell-out* up close."

"According to you, I sold out ten years ago."

"And fool that I am, I thought you had redeemed yourself."

Giving up the pretense of eating, Nick slammed his fork down on the table. "What the hell—" Nick cast a glance in Gabriel's direction. "Sorry, Reverend." He returned his attention to Vicki. "What the heck is your problem tonight?"

Vicki shot to her feet and tossed her napkin at his chest. "As if you don't know."

Nick stood. "Apparently I don't."

Angela looked back and forth at the man and woman leaning across her formal dining room table, and Gabriel who seemed to be simply taking it all in. She started to stand, to tiredly resume her position as coach between these two people who meant so much to her.

Angela noticed the movement of Gabriel's head. She turned to look at him directly, and he shook his head again. Was he telling her to stay out of it? One part of her said to do what she'd always done: separate and comfort. But considering that had never been successful, she decided instead to try his approach.

"I know you took on Yoshimoto as a client."

Nick frowned in confusion. "So what?"

"So what? So what?"

"Yeah, so what?"

Vicki braced her hands on her hips to keep from crawling across the table and popping the man she loved dead center in the mouth. "Another murderer, Nick. Just like Andy Pallister."

"Oh come on," Nick huffed in disbelief. "This is America, Vicki. The man is innocent until *proven* guilty. Regardless of what the media says."

"Come on, nothing," Vicki fumed. "The man's guilty as sin, Nick. *Just* like Andy Pallister." Vicki paused, and took a deep breath. "And, like Andy Pallister, I can prove it."

Nick folded his arms across his chest, his jaw clenched tightly as he considered her words. *Another impasse,* he thought. The last time they'd come to this place, Nick had ignored the evidence Vicki offered, and it ended up costing another woman her life. Could he be as wrong about Yoshimoto as he was about Andy Pallister?

"Okay," Nick said, before resuming his seat. "Go ahead, let me hear it."

Vicki's eyes widened in surprise. Was he actually willing to hear her out? She considered that this was probably just an attempt to appease her, but what if he was serious. What if he was really willing to listen to her? She had to take the chance.

She leaned forward and began. "Right after I got back in town, Tommy Morrison came by my place. Of course, I first thought he was there to try to take revenge on me in some way, but instead he had some information he felt the prosecutor's office should have. You see, Benny Brown was a friend of his . . ."

Vicki continued, and spelled out everything Tommy had told her, everything Peaches had told her, and everything Ellis had been able to uncover about the businessman. Nick listened attentively, interrupting with the occasional question.

Neither of them noticed when Gabriel and Angela crept out of the dining room. But when Vicki noticed the time on her wristwatch, a full ninety minutes had passed.

Once she finished, Vicki sat back and waited. When the silence had lasted for several seconds, Nick rose with his plate. "I'm going to heat up my food. Want me to heat your plate?"

Vicki's eyebrows furrowed. "What? No. What are you going to do, Nick?"

Nick tilted his head. "I told you, I'm going to heat my food." He started toward the kitchen. Vicki jumped up and blocked his path. "Don't play games, Nick. You know what I mean. What are you going to do about the Yoshimoto case?"

He shrugged as if it mattered little. "Drop it, of course."

Vicki felt her mouth fall open, a surge of gratification coursed through her body. "Just like that?" she said, in a half chuckle. "Because I asked you to?"

He leaned forward and touched his lips to hers. "Yes, just like that, but because I trust your judgment." He moved past her, carrying his plate into the kitchen. Nick placed his plate in the microwave for thirty seconds and leaned against the counter.

He wondered briefly if Vicki had any idea what it did to him to concede a battle before it began. Especially since part of him still wanted the case, the challenge of it. But given what Vicki had told him, he was no longer one hundred percent certain of Yoshimoto's innocence. That alone was reason enough to drop it. That and the look of awe and happiness in Vicki's eyes when he announced he would give it up.

It had taken him almost eight years to get it right, Nick thought. But this time, he was certain he'd made the right choice. Now came the hard part, informing his client of his decision.

***

Yoshimoto stood with his hands locked behind his back, staring out the window of his high-rise office. The tic below his left eye and the firm set of his jaw were the only indications of his displeasure.

Apparently he'd underestimated the American legal system. He was still unsure of how the city of Chicago prosecutor John Ellis and his staff had managed to tie his name to the liquor store massacre. When he was notified of the prosecutor's indictment, he'd immediately thought of Nick Wilcox. The man's exemplary record, charismatic presence, and sharp mind were well known by all. But Yoshimoto was more impressed by his intense desire to win. Something Yoshimoto understood well.

He chuckled to think of the irony behind being represented by the same man who'd represented the innocent man, Tommy Morrison, when he was accused of the same crime. But for all his planning, Yoshimoto never could have anticipated the visit he'd received earlier that morning. Never did he imagine that Nick Wilcox, whose rapacity was as legendary as his brilliance, would turn him down. *He would dare to defy me? I am Yoshimoto!*

He took a deep breath in an attempt to maintain his much-prided self-control. For one brief moment earlier that morning, immediately after Nick stated his position, Yoshimoto had lost that control and told the other man in vivid detail what he would do to him and his family if he tried to renege on their agreement.

After recovering from the shock of such a horrific declaration, the younger man turned and in a few long strides crossed the room to the doorway. He stopped and turned to face Yoshimoto. His large, dark form loomed in the entryway like an angry giant.

"If you want to fight me, Yoshimoto, you're welcome to try. But if you go near my family, or anyone I know, I'll destroy you," Nick said through clenched teeth before storming away.

Yoshimoto knew there was no way he could compel the man to represent him without exposing more of his true character, especially since the attorney had been vague in his reasons for rejecting the case. He assumed someone had convinced Nick of his guilt. It was one of Nick Wilcox's rules of morality. He never represented clients whom he knew for certain were guilty.

Yoshimoto knew he could easily find another greedy attorney to replace this one; they were a dime a dozen. But that was not the point. No one told him no. No one. This insult could not go unpunished.

Finding out Veronica Cole had her own axe to grind was simply icing on the cake. After an extensive and informative conversation with the female attorney, Yoshimoto decided they would try to destroy Nick Wilcox her way—first. But if that did not work they would use his fool-proof alternative. And that is the method which he was presently contemplating.

"You asked for me, sir?" A deep voice came from the other side of the room, near the door.

"Yes," Yoshimoto answered without turning toward the voice. His eyes were still focused on the blue summer sky outside his window. "I need you to take care of a little matter for me."

Yoshimoto spent the next few minutes giving the other man explicit orders, before dismissing him without once laying his eyes on him. He knew he could trust his underling to carry out his request as it was laid out to him. One way or the other, by the end of the week, Nick Wilcox would be properly chastised for his insult to Yoshimoto.

CHAPTER NINETEEN

Vicki pushed her cart along the aisle, trying without much success to ignore the rows and rows of cookies, which seemed to be speaking to her. *"Pssst. Over here,"* called a blue and white bag of Oreo's. *"You know you want me,"* whispered a red bag of Chips Ahoy. She kept her head facing straight toward the end of the aisle and vowed never to shop on an empty stomach again. She was determined she would fit into her beautiful ivory lace wedding gown if it killed her. She forced herself to concentrate on the beautiful line of pearl buttons that lined the waistline, and the tight-fitting arms.

Clearing the endless corridor, she turned in the direction of the check-out lanes. refusing to examine her grocery cart filled with typical nutritional foodstuffs, and a heaping helping of the not-so-nutritional foodstuffs. *Okay,* she thought, *so nobody's perfect.*

Standing behind an elderly lady who seemed to have picked today to redeem all her coupons, Vicki leaned across her crowded basket, eyeballing a bag of potato chips buried beneath a dozen eggs. She was considering digging it out when something familiar flashed in her peripheral vision.

She turned toward a tabloid magazine. On the cover was the pretty attorney Nick had introduced her to at the courthouse a few weeks ago. An old friend, he had called her. "The mother of Nick Wilcox's love child," is what the tabloid was calling her.

"What?" Ignoring the startled cashier and customers, Vicki leafed through the magazine and skimmed through the article. She turned to leave, her basket of groceries completely forgotten, but soon realized she was trapped between the elderly lady in front and a woman with three rambunctious small children behind her. She had no choice but to wait, and while she did she finished the article and managed to calm her nerves at the same time.

By the end of the story, Vicki knew it for the lie it was. According to the article, the time at which Veronica's Cole's child was conceived was during the time Nick had been in Hope, Arkansas, with her. If anyone was carrying a child conceived by Nick during that time, Vicki thought, it would have been herself, *not* Veronica Cole.

By the time Vicki arrived back at Nick's apartment, she was convinced this crazy story was somehow tied into the threat Yoshimoto had made against Nick.

Using the key Nick had given her, she swept into the apartment like a force of nature. She was ranting long before she found him in the laundry room emptying a load of clothes from the dryer.

"I knew it. I knew there was something wrong with that woman when I met her. I knew it."

Nick stood, taking in her frazzled appearance and angry scowl. "Baby, what's wrong?"

She shoved the magazine at his chest and continued

her tirade. "Something in her eyes wasn't right. I knew she was crazy. I knew it."

Nick continued to read, trying to take in the shocking fabrication. In the void of his silence, Vicki continued. "She can't actually think she's gonna get away with this?"

"I don't think getting away with it is the goal. She wants to stir up trouble." Nick leaned back against the warm dryer with arms folded across his chest watching as Vicki frantically paced back and forth.

"But it's a lie. A blatant lie. I *knew* something wasn't right about her."

Nick arched a well-shaped eyebrow. "You knew it, huh?" he asked with more than a bit of skepticism.

"The way she kept looking at you like she wanted to jump on you. I should've taken her out right then and there." Her small hands were fisted at her side, and she huffed in repressed rage. She was outraged on his behalf, and Nick tried not to smile.

She'd stormed in the front door and immediately began defending him and berating the "blatant liar." It took Nick a minute to catch on to what she was saying, the incriminating story right there in black and white. Complete with colored pictures of a pregnant Veronica. Any attorney worth his salt knew that a well-placed lie was much more dangerous than a little-known truth.

She placed her hands on her hips. "Yes, I knew it." In her anger she had begun to shriek.

"Well, if you *knew it,*" Nick mimicked her higher-pitched voice, before resuming his natural rich baritone, "why the hell didn't you tell me?"

Vicki finally came to a stop directly in front of him. Placing her hands on her hips she stood glaring up at him. "I knew she was crazy, Nick. I did not know she had a death wish."

Nick moved forward and wrapped her in his arms. "Uh, maybe I shouldn't hear anymore. If you're saying what I think you're saying, I may have to represent you. As your attorney I must request that you keep your criminal intentions to yourself." He kissed the top of her head.

She wrapped her arms around his back and took a deep breath to soak him up. His warmth, his masculine scent, and his strength. Everything that made Nick *Nick*. Everything that made him the man she loved. "I'm glad you can find some humor in this." Her voice was muffled against his chest.

"After Pete Marlow, Yoshimoto, and now Veronica, I have to laugh," he huffed. "It's either that or cry."

Later, after a call to Roland Maxwell, both Nick and Vicki were feeling better. They relayed the fallacy of the story to him and answered all his pertinent questions. Roland told Nick to rest assured, and that he would take care of it. That was all he'd said, but Nick knew with Roland Maxwell's resources both media-related and financial that simple assurance was enough.

By the end of the week the story had peaked, and every major city in the country was talking about Nick Wilcox. But not in the way Veronica and Yoshimoto intended. They spoke of the plot by a jilted admirer and a vindictive client to smear his good name with lies. Thanks to the plotting pair, Nick's popularity was at an all-time high.

"Very good, Ms. Peaches," Yoshimoto gave her a slight bow in approval of her latest work. His eyes devoured the work, taking in her unique use of vibrant color.

Yoshimoto had an eye for art, and he knew that given time for growth this young artist would one day make a huge impact on the art world, and he would be the primary holder of most of her early works.

He'd spotted the current work when it was just partially finished, the last time he was in her studio. He wrote her a significant check and paid for it on the spot. Two months later and he knew it was a wise investment. His art collection was a source of great comfort in these times of legal woes.

"I'm glad you like it," Peaches called from her position on the other side of the studio. She was mixing a new batch of paint; if she could get rid of Yoshimoto, she would still have a few hours of good sunlight in which to work.

Every since her conversation with Vicki, she'd made a conscious effort to avoid Yoshimoto, but her current work was paid for long ago and she could not rightly keep him away from it. Not that he would've let her; he'd been hounding her for the past month as to the progress of it.

Yoshimoto's cell phone rang. "Yoshimoto, " he answered on the second ring.

Peaches wasn't trying to eavesdrop, but the words "the lawyer girlfriend," caught her attention. She picked up her roll of wrapping paper and moved up behind Yoshimoto, trying to hear more.

"Yes, tonight. I want it done tonight." Yoshimoto was too absorbed in the conversation to notice Peaches standing behind him. "Leave our mark for him to find, but make sure it looks accidental to the police." Yoshimoto nodded adamantly. "Very good." He flipped off his cell phone and turned to find Peaches directly behind him. His dark eyes raked over her tiny form, studying her intensely. "What are you doing?"

Peaches smiled and held up the roll of paper. "I was going to wrap it," she moved around the man, closer to the painting. "But then I realized the paint is still settling. Maybe you should leave it for another day or two."

The distraction worked, Yoshimoto's attention immediately reverted to his newest treasure and he frowned as he considered her words. She was right, if the paint was not settled, the original image could be distorted.

"All right, I'll send someone to pick it up Friday." Yoshimoto knew that by nightfall he would be well away from Chicago. He wanted to collect the painting today so it could be packed along with his other precious possessions. But he wasn't willing to take it at the risk of it being ruined.

Several minutes later, Peaches stood against the wall peeking out one of her large warehouse windows. She watched Yoshimoto climb into his limousine and drive away. She did not move until she watched the car turn the corner. She rushed across the room to her small office and picked up the phone. Even as she dialed the numbers, Peaches silently prayed that she had misunderstood what she heard.

Vicki took one final look around her office before locking the door. She'd been with the city of Chicago for almost eight years. It had been one of the few constants in her life during the period of reconstruction after her break up with Nick. But that era was coming to an end.

In a way it seemed fitting that her life here was also ending. Nick was the reason she'd come to Chicago all those years ago, and now he was the reason she was leaving. Time to begin again, and this time they would get it right.

She started down the hall toward Ellis's office, planning to drop off the remainder of her files and say her final good-bye. Some of her co-workers had thrown her a going away luncheon earlier, but Ellis had not been able to attend. Besides, she thought, she needed to say good-bye to him in private. This man who'd given her opportunity and support when she'd needed it most.

The light coming from beneath the door was a familiar sight. Ellis often worked well into the evening hours. She knocked once, twice, no answer. She cracked the door a fraction.

"Ellis?" she peeked around the corner. The back of the desk chair was facing the door, but she could see the light emanating from beyond it that indicated the computer monitor was on. There was no sign of Ellis. She looked around the empty office before entering taking in the odd-shaped bottle on a side table near the leather sofa. Thinking that maybe he was in the bathroom, she decided to wait.

Vicki was halfway across the room when she sensed something was wrong. The door behind her shut quietly at the same time she realized someone was in the chair after all. Ellis's large body was slumped forward. From where she stood, Vicki could not tell if he was dead or alive. She gasped and spun around to face the door. A man stood blocking the entrance; he wore a black mask that revealed his dark eyes. His right hand cradled a small handgun, which was leveled at her chest.

"Don't worry," he said with a heavy accent. "Your friend will not die." The mask stretched when he smiled beneath it. "In that, he is more fortunate that you."

His black bodysuit was nondescript except for the symbol of a blood-red moon, sliced by a sword. Vicki recognized the symbol right away, and an understanding of the situation came to her. This man was obviously sent by Yoshimoto with the orders to kill her.

She looked at the desk behind her, seeking something—anything—that could be used as a weapon. Her fingers tightened around a shell-shaped paperweight. She gripped it tight, and felt a morbid sense of satisfaction at the jagged edge that outlined the object.

She turned back toward her assailant and realized too late that he'd cross the room. Her arm went up with the intention of bringing it down as close to his head as she could get. The masked stranger's arm came up and blocked the blow. The gun fell from his hand as he used all his strength to wrestle her down.

Vicki wondered briefly why he had not shot her from across the room. As quick as the thought came, it was gone; all her attention was drawn into a life-or-death struggle. The killer's fingers closed around her wrist and he tried to shake the paperweight free.

Vicki held it with all her might, knowing it was the one thing standing between her and certain death. He brought his other hand around and attempted to pin her to the desk; Vicki instinctively brought her knee up and, with the help of angels, it found its target.

All thoughts of murder and mayhem disappeared as the man cupped his groin with both hands and fell forward. Vicki heard the sound of sirens in the distance and prayed they were headed in her direction. She moved around her attacker and raced across the room to the door. Swinging it open, she ran right into a wall of warm concrete. She looked up into Nick's worried face. All her mind needed was a moment of recognition before she threw herself into his arms.

"Nick." She wrapped her legs around his and nuzzled into his shoulder as if she could climb inside him. Using his big body to protect her from anything or anyone who could hurt her ever again.

He wrapped his arms around her. "Are you all right?" He cried into her hair. Nick noticed the man, who was beginning to recover on the other side of the room.

"Yes," she moaned against his neck. Without warning, her warm security was ripped away. Nick separated himself from her, and Vicki found herself standing on the opposite side of a closed door. "Nick!" She flung herself at the door, pounding against it. "Nick!" Small hands closed around her shoulders.

"It's okay," Peaches's voice cooed.

Feeling no shame, Vicki turned into her friend's arms and released the floodgate of tears she'd held back bravely until now.

From inside the office, the two women heard loud bumping and the sound of glass breaking. The hallway around them filled with activity. Police officers with weapons drawn charged toward them. The officer in front surmised the situation and kicked the door in.

The image that greeted everyone in the hallway was Nick standing straddled over the unconscious body of the masked murderer. "He's all yours." Nick smiled, despite the small stream of blood leaking from his bottom lip.

Vicki forced her way through the crowd and back into his arms.

He kissed the top of her head. "I know you had already taken care of him, but there were some things I wanted to *discuss* with him, personally."

"It's Yoshimoto, isn't it?" Vicki wanted to hear him confirm what she knew.

"Yes." He nodded in the direction of the bottle on the side table. "Peaches overheard his cell phone conversation with this guy." Nick used the toe of his shoe to nudge the body. "Apparently, he was supposed to feed you whatever is in that bottle and place your drugged body behind the wheel of your car and run it off the road. It was all supposed to look like an accident."

Vicki shivered, and understanding sank into her exhausted brain. "He would've gotten away with it, too."

"Yes." Nick squeezed her tighter, his tone was heavy with foreboding. "He would've."

"But we've got him now." She smiled up at him in satisfaction. But the smile faded when she saw the doubt in his eyes. "Don't we?"

Nick's mouth set in a tight line, his dark brows scrunched in anger. "Unfortunately, Yoshimoto has disappeared."

"Oh." Vicki's disappointment was palpable, but she tried to hide it. She was alive, Nick was alive, and they still had their future lives to live together. That was all that mattered.

She watched the prone body of Ellis being carried out on an EMS stretcher. Ellis turned his head to scowl at her and groaned in pain. Vicki thought it was the most pleasing sound she'd ever heard. Her friend would be okay.

"Nick?" Vicki reached out and wiped away the stream of blood that coated his now-swollen lip.

"Yes?"

"Thanks for believing me about Yoshimoto."

Despite the painful throbbing, Nick lowered his head and touched his lips to hers, certain that if anything could miraculously heal him, it was Vicki's kiss. "That's the way it's supposed to be, sweetheart. I believe in you and you believe in me."

Vicki wanted to deepen the kiss, but knew it would be painful for him. Instead she opted for a peck on his chin. She wrapped herself tightly around his body, determined to hold on for the rest of her life. "Always, my love, just the way it's suppose to be."

***

Blindfolded and helpless, Vicki held Silent Thunder's saddle knot as Nick led her slowly down the gravel path. She felt completely safe, with the man she loved leading her reins and the horse she'd known for a lifetime beneath her body. And although she couldn't see, she had a fairly good idea of where they were going. But why the blindfold? Nick had been very mysterious and very insistent upon it.

"Tell me again why I'm blindfolded?"

"I never told you the first time," came his playful response.

"Okay, so tell me now."

"Patience, patience, my love. We're almost there."

"Almost where?"

"I love a tenacious woman," he teased, bringing both horses to a stop.

Vicki listened to the noises of Nick sliding off of Wicked Ways and coming around to her side. Without a word, he lifted her around the waist and lowered her to the ground. He held her while she found her footing, and Vicki waited for the blindfold to come off. But instead, she felt Nick's strong hands stroking her arms.

"What are you doing?"

"I just realized what a compromising situation you're in." He pulled her against his body, and nibbled at her neck. "So helpless and vulnerable."

"You're a sick man, Nick Wilcox. Now remove this thing, or I will."

"Spoilsport," he mumbled as he removed the blindfold.

The first thing that came into clear vision was Nick's sinfully beautiful smile, but Vicki refused to allow herself to be distracted by that. Her eyes immediately jumped to the small shack over his shoulder.

Her mouth opened in surprise. "Oh, Nick." She circled around him to get a better look. "It's beautiful."

The small fishing lodge they'd used as a headquarters and love nest had been completely renovated. The wood-chipped outer covering had been repaired, leaving the cabin looking much as it would've when it was first built. The shingled roof was brand-new, as well as the windows. It was all framed by a beautifully landscaped yard. Now that it was mid-summer, flowers in every color and variety lined the little path leading to the new front door.

"You like it?"

"I love it. Who did it?"

"I did," Nick snapped. His voice was filled with indignation, as though the answer should've been obvious.

Vicki fought the urge to laugh as she swung around to face him. "Sorry, didn't know you were such an accomplished carpenter."

He took her hand. "You haven't seen anything yet." He led her to the front door. "Welcome to our hideaway." He opened the door with a dramatic flourish of his hand.

The first word that came to Vicki's mind was "home." That's what it looked like. That's what it felt like. "It's perfect, Nick."

"I thought with us living in Little Rock, we would probably be spending a lot more time here with out families. So we would need a place to stay when we do."

The small cabin had been transformed. Gone were the long work tables and rusty bunk beds. In their place was a small living area, fully decorated with furniture in corals and creams. The kitchenette had been redone as well, with new cabinets and new shiny white appliances.

A tall, discreet screen was in place, dividing the sleeping area from the living area and Vicki hurried around it to see. A large bed was in the corner, and behind it a large bay window looked out on the pond where they'd swam as children. He'd even managed to get a dark wooden nightstand and bureau in the small space. Vicki noted the colors were similar to those in the living room, but more masculine in appeal. Nick had obviously been very busy.

After the wedding and their brief vacation in Hawaii, Vicki's full focus had been on getting them settled into their new Little Rock home over the past several weeks. She'd not given much thought to the many trips Nick had been making to Hope. She'd just assumed he was checking on his aunt. But now, looking at the dramatic change to this place, it was amazing to see what he'd achieved in so short a time.

Vicki felt him come up behind her. "The salesman said this was his number one–selling mattress, but you never know how good a mattress is until you've slept on it."

Vicki felt his large arm snake around her waist, and another cupped her under her thighs. "Nick—don't!" But it was too late; her feet were already off the ground, and the feel of the firm mattress was soon beneath her back.

"Umm," he groaned, coming down on top of her. "I think the salesman was right," he whispered in her ear.

With the feel of his heavy body on hers, and the hard warmth now throbbing between her legs, the quality of the mattress was the last thing on her mind. She wrapped her arms around Nick's neck and found his mouth with hers. "Nick, this is so wonderful. I can't believe you did all this by yourself."

"You have got yourself one hell of a multi-faceted man, and don't you forget it," he mumbled against her lips.

Vicki laughed. "I doubt you'll ever let me."

Nick popped his fingers. "Oh, before I forget—" He reached over her head, and in doing so his body pushed hers farther into the mattress. The movement sent sparks of fire shooting through both of them, and Nick completely forgot whatever it was he was trying not to forget.

Soon, the couple was tearing at each other's clothes as if they'd never been skin to skin, never touched in the most intimate way, as if lovemaking was a new experience, which it felt like every time their bodies came together.

"I've always loved you, Vicki," Nick whispered in her ear, positioning his body to enter her. "I never stopped loving you, never!"

"I know, baby." Vicki opened her body as she opened her heart. "I never stopped loving you, either."

With one forward thrust, Nick entered her, and bound their bodies as their hearts and souls had been from the moment they met on the playground all those years ago.

Hours later, Vicki lay staring at the newly painted ceiling, realizing that in their haste to come together, neither had thought about the horses they'd basically abandoned outside. She started to move when Nick stopped her with his heavy arm across her chest.

"Before I was so wonderfully distracted, I was trying to give you this." He reached beneath the pillow and pulled out an envelope. Handing it to Vicki, he propped himself up on one elbow.

"What is this?"

"Read it."

Vicki watched his eyes for some clue as to what could be contained inside the cream envelope, but he intentionally kept his face expressionless.

She turned it over and opened it, taking out the folded letter inside. As she unfolded the letter, she realized what it was and felt her fingers begin to tremble, fearful of what it would say.

Nick grabbed her shaky hand. "It's okay," he whispered, looking into her eyes, "It's good news."

She unfolded the textured paper and began to read. The neat, simple heading read: National Register of Historic Places, along with a local Little Rock address.

> *Dear Mr. Wilcox,*
>   *After reviewing your Preliminary Information form . . .*
> *met the criteria . . . historical documentation, photographs,*
> *and maps contained . . . we would like to nominate the area*
> *described . . . the state historic preservation office will provide*
> *a certificate . . .*

Vicki's eyes skimmed over the information at lightning speed, until she came to the only portion of the letter that truly mattered.

> *Properties that are listed in the National Register are*
> *given protection under section 106 . . . qualify for federal*
> *rehabilitation tax incentives, preservation easements . . .*
> *park service grants . . .*

She continued to the end, and re-read the letter once more, feeling as if the weight of the world had been lifted. Until that moment, Vicki had not been aware of just how concerned she was for the future of their small town. And with one glance at Nick's creased brow, she saw the same relief reflected in his dark eyes.

With tears in her eyes, Vicki rolled over into Nick's

arms. "They're safe, Nick. Big Mama, Aunt Tilde, Mama, and all the farmers, they're all truly safe now."

He placed a gentle kiss on the center of her forehead. "Thanks to you."

"No, thanks to you. You're the one who knew what to do, and who to talk to. I couldn't have done this without you, Nick."

"Us, Vicki. We're a team, remember?"

Vicki chuckled. "The ying and the yang?"

Nick lay staring down into the face of the woman who'd most affected his life. He wondered at the path his life would've taken without her. Life without a conscience, he thought, for that's what Vicki represented. She kept him grounded, and ethical. And he knew in his heart she always would.

He wrapped her tightly in his arms and took possession of her mouth for one breath-catching kiss, before staring intently into her eyes. "Which am I?"

Vicki, still recovering from the kiss, took a moment to breathe. "Does it matter?" she whispered.

"No, baby, as long as I can always be some part of you, nothing else matters." He rolled her onto her back and proceeded to match his actions to his words.

EPILOGUE

Little Rock, Arkansas
A few weeks later . . .

Nick stood with his long arms slung loosely around Vicki's shoulders. The pair was staring up at the plexiglas sign being lifted above their heads.

"Are you sure about this?" Vicki asked her new husband.

Nick smiled and placed a kiss on top of her head. "Positive."

She tilted her face to look up at him. "You would've made a great attorney general."

"So would you."

Two workmen on the top ledge lifted the sign from the crane and positioned it against the building.

"You know, this will never have the prestige you would've had as AG." Vicki bit her lip nervously. She and Nick had discussed this in detail for several weeks, but she couldn't help harboring a secret fear that he would one day regret it.

Nick turned Vicki to face him, and lifted her chin to

look directly into her eyes. "Being your husband is all the prestige I need." His mouth lowered to hers, and with practiced ease her lips parted beneath his.

"Is this good?" one of the workmen called down.

Nick smiled and made the okay symbol. "Perfect," he called back.

The elegantly scripted cream and black sign hung perfectly positioned above their newest real estate purchase. It read: WILCOX & WILCOX, ATTORNEYS AT LAW

The sounds of the busy city surrounded them, but they stood isolated in their bubble of love and contentment. Vicki was oblivious to the noise and chaos, or the workmen making their way down from the building. She felt the warmth of the strong masculine body beside her, and the presence of a love she'd held in her heart for most of her life.

Nick pulled Vicki close to his side while mentally reciting the latest addition to the Nick Wilcox rules to live by: *Never forget the past, for if you do you're bound to repeat it.* A mistake Nick realized he had almost made.

"Ready to go back inside—partner?" Vicki smiled.

Nick smiled in return. Little did either know their smiles were prompted by completely different thoughts. Vicki was eager to begin unpacking their furniture and get their new venture off the ground. Nick, on the other hand, was thinking about his brand-new oak desk, how good Vicki was looking in her snug-fitting red silk coat-dress, and the fact that their new office had yet to be christened properly.

"Ready when you are," he said, taking her hand and leading her into their future.

Dear Reader,

I hope you have enjoyed meeting Vicki and Nick and their unique circle of family and friends. This is my second endeavor in the world of writing, and I must admit, I like it!

I love the process of beginning to create interesting and lovable characters, then watching them take over the keyboard and create themselves before my very eyes. The end of the story is usually as much of a surprise to me as it is to you.

I would like to apologize for taking creative liberties with the application process for registering historical properties. Unfortunately, in truth, my fictional town would not have met the criteria for the National Register of Historic Places. Their criteria would require it to have been the birth home of a historic figure, or the place of a historically significant occurrence.

Also, although there is a Hope, Arkansas, on the map, it in no way resembles my small mountainous town. I just loved the name.

In my own way, *Déjà Vu* was my tribute to the strong maternal figure that has always been such a prominent part of the black family. Sometimes she was there in the form of a mother, grandmother, aunt, sister or friend— but the point is she was always there. In this world of constant challenge, young people, especially young women, need these role models now more than ever.

I have started writing a sequel to *Déjà Vu*, Angela and Gabriel's story. I think it will be interesting to see if Big Mama can help Angela's poor cooking skills. Thank you so much for your support, and I hope to continue to provide you with interesting and entertaining stories.

Also, a heartfelt thanks to everyone who has read and enjoyed my first book *Love's Inferno*. Please feel free to contact me at www.elaineoverton.com. I would love to hear your comments.